Jaffery

by

William John Locke

Double9
BOOKS

Jaffery
by William John Locke

Copyright © 2024

All Rights reserved.

ISBN: 978-93-62206-05-3

Published by

DOUBLE 9 BOOKS

2/13-B, Ansari Road
Daryaganj, New Delhi – 110002
info@double9books.com
www.double9books.com
Tel. 011-40042856

ABOUT THE AUTHOR

William John Locke was a British author, dramatist, and playwright who is best known for his short tales. On March 20, 1863, he was born in Cunningsbury St. George, Christ Church, Demerara, British Guiana. He was the oldest child of Barbados bank manager John Locke and Sarah Elizabeth Locke, who was also his first wife. His family relocated to Trinidad & Tobago in 1864. His half-sister Anna Alexandra Hyde (née Locke) passed away at age 25 while giving birth. Locke received an honors degree in mathematics from Cambridge University in 1884. When he was a teenager, he called math "an absolutely pointless and inhuman subject." He resided in London and served at the Royal Institute of British Architects' secretary from 1897 to 1907. His books The Morals of Marcus Ordeyne (1905), The Beloved Vagabond (1906), and At the Gate of Samaria (1894) were well-received in both Britain and America. Locke wed Aimee Maxwell Close (née Heath), the ex-wife of Percy Hamilton Close, on May 19, 1911, in Chelsea, London. James Douglas and Alice Baines both attended the wedding. On May 15, 1930, Locke passed away from cancer at 67 avenues Desbordes-Valmore in Paris, France.

CONTENTS

TO MY WIFE

This book on which it has pleased you to bestow your especial affection I dedicate to you with my love. It is a memory of many happy hours and many dreams that we have shared.

You remember how it was begun, one spring morning two years ago, with the opening scene of the first chapter gay before my eyes as I wrote. You remember the excitement of ending it before the Christmas of 1913; so that we could start with free consciences, early in the New Year, on our Egyptian journey.

C'est bien loin, tout cela! War overtook it in its serial course; and now, in book form, it must go out to the world as an expression of the moods and fancies almost of a past incarnation.

These dream figures with whom we delighted, like children, to people our home, are now replaced by other guests tragically real, as big-hearted as those most loved of our shadow-folk. Yet sometimes they seem still to live. . . . While correcting the final proofs we have been tempted to modify the end, to bring the story of Jaffery more or less up to date; but we have felt that any addition would be out of key, so far are we from that happy Christmastide when, in gaiety of heart, I wrote the last words.

Yet we know, you and I, that Jaffery Chayne is even now over there, across the Channel, no longer writing of war, but doing his soldier's work in the thick of it, like a gallant gentleman. And don't you feel that one day he will come again and we shall hear his mighty voice thundering across the lawn. . . ?

W.J.L.

CHAPTER I

I received a letter the day before yesterday from my old friend, Jaffery Chayne, which has inspired me to write the following account of that dear, bull-headed, Pantagruelian being. I must say that I have been egged on to do so by my wife, of whom hereafter. A man of my somewhat urbane and dilettante temperament does not do these things without being worried into them. I had the inspiration, however. I told Barbara (my wife), and she agreed, at the time, dutifully, that I ought to record our friend Jaffery's doings. But now, womanlike, she declares that the first suggestion, the root germ of the idea, came from her; that the "egging on" is merely the vain man's way of misdefining a woman's serene insistence; that she has given me, out of her intimate knowledge, all the facts of the story—although Jaffery Chayne and Adrian Boldero and poor Tom Castleton, and others involved in the imbroglio, counted themselves as my bosom cronies, while she, poor wretch (a man must get home somewhere), was in the nursery; and that, finally, if she had been taught English grammar and spelling at school, she would have dispensed entirely with my pedantic assistance and written the story herself. Anyhow, man-like, I am broad minded enough to proclaim that it doesn't very much matter. Man and wife are one. She thinks they are one wife. I know they are one husband. Between speculation and knowledge why so futile a thing as a quarrel? I proceed therefore to my originally self-appointed and fantastic task.

But on reflection, before beginning, I must honestly admit that if it had not been for Barbara I should write of these things with half-knowledge. Sex is a queer and incalculable solvent of human confidence. There are certain revelations that men will make only to a man, certain revelations likewise that women will make only to a man. On the other hand, a woman is told things by her sister women and her brother men which, but for her, would never reach a man's ears. So by combining the information obtained from our family encyclopædia under the feminine heading of China with that obtained under the masculine heading of Philosophy, I can, figuratively speaking, like the famous student, issue my treatise on Chinese Philosophy.

One miraculous morning in late May, not so very many years ago, when the parrot-tulips in my garden were expanding themselves wantonly you all were when I got my First at Cambridge? Everybody thought I hadn't done a stroke of work—but I had sweated like mad all the time."

This was quite true, the sudden brilliance of the end of Adrian's University career had dazzled the whole of his acquaintance. Barbara, impatient of retrospect, came to the all-important point.

"How does Doria take it?"

He turned on her and beamed. He was one of those dapper, slim-built men who can turn with quick grace.

"She's as pleased as Punch. Gave it to old man Jornicroft to read and insisted on his reading it. He's impressed. Never thought I had it in me. Can't see, however, where the commercial value of it comes in."

"Wait till you show him your first thumping cheque," sympathised my wife.

"I'm going to," he exclaimed boyishly. "I might have done it this afternoon. Wittekind was off his head with delight and if I had asked him to give me a bogus cheque for ten thousand to show to old man Jornicroft, he would have written it without a murmur."

"How much did he really write a cheque for this afternoon?" I asked, knowing (as I have said before) my Adrian.

Barbara looked shocked. "Hilary!" she remonstrated.

But Adrian laughed in high good humour. "He gave me a hundred pounds on account."

"That won't impress Mr. Jornicroft at all," said I.

"It impressed my tailor, who cashed it, deducting a quarter of his bill."

"Do you mean to say, my dear Adrian," I questioned, "that you went to your tailor with a cheque for a hundred pounds and said, `I want to pay you a quarter of what I owe you, will you give me change?'"

"Of course."

"But why didn't you pass the cheque through your banking account and post him your own cheque?"

"Did you ever hear such an innocent?" he cried gaily. "I wanted to impress him, I did. One must do these things with an air. He stuffed my pockets with notes and gold—there has never been any one so all over money as I am at this particular minute—and then I gave him an order for half-a-dozen suits straight away."

"Good God!" I cried aghast. "I've never had six suits of clothes at a time since I was born."

"And more shame for you. Look!" said he, drawing my wife's attention to my comfortable but old and deliberately unfashionable raiment. "I love you, my dear Barbara, but you are to blame."

"Hilary," said my wife, "the next time you go to town you'll order half-a-dozen suits and I'll come with you to see you do it. Who is your tailor, Adrian?"

He gave the address. "The best in London. And if you go to him on my introduction—Good Lord!"—it seemed to amuse him vastly—"I can order half-a-dozen more!"

All this seemed to me, who am not devoid of a sense of humour and an appreciation of the pleasant flippancies of life, somewhat futile and frothy talk, unworthy of the author of "The Diamond Gate" and the lover of Doria Jornicroft. I expressed this opinion and Barbara, for once, agreed with me.

"Yes. Let us be serious. In the first place you oughtn't to allude to Doria's father as 'old man Jornicroft.' It isn't respectful."

"But I don't respect him. Who could? He is bursting with money, but won't give Doria a farthing, won't hear of our marriage, and practically forbids me the house. What possible feeling can one have for an old insect like that?"

"I've never seen any reason," said Barbara, who is a brave little woman, "why Doria shouldn't run away and marry you."

"She would like a shot," cried Adrian; "but I won't let her. How can I allow her to rush to the martyrdom of married misery on four hundred a year, which I don't even earn?"

I looked at my watch. "It's time, my friends," said I, "to dress for dinner. Afterwards we can continue the discussion. In the meanwhile I'll order up some of the '89 Pol Roger so that we can drink to the success of the book."

"The '89 Pol Roger?" cried Adrian. "A man with '89 Pol Roger in his cellar is the noblest work of God!"

"I was thinking," Barbara remarked drily, "of asking Doria to spend a few days here next week."

"All I can say is," he retorted, with his quick turn and smile, "that you are the Divinity Itself."

So, a short time afterwards, a very happy Adrian sat down to dinner and brought a cultivated taste to the appreciation of a now, alas! historical wine, under whose influence he expanded and told us of the genesis and the making of "The Diamond Gate."

Now it is a very odd coincidence, one however which had little, if anything, to do with the curious entanglement of my friend's affairs into which I was afterwards drawn, but an odd coincidence all the same, that on passing from the dining room with Adrian to join Barbara in the drawing room, I found among the last post letters lying on the hall table one which, with a thrill of pleasure, I held up before Adrian's eyes.

"Do you recognise the handwriting?"

"Good Lord!" cried he. "It's from Jaffery Chayne. And" — he scanned the stamp and postmark — "from Cettinje. What the deuce is he doing there?"

"Let us see!" said I.

I opened the letter and scanned it through; then I read it aloud.

"Dear Hilary,

"A line to let you know that I'm coming back soon. I haven't quite finished my job—"

"What was his job?"

"Heaven knows," I replied. "The last time I heard from him he was cruising about the Sargasso Sea."

I resumed my reading.

"—for the usual reason, a woman. If it wasn't for women what a thundering amount of work a man could get through. Anyhow—I'm coming back, with an encumbrance. A wife. Not my wife, thank Olympus, but another man's wife—"

"Poor old devil!" cried Adrian. "I knew he would come a mucker one of these days!"

"Wait," said I, and I read—

"—poor Prescott's wife. I don't think you ever knew Prescott, but he was a good sort. He died of typhoid. Only quaggas and yaks and other iron-gutted creatures like myself can stand Albania. I'm escorting her to England, so look out for us. How's everybody? Do you ever hear of Adrian? If so, collar him. I want to work the widow off on him. She has a goodish deal of money and is a kind of human dynamo. The best thing in the world for Adrian."

Adrian confounded the fellow. I continued—

"Prepare then for the Dynamic Widow. Love to Barbara, the fairy grasshopper—"

"Who's that?"

"My daughter, Susan Freeth. The last time he saw her, she was hopping about in a green jumper—Barbara would give you the elementary costume's commercial name."

"—and yourself," I read. "By the way, do you know of a granite-built, iron-gated, portcullised, barbicaned, really comfortable home for widows?

Yours, Jaffery."

Without waiting for comment from Adrian, I went with the letter into the drawing room, he following. I handed it to Barbara, who ran it through.

"That's just like Jaffery. He tells us nothing."

"I think he has told us everything," said I.

"But who and what and whence is this lady?"

"Goodness knows!" said I.

"Therefore, he has told us nothing," retorted Barbara. "My own belief is that she's a Brazilian."

"But what," asked Adrian, "would a lone Brazilian female be doing in the Balkans?"

"Looking for a husband, of course," said Barbara.

And like all wise men when staggered by serene feminine asseveration we bowed our heads and agreed that nothing could be more obvious.

CHAPTER II

Some weeks passed; but we heard no more of Jaffery Chayne. If he had planted his widow there, in Cettinje, and gone off to Central Africa we should not have been surprised. On the other hand, he might have walked in at any minute, just as though he lived round the corner and had dropped in casually to see us.

In the meantime events had moved rapidly for Adrian. Everybody was talking about his book; everybody was buying it. The rare phenomenon of the instantaneous success of a first book by an unknown author was occurring also in America. Golden opinions were being backed by golden cash. Adrian continued to draw on his publishers, who, fortunately for them, had an American house. Anticipating possible alluring proposals from other publishers, they offered what to him were dazzling and fantastic terms for his next two novels. He accepted. He went about the world wearing Fortune like a halo. He achieved sudden fame; fame so widespread that Mr. Jornicroft heard of it in the city, where he promoted (and still promotes) companies with monotonous success. The result was an interview to which Adrian came wisely armed with a note from his publisher as to sales up to date, and the amazing contract which he had just signed. He left the house with a father's blessing in his ears and an affianced bride's kisses on his lips. The wedding was fixed for September. Adrian declared himself to be the happiest of God's creatures and spent his days in joy-sodden idleness. His mother, with tears in her eyes, increased his allowance.

The book that created all this commotion, I frankly admit, held me spellbound. It deserved the highest encomiums by the most enthusiastic reviewers. It was one of the most irresistible books I had ever read. It was a modern high romance of love and pity, of tears iridescent with laughter, of strong and beautiful though erring souls; it was at once poignant and tender; it vibrated with drama; it was instinct with calm and kindly wisdom. In my humility, I found I had not known my Adrian one little bit. As the shepherd of old who had a sort of patronizing affection for the irresponsible, dancing, flute-playing, goat-footed creature of the woodland was stricken with panic when he recognised the god, so was I convulsed when I recognised the genius of my friend Adrian. And the fellow still went on dancing and flute-playing and I stared at him open-mouthed.

Mr. Jornicroft, who was a widower, gave a great dinner party at his house in Park Crescent, in honour of the engagement. My wife and I attended, fishes somewhat out of water amid this brilliant but solid assembly of what it pleased Barbara to call "merchantates." She expressed a desire to shrink out of the glare of the diamonds; but she wore her grandmother's pearls, and, being by far the youngest and prettiest matron present, held her own with the best of them. There were stout women, thin women, white-haired women, women who ought to have been white-haired, but were not; sprightly and fashionable women; but besides Barbara, the only other young woman was Doria herself.

She took us aside, as soon as we were released from the formal welcome of Mr. Jornicroft, a thickset man with a very bald head and heavy black moustache.

"The sight of you two is like a breath of fresh air. Did you ever meet with anything so stuffy?"

Now, considering that all these prosperous folks had come to do her homage I thought the remark rather ungracious.

"It's apt to be stuffy in July in London," I said.

She laid her hand on Barbara's wrist and pointed at me with her fan.

"He thinks he's rebuking me. But I don't care. I'm glad to see him all the same. These people mean nothing but money and music-halls and bridge and restaurants—I'm so sick of it. You two mean something else."

"Don't speak sacrilegiously of restaurants, even though you are going to marry a genius," said I. "There is one in Paris to which Adrian will take you straight—like a homing bird."

"Wherever Adrian takes me, it will be beautiful," she said defiantly.

My little critical humour vanished, for she looked so valiantly adorable in her love for the man. She was very small and slenderly made, with dark hair, luminous eyes, and ivory-white complexion, a sensitive nose and mouth, a wisp of nerves and passion. She carried her head high and, for so diminutive a person, appeared vastly important.

Adrian, released from an ex-Lady Mayoress, came up all smiles, to greet us. Doria gave him a glance which in spite of my devotion to Barbara and my abhorrence of hair's breadth deviation from strict monogamy dealt me a pang of unregenerate jealousy. There is only one man in the universe worthy of being so regarded by a woman; and he is oneself. Every true-minded man will agree with me. She was inordinately proud of him; proud too of herself in that she had believed in him and given him her love long before he became famous. Adrian's eyes softened as they met the glance. He turned to Barbara.

"It's in a crowd like this that she looks so mysterious—an Elemental; but whether of Earth, Air, Fire or Water, I shall spend my life trying to discover."

The faintest flush possible mounted to that pure ivory-white cheek of hers. She laughed and caught me by the arm.

"I must carry you to Lady Bagshawe—you're taking her in to dinner. Her husband is Master of the Organ-Grinders' Company—"

"No, no, Doria," said I.

"—Well, it's some city company—I don't know—and she is a museum of diseases and a gazetteer of cure places. Now you know where you are."

She led me to Lady Bagshawe. Soon afterwards we trooped down to dinner, during which I learned more of my inside than I knew before, and more of that of Lady Bagshawe than any of her most fervent adorers in their wildest dreams could have ever hoped to ascertain; during which, also, I endeavoured to convince an unknown, but agreeable lady on my left that I did not play polo, whereat, it seemed, her eight brothers were experts; and that Omar Khayyam was a contemporary not of the Prophet Isaiah, but of William the Conqueror. As for the setting—I am not an observant man—but I had an impression of much gold and silver and rare flora on the table, great gold frames enclosing (I doubt not) costly pictures on the walls, many desirable jewels on undesirable bosoms, strong though unsympathetic masculine faces, and such food and drink as Lucullus, poor fellow, did not live long enough to discover.

When the ladies retired, and we moved up towards our host, I found myself between two groups; one discussing the mercantile depravity of a gentleman called Wilmot, of whom I had never heard, the other arguing on dark dilemmas connected with an Abyssinian loan. A vacant chair happening to be by my side, Adrian, glass in hand, came round the table and sat down.

"How are you getting on?"

"Well," said I. "Very well." I sipped my port. I recognised Cockburn 1870.

"You seemed rather at a loose end."

"When one has 1870 port to drink," said I, "why fritter away its flavour in vain words?"

"It is damned good port," Adrian admitted.

"Earth holds nothing better," said I.

We lapsed into silence amid the talk on each side of us. I confess that I rather surrendered myself to the wine. A little taper for cigarettes happened to be in front of me; I held my glass in its light and lost myself in the wine's pure depths of mystery and colour; and my mind wandered to the lusty sunshine of "Lusitanian summers" that was there imprisoned. I inhaled its fragrance, I accepted its exquisite and spacious generosity. Wine, like bread and oil—"God's three chief words"—is a thing of itself—a thing of earth and air and sun—one of the great natural things, such as the stars and the flowers and the eyes of a dog. Even the most mouth-twisting new wine of Northern Italy has its fascination for me, in that it is essentially something apart from the dust and empty racket of the world; how much more then this radiant vintage suddenly awakened from its slumber in the darkness of forty years. So I mused, as I think an honest man is justified in musing, soberly, over a great wine, when suddenly my left eye caught Adrian's face. He too was musing; but musing on unhappy things, for a hand seemed to have swept his face and wiped the joy from it. He was gazing at his half-emptied glass, with the short stem of which his fingers were nervously toying. There was a quick snap. The stem broke and the wine flowed over the cloth. He started, and with a flash the old Adrian came back, manifesting itself in his smiling dismay, his boyish apology to Mr. Jornicroft for smashing a rare glass, spoiling the tablecloth and wasting precious wine. The incident served to disequilibrate, as one might say, the two discussions on Wilmot and Abyssinia. Coffee came and liqueurs. I bade farewell to Lusitanian dreams and found myself in heart to heart conversation with my neighbour on the right, a florid, simple-minded sugar-broker, a certain next-year's Sheriff of the City of London, whose consuming ambition was to become a member of the Athenæum Club. When I informed him that I was privileged to enter that Valley of Dry Bones—my late father, an eminent Assyriologist and a disastrous Master of Fox hounds, had put me up for all sorts of weird institutions, I think, before I was born—my sugar broker almost fell at my feet and worshipped me. Although I told him that the premises were overrun with Bishops and that we had laid down all kinds of episcopicide to no avail, he refused to be disillusioned. I told him that on the occasion of my last visit to the Megatherium—Thackeray, I explained—a Royal Academician, with whom I had a slight acquaintance, reading desolate "The Hibbert Journal" in the smoking-room, embraced me as fondly as the austerity of the place permitted and related a non-drawing-room story which was current at my preparatory school—and that in the library I ran into an equally desolate, though even less familiar Archdeacon, who seized me, like the Ancient Mariner, and never let me go until he had impressed upon my mind the name and address of the only man in London who could cut clerical gaiters. But the simple child of sugar would have his way. There was but one Valhalla in London, and it was built by Decimus Burton.

After that we joined the ladies for an unimportant half hour or so, and then Barbara and I took our leave. As we were motoring home—we live some thirty miles out of London—we discussed the dinner party, according to the way of married folks, home-bound after a feast, and I mentioned the trivial incident of Adrian and the broken glass. Why should his face have been so haggard when he had everything to make him happy?

"He was thinking of Mr. Jornicroft's previous insulting behaviour."

"How do you know?"

"He told me," said Barbara.

"I never knew Adrian to be seriously vindictive," said I.

"It strikes me, my dear," replied Barbara, taking my hand, "that you are an old ignoramus."

And this from a woman who actively glories in not knowing how many "r's" there are in "harassed."

She nestled up to me. "We're not going abroad in August, are we?"

"What?" I cried, "leave the English country during the only part of the year that is not 'deformed with dripping rains or withered by a frost'? Certainly not."

"But we did last year, and the year before."

"Pure accident. The year before, Susan was recovering from the measles and you had some pretty frocks which you thought would look lovely at Dinard. And last year you also had some frocks and insisted that Houlgate was the only place where Susan could avoid being stricken down by scarlet-fever."

"Anyhow," said my wife, "we're not going away this year, for I've fixed up with Doria and Adrian to spend August at Northlands."

"Why didn't you tell me so at once? Why did you ask me whether we were going away?"

"Because I knew we weren't," she answered.

In putting two questions at the same time, I blundered. The first was a poser and might have elicited some interesting revelation of feminine mental process. In forlorn hope I repeated it.

"Why, I've told you, stupid," said Barbara. "You've no objection to their coming, have you?"

"Good Lord, no. I'm delighted."

"From the way you've argued, any one would have thought you didn't want them."

Outraged by the illogic, I gasped; but she broke into a laugh.

"You silly old Hilary," she said. "Don't you see that Doria must get her trousseau together and Adrian must find a house or a flat, that has to be decorated and furnished, and the poor child hasn't a mother or any sensible woman in the world to look after her but me?"

"I see," said I, "that you intend having the time of your life."

My prevision proved correct. In August came the engaged couple and every day Barbara took them up to town and whirled them about from house-agent to house-agent until she found a flat to suit them, and then from emporium to emporium until she found furniture to suit the flat, and from raiment-vendor to raiment-vendor until she equipped Doria to suit the furniture. She used to return almost speechless with exhaustion; but pantingly and with the glaze of victory in her eyes, she fought all her battles o'er again and told of bargains won. In the meantime had it not been for Susan, I should have lived in the solitude of an anchorite. We spent much time in the garden which we (she less conscious of irony than I) called our desert island. I was Robinson Crusoe and she was Man Friday, and on the whole we were quite happy; perhaps I should have been happier in a temperature of 80° in the shade if I had not been forced to wear the Polar bear rug from the drawing-room in representation of Crusoe's goatskins. I did suggest that I should be Robinson Crusoe's brother, who wore ordinary flannels, and that she should be Woman Wednesday. But Susan saw through the subterfuge and that game didn't work. One afternoon, however, Barbara, returning earlier than usual, caught us at it and expressing horror and indignation at the uses to which the bearskin was put, metaphorically whipped me and sent me to bed as being the elder of the naughty ones. After that we played at fairies in a glade, which was much cooler.

It was in the evenings that I was loneliest; for then Barbara went early to bed, and the lovers strolled about together in the moonlight. With the intention, half-malicious, half-pitiful, of filling up my time, Doria taught me a new and complicated Patience. Then finally, when Doria, having spent a couple of polite minutes in the drawing-room, had retired, and when I was tired out from the strain of the day and half-asleep through weariness, Adrian would mix himself the longest possible brandy and soda, light the longest possible cigar and try to keep me up all night listening to his conversation.

At last, one Friday evening, while I was engaged in my forlorn and unprofitable game, the butler entered the drawing-room with unperturbed announcement:

"Mr. Chayne on the telephone, sir."

I sent the card table flying amid the wreckage of my lay-out and rushed to the telephone.

"Hullo! That you, Jaff?"

"Yes, old man. Very much me. A devil of a lot of me. How are you?"

His strong bass boomed through the receiver. I have always found a queer comfort in Jaffery's voice. It wraps you round about in thundering waves. We exchanged the commonplaces of delighted greeting. I asked:

"When did you arrive?"

"A couple of days ago."

"Why on earth didn't you let me know at once?"

I heard him laugh. "I'll tell you when I see you. By the way, can Barbara have me for the week-end?"

This was like Jaffery. Most men would have asked me, taking Barbara for granted.

"Barbara would have you for the rest of time," said I. "And so would Susan. I'll expect you by the 11 o'clock train."

"Right," said he.

"And, I say!"

"Yes?"

"Talking of fair ladies — what about — ?"

"Oh, Hell!" came Jaffery's great voice. "She's here right enough."

"Where?" I asked.

"The Savoy. So is Euphemia — "

Euphemia was Jaffery's unmarried sister, as like to her brother as a little wizened raisin is to a fat, bursting muscat grape.

"Euphemia has taken her on. Wants to convert her."

"Good Lord!" I cried. "Is she a Turk?"

"She's a problem." And his great laugh vibrated in my ears.

"Why not bring her down with Euphemia?"

"I want a couple of days off. I want a good quiet time, with no female women about save Barbara and my fairy grasshopper whom, as you know, I love to distraction."

"But will Euphemia be all right with her?"

I had not the faintest notion what kind of a creature the "problem" was.

"Right as rain. Euphemia has fixed up to take her to-morrow night to a lecture on Tolstoi at the Lyceum Club, and to the City Temple on Sunday. Ho! ho! ho!"

His Homeric laughter must have shattered the Trunk Telephone system of Great Britain, for after that there was silence cold and merciless. Well, perhaps it was just as well, for if we had been allowed to converse further I might have told him that another female woman, Doria Jornicroft, was staying at Northlands, and he might not have come. Jaffery was always a queer fish where women were concerned. Not a chilly, fishy fish, but a sort of Laodicean fish, now hot, now cold. I have seen him shrink like a sensitive plant in the presence of an ingenue of nineteen and royster in Pantagruelian fashion with a mature member of the chorus of the Paris Opera; I ham e also known him to fly, a scared Joseph, from the allurements of the charming wife of a Right Honourable Sir Cornifer Potiphar, G.C.M.G., and sigh like a furnace in front of an obdurate little milliner's place of business in Bond Street. I do not, for the world, wish it to be supposed that I am insinuating that my dear old Jaffery had no morals. He had—lots of them. He was stuffed with them. But what they were, neither he nor I nor any one else was ever able to define. As a general rule, however, he was shy of strange women, and to that category did Doria belong.

When the lovers came in I told them my news. Adrian expressed extravagant delight. A little tiny cloud flitted over Doria's brow.

"Shall I like him?" she asked.

"You'll adore him," cried Adrian.

"I'll try to, dear, because he seems to mean so much to you. Are you going up to town with us to-morrow?"

"There's only a morning's fitting at a dressmaker—no place for me," he laughed. "I'll stay and welcome old Jaffery."

Again the most transient of tiny little clouds. But I could not help thinking that if Jaffery had been a woman instead of a mere man, there would have been a thunderstorm.

When we were alone Adrian threw himself into a chair.

"Women are funny beings," he said. "I do believe Doria is jealous of old Jaffery."

"You have every reason to be proud," said I, "of your psychological acumen."

CHAPTER III

A fair-bearded, red-faced, blue-eyed, grinning giant got out of the train and catching sight of us ran up and laid a couple of great sun-glazed hands on my shoulders.

"Hullo! hullo! hullo!" he shouted, and gripping Adrian in his turn, shouted it again. He made such an uproar that people stuck wondering heads out of the carriage windows. Then he thrust himself between us, linked our arms in his and made us charge with him down the quiet country platform. A porter followed with his suit-case.

"Why didn't you tell me that the Man of Fame was with you?"

"I thought I'd give you a pleasant surprise," said I.

"I met Robson of the Embassy in Constantinople—you remember Robson of Pembroke—fussy little cock-sparrow—he'd just come from England and was full of it. You seem to have got 'em in the neck. Bully! Bully!"

Adrian took advantage of the narrow width of the exit to release himself and I, who went on with Jaffery, looking back, saw him rub himself ruefully, as though he had been mauled by a bear.

"And how's everybody?" Jaffery's voice reverberated through the subway. "Barbara and the fairy grasshopper? I'm longing to see 'em. That's the pull of being free. You can adopt other fellows' wives and families. I'm coming home now to my adopted wife and daughter. How are they?"

I answered explicitly. He boomed on till we reached the station yard, where his eye fell upon a familiar object.

"What?" cried he. "Have you still got the Chinese Puffhard?"

The vehicle thus disrespectfully alluded to was an ancient, ancient car, the pride of many a year ago, which sentiment (together with the impossibility of finding a purchaser) would not allow me to sell. It had been a splendid thing in those far-off days. It kept me in health. It made me walk miles and miles along unknown and unfrequented roads. In the aggregate I must have spent months of my life doing physical culture exercises underneath it. You got into it at the back; it was about ten feet high, and you started it at the side by a handle in its midriff. But I loved it. It still went, if treated kindly. Barbara loathed it and insulted it, so that with her as passenger, it sulked and refused to go. But Susan's adoration surpassed even mine. Its demoniac groans and rattles and convulsive quakings appealed to her unspoiled sense of adventure.

"Barbara has gone away with the Daimler," said I, "and as I don't keep a fleet of cars, I had to choose between this and the donkey-cart. Get in and don't be so fastidious—unless you're afraid—"

He took no account of my sarcasm. His face fell. He made no attempt to enter the car.

"Barbara gone away?"

I burst out laughing. His disappointment at not being welcomed by Barbara at Northlands was so genuine and so childishly unconcealed.

"She'll be back in time for lunch. She had to run up to town on business. She sent you her love and Susie will do the honours."

His face brightened. "That's all right. But you gave me a shock. Northlands without Barbara—" He shook his head.

We drove off. The Chinese Puffhard excelled herself, and though she choked asthmatically did not really stop once until we were half way up the drive, when I abandoned her to the gardeners, who later on harnessed the donkey to her and pulled her into the motor-house. We dismounted, however, in the drive. A tiny figure in a blue smock came scuttling over the sloping lawn. The next thing I saw was the small blue patch somewhere in the upland region of Jaffery's beard. Then boomed forth from him idiotic exclamations which are not worth chronicling, accompanied by a duet of bass and treble laughter. Then he set her astride of his bull neck and pitched his soft felt hat to Adrian to hold.

"Hang on to my hair. It won't hurt," he commanded.

She obeyed literally, clawing two handfuls of his thick reddish shock in her tiny grasp, and Jaffery lumbered along like an elephant with a robin on his head, unconscious of her weight. We mounted to the terrace in front of the house and having established my guests in easy chairs, I went indoors to order such drink as would be refreshing on a sultry August noon. When I returned I found Jaffery, with Susan on his knee, questioning Adrian, after the manner of a primitive savage, on the subject of "The Diamond Gate," and Adrian, delighted at the opportunity, dazzling our simple-minded friend with publisher's statistics.

"And you're writing another? Deep down in another?" asked Jaffery. "Do you know, Susie, Uncle Adrian has just got to take a pen and jab it into a piece of paper, and—tchick!—up comes a golden sovereign every time he does it."

Susan turned her serene gaze on Adrian. "Do it now," she commanded.

"I haven't got a pen," said he.

"I'll fetch you one from Daddy's study," she said, sliding from Jaffery's knee.

Both Jaffery and Adrian looked scared. I, who was not the father of a feminine thing of seven years old for nothing, interposed, I think, rather tactfully.

"Uncle Adrian can only do it with a great gold pen, and poor old daddy hasn't got one."

"I call that silly," replied my daughter. "Uncle Jaffery, have you got one?"

"No," said he, "You have to be born, like Uncle Adrian, with a golden pen in your mouth."

The lucky advent of the Archangel Gabriel, with a grin on his face and a doll in his mouth—the Archangel Gabriel, commonly known as Gabs, and so termed on account of his archi-angelic disposition, a hideous mongrel with a white patch over one eye and a brown patch over the other, with the nose of a collie and the legs of a Great Dane and the tail of a fox-terrier, whose mongreldom, however, Adrian repudiated by the bold assertion that he was a Zanzibar bloodhound—the lucky advent of this pampered and over-affectionate quadruped directed Susan's mind from the somewhat difficult conversation. She ran off, forthwith, to the rescue or her doll; but later (I heard) her nurse was sore put to it to explain the mystery of the golden pen.

"So much for Adrian. I'm tired of the auriferous person," said I, waving a hand. "What about yourself? What about the dynamic widow?"

"Oh, damn the dynamic widow," he replied, corrugating his serene and sunburnt forehead. "I've come down here to forget her. I'll tell you about her later." Then he grinned, in his silly, familiar way, showing two rows of astonishingly white, strong teeth, between the hair on lip and chin.

"Well," said I, "at any rate give some account of yourself. What were you doing in Albania, for instance?"

"Prospecting," said he.

"In what—gold, coal, iron?"

"War," said he. "There's going to be a hell of a bust-up one of these days—and one of these days very soon—in the Balkans. From Scutari to Salonica to Rodosto, the whole blooming triangle—it's going to be a battlefield. The war correspondent who goes out there not knowing his ground will be a silly ass. The slim statesman like me won't. See? So poor old Prescott—you must know Prescott of Reuter's?—anyhow that was the chap—poor old Prescott and I went out exploring. When he pegged out with enteric I hadn't finished, so I dumped his widow down at Cettinje where I have some pals, and started out again on my own. That's all."

He filled another pint tumbler with the iced liquid (one always had to provide largely for Jaffery's needs) and poured it down his throat.

"I don't call that a very picturesque account of your adventures," said Adrian.

Jaffery grinned. "I'll tell you all sorts of funny things, if you'll give me time," said he, wiping his lips with a vast red and white handkerchief about the size of a ship's Union Jack.

But we did not give him time; we plied him with questions and for the next hour he entertained us pleasantly with stories of his wanderings. He had a Rabelaisian way of laughing over must of his experiences, even those which had a touch of the gruesome, and the laughter got into his speech, so that many amusing episodes were told in the roars of a hilarious lion.

Presently the familiar sound of the horn announced the return of Barbara. We sprang to our feet and descended to meet the car at the front porch. Jaffery, grinning with delight, opened the door, appeared to lift a radiant Barbara out of the car like a parcel and almost hugged her. And there they stood holding on to each other's hands and smiling into each other's faces and saying how well they looked, regardless of the fact that they were blocking the way for Doria, who remained in the car, I had to move them on with the reminder that they had the whole week-end for their effusions. Adrian helped Doria to alight, and to Doria then, for the first time, was presented Jaffery Chayne. Jaffery blinked at her oddly as he held her little gloved fingers in his enormous hand. And, indeed, I could excuse him; for she was a very striking object to come suddenly into the immediate range of a man's vision, with her chiffon and her slenderness, and her black hat beneath which her great eyes shone from the startling, nervous, ivory-white face.

She smiled on him graciously. "I'm so glad to meet you." Then after a fraction of a second came the explanation. "I've heard so much of you."

He murmured something into his beard. Meeting his childlike gaze of admiration, she turned away and put her arm round Barbara's waist. The ladies went indoors to take off their things, accompanied by Adrian, who wanted a lover's word with Doria on the way. Jaffery followed her with his eyes until she had disappeared at the corner of the hall-stairs. Then he took me by the arm and led me up towards the terrace.

"Who is that singularly beautiful girl?" he asked.

"Doria Jornicroft," said I.

"She's the most astonishing thing I've ever seen in my life."

"I wouldn't find her too astonishing, if I were you," said I with a laugh, "because there might be complications. She's engaged to Adrian."

He dropped my arm. "Do you mean—she's going to marry him?"

"Next month," said I.

"Well, I'm damned," said Jaffery. I asked him why. He did not enlighten me. "Isn't he a lucky devil?" he asked, instead. "The most pestilentially lucky devil under the sun. But why the deuce didn't you tell me before?"

"You expressed such a distaste for female women that we thought we would give you as long a respite as possible."

"That's all very well," he grumbled. "But if I had known that Adrian's fiancée was knocking around I'd have lumped her in my heart with Barbara and Susie."

"You're not prevented from doing that now," said I.

His brow cleared. "True, sonny." He broke into a guffaw. "Fancy old Adrian getting married!"

"I see nothing funny in it," said I. "Lots of people get married. I'm married."

"Oh, you—you were born to be married," he said crushingly.

"And so are you," I retorted.

"I? I tie myself to the stay-strings of a flip of a thing in petticoats, whom I should have to swear to love, honour and obey—?"

"My good fellow," I interrupted, "it is the woman who swears obedience."

"And the man practises it. Ho! Ho! Ho!"

His laughter (at this very poor repartee) so resounded that the adventitious cow, in the field some hundred yards away, lifted her tail in the air and scampered away, in terror.

"And as to the stay-strings, to continue your delicate metaphor, you can always cut them when you like."

"Yes. And then there's the devil to pay. She shows you the ends and makes you believe they're dripping blood and tears. Don't I know 'em? They're the same from Cape Horn to Alaska, from Dublin to Rio."

He bellowed forth his invective. He had no quarrel with marriage as an institution. It was most useful and salutary—apparently because it provided him, Jaffery, with comfortable conditions wherein to exist. The multitude of harmless, necessary males (like myself) were doomed to it. But there was a race of Chosen Ones, to which he belonged, whose untamable and omni-concupiscent essence kept them outside the dull conjugal pale. For such as him, nineteen hundred women at once, scattered within the regions of the seven circumferential seas. He loved them all. Woman as woman was the joy of the earth. It was only the silly spectrum of civilisation that broke Woman up into primary colours—black, yellow, brunette, blonde—he damned civilisation.

"To listen to you," said I, when he paused for breath, "one would think you were a devil of a fellow."

"I am," he declared. "I'm a Universalist. At any rate in theory, or rather in the conviction of what best suits myself. I'm one of those men who are born to be free, who've got to fill their lungs with air, who must get out into the wilds if they're to live—God! I'd sooner be snowed up on a battlefield than smirk at a damned afternoon tea-party any day in the week! If I want a woman, I like to take her by her hair and swing her up behind me on the saddle and ride away with her—"

"Lord! That's lovely," said I. "How often have you done it?"

"I've never done that exactly, you silly ass," said he. "But that's my attitude, my philosophy. You see how impossible it would be for me to tie myself for life to the stay-strings of one flip of a thing in petticoats."

"You're a blessed innocent," said I.

Adrian sauntering through the French window of my library joined us on the terrace. Jaffery, forgetful of his attitude, his philosophy, caught him by the shoulders and shook him in pain-dealing exuberance. Old Adrian was going to be married. He wished him joy. Yet it was no use his wishing him joy because he already had it—it was assured. That exquisite wonder of a girl. Adrian was a lucky devil, a pestilentially lucky devil. He, Jaffery, had fallen in love with her on sight. . . .

"And if I hadn't told him that Miss Jornicroft was engaged to you," said I, "he would have taken her by the hair of her head and swung her up behind him on the saddle and ridden away with her. It's a little way Jaffery has."

In spite of sunburn, freckles and pervading hairiness of face, Jaffery grew red.

"Shut up, you silly fool!" said he, like the overgrown schoolboy that he was.

And I shut up—not because he commanded, but because Barbara, like spring in deep summer, and Doria, like night at noontide, appeared on the terrace.

Soon afterwards lunch was announced. By common conspiracy Jaffery and Susan upset the table arrangements, insisting that they should sit next each other. He helped the child to impossible viands, much to my wife's dismay, and told her apocalyptic stories of Bulgaria, somewhat to her puzzledom, but wholly to her delight. But when he proposed to fill her silver mug (which he, as godfather, had given her on her baptism) with the liquefied dream of Paradise that Barbara, *sola mortalium*, can prepare, consisting of hock and champagne and fruits and cucumber and borage and a blend of liqueurs whose subtlety transcends human thought, Barbara's Medusa glare petrified him into a living statue, the crystal jug of joy poised in his hand.

"Why mayn't I have some, mummy?"

"Because Uncle Jaff's your godfather," said I. "And your mother's hock-cup is a sinful lust of the flesh. Spare the child and fill up your own glass."

"Don't you know," said Barbara, "that this is Berkshire, not the Balkans? We don't intoxicate infants here to make a summer holiday!"

At this rebuke he exchanged winks with my daughter, and refusing a handed dish of cutlets asked to be allowed to help himself to some cold beef on the sideboard. The butler's assistance he declined. No Christian butler could carve for Jaffery Chayne. After a longish absence he returned to the table with half the joint on his plate. Susan regarded it wide-eyed.

"Uncle Jaff, are you going to eat all that?" she asked in an audible whisper.

"Yes, and you too," he roared, "and mummy and daddy and Uncle Adrian, if I don't get enough to eat!"

"And Aunt Doria?"

Again he reddened—but he turned to Doria and bowed.

"In my quality of ogre only—a *bonne bouche*," said he.

It was said very charmingly, and we laughed. Of course Susan began the inevitable question, but Barbara hurriedly notified some dereliction with regard to gravy, and my small daughter was, so to speak, hustled out of the conversation. Jaffery by way of apology for his Gargantuan appetite discoursed on the privations of travel in uncivilised lands. A lump of sour butter for lunch and a sardine and a hazelnut for dinner. We were to fancy the infinite accumulation of hunger-pangs. And as he devoured cold beef and talked, Doria watched him with the somewhat aloof interest of one who stands daintily outside the railed enclosure of a new kind of hippopotamus.

The meal over we sought the deep shade of the terrace which faces due east. Jaffery, in his barbaric fashion, took Doria by the elbow and swept her far away from the wistaria arbour beneath which the remaining three of us were gathered, and when he fondly thought he was out of earshot, he set her beside him on the low parapet. My wife, with the responsibilities of all the Chancelleries of Europe knitted in her brow, discussed wedding preparations with Adrian. I, to whom the quality of the bath towels wherewith Adrian and his wife were to dry themselves and that of the sheets between which their housemaid was to lie, were matters of black and awful indifference, gave my more worthily applied attention to one of a new brand of cigars, a corona corona, that had its merits but lacked an indefinable soul-satisfying aroma; and I was on the pleasurable and elusive point of critical formulation, when Jaffery's voice, booming down the terrace, knocked the discriminating nicety out of my head. I lazily shifted my position and watched the pair.

"You're subtle and psychological and introspective and analytic and all that," Jaffery was saying—his light word about an ogre at lunch was not a bad one; sitting side by side on the low parapet they looked like a vast red-bearded ogre and a feminine black-haired elf—she had taken off her hat—engaged in a conversation in which the elf looked very much on the defensive—"and you're always tracking down motives to their roots, and you're not contented, like me, with the jolly face of things—"

"For an accurate diagnosis," I reflected, "of an individual woman's nature, the blatant universalist has his points."

"Whereas, I, you see," he continued, "just buzz about life like a dunderheaded old bumble-bee. I'm always busting myself up against glass panes, not seeing, as you would, the open window a few inches off. Do you see what I'm driving at?"

Apparently she didn't; for while she was speaking, he threw away his corona corona—a dream of a cigar for nine hundred and ninety-nine men out of a thousand (I glanced at Adrian who had religiously preserved two inches of ash on his)—and hauled out pipe and tobacco-pouch. I could not hear what she said. When she had finished, he edged a span nearer.

"What I want you to understand," said he, "is that I'm a simple sort of savage. I can't follow all these intricate henry Jamesian complications of feeling. I've had in my life"—he stuck pouch and pipe on the stone beside him—"I've had in my life just a few men I've loved—I don't count women—men—men I've cared for, God knows why. Do you know why one cares for people?"

She smiled, shrugged her shoulders and shook her head.

"The latest was poor Prescott—he has just pegged out—you'll hear soon enough about Prescott. There was Tom Castleton—has Adrian told you about Castleton—?"

Again she shook her head.

"He will—of course—a wonder of a fellow—up with us at Cambridge. He's dead. There only remains Hilary, our host, and Adrian."

As far as I could gather—for she spoke in the ordinary tones of civilised womanhood, whereas Jaffery, under the impression that he was whispering confidentially, bellowed like an honest bull—as far as I could gather, she said:

"You must have met hundreds of men more sympathetic to you than Mr. Freeth and Adrian."

"I haven't," he cried. "That's the funny devil of it. I haven't. If I was struck a helpless paralytic with not a cent and no prospect of earning a cent, I know I could come to those two and say, 'Keep me for the rest of my life'—and they would do it"

"And would you do the same for either of them?"

Jaffery rose and stuffed his hands in his jacket pockets and towered over her.

"I'd do it for them and their wives and their children and their children's children."

He sat down again in confusion at having been led into hyperbole. But he took her shoulders in his huge but kindly hands, somewhat to her alarm—for, in her world, she was not accustomed to gigantic males laying unceremonious hold of her—

"All I wanted to convey to you, my dear girl, is this—that if Adrian's wife won't look on me as a true friend, I'm ready to go away and cut my throat"

Doria smiled at him with pretty civility and assured him of her willingness to admit him into her inner circle of friends; whereupon he caught up his pouch and pipe and lumbered down the terrace towards us, shouting out his news.

"I've fixed it up with Doria"—he turned his head—"I can call you Doria, can't I?" She nodded permission—what else could she do? "We're going to be friends. And I say, Barbara, they'll want a wedding-present. What shall I give 'em? What would you like?"

The latter question was levelled direct at Doria, who had followed demurely in his footsteps. But it was not answered; for from the drawing-room there emerged Franklin, the butler, who marched up straight to Jaffery.

"A lady to see you, sir"

"A lady? Good God! What kind of a lady?"

He stared at Franklin, in dismay.

"She came in a taxi, sir. The driver mistook the way, and put her down at the back entrance. She would not give her name."

"Tall, rather handsome, dressed in black?"

"Yes, sir."

"Lord Almighty!" cried Jaffery, including us all in the sweep of a desperate gaze. "It's Liosha! I thought I had given her the slip."

Barbara rose, and confronted him. "And pray who is Liosha?"

Adrian hugged his knee and laughed:

"The dynamic widow," said he.

"I'll go and see what in thunder she wants," said Jaffery.

But Barbara's eyes twinkled. "You'll do nothing of the sort. She has no business to come running after you like this. She must be taught manners. Franklin, will you show the lady out here?"

She drew herself up to her full height of five feet nothing, thereby demonstrating the obvious fact that she was mistress in her own house.

Presently Franklin reappeared.

"Mrs. Prescott," said he.

CHAPTER IV

That there should have been in the uncommon-tall young woman of buxom stateliness and prepossessing features, attired (to the mere masculine eye) in quite elegant black raiment—a thing called, I think, a picture hat, broad-brimmed with a sweeping ostrich feather, tickled my especial fancy, but was afterwards reviled by my wife as being entirely unsuited to fresh widowhood—what there should have been in this remarkable Junoesque young person who followed on the heels of Franklin to strike terror into Jaffery's soul, I could not, for the life of me, imagine. In the light of her personality I thought Barbara's *coup de théâtre* rather cruel. . . . Of course Barbara received her courteously. She, too, was surprised at her outward aspect, having expected to behold a fantastic personage of comic opera.

"I am very pleased to see you, Mrs. Prescott."

Liosha—I must call her that from the start, for she exists to me as Liosha and as nothing else—shook hands with Barbara, making a queer deep formal bow, and turned her calm, brown eyes on Jaffery. There was just a little quarter second of silence, during which we all wondered in what kind of outlandish tongue she would address him. To our gasping astonishment she said with an unmistakable American intonation: "Mr. Chayne, will you have the kindness to introduce me to your friends?"

I broke into a nervous laugh and grasped her hand "Pray allow me. I am Mr. Freeth, your much honoured host, and this is my wife, and . . . Miss Jornicroft . . . and Mr. Boldero. Mr. Chayne has been deceiving us. We thought you were an Albanian."

"I guess I am," said the lady, after having made four ceremonious bows, "I am the daughter of Albanian patriots. They were murdered. One day I'm going back to do a little murdering on my own account."

Barbara drew an audible short breath and Doria instinctively moved within the protective area of Adrian's arm. Jaffery, with knitted brow, leaned against one of the posts supporting the old wistaria arbour and said nothing, leaving me to exploit the lady.

"But you speak perfect English," said I.

"I was raised in Chicago. My parents were employed in the stockyards of Armour. My father was the man who slit the throats of the pigs. He was a dandy," she said in unemotional tones—and I noticed a little shiver of repulsion ripple through Barbara and Doria. "When I was twelve, my father kind of inherited lands in Albania, and we went back. Is there anything more you'd like to know?"

She looked us all up and down, rather down than up, for she towered above us, perfectly unconcerned mistress of the situation. Naturally we made mute appeal to Jaffery. He stirred his huge bulk from the post and plunged his hands into his pockets.

"I should like to know, Liosha," said he, in a rumble like thunder, "why you have left my sister Euphemia and what you are doing here?"

"Euphemia is a damn fool," she said serenely. "She's a freak. She ought to go round in a show."

"What have you been quarrelling about?" he asked.

"I never quarrel," she replied, regarding him with her calm brown eyes. "It is not dignified."

"Then I repeat, most politely, Liosha—what are you doing here?"

She looked at Barbara. "I guess it isn't right to talk of money before strangers."

Barbara smiled—glanced at me rebukingly. I pulled forward a chair and invited the lady to sit—for she had been standing and her astonishing entrance had flabbergasted ceremonious observance out of me. Whilst she was accepting my belated courtesy, Barbara continued to smile and said:

"You mustn't look on us as strangers, Mrs. Prescott. We are all Mr. Chayne's oldest and most intimate friends."

"Do tell us what the row was?" said Jaffery.

Liosha took calm stock of us, and seeing that we were a pleasant-faced and by no means an antagonistic assembly—even Doria's curiosity lent her a semblance of a sense of humour—she relaxed her Olympian serenity and laughed a little, shewing teeth young and strong and exquisitely white.

"I am here, Jaff Chayne," she said, "because Euphemia is a damn fool. She took me this morning to your big street—the one where all the shops are—"

"My dear lady," said Adrian, "there are about a hundred miles of such streets in London."

"There's only one—" she snapped her fingers, recalling the name— "only one Regent Street, I ever heard of," she replied crushingly. "It was Regent Street. Euphemia took me there to shew me the shops. She made me mad. For when I wanted to go in and buy things she dragged me away. If she didn't want me to buy things why did she shew me the shops?" She bent forward and laid her hand on Barbara's knee. "She must he a damn fool, don't you think so?"

Said Barbara, somewhat embarrassed:

"It's an amusement here to look at shops without any idea of buying."

"But if one wants to buy? If one has the money to buy?—I did not want anything foolish. I saw jewels that would buy up the whole of Albania. But I didn't want to buy up Albania. Not yet. But I saw a glass cage in a shop window full of little chickens, and I said to Euphemia: 'I want that. I must have those chickens.' I said, 'Give me money to go in and buy them.' Do you know, Jaff Chayne, she refused. I said, 'Give me my money, my husband's money, this minute, to buy those chickens in the glass cage.' She said she couldn't give me my husband's money to spend on chickens."

"That was very foolish of her," said Adrian solemnly, "for if there's one thing the management of the Savoy Hotel love, it's chicken incubators. They keep a specially heated suite of apartments for them."

"I was aware of it," said Liosha seriously. "Euphemia was not. She knows less than nothing. I asked her for the money. She refused. I saw an automobile close by. I entered. I said, 'Drive me to Mr. Jaff Chayne, he will give me the money.' He asked where Mr. Jaff Chayne was. I said he was staying with Mr. Freeth, at Northlands, Harston, Berkshire. I am not a fool like Euphemia. I remember. I left Euphemia standing on the sidewalk with her mouth open like that"—she made the funniest grimace in the world—"and the automobile brought me here to get some money to buy the chickens." She held out her hand to Jaffery.

"Confound the chickens," he cried. "It's the taxi I'm thinking of— ticking out tuppences, to say nothing of the mileage. Liosha," said he, in a milder roar, "it's no use thinking of buying chickens this afternoon. It's Saturday and the shops are shut. You go home before that automobile has ticked out bankruptcy and ruin. Go back to the Savoy and make your peace with Euphemia, like a good girl, and on Monday I'll talk to you about the chickens."

She sat up straight in her chair.

"You must take me somewhere else. I've got no use for Euphemia."

"But where else can I take you?" cried Jaffery aghast.

"I don't know. You know best where people go to in England. Doesn't he?" She included us all in a smile.

"But you must go back to Euphemia till Monday, at any rate."

"And she has arranged such a nice little programme for you," said Adrian. "A lecture on Tolstoi to-night and the City Temple to-morrow. Pity to miss 'em."

"If I saw any more of Euphemia, I might hurt her," said Liosha.

"Oh, Lord!" said Jaffery. "But you must go somewhere." He turned to me with a groan. "Look here, old chap. It's awfully rough luck, but I must take her back to the Savoy and mount guard over her so that she doesn't break my poor sister's neck."

"I wouldn't go so far as that," said Liosha.

"How far would you go?" Adrian asked politely, with the air of one seeking information.

"Oh, shut up, you idiot," Jaffery turned on him savagely. "Can't you see the position I'm in?"

"I'm very sorry you're angry, Jaff Chayne," said Liosha with a certain kind dignity. "But these are your friends. Their house is yours. Why should I not stay here with you?"

"Here? Good God!" cried Jaffery.

"Yes, why not?" said Barbara, who had set out to teach this lady manners.

"The very thing," said I.

Jaffery declared the idea to be nonsense. Barbara and I protested, growing warmer in our protestations as the argument continued. Nothing would give us such unimaginable pleasure as to entertain Mrs. Prescott. Liosha laid her hand on Jaffery's arm.

"But why shouldn't they have me? When a stranger asks for hospitality in Albania he is invited to walk right in and own the place. Is it refused in England?"

"Strangers don't ask," growled Jaffery.

"It would make life much more pleasant if they did," said Barbara, smiling. "Mrs. Prescott, this bear of a guardian or trustee or whatever he is of yours, makes a terrible noise—but he's quite harmless."

"I know that," said Liosha.

"He does what I tell him," the little lady continued, drawing herself up majestically beside Jaffery's great bulk. "He's going to stay here, and so will you, if you will so far honour us."

Liosha rose and bowed. "The honour is mine."

"Then will you come this way—I will shew you your room."

She motioned to Liosha to precede her through the French window of the drawing-room. Before disappearing Liosha bowed again. I caught up Barbara.

"My dear, what about clothes and things?"

"My dear," she said, "there's a telephone, there's a taxi, there's a maid, there's the Savoy hotel, and there's a train to bring back maid and clothes."

When Barbara takes command like this, the wise man effaces himself. She would run an Empire with far less fuss than most people devote to the running of a small sweet-stuff shop. I smiled and returned to the others. Jaffery was again filling his huge pipe.

"I'm awfully sorry, old man," he said gloomily.

Adrian burst out laughing "But she's immense, your widow! The most refreshing thing I've seen for many a day. The way she clears the place of the cobwebs of convention! She's great. Isn't she, Doria?"

"I can quite understand Mr. Chayne finding her an uncomfortable charge."

"Thank you," said Jaffery, with rather unnecessary vehemence. "I knew you would be sympathetic." He dropped into a chair by her side. "You can't tell what an awful thing it is to be responsible for another human being."

"Heaps of people manage to get through with it—every husband and wife—every mother and father."

"Yes; but not many poor chaps who are neither father nor husband are responsible for another fellow's grown-up widow."

Doria smiled. "You must find her another husband."

"That's a great idea. Will you help me? Before I knew of Adrian's great good fortune, I wrote to Hilary—ho! ho! ho! But we must find somebody else."

"Has she any money?" asked Doria, who smiled but faintly at the jocular notion of a Liosha-bound Adrian.

"Prescott left her about a thousand a year. He was pretty well off, for a war-correspondent."

"I don't think she'll have much difficulty. Do you know," she added, after a moment or two of reflection, "if I were you, I would establish her in a really first-class boarding-house."

"Would that be a good way?" Jaffery asked simply.

She nodded. "The best. She seems to have fallen foul of your sister."

"The dearest old soul that ever lived," said Jaffery.

"That's why. I'm sure I know your sister perfectly. The daughter of an Albanian patriot who used to kill pigs in Chicago—why, what can your poor sister do with her? Your sister is much older than you, isn't she?"

"Ten years. How did you guess?"

Doria smiled with feminine wisdom. "She's the gentlest maiden lady that ever was. It's only a man that could have thought of saddling her with our friend. Well—that's impossible. She would be the death of your sister in a week. You can't look after her yourself—that wouldn't be proper."

"And it would be the death of me too!" said Jaffery.

"You can't leave her in lodgings or a flat by herself, for the poor woman would die of boredom. The only thing that remains is the boarding-house."

Jaffery regarded her with the open-eyed adoration of a heathen Goth receiving the Gospel from Saint Ursula.

"By Jove!" he murmured. "You're wonderful."

"Let us stretch our legs, Hilary," said Adrian, who had not displayed enthusiastic interest in the housing of Liosha.

So we went off, leaving the two together, and we discoursed on the mystic ways of women, omitting all reference, as men do, to the exceptional paragon of femininity who reigned in our respective hearts. Perhaps we did a foolish thing in thus abandoning saint and hungry convert to their sympathetic intercourse. The saint could hold her own; she had vowed herself to Adrian, and she belonged to the type for whom vows are irrefragable; but poor old Jaffery had made no vows, save of loyalty to his friends; which vows, provided they are kept, are perfectly consistent with a man's falling hopelessly, despairingly in love with his friend's affianced bride. And, as far as Barbara and myself have been able to make out, it was during this intimate talk that Jaffery fell in love with Doria. Of course, what the French call *le coup de foudre*, the thunderbolt of love had smitten him when he had first beheld Doria alighting from the motor-car. But he did not realise the stupefying effect of this bang on the heart till he had thus sat at her little feet and drunk in her godlike wisdom.

The fairy tales are very true. The rumbustious ogre has a hitherto undescribed, but quite imaginable, gap-toothed, beetle-browed ogress of a wife. Why he married her has never been told. Why the mortal male whom we meet for the first time at a dinner party has married the amazing mortal female sitting somewhere on the other side of the table is an insoluble mystery, and if we can't tell even why men mate, what can we expect to know about ogres? At all events, as far as the humdrum of matrimony is concerned, the fairy tales are truer than real life. The ogre marries his ogress. It is like to like. But when it comes to love—and if love were proclaimed and universally recognised as humdrum, there would never be a tale, fairy or otherwise, ever told again in the world worth the hearing—we have quite a different condition of affairs. Did you ever hear of an ogre sighing himself to a shadow for love of a gap-toothed ogress? No. He goes out into the fairy world, and, sending his ogress-wife to Jericho, becomes desperately enamoured of the elfin princess. There he is, great, ruddy, hairy wretch: there she is, a wraith of a creature made up of thistledown and fountain-bubbles and stars. He stares at her, stretches out his huge paw to grab a fairy, feathery tress of her dark hair. Defensive, she puts up her little hand. Its touch is an electric shock to the marauder. He blinks, and rubs his arm. He has a mighty respect for her. He could take her up in his fingers and eat her like a quail—the one satisfactory method of eating a quail is unfortunately practised only by ogres—but he does not want to eat her. He goes on his knees, and invites her to chew any portion of him that may please her dainty taste. In short he makes the very silliest ass of himself, and the elfin princess, who of course has come into contact with the Real Beautiful Young Man of the Story Books, won't have anything to do with the Ogre; and if he is more rumbustious than he ought to be, generally finds a way to send him packing. And so the poor Ogre remains, planted there. The Fairy Tales, I remark again, are very true in demonstrating that the Ogre loves the elf and not the Ogress. But all the same they are deucedly unsympathetic towards the poor Ogre. The only sympathetic one I know is Beauty and the Beast; and even that is a mere begging of the question, for the Beast was a handsome young nincompoop of a Prince all the time!

Barbara says that this figurative, allusive adumbration of Jaffery's love affair is pure nonsense. Anything less like an ogre than our overgrown baby of a friend it would be impossible to imagine. But I hold to my theory; all the more because when Adrian and I returned from our stroll round the garden, we found Jaffery standing over her, legs apart, like a Colossus of Rhodes, and roaring at her like a sucking dove. I noticed a scared, please-don't-eat-me look in her eyes. It was the ogre (trying to make himself agreeable) and the princess to the life.

Presently tea was brought out, and with it came Barbara, a quiet laugh about her lips, and Liosha, stately and smiling. My wife to put her at her ease (though she had displayed singularly little shyness), after dealing with maid and taxi, had taken her over the house, exhibited Susan at tea in the nursery, and as much of Doria's trousseau as was visible in the sewing-room. The approaching marriage aroused her keen interest. She said very little during the meal, but smiled embarrassingly on the engaged pair. Jaffery stood glumly devouring cucumber sandwiches, till Barbara took him aside.

"She's rather a dear, in spite of everything, and I think you're treating her abominably."

Jaffery grew scarlet beneath the brick-coloured glaze.

"I wouldn't treat any woman abominably, if I could help it."

"Well, you can help it—" and taking pity on him, she laughed in his face. "Can't you take her as a joke?"

He glanced quietly at the lady. "Rather a heavy one," he said.

"Anyhow come and talk to us and be civil to her. Imagine she's the Vicar's wife come to call."

Jaffery's elementary sense of humour was tickled and he broke out into a loud guffaw that sent the house cat, a delicate mendicant for food, scuttling across the lawn. The sight of the terror-stricken animal aroused the rest of the party to harmless mirth.

"Tell me, Mrs. Prescott," said Adrian, "was he allowed to do that in Albania?"

"I guess there aren't many things Jaff Chayne can't do in Albania," replied Liosha. "He has the *bessas* that carry him through and he's as brave as a lion."

"I suppose you like brave men?" said Doria.

"A woman who married a coward would be a damn fool—especially in Albania. I guess there aren't many in my mountains."

"I wish you would tell us about your mountains," said Barbara pleasantly.

"And at the same time," said I, "Jaff might let us hear his story. That is to say if you have no objection, Mrs. Prescott."

"With us," said Liosha, "the guest is expected to talk about himself; for if he's a guest he's one of the family."

"Shall I go ahead then?" asked Jaffery, "and you chip in whenever you feel like it?"

"That would be best," replied Liosha.

And having lit a cigarette and settled herself in her deck-chair, she motioned to Jaffery to proceed. And there in the shade of the old wistaria arbour, surrounded by such dainty products of civilisation as Adrian (in speckless white flannels and violet socks) and the tea-table (in silver and egg-shell china) this pair of barbarians told their tale.

CHAPTER V

It is some years now since that golden August afternoon, and my memory of the details of the story of Liosha as told by Jaffery and illustrated picturesquely by the lady herself is none of the most precise. Incidentally I gathered, then and later in the smoking-room from Jaffery alone, a prodigious amount of information about Albania which, if I had imprisoned it in writing that same evening as the perfect diarist is supposed to do, would have been vastly useful to me at the present moment. But I am as a diarist hopelessly imperfect. I stare, now, as I write, at the bald, uninspiring page. This is my entry for Aug. 4th, 19—.

"Weighed Susan. 4 st. 3.

"Met Jaffery at station.

"Albanian widow turned up unexpectedly after lunch. Fine woman. Going to be a handful. Staying week-end. Story of meeting and Prescott marriage.

"Promised Susan a donkey ride. Where the deuce does one get donkeys warranted quiet and guaranteed to carry a lady? *Mem:* Ask Torn Fletcher.

"*Mem:* Write to Launebeck about cigars."

Why I didn't write straight off to Launebeck about the cigars, instead of "mem-ing" it, may seem a mystery. It isn't. It is a comfortable habit of mine. Once having "mem-ed" an unpleasant thing in my diary, the matter is over. I dismiss it from my mind. But to return to Liosha—I find in my entry of sixty-two words thirty-five devoted to Susan, her donkey and the cigars, and only twenty-seven to the really astonishing events of the day. Of course I am angry. Of course I consult Barbara. Of course she pats the little bald patch on the top of my head and laughs in a superior way and invents, with a paralysing air of verity, an impossible amplification of the "story of meeting and Prescott marriage." And of course, the frivolous Jaffery, now that one really wants him, is sitting astride of a cannon, and smoking a pipe and, notebook and pencil in hand, is writing a picturesque description of the bungling decapitation by shrapnel of the general who has just been unfolding to him the whole plan of the campaign, and consequently is provokingly un-getatable by serious persons like myself[A].

[A] Hilary is writing at the end of the late Balkan war.— W.J.L.

So for what I learned that day I must trust to the elusive witch, Memory. I have never been to Albania. I have never wanted to go to Albania. Even now, I haven't the remotest desire to go to Albania. I should loathe it. Wherever I go nowadays, I claim as my right bedroom and bath and viands succulent to the palate and tender to the teeth. My demands are modest. But could I get them in Albania? No. Could one travel from Scutari to Monastir in the same comfort as one travels from London to Paris or from New York to Chicago? No. Does any sensible man of domestic instincts and scholarly tastes like to find himself halfway up an inaccessible mountain, surrounded by a band of moustachioed desperadoes in fustanella petticoats engirdled with an armoury of pistols, daggers and yataghans, who if they are unkind make a surgical demonstration with these lethal implements, and if they are smitten with a mania of amiability, hand you over, for superintendence of your repose, to an army of satellites of whom you are only too glad to call the flea brother? I trow not. Personally, I dislike mountains. They were made for goats and cascades and lunatics and other irresponsible phenomena of nature. They have their uses, I admit, as windscreens and water-sheds; and beheld from the valley they can assume very pretty colours, owing to varying atmospheric conditions; and the more jagged and unenticing they are, the greater is their specious air of stupendousness. . . . At any rate they are hindrances to convenient travel and so I go among them as little as possible.

To judge from the fervid descriptions given us by Jaffery and Liosha, Albania must be a pestilentially uncomfortable place to live in. It is divided into three religious sects, then re-divided into heaven knows how many tribes. What it will be when it gets autonomy and a government and a parliament and picture-palaces no one yet knows. But at the time when my two friends met it was in about as chaotic a condition as a jungle. Some tribes acknowledged the rule of the Turk. Others did not. Every mountainside had a pretty little anarchical system of its own. Every family had a pretty little blood feud with some other family. Accordingly every man was handy with knife and gun and it was every maiden's dream to be sold as a wife to the most bloodthirsty scoundrel in the neighbourhood. At least that was the impression given me by Liosha.

When the tragedy occurred she herself was about to be sold to a prosperous young cutthroat of whom she had seen but little, as he lived, I gathered, a couple of mountains off. They had been betrothed years before. The price her father demanded was high. Not only did he hold a notable position on his mountain, but he had travelled to the fabulous land of America and could read and write and could speak English and could handle a knife with peculiar dexterity. Again, Liosha was no ordinary Albanian maiden. She too had seen the world and could read and write and speak English. She had a will of her own and had imbibed during her Chicago childhood curiously un-Albanian notions of feminine independence. Being beautiful as well, she ranked as a sort of prize bride worth (in her father's eyes) her weight in gold.

It was to try to reduce this excessive valuation that the young cutthroat visited his father's house. During the night two families, one of whom had a feud with the host and another with the guest, each attended by an army of merry brigands, fell upon the sleeping homestead, murdered everybody except Liosha, who managed to escape, plundered everything plunderable, money, valuables, household goods and live stock, and then set fire to the house and everything within sight that could burn. After which they marched away singing patriotic hymns. When they had gone Liosha crept out of the cave wherein she had hidden, and surveyed the scene of desolation.

"I tell you, I felt just mad," said Liosha at this stage of the story.

I remember Barbara and Doria staring at her open-mouthed. Instead of fainting or going into hysterics or losing her wits at the sight of the annihilation of her entire kith and kin—including her bridegroom to be—and of her whole worldly possessions, Liosha "felt just mad," which as all the world knows is the American vernacular for feeling very angry.

"It was enough to turn any woman into a raving lunatic," gasped Barbara.

"Guess it didn't turn me," replied Liosha contemptuously.

"But what did you do?" asked Dora.

"I sat down on a stone and thought how I could get even with that crowd." She bit her lip and her soft brown eyes hardened.

Where the lonely figure in black and white sat brooding.

"And that's where we came in, don't you see?" interposed Jaffery hastily.

You can imagine the scene. The two Englishmen, one gigantic, red and hairy, the other wiry and hawk-like, jogging up the mountain path on ragged ponies and suddenly emerging onto that plateau of despair where the lonely figure in black and white sat brooding.

Under such unusual conditions, it was not difficult to form acquaintance. She told her story to the two horror-stricken men. British instinct cried out for justice. They would take her straight to the Vali or whatever authority ruled in the wild land, so that punishment should be inflicted on the murderers. But she laughed at them. It would take an army to dislodge her enemies from their mountain fastnesses. And who could send an army but the Sultan, a most unlikely person to trouble his head over the massacre of a few Christians? As for a local government, the *mallisori*, the mountain tribes, did not acknowledge any. The Englishmen swore softly. Liosha nodded her head and agreed with them. What was to be done? The Englishmen, after giving her food and drink which she seemed to need, offered their escort to a place where she could find relations or friends. Again she laughed scornfully.

"All my relations lie there"—she pointed to the smoking ruins. "And I have no friends. And as for your escorting me—why I guess it would be much more use my escorting you."

"And where would you escort us?"

"God knows," she said.

Whereupon they realised that she was alone in the wide world, homeless and penniless, and that for a time, at least, they were responsible to God and man for this picturesque Albanian damsel who spoke the English of the stockyards of Chicago. Again what was to be done? They could take her back to Scutari, whence they had come, in the hope of finding a Roman Catholic sisterhood. The proposal evoked but lukewarm enthusiasm. Liosha being convinced that they would turn her into a nun—the last avocation in the world she desired to adopt. Her simple idea was to go out to America, like her father, return with many bags of gold and devote her life to the linked sweetness of a gradual extermination of her enemies. When asked how she would manage to amass the gold she replied that she would work in the packing-houses like her mother. But how, they asked, would she get the money to take her to Chicago? "It must come from you!" she said. And the men looked at each other, feeling mean dogs in not having offered to settle her there themselves. Then, being a young woman of an apparently practical mind, she asked them what they were doing in Albania. They explained. They were travellers from England, wandering for pleasure through the Balkans. They had come from Scutari, as far as they could, in a motor-car. Liosha had never heard of a motor-car. They described it as a kind of little railway-engine that didn't need rails to run upon. At the foot of the mountains they had left it at a village inn and bought the ragged ponies. They were just going ahead exploring.

"Do you know the way?" she asked with a touch of contempt.

They didn't.

"Then I guess I'll guide you. You pay me wages every day until you're tired and I'll use the money to go out to Chicago." And seeing them hesitate, she added: "No one's going to hurt me. A woman is safe in Albania. And if I'm with you, no one will hurt you. But if you go on by yourselves you'll very likely get murdered."

Fantastic as was her intention, they knew that, as far as they themselves were concerned, she spoke common-sense. So it came to pass that Liosha, having left them for a few moments to take grim farewell of the charred remains of her family lying hidden beneath the smouldering wreckage, returned to them with a calm face, mounted one of the ponies and pointing before her, led the way into the mountains.

Now, if old Jaff would only sit down and write this absurd Odyssey in the vivid manner in which he has related bits of it to me, he would produce the queerest book of travel ever written. But he never will. As a matter of fact, although he saw Albania as few Westerners have done and learned useful bits of language and made invaluable friends, and although he appreciated the journey's adventurous and humorous side, it did not afford him complete satisfaction. A day or two after their start, Prescott began to shew signs of peculiar interest in their guide. In spite of her unquestioning readiness to shoulder burdens, Prescott would run to relieve her. Liosha has assured me that Jaffery did the same—and indeed I cannot conceive Jaffery allowing a female companion to stagger along under a load which he could swing onto his huge back and carry like a walnut. To go further— she maintains that the two quarrelled dreadfully over the alleviation of her labours, so much so, that often before they had ended their quarrel, she had performed the task in dispute. This of course Jaffery has blusteringly denied. She was there, paid to do certain things, and she had to do them. The way Prescott spoiled her and indulged her, as though she were a little dressed-up cat in a London drawing-room, instead of a great hefty woman accustomed to throw steers and balance a sack of potatoes on her head, was simply sickening. And it became more sickening still as Prescott's infatuation clouded more and more the poor fellow's brain. Jaffery talked (not before Liosha, but to Adrian and myself, that night, after the ladies had gone to bed) as if the girl had woven a Vivien spell around his poor friend. We smiled, knowing it was Jaffery's way. . . .

At all events, whether Jaffery was jealous or not, it is certain that Prescott fell wildly, blindly, overwhelmingly in love with Liosha. Considering the close intimacy of their lives; considering that they were in ceaseless contact with this splendid creature, untrammelled by any convention, daughter of the earth, yet chaste as her own mountain winds; and considering that both of them were hot-blooded men, the only wonder is that they did not fly at each other's throats, or dash in each other's heads with stones, after the fashion of prehistoric males. It is my well-supported conviction, however, that Jaffery, honest old bear, seeing his comrade's very soul set upon the honey, trotted off and left him to it, and made pretence (to satisfy his ursine conscience) of growling his sarcastic disapproval.

"The devil of it was," he declared that night, with a sweep of his arm that sent a full glass of whiskey and soda hurtling across space to my bookshelves and ruining some choice bindings—"the devil of it was," said he, after expressing rueful contrition, "that she treated him like a dog, whereas I could do anything I liked with her. But she married him."

Of course she married him. Most Albanian young women in her position would have married a brave and handsome Englishman of incalculable wealth—even if they had not Liosha's ulterior motives. And beyond question Liosha had ulterior motives. Prescott espoused her cause hotly. He convinced her that he was a power in Europe. As a Reuter correspondent he did indeed possess power. He would make the civilised world ring with this tale of bloodshed and horror. He would beard Sultans in their lairs and Emperors in their dens. He would bring down awful vengeance on the heads of her enemies. How Sultans and Emperors were to do it was as obscure as at the horror-filled hour of their first meeting. But a man vehemently in love is notoriously blind to practical considerations. Prescott put his life into her hands. She accepted it calmly; and I think it was this calmness of acceptance that infuriated Jaffery. If she had been likewise caught in the whirlpool of a mad passion, Jaffery would have had nothing to say. But she did not (so he maintained) care a button for Prescott, and Prescott would not believe it. She had promised to marry him. That ideal of magnificent womanhood had promised to marry him. They were to be married—think of that, my boy!—as soon as they got back to Scutari and found a British Consul and a priest or two to marry them. "Then for God's sake," roared Jaffery, "let us trek to Scutari. I'm fed up with playing gooseberry. The Giant Gooseberry. Ho! ho! ho!"

So they shortened their projected journey and, making a circuit, picked up the motor-car—a joy and wonder to Liosha. She wanted to drive it—over the rutted wagon-tracks that pass for roads in Albania—and such was Prescott's infatuation that he would have allowed her to do so. But Jaffery sat an immovable mountain of flesh at the wheel and brought them safely to Scutari. There arrangements were made for the marriage before the British Vice-Consul. On the morning of the ceremony Prescott fell ill. The ceremony was, however, performed. Towards evening he was in high fever. The next morning typhoid declared itself. In two or three days he was dead. He had made a will leaving everything to his wife, with Jaffery as sole executor and trustee.

This sorry ending of poor Prescott's romance—I never knew him, but shall always think of him as a swift and vehement spirit—was told very huskily by Jaffery beneath the wistaria arbour. Tears rolled down Barbara's and Doria's cheeks. My wife's sympathetic little hand slid into Liosha's. With her other hand Liosha fondled it. I am sure it was rather gratitude for this little feminine act than poignant emotion that moistened Liosha's beautiful eyes.

"I haven't had much luck, have I?"

"No, my poor dear, you haven't," cried Barbara in a gush of kindness.

In the course of a few weeks to have one's affianced husband murdered and one's legal though nominal husband spirited away by disease, seemed in the eyes of my gentle wife to transcend all records of human tragedy. Very soon afterwards she made a pretext for taking Liosha away from us, and I had the extraordinary experience of seeing my proud little Barbara, who loathes the caressive insincerities prevalent among women, cross the lawn with her arm around Liosha's waist.

The rest of the bare bones of the story I have already told you. Jaffery, after burying his poor comrade, took ship with Liosha and went to Cettinje, where he entrusted her to the care of old friends of his, the Austrian Consul and his wife, and made her known as the widow of Prescott of Reuter's to the British diplomatic authorities. Then having his work to do, he started forth again, a heavy-hearted adventurer, and, when it was over, he picked up Liosha, for whom Frau von Hagen had managed to procure a stock of more or less civilised raiment, and brought her to London to make good her claim, under Prescott's will, to her dead husband's fortune.

Now this is Jaffery all over. Put him on a battlefield with guns going off in all directions, or in a shipwreck, or in the midst of a herd of crocodiles, and he will be cool master of the situation, and will telegraph to his newspaper the graphic, nervous stuff of the born journalist; but set him a simple problem in social life, which a child of fifteen would solve in a walk across the room, and he is scared to death. Instead of sending for Barbara, for instance, when he arrived in London, or any other sensible woman, say, like Frau von Hagen of Cettinje, he drags poor Euphemia, a timid maiden lady of forty-five, from her tea-parties and Bible-classes and Dorcas-meetings at Tunbridge Wells, and plants her down as guide, philosopher and friend to this disconcerting product of Chicago and Albania. Of course the poor lady was at her wits' ends, not knowing whether to treat her as a new-born baby or a buffalo. With equal inevitability, Liosha, unaccustomed to this type of Western woman, summed her up in a drastic epithet. And in the meanwhile Jaffery went about tearing hair and beard and cursing the fate that put him in charge of a volcano in petticoats.

"I have a great regard for Euphemia," said Barbara, later in the day— they were walking up and down the terrace in, the dusk before dinner— "but I have some sympathy with Liosha. Tolstoi! My dear Jaffery! And the City Temple! If she wanted to take the girl to church, why not her own church, the Brompton Oratory or Farm Street?"

"Euphemia wouldn't attend a Popish place of worship—she still calls it Popish, poor dear—to save her soul alive, or anybody else's soul," replied Jaffery.

"Then pack her off at once to Tunbridge Wells," said Barbara. "She's even more helpless than you, which is saying a great deal. I'll see to Liosha."

Jaffery protested. It was dear of her, sweet of her, miraculous of her, but he couldn't dream of it.

"Then don't," she retorted. "Put it out of your mind. And there's Franklin. Come to dinner."

"I'm not a bit hungry," he said gloomily.

We dined; as far as I was concerned, very pleasantly. Liosha, who sat on my right, refreshingly free in her table manners (embarrassingly so to my most correct butler), was equally free in her speech. She provided me with excellent entertainment. I learned many frank truths about Albanian women, for whom, on account of their vaccine subjection, she proclaimed the most scathing contempt. Her details, in architectural phrase, were full size. Once or twice Doria, who sat on my left, lowered her eyes disapprovingly. At her age, her mother would have been shocked; her grandmother would have blushed from toes to forehead; her great-grandmother might have fainted. But Doria, a Twentieth Century product, on the Committee of a Maternity Home and a Rescue Laundry, merely looked down her nose . . . I gathered that Liosha, for all her yearning to shoot, flay alive, crucify and otherwise annoy her enemies, did not greatly regret the loss of the distinguished young Albanian cutthroat who was her affianced. Had he lived she would have spent the rest of her days in saying, like Melisande, "I am not happy." She would have been an instrument of pleasure, a producer of children, a slaving drudge, while he went triumphantly about, a predatory ravisher, among the scattered Bulgarian peasantry. In fact, she expressed a whole-hearted detestation for her betrothed. I am pretty sure, too, that the death of her father did not leave in her life the aching gap that it might have done.

You see, it came to this. Her father, an American-Albanian, wanted to run with the hare of barbarism and hunt with the hounds of civilisation. His daughter (woman the world over) was all for hunting. He had spent twenty years in America. By a law of gravitation, natural only in that Melting Pot of Nations, Chicago, he had come across an Albanian wife. . . .

Chicago is the Melting Pot of the nations of the world. Let me tell you a true tale. It has nothing whatever to do with Jaffery Chayne or Liosha—except perhaps to shew that there is no reason why a Tierra del Fuegan foundling should not run across his long-lost brother on Michigan Avenue, and still less reason why Albanian male should not meet Albanian female in Armour's stockyards. And besides, considering that I was egged on, as I said on the first page, to write these memoirs, I really don't see why I should not put into them anything I choose.

An English novelist of my acquaintance visiting Chicago received a representative of a great daily newspaper who desired to interview him. The interviewer was a typical American reporter, blue-eyed, high cheekboned, keen, nervous, finely strung, courteous, intensely alive, desirous to get to the heart of my friend's mystery, and charmingly responsive to his frank welcome. They talked. My friend, to give the young man his story, discoursed on Chicago's amazingly solved problem of the conglomeration of all the races under Heaven. To point his remarks and mark his contrasts he used the words "we English" and "you Americans." After a time the young man smiled and said: "But am not an American—at least I'm an American citizen, but I'm not a born American."

"But," cried my friend, "you're the essence of America."

"No," said the young man, "I'm an Icelander."

Thus it was natural for Liosha's father to find an Albanian wife in Chicago. She too was superficially Americanised. When they returned to Albania with their purely American daughter, they at first found it difficult to appear superficial Albanians. Liosha had to learn Albanian as a foreign language, her parents and herself always speaking English among themselves. But the call of the blood rang strong in the veins of the elders. Robbery and assassination on the heroic scale held for the man an irresistible attraction, and he acquired great skill at the business; and the woman, who seems to have been of a lymphatic temperament, sank without murmuring into the domestic subjection into which she had been born. It was only Liosha who rebelled. Hence her complicated attitude towards life, and hence her entertaining talk at the dinner table.

I enjoyed myself. So, I think, did everybody. When the ladies rose, Jaffery, who was nearest the door, opened it for them to pass out, Barbara, the last, lingered for a second or two and laid her hand on Jaffery's arm and looked up at him out of her teasing blue eyes.

"My dear Jaff," she said, "what kind of a dinner do you eat when you *are* hungry?"

CHAPTER VI

Barbara having freed Jaffery from immediate anxieties with regard to Liosha, easily persuaded him to pay a longer visit than he had proposed. A telephonic conversation with a first distracted, then conscience-smitten and then much relieved Euphemia had for effect the payment of bills at the Savoy and the retreat of the gentle lady to Tunbridge Wells. Liosha remained with us, pending certain negotiations darkly carried on by my wife and Doria in concert. During this time I had some opportunity of observing her from a more philosophic standpoint and my judgment was—I will not say formed—but aided by Barbara's confidential revelations. When not directly thwarted, she seemed to be good-natured. She took to Susan—a good sign; and Susan took to her—a better. Finding that her idea of happiness was to sprawl about the garden and let the child run over her and inveigle her into childish games and call her "Loshie" (a disrespectful mode of address which I had all the pains in the world in persuading Barbara to permit) and generally treat her as an animate instrument of entertainment, we smoothed down every obstacle that might lie in this particular path to beatitude. So many difficulties were solved. Not only were we spared the problem of what the deuce to do with Liosha during the daytime, but also Barbara was able to send the nurse away for a short and much needed holiday. Of course Barbara herself undertook all practical duties; but when she discovered that Liosha experienced primitive delight in bathing Susan— Susan's bath being a heathen rite in which ducks and fish and swimming women and horrible spiders played orgiac parts, and in getting up at seven in the morning—("Good God! Is there such an hour?" asked Adrian, when he heard about it)—in order to breakfast with Susan, and in dressing and undressing her and brushing her hair, and in tramping for miles by her side while with Basset, her vassal, in attendance, Susan rode out on her pony; when Barbara, in short, became aware of this useful infatuation, she pandered to it, somewhat shamelessly, all the time, however, keeping an acute eye on the zealous amateur. If, for instance, Liosha had picked a bushel of nectarines and had established herself with Susan, in the corner of the fruit garden, for a debauch, which would have had, for consequence, a child's funeral, Barbara, by some magic of motherhood, sprang from the earth in front of them with her funny little smile and her "Only one—and a very ripe one—for Susan, dear Liosha." And in these matters Liosha was as much overawed by Barbara as was Susan.

This, I repeat, was a good sign in Liosha. I don't say that she would have fallen captive to any ordinary child, but Susan being my child was naturally different from the vulgar run of children. She was *rarissinia avis* in the lands of small girls—one of the few points on which Barbara and I are in unclouded agreement. No one could have helped falling captive to Susan. But, I admit, in the case of Liosha, who was an out-of-the-way, incalculable sort of creature—it was a good sign. Perhaps, considering the short period during which I had her under close observation, it was the best sign. She had grievous faults.

One evening, while I was dressing for dinner, Barbara burst into my dressing-room.

"Reynolds has given me notice."

"Oh," said I, not desisting (as is the callous way of husbands the world over) from the absorbing and delicate manipulation of my tie. "What for?"

"Liosha has just gone for her with a pair of scissors."

"Horrible!" said I, getting the ends even. "I can imagine nothing more finnikin in ghastliness than to cut anybody's throat with nail scissors, especially when the subject is unwilling."

Barbara pished and pshawed. It was no occasion for levity.

"I agree," said I. The dressing hour is the calmest and most philosophic period of the day.

Barbara came up to me blue eyed and innocent, and with a traitorous jerk, undid my beautiful white bow.

"There, now listen."

And I, dilapidated wretch, had to listen to the tale of crime. It appeared that Reynolds, my wife's maid, in putting Liosha into a ready-made gown—a model gown I believe is the correct term—insisted on her being properly corseted. Liosha, agonisingly constricted, rebelled. The maid was obdurate. Liosha flew at her with a pair of scissors. I think I should have done the same. Reynolds bolted from the room. So should I have done. I sympathised with both of them. Reynolds fled to her mistress, and, declaring it to be no part of her duty to wait on tigers, gave notice.

"We can't lose Reynolds," said I.

"Of course we can't."

"And we can't pack Liosha off at a moment's notice, so as to please Reynolds."

"Oh, you're too wise altogether," said my wife, and left me to the tranquil completion of my dressing.

Liosha came down to dinner very subdued, after a short, sharp interview with Barbara, who, for so small a person, can put on a prodigious air of authority. As a punishment for bloodthirsty behaviour she had made her wear the gown in the manner prescribed by Reynolds; and she had apologised to Reynolds, who thereupon withdrew her notice. So serenity again prevailed.

In some respects Liosha was very childish. The receipt of letters, no matter from whom—even bills, receipts and circulars—gave her overwhelming joy and sense of importance. This harmless craze, however, led to another outburst of ferocity. Meeting the postman outside the gate she demanded a letter. The man looked through his bundle.

"Nothing for you this morning, ma'am."

"I wrote to the dressmaker yesterday," said Liosha, "and you've got the reply right there."

"I assure you I haven't," said the postman.

"You're a liar," cried Liosha, "and I guess I'm going to see."

Whereupon Liosha, who was as strong as a young horse, sprang to death-grapple with the postman, a puny little man, pitched him onto the side of the road and calmly entered into felonious possession of His Majesty's mails. Then finding no letter she cast the whole delivery over the supine and gasping postman and marched contemptuously into the house.

The most astonishing part of the business was that in these outbreaks of barbarity she did not seem to be impelled by blind rage. Most people who heave a postman about a peaceful county would do so in a fit of passion, through loss of nerve-control. Not so Liosha. She did these things with the bland and deadly air of an inexorable Fate.

The perspiration still beads on my brow when I think of the cajoling and bribing and blustering and lying I had to practise in order to hush up the matter. As for Liosha, both Jaffery and I rated her soundly. I explained loftily that not so many years ago, transportation, lifelong imprisonment, death were the penalties for the felony which she had committed.

Jaffery, considerably disconcerted, handled the cleek.

"You ought to have a jolly good thrashing," roared Jaffery.

At this Liosha, who had endured our abuse with the downcast eyes of angelic meekness, took a golfclub from a bag lying on the hall table and handed it to the red-bearded giant.

"I guess I do," she said. "Beat me."

And, as I am a living man, I swear that if Jaffery had taken her at her word and laid on lustily she would have taken her thrashing without a murmur. What was one to do with such a woman?

Jaffery, considerably disconcerted, fingered the cleek. Gradually she raised her glorious eyes to him, and in them I was startled to see the most extraordinary doglike submission. He frowned portentously and shook his head. Her lips worked, and after a convulsive sob or two, she threw herself on the ground, clasped his knees, and to our dismay burst into a passion of weeping. Barbara, rushing into the hall at this juncture, like a fairy tornado, released us from our embarrassing position. She annihilated us with a sweeping glance of scorn.

"Oh, go away, both of you, go away!"

So we went away and left her to deal with Liosha.

Save for such little excursions and alarms the days passed very pleasantly. Jaffery spent most of the sweltering hours of daylight (it was a blazing summer) in playing golf on the local course. Adrian and Doria trod the path of the perfect lovers, while I, to justify my position as President of the Hafiz Society, worked hard at a Persian Grammar. Barbara, the never idle, was in the meantime arranging for Liosha's future. Her organising genius had brought Doria's suggestion as to the First Class London Boarding House into the sphere of practical things. The Boarding House idea alone would not work; but, combine it with Mrs. Considine, and the scheme ran on wheels.

"Even you," said Barbara, as though I were a sort of Schopenhauer, a professional disparager of her sex—"even you have a high opinion of Mrs. Considine."

I had. Every one had a high opinion of Mrs. Considine. She was not very beautiful or very clever or very fascinating or very angelic or very anything—but she was one of those women of whom everybody has a high opinion. The impoverished widow of an Indian soldierman, with a son soldiering somewhere in India, she managed to do a great deal on very small means. She was a woman of the world, a woman of character. She knew how to deal with people of queer races. Heaven indicated her for appointment by Barbara as Liosha's duenna in the Boarding House. Mrs. Considine, herself compelled to live in these homes for the homeless, gladly accepted the proposal, came down, interviewed her charge, who happened then to be in a mood of meekness indescribable, and went away, so to speak, with her contract in her pocket. It was part of the programme that Mrs. Considine should tactfully carry on Liosha's education, which had been arrested at the age of twelve, instil into her a sense of Western decorum, extend her acquaintance, and gradually root out of her heart the yearning to do her enemies to death. It was a capital programme; and I gave it the benediction of a smile, in which, seeing Barbara's shrewd blue eyes fixed on me, I suppressed the irony.

When this was all settled Jaffery proclaimed himself the most care-free fellow alive. His hitherto grumpy and resentful attitude towards Liosha changed. He established himself as fellow slave with her under the whip of Susan's tyranny. It did one good to see these two magnificent creatures sporting together for the child's, and incidentally their own, amusement. For the first time during their intercourse they met on the same plane.

"She's really quite a good sort," said Jaffery.

But if it was pleasant to see him with Liosha, it was still more touching to watch his protective attitude towards Doria. He seemed so anxious to do her service, so deferential to her views, so puzzle-headedly eager to reconcile them with his own. She took upon herself to read him little lectures.

"Don't you think you're rather wasting your life?" she asked him one day.

"Do you think I am?"

"Yes."

"Oh! But I work hard at my job, you know," he said apologetically— "when there's one for me to do. And when there isn't I kind of prepare myself for the next. For instance I've got to keep myself always fit."

"But that's all physical and outside." She smiled, in her little superior way. "It's the inside, the personal, the essential self that matters. Life, properly understood, is a process of self-development. If a human being is the same at the end of a year as he was at the beginning he has made no spiritual progress."

Jaffery pulled his red beard. "In other words, he hasn't lived," said he.

"Precisely."

"And you think that I'm just the same sort of old animal from one year's end to another and that I don't progress worth a cent, and so, that I don't live."

"I don't want to say quite that," she replied graciously. "Every one must advance a little bit unless they deteriorate. But the conscious striving after spiritual progress is so necessary—and you seem to put it aside. It is such waste of life."

"I suppose it is, in a way," Jaffery admitted.

She pursued the theme, a flattered Egeria. "You see—well, what do you do? You travel about in out-of-the-way places and make notes about them in case the knowledge may be useful to you in the future. When you come across anything to kill, you kill it. It also pleases you to come across anything that calls for an exercise of strength. When there is a war or a revolution or anything that takes you to your real work, as you call it, you've only got to go through it and report what you see."

"But that's just the difficulty," cried Jaffery. "It isn't every chap that's tough enough to come out rosy at the end of a campaign. And it isn't every chap that can see the things he ought to write about. That's when the training comes in."

Again she smiled. "I've no idea of belittling your profession, my dear Jaffery. I think it's a noble one. But should it be the Alpha and Omega of things? Don't you see? The real life is intellectual, spiritual, emotional. What are your ideals?"

Jaffery looked at her ruefully. Beneath those dark pools of eyes lay the spirituality that made her a mystery so sacred. He, great hulking fellow, was a gross lump of clay. Ideals?

"I don't suppose I have any," said he.

"But you must. Everybody has, to a certain extent."

"Well, to ride straight and tell the truth—like the ancient Persians, I suppose it was the Persians—anyway it's a sort of rough code I've got."

"Have you read Nietzsche?" she asked suddenly.

He frowned perplexedly. "Nietzsche—that's the mad superman chap, isn't it? No. I've not read a word."

"I do wish you would. You'll find him so exhilarating. You might possibly agree with a lot of what he says. I don't. But he sets you thinking."

She sketched her somewhat prim conception of the Nietzschean philosophy, and after listening to it in dumb wonder, he promised to carry out her wishes. So, when I came down to my library that evening dressed for dinner, I found him, still in morning clothes, with "Thus Spake Zarathustra" on his knees, and a bewildered expression on his face.

"Have you read this, Hilary?" he asked.

"Yes," said I.

"Understand it?"

"More or less."

"Gosh!" said he, shutting the book, "and I suppose Doria understands it too, or she wouldn't have recommended it. But," he rose ponderously and looked down on me with serious eyes—"what the Hell is it all about?"

I drew out my watch. "The five seconds that you have before rushing up-stairs to dress," said I, "don't give me adequate time to expound a philosophic system."

Now if Adrian or I had talked to Jaffery about soul-progression and the Will to Power and suggested that he was missing the essentials of life, we should have been met with bellows of rude and profane derision. I don't believe he had even roughly considered what kind of an individuality he had, still less enquired into the state of his spiritual being. But the flip of a girl he professed so much to despise came along and reduced him to a condition of helpless introspection. I cannot say that it lasted very long. Psychology and metaphysics and æsthetics lay outside Jaffery's sphere. But while seeing no harm in his own simple creed of straight-riding and truth-speaking, he added to it an unshakable faith in Doria's intellectual and spiritual superiority. On his first meeting with her he had disclaimed the subtler mental qualities, videlicet his similitude of the bumble-bee; now, however, he went further, declaring himself, to a subrident host, to be a chuckle-headed ass, only fit to herd with savages. He would listen, with childlike envy, to Adrian, glib of tongue, exchanging with Doria the shibboleths of the Higher Life. He had been considerably impressed by Adrian as the author of a successful novel; but Adrian as a co-treader of the stars with Doria, appeared to him in the light of an immortal.

Adrian and I, when alone, laughed over old Jaff, as we had laughed over him for goodness knows how many years. I, who had guessed (with Barbara's aid) the incidence of the thunderbolt, found in his humility something pathetic which was lost to Adrian. The latter only saw the blustering, woman-scorning hulk of thews and sinews, at the mercy of anything in petticoats, from Susan upward. I disagreed. He was not at the mercy of Liosha.

"You burrowing mole," cried Adrian one morning in the library, Jaffery having gone off to golf, "can't you see that he goes about in mortal terror of her?"

"No such thing!" I retorted hotly. "He has regarded her as an abominable nuisance—a millstone round his neck—a responsibility—"

"A huntress of men," he interrupted. "Especially an all too probable huntress of Jaffery Chayne. With Susan and Barbara and Doria he knows he's safe—spared the worst—so he yields and they pick him up—look at him and stand him on his head and do whatever they darn well like to him; but with Liosha he knows he isn't safe. You see," Adrian continued, after having lit a cigarette, "Jaffery's an honourable old chap, in his way. With Liosha, his friend Prescott's widow, it would be a question of marriage or nothing."

"You're talking rubbish," said I. "Jaffery would just as soon think of marrying the Statue of Liberty in New York Harbour."

"That's what I'm telling you," said Adrian. "He's in a mortal funk lest his animated Statue of Liberty should descend from her pedestal and with resistless hands take him away and marry him."

"For one who has been hailed as the acutest psychologist of the day," said I, "you seem to have very limited powers of observation."

For some unaccountable reason Adrian's pale face flushed scarlet. He broke out vexedly:

"I don't see what my imaginative work has got to do with the trivialities of ordinary life. As a matter of fact," he added, after a pause, "the psychology in a novel is all imagination, and it's the same imaginative faculty that has been amusing itself with Jaffery and this unqualifiable lady."

"All right, my dear man," said I, pacifically. "Probably you're right and I'm wrong. I was only talking lightly. And speaking of imagination—what about your next book?"

"Oh, damn the next book," said he, flicking the ash off his cigarette. "I've got an idea, of course. A jolly good idea. But I'm not worrying about it yet."

"Why?" I asked.

He threw his cigarette into the grate. How, in the name of common sense, could he settle down to work? Wasn't his head full of his approaching marriage? Could he see at present anything beyond the thing of dream and wonder that was to be his wife? I was a cold-blooded fish to talk of novel-writing.

"But you'll have to get into it sometime or other," said I.

"Of course. As soon as we come back from Venice, and settle down to a normal life in the flat."

"What does Doria think of the new idea?"

Thousands who knew him not were looking forward to Adrian Boldero's new book. We, who loved him, were peculiarly interested. Somehow or other we had not touched before so intimately on the subject. To my surprise he frowned and snapped impatient fingers.

"I haven't told Doria anything about it. It isn't my way. My work's too personal a thing, even for Doria. She understands. I know some fellows tell their plots to any and everybody—and others, if they don't do that, lay bare their artistic souls to those near and dear to them. Well, I can't. A word, no matter how loving, of adverse criticism, a glance even that was not sympathetic would paralyse me, it would shatter my faith in the whole structure I had built up. I can't help it. It's my nature. As I told you two or three months ago, it has always been my instinct to work in the dark. I instanced my First at Cambridge. How much more powerful is the instinct when it's a question of a vital created thing like a novel? My dear Hilary, you're the man I'm fondest of in the world. You know that. But don't worry me about my work. I can't stand it. It upsets me. Doria, heart of my heart and soul of my soul, has promised not to worry me. She sees I must be free from outside influences—no matter how closely near—but still outside. And you must promise too."

"My dear old boy," said I, somewhat confused by this impassioned exposition of the artistic temperament, "you've only got to express the wish—"

"I know," said he. "Forgive me." He laughed and lit another cigarette. "But Wittekind and the editor of *Fowler's* in America—I've sold him the serial rights—are shrieking out for a synopsis. I'm damned if I'm going to give 'em a synopsis. They get on my nerves. And—we're intimate enough friends, you and I, for me to confess it—so do our dearest Barbara and old Jaff, and you yourself, when you want to know how I'm getting on. Look, dear old Hilary"—he laughed again and threw himself into an armchair—"giving birth to a book isn't very much unlike giving birth to a baby. It's analogical in all sorts of ways. Well, some women, as soon as the thing is started, can talk quite freely—sweetly and delicately—I haven't a word to say against them—to all their women friends about it. Others shrink. There's something about it too near their innermost souls for them to give their confidence to anyone. Well, dear old Hilary—that's how I feel about the novel."

He spoke from his heart. I understood—like Doria.

"Elizabeth Barrett Browning calls it 'the sorrowful, great gift,'" said I. "We who haven't got it can only bow to those who have."

Adrian rose and took a few strides about the library.

"I'm afraid I've been talking a lot of inflated nonsense. It must sound awfully like swelled head. But you know it isn't, don't you?"

"Don't he an idiot," said I. "Let us talk of something else."

We did not return to the subject.

In the course of time came Mrs. Considine to carry off Liosha to the First Class Boarding House which she had found in Queen's Gate. Liosha left us full of love for Barbara and Susan and I think of kindly feeling for myself. A few days afterwards Jaffery went off to sail a small boat with another lunatic in the Hebrides. A little later Doria and Adrian went to pay a round of short family visits beginning with Mrs. Boldero. So before August was out, Barbara and Susan and I found ourselves alone.

"Now," said I, "I can get through some work."

"Now," said Barbara, "we can run over to Dinard."

"What?" I shouted.

"Dinard," she said, softly. "We always go. We only put it off this year on account of visitors."

"We definitely made up our minds," I retorted, "that we weren't going to leave this beautiful garden. You know I never change my mind. I'm not going away."

Barbara left the room, whistling a musical comedy air.

We went to Dinard.

CHAPTER VII

There is a race of gifted people who make their livelihood by writing descriptions of weddings. I envy them. They can crowd so many pebbly facts into such a small compass. They know the names of everybody who attended from the officiating clergy to the shyest of poor relations. With the cold accuracy of an encyclopædia, and with expert technical discrimination, they mention the various fabrics of which the costumes of bride and bridesmaids were composed. They catalogue the wedding presents with the correct names of the donors. They remember what hymns were sung and who signed the register. They know the spot chosen for the honeymoon. They know the exact hour of the train by which the happy pair departed. Their knowledge is astonishing in its detail. Their accounts naturally lack imagination. Otherwise they would not be faithful records of fact. But they do lack colour, the magic word that brings a scene before the eye. Perhaps that is why they are never collected and published in book form.

Now I have been wondering how to describe the wedding of Doria and Adrian. I have recourse to Barbara.

"Why, I have the very thing for you," she says, and runs away and presently reappears with a long thing like a paper snake. "This is a full report of the wedding. I kept it. I felt it might come in useful some day," she cried in triumph. "You can stick it in bodily."

I began to read in hope the column of precise information. I end it in despair. It leaves me admiring but cold. It fails to conjure up to my mind the picture of a single mortal thing. Sadly I hand it back to Barbara.

"I shan't describe the wedding at all," I say.

And indeed why should I? Our young friends were married as legally and irrevocably as half a dozen parsons in the presence of a distinguished congregation assembled in a fashionable London church could marry them. Of what actually took place I have the confused memory of the mere man. I know that it was magnificent. All the dinner parties of Mr. Jornicroft were splendidly united. Adrian's troops of friends supported him. Doria, dark eyed, without a tinge of colour in the strange ivory of her cheek, looked more elfin than ever beneath the white veil. Jaffery, who was best man, vast in a loose frock coat, loomed like a monstrous effigy by the altar-rails. Susan, at the head of the bridesmaids, kept the stern set face of one at grapple with awful responsibility. She told her mother afterwards that a pin was running into her all the time. . . . Well, I, for one, signed the register and I kissed the bride and shook hands with Adrian, who adopted the poor nonchalant attitude of one accustomed to get married every day of his life. Driving from church to reception with Barbara, I railed, in the orthodox manner of the superior husband, at the modern wedding.

"A survival of barbarism," said I. "What is the veil but a relic of marriage by barter, when the man bought a pig in a poke and never knew his luck till he unveiled his bride? What is the ring but the symbol of the fetters of slavery? The rice, but the expression of a hope for a prolific union? The satin slipper tied on to the carriage or thrown after it? Good luck? No such thing. It was once part of the marriage ceremony for the bridegroom to tap the wife with a shoe to symbolise his assertion of and her acquiescence in her entire subjection."

"Where did Lady Bagshawe get that awful hat?" said Barbara sweetly. "Did you notice it? It isn't a hat; it's a crime."

I turned on her severely. "What has Lady Bagshawe's hat to do with the subject under discussion? Haven't you been listening?"

She squeezed my hand and laughed. "No, you dear silly, of course not."

Another instance of the essential inconvincibility of woman.

It was Jaffery Chayne, who, on the pavement before the house in Park Crescent, threw the satin slipper at the departing carriage. He had been very hearty and booming all the time, the human presentment of a devil-may-care lion out for a jaunt, and his great laugh thundering cheerily above the clatter of talk had infected the heterogeneous gathering. Unconsciously dull eyes sparkled and pursy lips vibrated into smiles. So gay a wedding reception I have never attended, and I am sure it was nothing but Jaffery's pervasive influence that infused vitality into the deadly and decorous mob. It was a miracle wrought by a rich Silenic personality. I had never guessed before the magnetic power of Jaffery Chayne. Indeed I had often wondered how the overgrown and apparently irresponsible schoolboy who couldn't make head or tail of Nietzsche and from whom the music of Shelley was hid, had managed to make a journalistic reputation as a great war and foreign correspondent. Now the veil of the mystery was drawn an inch or two aside. I saw him mingle with an alien crowd, and, by what On the surface appeared to be sheer brute full-bloodedness, compel them to his will. The wedding was not to be a hollow clang of bells but a glad fanfare of trumpets in all hearts. In order that this wedding of Adrian and

Doria should be memorable he had instinctively put out the forces that had carried him unscathed through the wildest and fiercest of the congregations of men. He could subdue and he could create. In the most pithless he had started the working of the sap of life.

As for his own definite part of best man, he played it with an Elizabethan spaciousness. . . . There was no hugger-mugger escape of travel-clad bride and bridegroom. He contrived a triumphal progress through lines of guests led by a ruddy giant, Master of the Ceremonies, exuding Pantagruelian life. Joyously he conducted them to their glittering carriage and pair— and, unconscious of anthropological truth, threw the slipper of woman's humiliation. The carriage drove off amid the cheers of the multitude. Jaffery stood and watched it until it disappeared round the curve. In my eagerness to throw the unnecessarily symbolic rice I had followed and stayed a foot or two away from him; and then I saw his face change—just for a few seconds. All the joyousness was stricken from it; his features puckered up into the familiar twists of a child about to cry. His huge glazed hands clenched and unclenched themselves. It was astonishing and very pitiful. Quickly he gulped something down and turned on me with a grin and shook me by the shoulders.

"Now I'm the only free man of the bunch. The only one. Don't you wish you were a bachelor and could go to Hell or Honolulu—wherever you chose without a care? Ho! ho! ho!" He linked his arm in mine, and said in what he thought was a whisper: "For Heaven's sake let us go in and try to find a real drink."

We went into a deserted smoking-room where decanters and siphons were set out. Jaffery helped himself to a mighty whisky and soda and poured it down his throat.

"You seemed to want that," said I, drily.

"It's this infernal kit," said he, with a gesture including his frock coat and patent leather boots. "For gossamer comfort give me a suit of armour. At any rate that's a man's kit."

I made some jesting answer; but it had been given to me to see that transient shadow of pain and despair, and I knew that the discomfort of the garments of civilisation had nothing to do with the swallowing of the huge jorum of alcohol.

Of course I told Barbara all about it—it is best to establish your wife in the habit of thinking you tell her everything—and she was more than usually gentle to Jaffery. We carried him down with us to Northlands that afternoon, calling at his club for a suit-case. In the car he tucked a very tired and comfort-desiring Susan in the shelter of his great arm. There was something pathetically tender in the gathering of the child to him. Barbara with her delicate woman's sense felt the harmonics of chords swept within him. And when we reached home and were alone together, she said with tears very near her eyes:

"Poor old Jaff. What a waste of a life!"

"My dear," I replied, "so said Doria. But you speak with the tongue of an angel, whereas Doria, I'm afraid, is still earth-bound."

The tear fell with a laugh. She touched my cheek with her hand.

"When you're intelligent like that," she said, "I really love you."

For a mere man to be certified by Barbara as intelligent is praise indeed.

"I wonder," she said, a little later, "whether those two are going to be happy?"

"As happy," said I, "as a mutual admiration society of two people can possibly be."

She rebuked me for a tinge of cynicism in my estimate. They were both of them dears and the marriage was genuine Heaven-made goods. I avowed absolute agreement.

"But what would have happened," she said reflectively, "if Jaffery had come along first and there had been no question of Adrian. Would they have been happy?"

Then I found my opportunity. "Woman," said I, "aren't you satisfied? You have made one match—you, and you'll pardon me for saying so, not Heaven—and now you want to unmake it and make a brand-new hypothetical one."

"All your talk," she said, "doesn't help poor Jaffery."

I put my hand to my head to still the flickering in my brain, kissed her and retired to my dressing-room. Barbara smiled, conscious of triumph over me.

During dinner and afterwards in the drawing-room, she played the part of Jaffery's fairy mother. She discussed his homelessness—she had an eerie way of treading on delicate ground. A bed in a tent or a club or an inn. That was his home. He had no possessions.

"Good Lord!" cried Jaffery. "I should think I have. I've got about three hundred stuffed head of game stored in the London Repository, to say nothing of skins and as fine a collection of modern weapons as you ever saw. I could furnish a place in slap-up style to-morrow."

"But have you a chest of drawers or a pillow slip or a book or a dinner plate or a fork?"

"Thousands, my dear," said Jaffery. "They're waiting to be called for in all the shops of London."

He laughed his great laugh at Barbara's momentary discomfiture. I laughed too, for he had scored a point. When a man has, say, a thousand pounds wherewith to buy that much money's worth of household clutter, he certainly is that household clutter's potential owner. Between us we developed this incontrovertible proposition.

"Then why," said Barbara, "don't you go at once to Harrod's Stores and purchase a comfortable home?"

"Because, my dear Barbara," said Jaffery, "I'm starting off for the interior of China the day after to-morrow."

"China?" echoed Barbara vaguely.

"The interior of China?" I reëchoed, with masculine definiteness.

"Why not? It isn't in Neptune or Uranus. You wouldn't go into hysterics if I said I was going to Boulogne. Let him come with me, Barbara. It would do him a thundering lot of good."

At this very faintly humorous proposal he laughed immoderately. I need not say that I declined it. I should be as happy in the interior of China as on an Albanian mountain. I asked him how long he would be away.

"A year or two," he replied casually.

"It must be a queer thing," said I, "to be born with no conception of time and space."

"A couple of years pass pretty quick," said Jaffery.

"So does a lifetime," said I.

Well, this was just like Jaffery. No sooner home amid the amenities of civilisation than the wander-fever seizes him again. In vain he pleaded his job, the valuable copy he would send to his paper. I proved to him it was but the mere lust of savagery. And he could not understand why we should be startled by the announcement that within forty-eight hours he would be on his way to lose himself for a couple of years in Crim Tartary.

"Suppose I sprang a thing like that on you," said I. "Suppose I told you I was starting to-morrow morning for the South Pole. What would you say?"

"I should say you were a liar. Ho! ho! ho!"

In his mirth he rubbed his hands and feet together like a colossal fly. The joke lasted him for the rest of the evening.

So, the next morning Jaffery left us with a "See you as soon as ever I get back," and the day after that he sailed for China. We felt sad; not only because Jaffery's vitality counted for something in the quiet backwater of our life, but also because we knew that he went away a less happy man than he had come. This time it was not sheer *Wanderlust* that had driven him into the wilderness. He had fled in the blind hope of escaping from the unescapable. The ogre to whatsoever No Man's Land he betook himself would forever be haunted by the phantom of the elf. . . . It was just as well he had gone, said Barbara.

A man of intense appetites and primitive passions, like Jaffery, for all his loyalty and lovable childishness, was better away from the neighbour's wife who had happened to engage his affections. If he lost his head. . . .

I had once seen Jaffery lose his head and the spectacle did not make for edification. It was before I was married, when Jaffery, during his London sojourn, had the spare bedroom in a set of rooms I rented in Tavistock Square. At a florist's hard by, a young flower seller—a hussy if ever there was one—but bewitchingly pretty—carried on her poetical avocation; and of her did my hulking and then susceptible friend become ragingly enamoured. I repeat, she was a hussy. She had no intention of giving him more than the tip of her pretty little shoe to kiss; but Jaffery, reading the promise of secular paradise in her eyes, had no notion of her little hard intention. He squandered himself upon her and she led him a dog's life. Of course I remonstrated, argued, implored. It was like asking a hurricane politely not to blow. Her name I remember was Gwenny. One summer evening she had promised to meet him outside the house in Tavistock Square—he had arranged to take her to some Earl's Court Exhibition, where she could satiate a depraved passion for switch-backs, water-chutes and scenic railways. At the appointed hour Jaffery stood in waiting on the pavement. I sat on the first floor balcony, alternately reading a novel and watching him with a sardonic eye. Presently Gwenny turned the corner of the square—our house was a few doors up—and she appeared, on the opposite side of the road, by the square railings. But Gwenny was not alone. Gwenny, rigged out in the height of Bloomsbury florists' fashion, was ostentatiously accompanied by a young man, a very scrubby, pallid, ignoble young man; his arm was round her waist, and her arm was around his, in the approved enlinkment of couples in her class who are keeping company, or, in other words, are, or are about to be, engaged to be married. A curious shock vibrated through Jaffery's frame. He flamed red. He saw red. Gwenny shot a supercilious glance and tossed her chin. Jaffery crossed the road and barred their path. He fished in his pocket for some coins and addressed the scrubby man, who, poor wretch, had never heard of Jaffery's existence.

"Here's twopence to go away. Take the twopence and go away. Damn you—take the twopence."

The man retreated in a scare.

"Won't you take the twopence? I should advise you to."

Anybody but a born fool or a hero would have taken the twopence. I think the scrubby man had the makings of a hero. He looked up at the blazing giant.

"You be damned!" said he, retreating a pace.

Then, suddenly, with the swiftness of a panther, Jaffery sprang on him, grasped him in the back by a clump of clothes—it seemed, with one hand, so quickly was it done—and hurled him yards away over the railings. I can still see the flight of the poor devil's body in mid air until it fell into a holly-bush. With another spring he turned on the paralysed Gwenny, caught her up like a doll and charged with her now screaming violently against the shut solid oak front door. A flash of instinct suggested a latchkey. Holding the girl anyhow, he fumbled in his pocket. It was an August London evening. The Square was deserted; but at Gwenny's shrieks, neighbouring windows were thrown up and eager heads appeared. It was very funny. There was Jaffery holding a squalling girl in one arm and with the other exploring available pockets for his latchkey. I had one of the inspirations of my life. I rushed into my bedroom, caught up the ewer from my washstand, went out onto the extreme edge of the balcony and cast the gallon or so of water over the heads of the struggling pair. The effect was amazing. Jaffery dropped the girl. The girl, once on her feet, fled like a cat. Jaffery looked up idiotically. I flourished the empty jug. I think I threatened to brain him with it if he stirred. Then people began to pour out of the houses and a policeman sprang up from nowhere. I went down and joined the excited throng. There was a dreadful to-do. It cost Jaffery five hundred pounds to mitigate the righteous wrath of the young man in the holly-bush, and save himself from a dungeon-cell. The scrubby young man, who, it appeared, had been brought up in the fishmongering trade, used the five hundred pounds to set up for himself in Ealing, where very shortly afterwards Gwenny joined him, and that, save an enduring ashamedness on the part of Jaffery, was the end of the matter.

So, if Jaffery did lose his head over Doria, there might be the devil to pay. We sighed and reconciled ourselves to his exile in Crim Tartary. After all, it was his business in life to visit the dark places of the earth and keep the world informed of history in the making. And it was a business which could not possibly be carried on in the most cunningly devised home that could be purchased at Harrod's Stores.

CHAPTER VIII

In the course of time Adrian and Doria returned from Venice, their heads full of pictures and lagoons and palaces, and took proud possession of their spacious flat in St. John's Wood. They were radiantly happy, very much in love with each other. Having brought a common vision to bear upon the glories of nature and art which they had beheld, they were spared the little squabbles over matters of æsthetic taste which often are so disastrous to the serenity of a honeymoon. Touchingly they expounded their views in the first person plural. Even Adrian, whom I must confess to have regarded as an unblushing egotist, seldom delivered himself of an egotistical opinion. "We don't despise the Eclectics," said he. And—"We prefer the Lombardic architecture to the purely Venetian," said Doria. And "we" found good in Italian wines and "we" found nothing but hideousness in Murano glass. They were, therefore, in perfect accord over decoration and furnishing. The only difference I could see between them was that Adrian loved to wallow in the comfort of a club or another person's house, but insisted on elegant austerity in his own home, whereas Doria loved elegant austerity everywhere. So they had a pure Jacobean entrance hall, a Louis XV drawing-room, an Empire bedroom, and as far as I could judge by the barrenness of the apartment, a Spartan study for Adrian.

On our first visit, they triumphantly showed us round the establishment. We came last to the study.

"No really fine imaginative work," said Adrian, with a wave of the hand indicating the ascetic table and chair, the iron safe, the bookcase and the bare walls—"no really fine imaginative work can be done among luxurious surroundings. Pictures distract one's attention, arm-chairs and sofas invite to sloth. This is my ideal of a novelist's workshop."

"It's more like a workhouse," said Barbara, with a shiver. "Or a condemned cell. But even a condemned cell would have a plank bed in it."

"You don't understand a bit," said Doria, with a touch of resentment at adverse criticism of her paragon's idiosyncrasies, "although Adrian has tried to explain it to you. It's specially arranged for concentration of mind. If it weren't for the necessity of having something to sit upon and something to write at and a few necessary reference books and a lock-up place, we should have had nothing in the room at all. When Adrian wants to relax and live his ordinary human life, he only has to walk out of the door and there he is in the midst of beautiful things."

"Oh, I quite see, dear," said Barbara, with a familiar little flash in her blue eyes. "But do you think a leather seat for that hard wooden chair—what the French call a *rond-de-cuir*—would very greatly impair the poor fellow's imagination?"

"It might be economical, too," said I, "in the way of saving shininess!—"

Adrian laughed. "It does look a bit hard, darling," said he.

"We'll get a leather seat to-day," replied Doria.

But she did not smile. Evidently to her the spot on which Adrian sat was sacrosanct. The room was the Holy of Holies where mortal man put on immortality. Flippant comment sounded like blasphemy in her ears. She even grew somewhat impatient at our lingering in the august precincts, although they had not yet been consecrated by inspired labour. Their unblessed condition was obvious. On the large library table were a couple of brass candlesticks with fresh candles (Adrian could not work by electric light), a couple of reams of scribbling paper, an inkpot, an immaculate blotting pad, three virgin quill pens (it was one of Adrian's whimsies to write always with quills), lying in a brass dish, and an office stationery case closed and aggressively new. The sight of this last monstrosity, I thought, would play the deuce with my imagination and send it on a devastating tour round the Tottenham Court Road, but not having the artistic temperament and catching a glance of challenge from Doria, I forebore to make ignorant criticism.

In the bedroom while Barbara was putting on her veil and powdering her nose (this may be what grammarians call a *hysteron proteron*—but with women one never can tell)—Doria broke into confidences not meet for masculine ears.

"Oh, darling," she cried, looking at Barbara with great awe-stricken eyes, "you can't tell what it means to be married to a genius like Adrian. I feel like one of the Daughters of Men that has been looked upon by one of the Sons of God. It's so strange. In ordinary life he's so dear and human—responsive, you know, to everything I feel and think—and sometimes I quite forget he's different from me. But at others, I'm overwhelmed by the thought of the life going on inside his soul that I can never, never share—I can only see the spirit that conceived 'The Diamond Gate'—don't you understand, darling?—and that is even now creating some new thing of wonder and beauty. I feel so little beside him. What more can I give him beyond what I have given?"

Barbara took the girl's tense face between her two hands and smiled and kissed her.

"Give him," said she, "ammoniated quinine whenever he sneezes."

Then she laughed and embraced the Heavenly One's wife, who, for the moment, had not quite decided whether to feel outraged or not, and discoursed sweet reasonableness.

"I should treat your genius, dear, just as I treat my stupid old Hilary."

She proceeded to describe the treatment. What it was, I do not know, because Barbara refused to tell me. But I can make a shrewd guess. It's a subtle scheme which she thinks is hidden from me; but really it is so transparent that a babe could see through it. I, like any wise husband, make, however, a fine assumption of blindness, and consequently lead a life of unruffled comfort.

Whether Doria followed the advice I am not certain. I have my doubts. Barbara has never knelt by the side of her stupid old Hilary's chair and worshipped him as a god. She is an excellent wife and I've no fault to find with her; but she has never done that, and she is the last woman in the world to counsel any wife to do it. Personally, I should hate to be worshipped. In worship hours I should be smoking a cigar, and who with a sense of congruity can imagine a god smoking a cigar? Besides, worship would bore me to paralysis. But Adrian loved it. He lived on it, just as the new hand in a chocolate factory lives on chocolate creams. The more he was worshipped the happier he became. And while consuming adoration he had a young Dionysian way of inhaling a cigarette—a way which Dionysus, poor god, might have exhibited, had tobacco grown with the grape on Mount Cithaeron—and a way of exhaling a cloud of smoke, holier than the fumes of incense in the nostrils of the adorer, which moved me at once to envy and exasperation.

Yes, there he would sprawl, whenever I saw them together, either in their own flat or at our house (more luxuriously at Northlands than in St. John's Wood, owing to the greater prevalence of upholstered furniture), cigarette between delicate fingers, paradox on his tongue and a Christopher Sly beatitude on his face, while Doria, chin on palm, and her great eyes set on him, drank in all the wonder of this miraculous being.

I said to Barbara: "She's making a besotted idiot of the man."

Barbara professed rare agreement. But . . . the woman's point of view.
. . .

"I don't worry about him," she said. "It's of her I'm thinking. When she has turned him into the idiot—"

"She'll adore him all the more," I interrupted.

"But when she finds out the idiot she has made?"

"No woman has ever done that since the world began," said I. "The unwavering love of woman for her home-made idiot is her sole consistency."

Barbara with much puckering of brow sought for argument, but found none, the proposition being incontrovertible. She mused for a while and then, quickly, a smile replaced the frown.

"I suppose that is why I go on loving you, Hilary dear," she said sweetly.

I turned upon her, with my hand, as it were, on the floodgates of a torrent of eloquence; but with her silvery mocking laugh she vanished from the apartment. She did. The old-fashioned high-falutin' phrase is the best description I can give of the elusive uncapturable nature of this wife of mine. It is a pity that she has so little to do with the story of Jaffery which I am trying to relate, for I should like to make her the heroine. You see, I know her so well, or imagine I do, which comes to the same thing, and I should love to present you with a solution, of this perplexing, exasperating, adorable, high-souled conundrum that is Barbara Freeth. But she, like myself, is but a *raisonneur* in the drama, and so, reluctantly, I must keep her in the background. *Paullo majora canamus.* Let us come to the horses.

All this, time we had not lost sight of Liosha. As deputies for the absent trustee we received periodical reports from the admirable Mrs. Considine, and entertained both ladies for an occasional week-end. On the whole, her demeanour in the Queen's Gate boarding-house was satisfactory. At first trouble arose over a young curly haired Swiss waiter who had won her sympathy in the matter of a broken heart. She had entered the dining-room when he was laying the table and discovered him watering the knives and forks with tears. Unaccustomed to see men weep, she enquired the cause. He dried his eyes with a napkin and told a woeful tale of a faithless love in Neuchatel, a widow plump and well-to-do. He had looked forward to marry her at the end of the year, and to pass an unruffled life in the snugness of the *delicatessen* shop which she conducted with such skill; but now alas, she had announced her engagement to another, and his dream of bliss among the chitterlings and liver-sausages was shattered. Herr Gott! what was he to do? Liosha counselled immediate return to Neuchatel and assassination of his rival. To kill another man for her was the surest way to a woman's heart. The waiter approved the scheme, but lacked the courage—also the money to go to Neuchatel. Liosha, espousing his cause warmly, gave him the latter at once. The former she set to work to instil into him. She waylaid him at odd corners in odd moments, much to the scandal of the guests, and sought to inspire him with the true Balkan spirit. She even supplied him with an Albanian knife, dangerously sharp. At last, the poor craven, finding himself unwillingly driven into crime, sought from the mistress of the boarding-house protection against his champion. Mrs. Considine, called into consultation, was informed that Mrs. Prescott must either cease from instigating the waiters to commit murder or find other quarters. Liosha curled a contemptuous lip.

"If you think I'm going to have anything more to do with the little skunk, you're mistaken."

And that evening when Josef, serving coffee in the drawing-room, approached her with the tray, she waved him off.

"See here," she said calmly, "just you keep out of my way or I might tread on you."

Whereupon the terrified Josef, amid the tittering hush of the genteel assembly, bolted from the room, and then solved the whole difficulty by bolting from the house, never to return.

When taken to task by Barbara over the ethics of this matter, Liosha shrugged her shoulders and laughed.

"I guess," she said, "if a man loves a woman strongly enough to cry for her, he ought to know what to do with the guy that butted in, without being told."

"But you don't seem to understand what a terrible thing it is to take the life of a human being," said Barbara.

"I can understand how you feel," Liosha admitted. "But I don't feel about it the same as you. I've been brought up different."

"You see, my dear Barbara," I interposed judicially, "her father made his living by slaughter before she was born. When he finished with the pigs he took on humans who displeased him."

"And they were worse than the pigs," said Liosha.

Barbara sighed, for Liosha remained unconvinced; but she extracted a promise from our fair barbarian never to shoot or jab a knife into anyone before consulting her as to the propriety of so doing.

But for this and for one or two other trivial lapses from grace, Liosha led a pretty equable existence at the boarding-house. If she now and then scandalised the inmates by her unconventional habits and free expressions of opinion, she compensated by affording them a chronic topic of conversation. A large though somewhat scornful generosity also established her in their esteem. She would lend or give anything she possessed. When one of the forlorn and woollen-shawled old maids fell ill, she sat up of nights with her, and in spite of her ignorance of nursing, which was as vast as that of a rhinoceros, magnetised the fragile lady into well-being. I think she was fairly happy. If London had been situated amid gorges and crags and ravines and granite cliffs she would have been completely so. She yearned for mountains. Mrs. Considine to satisfy this nostalgia took her for a week's trip to the English Lakes. She returned railing at Scawfell and Skiddaw for unimportant undulations, and declaring her preference for London. So in London she remained.

In these early stages of our acquaintance with Liosha, she counted in our lives for little more than a freakish interest. Even in the crises of her naughtiness anxiety as to her welfare did not rob us of our night's sleep. She existed for us rather as a toy personality whose quaint vagaries afforded us constant amusement than as an intense human soul. The working out of her destiny did not come within the sphere of our emotional sympathies like that of Adrian and Doria. The latter were of our own kind and class, bound to us not only by the common traditions of centuries, but by ties of many years' affection. It is only natural that we should have watched them more closely and involved ourselves more intimately in their scheme of things.

The first fine rapture of house-pride having grown calm, the Bolderos settled down to the serene beatitude of the Higher Life tempered by the amenities of commonplace existence. When Adrian worked, Doria read Dante and attended performances of the Intellectual Drama; when Adrian relaxed, she cooked dainties in a chafing dish and accompanied him to Musical Comedy. They entertained in a gracious modest way, and went out into cultivated society. The Art of Life, they declared, was to catch atmosphere, whatever that might mean. Adrian explained, with the gentle pity of one addressing himself to the childish intelligence.

"It's merely the perfect freedom of mental adaptation. To discuss pragmatism while eating oysters would be destructive to the enjoyment afforded by the delicate sense of taste, whereas, to let one's mind wander from the plane of philosophic thought when preparing for a Hauptmann or a Strindberg play would lead to nothing less than the disaster of disequilibrium."

Saying this he caught my cold, unsympathetic gaze, but I think I noticed the flicker of an eyelid. Doria, however, nodded, in wide-eyed approval. So I suppose they really did practise between themselves these modal gymnastics. They were all of a piece with the "atmospheres" evoked in the various rooms of the flat. To Barbara and myself, comfortable Philistines, all this appeared exceeding lunatic. But every married couple has a right to lay out its plan of happiness in its own way. If we had made taboo of irrelevant gossip between the acts of a serious play our evening would have been a failure. Theirs would have been, and, in fact, was a success. Connubial felicity they certainly achieved: and what else but an impertinence is a criticism of the means?

Easter came. They had been married six months. "The Diamond Gate" had been published for nearly a year and was still selling in England and America. Adrian flourishing his first half-yearly cheque in January had vowed he had no idea there was so much money in the world. He basked in Fortune's sunshine. But for all the basking and all the syllabus of the perfect existence, and all his unquestionable love for Doria, and all her worship for him together with its manifestation in her admirable care for his material well-being, Adrian, just at this Eastertide, began to strike me as a man lacking some essential of happiness. They spent a week or so with us at Northlands. Adrian confessed dog-weariness. His looks confirmed his words. A vertical furrow between the brows and a little dragging line at each corner of the mouth below the fair moustache forbade the familiar mockery in his pleasant face. In moments of repose the cross of strain, almost suggestive of a squint, appeared in his blue eyes. He was no longer debonair, no longer the lightly laughing philosopher, the preacher of paradox seeing flippancy in the Money Article and sorrowful wisdom in Little Tich. He was morose and irritable. He had acquired a nervous habit of secretly rubbing his thumbs swiftly over his finger-tips when Doria, in her pride, spoke of his work, which amounted almost to ill-breeding. It was only late at night during our last smoke that he assumed a semblance of the old Adrian; and by that time he had consumed as much champagne and brandy as would have rendered jocose the prophet Jeremiah.

He was suffering, poor fellow, from a nervous breakdown. From Doria we learned the cause. For the last three months he had been working at insane pressure. At seven he rose; at a quarter to eight he breakfasted; at half past he betook himself to his ascetic workroom and remained there till half-past one. At four o'clock he began a three-hour spell of work. At night a four hours' spell—from nine to one, if they had no evening engagement, from midnight to four o'clock in the morning if they had been out.

"But, my darling child!" cried Barbara, aghast when she heard of this maniacal time-table, "you must put your foot down. You mustn't let him do it. He is killing himself."

"No man," said I, in warm support of my wife, "can go on putting out creative work for more than four hours a day. Quite famous novelists whom I meet at the Athenæum have told me so themselves. Even prodigious people like Sir Walter Scott and Zola—"

"Yes, yes," said Doria. "But they were not Adrian. Every artist must be a law to himself. Adrian's different. Why—those two that you've mentioned—they slung out stuff by the bucketful. It didn't matter to them what they wrote. But Adrian has to get the rhythm and the balance and the beauty of every sentence he writes—to say nothing of the subtlety of his analysis and the perfect drawing of his pictures. My dear, good people"—she threw out her hands in an impatient gesture—"you don't know what you're talking about. How can you? It's impossible for you to conceive—it's almost impossible even for me to conceive—the creative workings of the mind of a man of genius. Four hours a day! Your mechanical fiction-monger, yes. Four hours a day is stamped all over the slack drivel they publish. But you can't imagine that work like Adrian's is to be done in this dead mechanical way."

"It is you that don't quite understand," I protested. "My admiration for Adrian's genius is second to none but yours. But I repeat that no human brain since the beginning of time has been capable of spinning cobwebs of fancy for twelve hours a day, day in and day out for months at a time. Look at your husband. He has tried it. Does he sleep well?"

"No."

"Has he a hearty appetite?"

"No."

"Is he a light-hearted, cheery sort of chap to have about the place?"

"He's naturally tired, after his winter's work," said Doria.

"He's played out," said I, "and if you are a wise woman, you'll take him away for a couple of months' rest, and when he gets back, see that he works at lower pressure."

Doria promised to do her best; but she sighed.

"You don't realise Adrian's iron will."

Once more I recognised with a shock that I did not know my Adrian. I used to think one could blow the thistledown fellow about whithersoever one pleased. Of the two, Doria seemed to have unquestionably the stronger will-power.

"Surely," said I, "you can twist him round your little finger."

Doria sighed again—and a wanly indulgent smile played about her lips.

"You two dear people are so sensible, that it makes me almost angry to see how you can't begin to understand Adrian. As a man, of course I have a certain influence over him. But as an artist—how can I? He's a thing apart from me altogether. I know perfectly well that thousands of artists' wives wreck their happiness through sheer, stupid jealousy of their husbands' art. I'm not such a narrow-minded, contemptible woman." She threw her little head up proudly. "I should loathe myself if I grudged one hour that Adrian gave to his work instead of to me."

This time Barbara and I sighed, for we realised how vain had been our arguments. Our considerably greater knowledge of life, our stark common-sense, our deep affection for Adrian counted as naught beside the fact that we had no experience whatever in the rearing of a genius.

That word "genius" came too often from Doria's lips. At first it irritated me; then I heard it with morbid detestation. In the course of a more or less intimate conversation with Adrian, I let slip a mild expression of my feelings. He groaned sympathetically.

"I wish to heaven she wouldn't do it," said he. "It puts a man into such a horrible false position towards himself. It's beautiful of her, of course—it's her love for me. But it gets on my nerves. Instead of sitting down at my desk with nothing in my mind but my day's work to slog through, I hear her voice and I have to say to myself, 'Go to. I am a genius. I mustn't write like any common fellow. I must produce the work of a genius.' It really plays the devil with me."

He walked excitedly about the library, flourishing a cigar and scattering the ash about the carpet. I am pernicketty in a few ways and hate tobacco ash on my carpet; every room in the house is an arsenal of ash trays. In normal mood Adrian punctiliously observed the little laws of the establishment. This scattering of cigar ash was a sign of spiritual convulsion.

"Have you explained the matter to Doria?" I asked.

He halted before me performing his new uncomfortable trick of slithering thumb over finger tips.

"No," he snapped. "How can I?"

I replied, mildly, that it seemed to be the simplest thing in the world. He broke away impatiently, saying that I couldn't understand.

"All right," said I, though what there was to understand in so elementary a proposition goodness only knows. I was beginning to resent this perpetual charge of non-intelligence.

"I think we had better clear out," he said. "I'm only a damned nuisance. I've got this book of mine on the brain"—he held up his head with both hands—"and I'm not a fit companion for anybody."

I adjured him in familiar terms not to talk rubbish. He was here for the repose of country things and freedom from day-infesting cares. Already he was looking better for the change. But I could not refrain from adding:

"You wrote 'The Diamond Gate' without turning a hair. Why should you worry yourself to death about this new book?"

When he answered I had the shivering impression of a wizened old man speaking to me. The slight cast I had noticed in his blue eyes became oddly accentuated.

"'The Diamond Gate,'" he said, peering at me uncannily, "was just a pretty amateur story. The new book is going to stagger the soul of humanity."

"I wish you weren't such a secretive devil," said I. "What's the book about? Tell an old friend. Get it off your mind. It will do you good."

I put my arm round his shoulders and my hand gave him an affectionate grip. My heart ached for the dear fellow, and I longed, in the plain man's way, to break down the walls of reserve, which like those of the Inquisition Chamber, I felt were closing tragically upon him.

"Come, come," I continued. "Get it out. It's obvious that the thing is suffocating you. I'll tell nobody—not even that you've told me—neither Doria nor Barbara—it will be the confidence of the confessional. You'll be all the better for it. Believe me."

He shrugged himself free from my grasp and turned away; his nervous fingers plucked unconsciously at his evening tie until it was loosened and the ends hung dissolutely over his shirt front.

"You're very good, Hilary," said he, looking at every spot in the room except my eyes. "If I could tell you, I would. But it's an enormous canvas. I could give you no idea—" The furrow deepened between his brows—"If I told you the scheme you would get about the same dramatic impression as if you read, say, the letter R, in a dictionary. I'm putting into this novel," he flickered his fingers in front of me—"everything that ever happened in human life."

I regarded him in some wonder.

"My dear fellow," said I, "you can't compress a Liebig's Extract of Existence between the covers of a six-shilling novel."

"I can," said he, "I can!" He thumped my writing table, so that all the loose brass and glass on it rattled. "And by God! I'm going to do it."

"But, my dearest friend," I expostulated, "this is absurd. It's megalomania—*la folie des grandeurs*."

"It's the divinest folly in the world," said he.

He threw a cigar stump into the fireplace and poured himself out and drank a stiff whisky and soda. Then he laughed in imitation of his familiar self.

"You dear prim old prig of a Hilary, don't worry. It's all going to come straight. When the novel of the eighteenth, nineteenth and twentieth centuries is published I guess you'll be proud of me. And now, good-night."

He laughed, waved his arm in a cavalier gesture and went from the room, slamming the door masterfully behind him.

CHAPTER IX

We kept the unreasonable pair at Northlands as long as we could, doing all that lay in our power to restore Adrian's idiotically impaired health. I motored him about the county; I took him to golf, a pastime at which I do not excel; and I initiated him into the invigorating mysteries of playing at robbers with Susan. We gave a carefully selected dinner-party or two, and accepted on his behalf a few discreet invitations. At these entertainments—whether at Northlands or elsewhere—we caused it to be understood that the lion, being sick, should not be asked to roar.

"It's so trying for him," said Doria, "when people he doesn't know come up and gush over 'The Diamond Gate'—especially now when his nerves are on edge."

On the occasion of our second dinner-party, the guests having been forewarned of the famous man's idiosyncrasies, no reference whatever was made to his achievements. We sat him between two pretty and charming women who chattered amusingly to him with what I, who kept an eye open and an ear cocked, considered to be a very subtly flattering deference. Adrian responded with adequate animation. As an ordinary clever, well-bred man of the world he might have done this almost mechanically; but I fancied that he found real enjoyment in the light and picturesque talk of his two neighbours. When the ladies left us, he discussed easy politics with the Member for our own division of the County. In the drawing-room, afterwards, he played a rubber at bridge, happened to hold good cards and smiled an hour away. When the last guest departed, he yawned, excused himself on the ground of healthy fatigue and went straight off to bed. Barbara and I congratulated ourselves on the success of our dinner-party. The next day Adrian went about as glum as a dinosaur in a museum, and conveyed, even to Susan's childish mind, his desire for solitude. His hang-dog dismalness so affected my wife, that she challenged Doria.

"What in the world is the matter with him, to-day?"

Doria drew herself up and flashed a glance at Barbara—they were both little bantams of women, one dark as wine, the other fair as corn. If ever these two should come to a fight, thought I who looked on, it would be to the death.

"Your friends are very charming, my dear, and of course I've nothing to say against them; but I was under the impression that every educated person in the English-speaking world knew my husband's name, and I consider the way he was ignored last night by those people was disgraceful."

"But, my dear Doria," cried Barbara, aghast, "we thought that Adrian was having quite a good time."

"You may think so, but he wasn't. Adrian's a gentleman and plays the game; but you must see it was very galling to him—and to me—to be treated like any stockbroker—or architect—or idle man about town."

"You are unfortunate in your examples," said I, intervening judicially. "Pray reflect that there are architects alive whose artistic genius is not far inferior to Adrian's."

"You know very well what I mean," she snapped.

"No, we don't, dear," said Barbara dangerously. "We think you're a little idiot and ought to be ashamed of yourself. We took the trouble to tell every one of those people that Adrian hated any reference to his work, and like decent folk they didn't refer to it. There—now round upon us."

The pallor deepened a shade in Doria's ivory cheek.

"You have put me in the wrong, I admit it. But I think it would have been better to let us know."

What could one do with such people? I was inclined to let them work out their salvation in their own eccentric fashion; but Barbara decided otherwise. When one's friends reached such a degree of lunacy as warranted confinement in an asylum, it was one's plain duty to look after them. So we continued to look after our genius and his worshipper, and we did it so successfully that before he left us he recovered his sleep in some measure, and lost the squinting look of strain in his eyes.

On the morning of their departure I mildly counselled him to temper his fine frenzy with common-sense.

"Knock off the night work," said I.

He frowned, fidgeted with his feet.

"I wish to God I hadn't to work at all," said he. "I hate it! I'd sooner be a coal-heaver."

"Bosh!" said I. "I know that you're an essentially idle beggar; but you're as proud as Punch of your fame and success and all that it means to you."

"What does it mean after all?"

"If you talk in that pessimistic way," I said, "you'll make me cry. Don't. It means every blessed thing in the world to you. At any rate it has meant Doria."

"I suppose that's true," he grunted. "And I suppose I am essentially idle. But I wish the damned thing would get written of its own accord. It's having to sit down at that infernal desk that gets on my nerves. I have the same horrible apprehension of it—always have—as one has before a visit to the dentist, when you know he's going to drill hell into you."

"Why do you work in such a depressing room?" I asked. "If I were shut up alone in it, I would stick my nose in the air and howl like a dog."

"Oh, the room's all right," said he. Then he looked away absently and murmured as if to himself, "It isn't the room."

"Then what is it?" I persisted.

He turned with a dreary sort of smile. "It's the born butterfly being condemned to do the work of the busy bee."

A short while afterwards we saw them drive off and watched the car disappear round the bend of the drive.

"Well, my dear," said I, "thank goodness I'm not a man of genius."

"Amen!" said Barbara, fervently.

As soon as they had settled down in their flat, Adrian began to work again, in the same unremitting fashion. The only concession he made to consideration of health was to go to bed immediately on his return from dinner-parties and theatres instead of spending three or four hours in his study. Otherwise the routine of toil went on as before. One afternoon, happening to be in town and in the neighbourhood of St. John's Wood, I called at the flat with the idea of asking Doria for a cup of tea. I also had in my pocket a letter from Jaffery which I thought might interest Adrian. The maid who opened the door informed me that her mistress was out. Was Mr. Boldero in? Yes; but he was working.

"That doesn't matter," said I. "Tell him I'm here."

The maid did not dare disturb him. Her orders were absolute. She could not refuse to admit me, seeing that I was already in the hall; but she stoutly refused to announce me. I argued with the damsel.

"I may have business of the utmost importance with your master."

She couldn't help it. She had her orders.

"But, my good Ellen," said I—the minx had actually been in our service a couple of years before!—"suppose the place were on fire, what would you do?"

She looked at me demurely. "I think I should call a policeman, sir."

"You can call one now," said I, "for I'm going to announce myself. Don't tell me I'll have to walk over your dead body first, for it won't do."

I know it is not looked upon as a friendly act to interrupt a man in his work and to disregard the orders given to his servants, but I was irritated by all this Grand Llama atmosphere of mysterious seclusion. Besides, I had been walking and felt just a little hot and dusty and thirsty, and I felt all the hotter, dustier and thirstier for my argument with Ellen.

"I'll announce myself," I said, and marched to the door of Adrian's study. It was locked. I rapped at the door.

"Who's there?" came Adrian's voice.

"Me. Hilary."

"What's the matter?"

"I happen to be a guest under your roof," said I, with a touch of temper.

"Wait a minute," said he.

I waited about two. Then the door was unlocked and opened and I strode in upon Adrian who looked rather pale and dishevelled.

"Why the deuce," said I, "did you keep me hanging about like that?"

"I'm sorry," he replied. "But I make it a fixed rule to put away my work"—he waved a hand towards the safe—"whenever anybody, even Doria, wants to come into the room."

I glanced around the cheerless place. There were no traces of work visible. Save that the quill pens and blotting pad were inky, his library table seemed as immaculate, as unstained by toil, as it did on the occasion of my first visit.

"You needn't have made all that fuss," said I. "I only dropped in for a second or two. I wanted to ask for a drink and to show you a letter from Jaffery."

"Oh, Jaffery!" He smiled. "How's the old barbarian getting on?"

"Tremendously. He's the guest of a Viceroy and living in sumptuousness. Read for yourself."

I took from my pocket letter and envelope. Now I am a man who keeps few letters and no envelopes. The second post bringing Jaffery's epistle had just arrived when I was leaving Northlands that morning, and it was but an accident of haste that the envelope had not been destroyed. I took the opportunity of tearing it up while Adrian was reading. With the pieces in my hand, I peered about the room.

"What are you looking for?" he asked.

"Your waste-paper basket."

"Haven't got such a thing."

I threw my litter into the grate.

"Why?"

"I'm not going to pander to the curiosity of housemaids," he replied rather irritably.

"What do you do with your waste paper, then?"

"Never have any," he said, with his eyes on Jaffery's letter.

"Good Lord!" I cried. "Do you pigeon-hole bills and money-lenders' circulars and second-hand booksellers' catalogues and all their wrappers?"

He folded up the letter, took me by the arm and regarded me with a smile of forced patience.

"My dear Hilary, can't you ever understand that this room is just a workshop and nothing else? Here I think of nothing but my novel. I would as soon think of conducting my social correspondence in the bathroom. If you want to see the waste-paper basket where I throw my bills and unanswered letters from duchesses, and the desk—I share it with Doria—where I dash off my brilliant replies to money-lenders, come into the drawing-room. There, also, I shall be able to give you a drink."

My eyes, following an unconscious glance from his, fell upon a new and hitherto unnoticed object—a little table, now startlingly obvious, in a corner of the all but unfurnished room, bearing a tray with half full decanter, syphon and glass.

"You've got all I want here," said I.

"No. That's mere stimulant. *Sapit lucernam*. It has a horrible flavour of midnight oil. There's not what you understand by a drink in it. Let's get out of the accursed hole."

He dragged me almost by force into the drawing-room, where he entertained me courteously. It was curious to observe how his manner changed in—I have to use the Boldero jargon—in the different atmosphere. He expounded the qualities of his whisky—a present from old man

Jornicroft, a rare blend which just a few "merchantates" (Barbara's word, he declared, was delicious) in Glasgow and Dundee and here and there a one in the City of London were able to procure. In its flavour, said he, lurked the mystery of strange and barbaric names. He showed me a Bonington water colour which he had picked up for a song. On enquiry as to the signification of a song as a unit of value, I learned that since eminent tenors and divas had sung into gramophones, the standard had appreciated.

"My dear man," he laughed, in answer to my protest. "I can afford it."

For the quarter of an hour that I spent with him in his own drawing-room, he was quite the old Adrian. I drove to Paddington Station under the influence of his urbanity. But in the train, and afterwards at home, I was teased by vague apprehensions. Hitherto I had loosely and playfully qualified his methods of work as lunatic, without a thought as to the exact significance of the term. Now a horrible thought harassed me. Had I been precise without knowing it?

Novelists may have their little idiosyncrasies, and the privacy of their working hours deserves respect; but none I have ever heard of are such fearful wildfowl as to need the precautions with which Adrian surrounded himself. Why should he put himself under lock and key? Why should he not allow human eye to fall, even from the distance prescribed by good manners, upon his precious manuscript? Why need he use care so scrupulous as not to expose even torn up bits of rough draft to the ancillary publicity of a waste-paper basket? Soundness of mind did not lie that way. The terms in which he alluded to his book were not those of a sane man filled with the joy of his creation. None of us, not even Doria, knew how the story was progressing. He had signed a contract with an American editor for serialisation to begin in July. Here we were in the middle of May, and not a page of manuscript had been delivered. Doria told Barbara that the editor had been cabling frenziedly. How much of the story was written? I recalled his wild talk at Easter about putting into the novel the whole of human life. I had jested with him, calling it a megalomaniac notion. But suppose, unwittingly, I had been right? I thought of the ghastly name physicians give to the malady and shivered.

Suddenly, a day or two afterwards, came news that, to some extent, relieved my mind.

While the Bolderos were at breakfast, a cable arrived from the Editor. It ran: "Unless half of manuscript is delivered to-day at London Office will cancel contract." Adrian read it, frowned and handed it to Doria. It seems that in all business matters she had his confidence.

"Well, dear?" she said, looking up at him.

He broke out angrily. "Did you ever hear such amazing insolence? I give this pettifogging tradesman the privilege of publishing my novel in his rubbishy periodical and he dares to dictate terms to me! Half a novel, indeed! As if it were half a bale of calico. The besotted fool! As well ask a clock-maker to deliver half a clock."

"Argument by analogy is rather dangerous," she said gently, seeking to turn aside his wrath with a smile. "It's not quite the same thing. Can't you give him something to go on with?"

"I can, but I won't. I'll see him damned first." He turned to the maid and demanded a telegraph form.

"What are you going to do?"

"I'm going to teach him a lesson. He thinks I'm going to be taken in by his bluff and run round with a brown paper parcel to Fleet Street or wherever his beastly office is. He's mistaken. There," he wrote the cable hurriedly and read it aloud, "'Shall not deliver anything. Only too glad to cancel contract.' He'll he the most surprised and disgusted man in America!"

"Need you put it quite like that?" said Doria.

"It's the only way to make him understand. He has been buzzing round me like a wasp for the past month. Now he's squashed. And now," said he, getting up and lighting a cigarette, "I'm not going to do another stroke of work for three months."

It was the news of this last announcement that relieved my mind: not the story of Adrian's intolerable treatment of the editor, which was of a piece with his ordinary attitude towards his own genius. The capriciousness of the resolution startled me; but I approved whole-heartedly. I would have counselled immediate change of scene, had not Adrian anticipated my advice by rushing off then and there to Cook's and taken tickets to Switzerland. Having some business in town, I motored up with Barbara earlier than I need have done, and we saw them off at Victoria Station. Adrian, in holiday spirits, talked rather loudly. Now that he was free from the horror of that bestial vampire sucking his blood—that was his way of referring to the long suffering and hardly used editor—life emerged from gloom into sunshine. Now his spirit could soar untrammelled. It had taken its leap into the Empyrean. He beheld his book beneath him dazzlingly clear. Three months communing with nature, three months solitude on the pure mountain heights, three months calm discipline of the soul—that was what he needed. Then to work, and in another three months, *currente calamo*, the book would be written.

"And what is Doria going to do on top of the Matterhorn?" asked my wife.

Doria cried out, "Oh, don't tease. We're not going near the Matterhorn. We're going to read beautiful books, and see beautiful things and think beautiful thoughts." She dragged Barbara a step or two aside. "Don't you think this is the best thing that could have happened?" she asked, with her anxious, earnest gaze.

"The very, very best, dear," replied Barbara gently.

And indeed it was. If ever a man realised himself to be on the verge of the abyss, I am sure it was Adrian Boldero. Some haunting fear was set at the back of his laughing eyes—the expression of an animal instinct for self-preservation which discounted the balderdash about the soaring yet disciplined soul.

I whispered to Doria: "Don't go too far into the wilds out of reach of medical advice."

"Why?"

"You're taking away a sick man."

"Do you really think so?"

"I do," said I.

She looked to right and left and then at me full in the face, and she gripped my hand.

"You're a good friend, Hilary. God knows I thank you."

From which I clearly understood that her passionately loyal heart was grievously sore for Adrian.

During their absence abroad, which lasted much longer than three months, we heard fairly regularly from Doria; twice or thrice from Adrian. After a time he grew tired of mountaintops and solitude and declared that his inspiration required steeping in the past, communion with the hallowed monuments of mankind. So they wandered about the old Italian cities, until he discovered that the one thing essential to his work was the gaiety of cosmopolitan society; whereupon they went the round of French watering-places, where Adrian played recklessly at baccarat and spent inordinate sums on food. And all the time Doria wrote glowingly of their doings. Adrian had put the book out of his head, was always in the best of spirits. He had completely recovered from the strain of work and was looking forward joyously to the final spurt in London and the achievement of the masterpiece.

Meanwhile we played the annual comedy of our August migration; the only change being that instead of Dinard we went to the West Coast of Scotland to stay with some of Barbara's relatives. One gleam of joy irradiated that grey and dismal sojourn—the news that Jaffery, his mission in Crim Tartary being accomplished, would be home for Christmas. Our host and hostess were sporting folk with red, weatherbeaten faces and a mania (which they expected us to share) for salmon-fishing in the pouring rain. As neither Barbara nor I were experts—I always trembled lest a strong young fish getting hold of the end of Barbara's line should whisk her over like a feather into the boiling current—and as for myself, I prefer the more contemplative art of bottom fishing from a punt in dry weather—our friends caught all the salmon, while we merely caught colds in the head. Many an hour of sodden misery was cheered by the whispered word of comfort: Jaffery would be home for Christmas. And when, at ten o'clock in the evening, just as we were beginning to awake from the nightmare of the day, and to desire sprightly conversation, our host and hostess fell into a lethargy, and staggered off to slumber, we beguiled the hour before bedtime with talk of Jaffery's homecoming.

At last we escaped and took the good train south. The Bolderos had already returned to London. They came to spend our first week-end at Northlands. Adrian professed to be in the robustest of health and to have not a care in the world. The holiday, said he, had done him incalculable good. Already he had begun to work in the full glow of inspiration. We thought him looking old and hag-ridden, but Doria seemed happy. She had her own reason for happiness, which she confided to Barbara. It would be early in the New Year. . . . Her eyes, I noticed, were filled with a new and wonderful love for Adrian. On the Sunday afternoon as we were sauntering about the garden, Adrian touched upon the subject in a man's shy way when speaking to his fellow man.

"Why," said I with a laugh, "that's just about the time you expect the book to be out."

He gave me a queer, slanting look. "Yes," said he, "they'll both be born together."

That night, to my consternation and sorrow, he went to bed quite fuddled with whisky.

CHAPTER X

Never shall I forget that Christmastide. Its shadow has fallen on every Christmas since then. And, in the innocent insolence of our hearts, we had planned such a merry one. It was the first since our marriage that we were spending at Northlands, for like dutiful folk we had hitherto spent the two or three festival days in the solid London house of Barbara's parents. Her father, Sir Edward Kennion, retired Permanent Secretary of a Government Office, was a courtly gentleman with a faultless taste in old china and wine, and Lady Kennion a charming old lady almost worthy of being the mother of Barbara. To speak truly, I had always enjoyed my visits. But when the news came that, for the sake of the dear lady's health, the Kennions were starting for Bermuda, in the middle of December, it did not strike us desolate. On the contrary Barbara clapped her hands in undisguised glee.

"It will do mother no end of good, and we can give Susan a real Christmas of her own."

So we laid deep schemes to fill the house to overflowing and to have a roystering time. First, for Susan's sake, we secured a widowed cousin of mine, Eileen Wetherwood, with her four children; and we sent out invitations to the *ban* and *arrière ban* of the county's juvenility, to say nothing of that of London, for a Boxing-day orgy. Having accounted satisfactorily for Susan's entertainment, we thought, I hope in a Christian spirit, of our adult circle. Dear old Jaffery would be with us. Why not ask his sister Euphemia? They had a mouse and lion affection for each other. Then there was Liosha. Both she and Jaffery met in Susan's heart, and it was Susan's Christmas. With Liosha would come Mrs. Considine, admirable and lonely woman. We trusted to luck and to Mrs. Considine's urbane influence for amenable relations between Liosha and Euphemia Chayne. With Jaffery in the house, Adrian and Doria must come. Last Christmas they had spent in the country with old Mrs. Boldero; old Mrs. Boldero was, therefore, summoned to Northlands. In the lightness of our hearts we invited Mr. Jornicroft. After the letter was posted my spirits sank. What in the world would we do with ponderous old man Jornicroft? But in the course of a few posts my gloom was lightened by a refusal. Mr. Jornicroft had been in the habit for many years of spending Christmas at the King's Hotel, Hastings, and had already made his arrangements.

"Who else is there?" asked Barbara.

"My dear," said I. "This is a modest country house, not an International Palace Hotel. Including Eileen's children and their governess and nurse and Doria's maid, we shall have to find accommodation for fifteen people."

"Nonsense!" she said. "We can't do it."

"Count up," said I.

I lit a cigar and went out into the winter-stricken garden, and left her reckoning on her fingers, with knitted brow. When I returned she greeted me with a radiantly superior smile.

"Who said it couldn't be done? I do wish men had some kind of practical sense. It's as easy as anything."

She unfolded her scheme. As far as my dazed wits could grasp it, I understood that I should give up my dressing-room, that the maids should sleep eight in a bed, that Franklin, our excellent butler, should perch in a walnut-tree and that planks should be put up in the bath-rooms for as many more guests as we cared to invite.

"That is excellent," said I, "but do you realise that in this house party there are only three grown men—three ha'porth of grown men" (I couldn't forbear allusiveness) "to this intolerable quantity of women and children?"

"But who is preventing you from asking men, dear? Who are they?"

I mentioned my old friend Vansittart; also poor John Costello's son, who would most likely be at a loose end at Christmas, and one or two others.

"Well have them, dear," said Barbara.

So four unattached men were added to the party. That made nineteen. When I thought of their accommodation my brain reeled. In order to retain my wits I gave up thinking of it, and left the matter to Barbara.

We were going to have a mighty Christmas. The house was filled with preparations. Susan and I went to the village draper's and bought beautifully coloured cotton stockings to hang up at her little cousins' bedposts. We stirred the plum pudding. We planned out everything that we should like to do, while Barbara, without much reference to us, settled what was to be done. In that way we divided the labour. Old Jaffery, back from China, came to us on the twentieth of December, and threw himself heart and soul into our side of the work. He took up our life just as though he had left it the day before yesterday—just the same sun-glazed hairy red giant, noisy, laughter-loving and voracious. Susan went about clapping her hands the day he arrived and shouting that Christmas had already begun.

The first thing he did was to clamour for Adrian, the man of fame. But the three Bolderos were not coming till the twenty-fourth. Adrian was making one last glorious spurt, so Doria said, in order to finish the great book before Christmas. We had not seen much of them during the autumn. Trivial circumstances had prevented it. Susan had had measles. I had been laid up with a wrenched knee. One side happened to be engaged when the other suggested a meeting. A trumpery series of accidents. Besides, Adrian, with his new lease of health and inspiration, had plunged deeper than ever into his work, so that it was almost impossible to get hold of him. On the few occasions when he did emerge from his work-room into the light of friendly smiles, he gave glowing accounts of progress. He was satisfying his poet's dreams. He was writing like an inspired prophet. I saw him at the beginning of December. His face was white and ghastly, the furrow had deepened between his brows, and the strained squint had become permanent in his eyes. He laughed when I repeated my warnings of the spring. Small wonder, said he, that he did not look robust; virtue was going from him into every drop of ink. He could easily get through another month.

"And then"—he clapped me on the shoulder—"my boy—you shall see! It will be worth all the *enfantement prodigieux*. You thought I was going off my chump, you dear old fuss-box. But you were wrong. So did Doria—for a week or two. Bless her! she's an artist's wife in ten million."

"Have you thought of a title?" I asked.

"'God'," said he. "Yes—'God'—short like that. Isn't it good?"

I cried out that it was in the worst possible taste. It would offend. He would lose his public. The Non-conformists and Evangelicals would be frightened by the very name. He lost his temper and scoffed at my Early Victorianism. "Little Lily and her Pet Rabbit" was the kind of title I admired. He was going to call it "God."

"My dear fellow, call it what you please," said I, anxious to avoid a duel of plates and glasses, for we were lunching on opposite sides of a table at his club.

"I please to call it," said he, "by the only conceivable title that is adequate to such a work." Then he laughed, with a gleam of his old charm, and filled up my wine glass. "Anyhow, Wittekind, who has the commercial end of things in view, thinks it's ripping." He lifted his glass. "Here's to 'God.'"

"Here's to the new book under a different name," said I.

When I told Barbara about this, she rather agreed with Wittekind. It all depended on the matter and quality of the book itself.

"Well, anyhow," said I, abhorrent of dissension, "thank Heaven the wretched composition's nearly finished."

On the morning of the twenty-third came my cousin Eileen and her offspring, and in the afternoon came Liosha and Mrs. Considine. Jaffery met his dynamic widow with frank heartiness, and for the hour before bedtime, there were wild doings in the nursery, in which neither my wife, nor my cousin, nor Mrs. Considine, nor myself were allowed to participate. When nurses sounded the retreat, our two Brobdingnagians appeared in the drawing-room, radiant, and dishevelled, with children sticking to them like flies. It was only when I saw Liosha, by the side of Jaffery, unconsciously challenging him, as it were, physical woman against physical man, with three children—two in her generous arms and one on her back—to his mere pair—that I realised, with the shock that always attends one's discovery of the obvious, the superb Olympian greatness of the creature. She stood nearly six feet to his six feet two. He stooped ever so little, as is the way of burly men. She held herself as erect as a redwood pine. The depth of her bosom, in its calm munificence, defied the vast, thick heave of his shoulders. Her lips were parted in laughter shewing magnificent teeth. In her brown eyes one could read all the mysteries and tenderness of infinite motherhood. Her hair was anyhow: a debauched wreckage of combs and wisps and hairpins. Her barbaric beauty seemed to hold sleekness in contempt. I wanted, just for the picture, half her bodice torn away. For there they stood, male and female of an heroic age, in a travesty of modern garb. Clap a pepperpot helmet on Jaffery, give him a skin-tight suit of chain mail, moulding all his swelling muscles, consider his red sweeping moustache, his red beard, his intense blue eyes staring out of a red face; dress Liosha in flaming maize and purple, leaving a breast free, and twist a gold torque through her hair, dark like the bronze-black shadows under autumn bracken; strip naked-fair the five nesting bits of humanity—it was an unpresented scene from Lohengrin or the Götterdämmerung.

I can only speak according to the impression produced by their entrance on an idle, dilettante mind. My cousin Eileen, a smiling lady of plump unimportance, to whom I afterwards told my fancy, could not understand it. Speaking entirely of physical attributes, she saw nothing more in Jaffery than an uncouth red bear, and considered Liosha far too big for a drawing-room.

When the children departed after an orgy of osculation, Jaffery surveyed with a twinkling eye the decorous quartette sitting by the fire. Then in his familiar fashion, he took his companion by the arm.

"They're too grown up for us, Liosha. Let's leave 'em. Come and I'll teach you how to play billiards."

So off they went, to the satisfaction of Barbara and myself. Nothing could be better for our Christmas merriment than such relations of comradeship. We had the cheeriest of dinners that evening. If only, said Jaffery, old Adrian and Doria were with us. Well, they were coming the next day, together with Euphemia and the four unattached men. As I said before, I had given up enquiring into the lodging of this host, but Barbara, doubtless, as is her magic way, had caused bedrooms and beds to smile where all had been blank before. She herself was free from any care, being in her brightest mood; and when Barbara gave herself up to gaiety she was the most delicious thing in the wide world.

In the morning the shadow fell. About eleven o'clock Franklin brought me a telegram into the library where Jaffery and I were sitting. I opened it.

"Terrible calamity. Come at once. Boldero."

I passed it to Jaffery. "My God!" said he, and we stared at each other. Franklin said:

"Any answer, sir?"

"Yes. 'Boldero. Coming at once.' And order the car round immediately—for London. Also ask Mrs. Freeth kindly to come here. Say the matter's important." Franklin withdrew. "It's Adrian," said I, my mind rushing back to my horrible apprehensions of the summer.

"Or Doria. I understood—" He waved a hand.

"Then Barbara must come."

"She would in any case. It may be Adrian, so I'll come too, if you'll let me."

Let the great, capable fellow come? I should think I would. "For Heaven's sake, do," said I.

Barbara entered swinging housewifely keys.

"I'm dreadfully busy, dear. What is it?"

Then she saw our two set faces and stopped short. Her quick eyes fell on the telegram which Jaffery had put down in the arm of a couch, and before we could do or say anything, she had snatched it up and read it. She turned pale and held her little body very erect.

"Have you ordered the car?"

"Yes. Jaffery's coming with us."

"Good, I'll get on my coat. Send Eileen to me. I must tell her about house things."

She went out. Jaffery laid his heavy hand on my shoulder.

"What a wonder of a wife you've got!"

"I don't need you to tell me that," said I.

We went downstairs to put on our coats and then round to the garage to hurry up the car.

"There's some dreadful trouble at Mr. Boldero's," I said to the chauffeur. "You must drive like the devil."

Barbara, veiled and coated, met us at the front door. She has a trick of doing things by lightning. We started; Barbara and Jaffery at the back, I sideways to them on one of the little chair seats. We had the car open, as it was a muggy day.... It is astonishing how such trivial matters stick in one's mind.... We went, as I had ordained, like the devil.

"Who sent that telegram?" asked Barbara.

"Doria," said I.

"I think it's Adrian," said Jaffery.

"I think," said Barbara, "it's that silly old woman, Adrian's mother. Either of the others would have said something definite. Ah!" she smote her knee with her small hand, "I hate people with spinal marrow and no backbone to hold it!"

We tore through Maidenhead at a terrific pace, the Christmas traffic in the town clearing magically before us. Sometimes a car on an errand of life or death is recognised, given way to, like a fire engine.

"What makes you so dead sure something's happened to Adrian?" Jaffery asked me as we thundered through the railway arch.

Then I remembered. I had told him little or nothing of my fears. Ever since I learned that Adrian was putting the finishing touches to his novel, I had dismissed them from my mind. Such accounts as I had given of Adrian had been in a jocularly satirical vein. I had mentioned his pontifical attitude, the magnification of his office, his bombastic rhetoric over the Higher Life and the Inspiration of the Snows, and, all that being part and parcel of our old Adrian, we had laughed. Six months before I would have told Jaffery quite a different story. But now that Adrian had practically won through, what was the good of reviving the memory of ghastly apprehensions?

"Tell me," said Jaffery. "There's something behind all this."

I told him. It took some time. We sped through Slough and Hounslow, and past the desolate winter fields. The grey air was as heavy as our hearts.

"In plain words," said Jaffery, "it's G.P.—General Paralysis of the Insane."

"That's what I fear," said I.

"And you?" He turned to Barbara.

"I too. Hilary has told you the truth."

"But Doria! Good God! Doria! It will kill her!"

Barbara put her little gloved fingers on Jaffery's great raw hand. Only at weddings or at the North Pole would Jaffery wear gloves.

"We know nothing about it as yet. The more we tear ourselves to pieces now, the less able we'll be to deal with things."

Through the bottle-neck of Brentford, the most disgraceful main entrance in the world into any great city, with bare room for a criminal double line of tramways blocked by heavy, horse-drawn traffic, an officially organised murder-trap for all save the shrinking pedestrian on the mean, narrow, greasy side-walk, we crawled as fast as we were able. Then through Chiswick, over Hammersmith Bridge, into the heart of London. All London to cross. Never had it seemed longer. And the great city was smitten by a blight. It was not a fog, for one could see clearly a hundred yards ahead. But there was no sky and the air was a queer yellow, almost olive green, in which the main buildings stood out in startling meanness, and the distant ones were providentially obscured. Though it was but little past noon, all the great shops blazed with light, but they illuminated singularly little the yellow murk of the roadway. The interiors were sharply clear. We could see swarms of black things, seething with ant-like activity amid a phantasmagoria of colours, draperies, curtains, flashes of white linen, streaks of red and yellow meat gallant with rosettes and garlands, instantaneous, glistening vistas of gold, silver and crystal, warm reflections of mahogany and walnut; on the pavements an agglutinated yet moving mass by the shop fronts, the inner stream a garish pink ribbon of faces, the outer a herd of subfuse brown. And in the roadway, through the translucent olive, the swirling traffic seemed like armies of ghosts mightily and dashingly charioted.

The darkness had deepened when we, at last, drew up at the mansions in St. John's Wood. No lights were lit in the vestibule, and the hall-porter emerged as from a cavern of despair. He opened the car-door and touched his peaked cap. I could see from the man's face that he had been expecting us. He knew us, of course, as constant visitors of the Bolderos.

"What's the matter?" I asked.

"Don't you know, sir?"

"No."

He glanced at Barbara, as if afraid to give her the shock of his news, and bent forward and whispered to me:

"Mr. Boldero's dead, sir."

I don't remember clearly what happened then. I have a vague memory of the man accompanying us in the lift and giving some unintelligible account of things. I was stunned. We had interpreted the ambiguous telegram in all other ways than this. Adrian was dead. That was all I could think of. The only coherent remark I heard the man make was that it was a dreadful thing to happen at Christmas. Barbara gripped my hand tight and did not say a word. The next phase I remember only too vividly. When the flat door opened, in a blaze of electric light, it was like a curtain being lifted on a scene of appalling tragedy. As soon as we entered we were sucked into it. A horrible hospital smell of anæsthetics, disinfectants—I know not what—greeted us.

The maid Ellen who had admitted us, red-eyed and scared, flew down the corridor into the kitchen, whence immediately afterwards emerged a professional nurse, who, carrying something, flitted into Doria's room. From the spare room came for a moment an elderly woman whom we did not know. The study door was flung wide open—I noticed that the jamb was splintered. From the drawing-room came sounds of awful moaning. We entered and found Adrian's mother alone, helpless with grief. Barbara sat by her and took her in her arms and spoke to her. But she could tell us nothing. I heard a man's step in the hall and Jaffery and I went out. He was a young man, very much agitated; he looked relieved at seeing us.

"I am a doctor," said he, "I was called in. The usual medical man is apparently away for Christmas. I'm so glad you've come. Is there a Mrs. Freeth here?"

"Yes. My wife," said I.

"Thank goodness—" He drew a breath. "There's no one here capable of doing anything. I had to get in the nurse and the other woman."

Jaffery had summoned Barbara from her vain task.

"Mrs. Boldero is very ill—as ill as she can be. Of course you were aware of her condition—well—the shock has had its not very uncommon effect."

"Life in danger?" Jaffery asked bluntly.

"Life, reason, everything. Tell me. I'm a stranger. I know nothing—I was summoned and found a man lying dead on the floor in that room"—he pointed to the study—"and a woman in a dreadful state. I've only had time to make sure that the poor fellow was dead. Could you tell me something about them?"

So we told him, the three of us together, as people will, who Adrian Boldero was, and how he and his genius were all this world and a bit of the next to his wife. How I managed to talk sensibly I don't know, for beating against the walls of my head was the thought that Adrian lay there in the room where I had seen the strange woman, lifeless and stiff, with the laughing eyes forever closed and the last mockery gone from his lips. Just then the woman appeared again. The young doctor beckoned to her and said a few words. Jaffery and I followed her into the death-chamber, leaving the doctor with Barbara. And then we stood and looked at all that was left of Adrian.

But how did it happen? It was not till long afterwards that I really knew more than the scared maid-servant and the porter of the mansions then told us. But that little more I will set down here.

For the past few days he had been working early and late, scarcely sleeping at all. The night before he had gone to bed at five, had risen sleepless at seven, and having dressed and breakfasted had locked himself in his study. The very last page, he told Doria, was to be written. He was to come down to us for Christmas, with his novel a finished thing. At ten o'clock, in accordance with custom, when he began to work early, the maid came to his door with a cup of chicken-broth. She knocked. There was no reply. She knocked louder. She called her mistress. Doria hammered . . . she shrieked. You know how swiftly terror grips a woman. She sent for the porter. Between them they raised a din to awaken—well—all but the dead. The man forced the door—hence the splinters on the jamb—and there they found Adrian, in the great bare room, hanging horribly over his writing chair, with not a scrap of paper save his blotting-pad in front of him. He must have died almost as soon as he had reached his study, before he had time to take out his manuscript from the jealous safe. That this was so the harassed doctor afterwards affirmed, when he could leave the living to make examination of the dead. Still later than that we heard the cause of death—a clot of blood on the brain. . . .

To go back . . . They found him dead. And then arose an unpicturable scene of horror. It seems that the cook, a stolid woman, on the point of starting for a Christmas visit, took charge of the situation, sent for the doctor, despatched the telegram to us, and with the help of the porter's wife, saw to

Adrian. The elder Mrs. Boldero collapsed, a futile mass of sodden hysteria. Much that was fascinating and feminine in Adrian came from this amiable and incapable lady.

We went into the dining-room and helped ourselves to whisky and soda—we needed it—and talked of the catastrophe. As yet, of course, we knew nothing of the clot of blood. Presently Barbara came in and put her hands on my shoulders.

"I must stay here, Hilary, dear. You must get a bed at your club. Jaffery will take the car and bring us what we want from Northlands, and will look after things with Eileen. And put off Euphemia and the others, if you can."

And that was the Christmas to which we had looked forward with such joyous anticipation. Adrian dead; his child stillborn: Doria hovering on the brink of life and death. I did what was possible on a Christmas eve in the way of last arrangements. But to-morrow was Christmas Day. The day after, Boxing Day. The day after that, Sunday. The whole world was dead. And all those awful days the thin yellow fog that was not fog but mere blight of darkness hung over the vast city.

God spare me such another Christmastide.

CHAPTER XI

The first stages of our grievous task were accomplished. We had buried Adrian in Highgate Cemetery with the yellow fog around us. His mother had been put into a train that would carry her to the quiet country cottage wherein she longed to be alone with her sorrow. Doria still lay in the Valley of the Shadow unconscious, perhaps fortunately, of the stealthy footsteps and muffled sounds that strike a note of agony through a house of death. And it was many days before she awoke to knowledge and despair. Barbara stayed with her.

We had found Adrian's will, leaving everything to Doria and appointing Jaffery and myself joint executors and trustees for his wife and the child that was to come, among his private papers in the Louis XV cabinet in the drawing-room. We had consulted his bankers and put matters in a solicitor's hands with a view to probate. Everything was in order. We found his own personal bills and receipts filed, his old letters tied up in bundles and labelled, his contracts, his publisher's returns, his lease, his various certificates neatly docketed. It was the private desk of a careful business man, rather than that of our old unmethodical Adrian. There are few things more painful than to pry into the intimacies of those we have loved; and Jaffery and I had to pry alone, because Doria, who might have saved our obligatory search from impertinence, lay, herself, on the Borderland.

All that we required for the simple settlement of his affairs had been found in the cabinet. On the list of assets for probate we had placed the manuscript of the new book, its value estimated on the sales of "The Diamond Gate." We had not as yet examined the safe in the study, knowing that it held nothing but the manuscript, and indeed we had not entered the forbidding room in which our poor friend had died. We kept it locked, out of half foolish and half affectionate deference to his unspoken wishes. Besides, Barbara, most exquisitely balanced of women, who went in and out of the death-chamber without any morbid repulsion, hated the door of the study to be left ajar, and, when it was closed, professed relief from an inexplicable maccabre obsession, and being an inmate of the flat its deputy lady in charge of nurses and servants and household things, she had a right to spare herself unnecessary nervous strain. But, all else having been done for the dead and for the living, the time now came for us to take the manuscript from the safe and hand it over to the publisher.

So, one dark morning, Jaffery and I unlocked the study-door and entered the gloom-filled, barren room. The curtains were drawn apart, and the blinds drawn up, and the windows framed squares of unilluminating yellow. It was bitterly cold. The fire had not been laid since the morning of the tragedy and the grate was littered with dim grey ash. The stale smell of the week's fog hung about the place. I turned on the electric light. With its white distempered, pictureless walls, and its scanty office furniture, the room looked inexpressibly dreary. We went to the library table. A quill pen lay on the blotting pad, its point in the midst of a couple of square inches of idle arabesques. On three different parts of the pad marked by singularly little blotted matter the quill had scrawled "God. A Novel. By Adrian Boldero." On a brass ash-tray I noticed three cigarettes, of each of which only about an eighth of an inch had been smoked. Jaffery, who had the key that used to hang at the end of Adrian's watch-chain, unlocked the iron safe. Its heavy door swung back and revealed its contents: Three shelves crammed from bottom to top with a chaos of loose sheets of paper. Nowhere a sign of the trim block of well-ordered manuscript.

"Pretty kind of hay," growled Jaffery, surveying it with a perplexed look. "We'll have our work cut out."

"It'll be all right," said I. "Lift out the top shelf as carefully as you can. You may be sure Adrian had some sort of method."

Onto the cleared library table Jaffery deposited three loose, ragged piles. We looked through them in utter bewilderment. Some of the sheets unnumbered, unconnected one with the other, were pages of definite manuscript; these we put aside; others contained jottings, notes, fragments of dialogue, a confused multitude of names, incomprehensible memoranda of incidents. Of the latter one has stuck in my memory. "Lancelot Sinlow seduces Guinevere the false 'Immaculata' and Jehovah steps in." Other sheets were covered with meaningless phrases, the crude drawings that the writing man makes mechanically while he is thinking over his work, and arabesques such as we found on the blotting pad.

"What the blazes is all this?" muttered Jaffery, his fingers in his beard.

"I can't make it out," said I. And then suddenly I laughed in great relief, remembering the absence of the waste-paper basket. We were turning over what evidently would have been its contents. I explained Adrian's whimsy.

"What a funny devil the poor old chap was," said Jaffery, with a laugh at the harmless foible of the artist who would not give even an incurious housemaid a clue to his mystery. "Well, clear the rubbish away, and we'll look at the second shelf."

The second shelf was more or less a replica of the first. There were more pages of consecutive composition—of such we sorted out perhaps a couple of hundred, but the rest were filled with the same incoherent scribble, with the same drawings, and with bits of scenarios of a dozen stories.

"The whole damn thing seems to be waste-paper basket," said Jaffery, standing over me. There was but one chair in the room—Adrian's famous wooden writing chair with the leathern pad for which Barbara had pleaded, the chair in which the poor fellow had died, and I was sitting in it, as I sorted the manuscript which rose in masses on the table.

"There's quite a lot of completed pages," said I, putting together those found on the two shelves. "Let us see what we can make of them."

We piled the obvious rubbish on the floor, and examined the salvage. We could make nothing of it. Jaffery wrinkled a hopeless brow.

"It will take weeks to fix it up."

"What licks me," said I, "is the difference between this and the old-maidish tidiness of his other papers. Anyhow let us go on."

In a little while we tried to put the sheets together in their order, going by the grammatical sequence of the end of one page with the beginning of the next, but rarely could we obtain more than three or four of such consecutive pages. We were confused, too, by at least a dozen headed "Chapter I."

"There's another shelf, anyhow," said Jaffery, turning away.

I nodded and went on with my puzzling task of collation. But the more I examined the more did my brain reel. I could not find the nucleus of a coherent story. A great shout from Jaffery made me start in my chair.

"Hooray! At last! I've got it! Here it is!"

He came with three thick clumps of manuscript neatly pinned together in brown paper wrappers and dumped them with a bang in front of me.

"There!" he cried, bringing down his great hand on the top of the pile.

"Thank God!" said I.

He removed his hand. Then, as he told me afterwards, I sprang to my feet with a screech like a woman's. For there, staring me in the face, on a white label gummed onto the brown paper, was the hand-written inscription:

"The Diamond Gate. A Novel—by Thomas Castleton."

"Look!" I cried, pointing; and Jaffery looked. And for a second or two we both stood stock-still.

The writing was Tom Castleton's; and the writing of the script hastily flung open by Jaffery was Tom Castleton's—Tom Castleton, the one genius of our boyish brotherhood, who had died on his voyage to Australia. There was no mistake. The great square virile hand was only too familiar—as different from Adrian's precise, academical writing as Tom Castleton from Adrian.

Then our eyes met and we realized the sin that had been committed.

There was the original manuscript of "The Diamond Gate." "The Diamond Gate" was the work not of Adrian Boldero, but of Tom Castleton. Adrian had stolen "The Diamond Gate" from a dead man. Not only from a dead man, but from the dead friend who had loved and trusted in him.

We stared at each other open-mouthed. At last Jaffery threw up his hands and, without a word, cleared the lowest shelf of the safe. Quickly we ran through the mass. We could not trust ourselves to speak. There are times when words are too idle a medium for interchange of thought. We found nothing different from the contents of the two upper shelves. The apparently coherent manuscript we placed with the rest. Again we examined it. A sickening fear gripped our hearts, and steadily grew into an awful certainty.

The great epoch-making novel did not exist.

It had never existed. Even if Adrian had lived, it would have had no possibility of existing.

"What in God's name has he been playing at?" cried Jaffery, in his great, hoarse bass.

"God knows," said I.

But even as I spoke, I knew.

I looked round the room which Barbara had once called the Condemned Cell. The ghastly truth of her prescience shook me, and I began to shudder with the horror of it, and with the hitherto unnoticed cold. I was chilled to the bone. Jaffery put his arm round my shoulders and hugged me kindly.

"Go and get warm," said he.

"But this?" I pointed to the litter.

"I'll see to it and join you in a minute."

He pushed me outside the door and I went into the drawing-room, where I crouched before a blazing fire with chattering teeth and benumbed feet and hands. I was alone. Doria had taken a faint turn for the better that morning and Barbara had run down to Northlands for the day. It was just as well she had gone, I thought. I should have a few hours to compose some story in mitigation of the tragedy.

Soon Jaffery returned with a glass of brandy, which I drank. He sat down on a low chair by the fire, his elbows on his knees and his shoulders hunched up, and the leaping firelight played queer tricks with the shadows on his bearded face, making him look old and seamed with coarse and innumerable furrows. But for the blaze the room was filled with the yellow darkness that was thickening outside; yet we did not think of turning on the lights.

"What have you done?" I asked.

"Locked the stuff up again," he replied. "This afternoon I'll bring a portmanteau and take it away."

"What are you going to do with it?"

"Leave that to me," said he.

What was in his mind I did not know, but, for the moment, I was very glad to leave it to him. In a vague way I comforted myself with the reflection that Jaffery was a specialist in crises. It was his job, as he would have said. In the ordinary affairs of life he conducted himself like an overgrown child. In time of cataclysm he was a professional demigod. He reassured me further.

"That's where I come in. Don't worry about it any more."

"All right," said I.

And for a while he said nothing and stared at the fire. Presently he broke the silence.

"What was the poor devil playing at?" he repeated. "What, in God's name?"

And then I told him. It took a long time. I was still in the cold grip of the horror of that condemned cell, and my account was none too consecutive. There was also some argument and darting up side-tracks, which broke the continuity. It was also difficult to speak of Adrian in terms that did not tear our hearts. As a despoiler of the dead, his offence was rank. But we had loved him; and we still loved him, and he had expiated his crime by a year's unimaginable torture.

Often have I said that I thought I knew my Adrian, but did not. Least of all did I know my Adrian then, as I sat paralysed by the revelation of his fraud. Even now, as I write, looking at things more or less in perspective, I cannot say that I know my Adrian. With all his faults, his poses, his superficialities, his secrecies, his egotisms, I never dreamed of him as aught but a loyal and honourable gentleman. When I think of him, I tremble before the awful isolation of the human soul. What does one man know of his brother? Yes; the coldest of poets was right: "We mortal millions live alone." It is only the unconquerable faith in Humanity by which we live that saves us from standing aghast with conjecture before those who are so near and dear to us that we feel them part of our very selves.

Adrian was dead and could not speak. What was it that in the first place made him yield to temptation? What kink in the brain warped his moral sense? God is his judge, poor boy, not I. Tom Castleton had put the manuscript of "The Diamond Gate" into his hands. Undoubtedly he was to arrange for its publication. Castleton's appointment to the professorship in Australia had been a sudden matter, as I well remember, necessitating a feverish scramble to get his affairs in order before he sailed. Why did not Adrian in the affectionate glow of parting send the manuscript straight off to a publisher? At first it was merely a question of despatching a parcel and writing a covering letter. Why were not parcel and letter sent? Merely through the sheer indolence that was characteristic of Adrian. Then came the news of Castleton's death. From that moment the poison of temptation must have begun to work. For years, in his easy way, he struggled against it, until, perhaps, desperate for Doria, he succumbed. What script, type-written or hand-written, he sent to Wittekind, the publisher of "The Diamond Gate," I did not learn till later. But why did he not destroy Tom Castleton's original manuscript? That was what Jaffery could not understand. Yet any one familiar with morbid psychology will tell you of a hundred analogical instances. Some queer superstition, some reflex action of conscience, some dim, relentless force compelling the hair shirt of penitence—that is the only way in which I, who do not pretend to be a psychologist, can explain the sustained act of folly.

And when the book blazed into instantaneous success, and he accepted it gay and debonair, what could have been the state of that man's soul? I remembered, with a shiver, the look on Adrian's face, at Mr. Jornicroft's dinner party, as if a hand had swept the joy from it, and the snapping of the stem of the wineglass. In the light of knowledge I looked back and recognised the feverishness of a demeanour that had been merely gay before. Well . . . he had been swept off his feet. If any man ever loved a woman passionately and devoutly, Adrian loved Doria. For what it may be worth, put that to his credit: he sinned for love of a woman. And the rest? The tragic rest? His undertaking to write another novel? Indomitable self-confidence was the keynote of the man. Careless, casual lover of ease that he was, everything he had definitely set himself to do heretofore, he had done.

As I have said, he had got his First Class at Cambridge, to the stupefaction of his friends. With the exception of a brilliant bar examination, he had done nothing remarkable afterwards, merely for lack of incentive. When the incentive came, the writing of a novel to eclipse "The Diamond Gate," I am absolutely certain that he had no doubt of his capacity.

When he married, I think his sunny nature dispelled the cloud of guilt. He looked forward with a gambler's eagerness to the autumn's work, the beginning of the apotheosis of his real imaginary self, the genius that was Adrian Boldero. And yet, behind all this light-hearted enthusiasm, must have run a vein of cunning, invariable symptom of an unbalanced mind, which prompted secrecy, the secrecy which he had always loved to practise, and inspired him with the idea of the mysterious, secret room. The latter originated in his brain as a fantastic plaything, an intellectual Bluebeard's chamber whose sanctity he knew his awe-stricken wife would respect. It developed into a bleak prison; and finally into the condemned cell.

As I said to Jaffery, on that morning of fog and firelight, in the midst of Adrian's artificial French Lares and Penates, dimly seen, like spindle-shanked ghosts of chairs and tables, just consider the mind-shattering facts. Here was a man whose whole literary output was a few precious essays and a few scraggy poems, who had never schemed out a novel before, not even, as far as I am aware, a short story; who had never, in any way, tested his imaginative capacity, setting out, in insane self-conceit, to write, not merely a commercial work of fiction, but a novel which would outrival a universally proclaimed work of genius. And he had no imaginative capacity. His mind was essentially critical; and the critical mind is not creative. He was a clever man. All critics are clever men; if they were just a little more, or just a little less than clever, they wouldn't be critics. Perhaps Adrian was, by a barleycorn, a little more; but he had a blind spot in his brain which prevented him from seeing that the power to do imaginative work in a literary medium is as much a special gift as the power to interpret human life on canvas. It was exactly the same thing as if you or I, who have not the remotest notion how to draw a man on horseback correctly, were to try to paint a Velasquez portrait. It did not seem to enter the poor fellow's head that the novelist, in no matter how humble a way, no matter how infinitesimal the invisible grain of muse may be, must have the especial, incommunicable gift, the queer twist of brain, if you like, but the essential quality of the artist.

And there the man had sat in that stark cell of a room, for all those months, whipping, in intolerable agony, a static imagination. He had never begun to get his central incident, his plot, his character scheme, such as all novelists must do. He had grasped at one elusive vision of life, after another. His mind had become a medley of tags of the comedy and tragedy of human things. The more confused, the more universal became the poor limited vision. The whole of illimitable life, he had told me in his flogged, crazed exaltation, was to be captured in this wondrous book. The pity of it!

How he had retained his sanity I cannot to this day understand—that is to say, if he had retained it. The hypothesis of madness comforted. I would give much to feel that he had really believed in his progress with the work, that his assurance of having come to the end was genuine. If he had deceived himself, God had been merciful. But if not, if he had sat down day after day, with the appalling consciousness of his impotence, there have been few of the sons of men to whom God had meted out, in this world, greater punishment for sin. It is incredible that he should have lasted so long alive. No wonder he could not sleep. No wonder he drank in secret. Barbara, who had gone through the household accounts, had already been staggered by the wine-merchant's bills for whisky. Had he stupefied himself day after day, night after night for the last few months? I cannot but hope that he did. At any rate God was merciful at last. He killed him.

Jaffery threw a couple of logs on the fire—the ship-logs that Adrian loved, and the sea-salts, barium, strontium and what-not, gave green and crimson and lavender flames.

"I've seen as much suffering in my time as any man living," he said. "A war-correspondent does. He sees samples of every conceivable sort of hell. But this sample I haven't struck before and it's the worst of the lot. My God! and only the day before yesterday I took him to be married."

"It was fifteen months ago, Jaff, and since then you've plucked hairs out of Prester John's beard, or been entertained by a Viceroy of China, which comes to the same thing. I was right in saying you had no idea of time or space."

He paid no attention to my poor, watery jest.

"It was the day before yesterday. And now he's dead and the child stillborn—"

I uttered a short cry which interrupted him. A memory had smitten me; that of his words in September, and of the queer slanting look in his eyes: "They'll both be born together."

I told Jaffery. "Was there ever such a ghastly prophecy?" I said. "Both stillborn together. The more one goes into the matter, the more shudderingly awful it is."

Jaffery nodded and stared into the fire.

"And she at the point of death—to complete the tragedy," he said below his breath.

Then suddenly he shook himself like a great dog.

"I would give the soul out of my body to save her," he cried with a startling quaver in his deep voice.

"I know you love her dearly, old man," said I, "but is life the best thing you can wish for her?"

"Why not?"

"Isn't it obvious? She recovers—she will, most probably, recover; Jephson said so this morning—she comes back to life to find what? The shattering of her idol. That will kill her. My dear old Jaff, it's better that she should die now."

Rugged lines that I had never seen before came into his brow, and his eyes blazed.

"What do you mean—shattering of idols?"

"She is bound to learn the truth."

He darted forward in his chair and gripped my knee in his mighty grasp, so that I winced with pain.

"She's not going to learn the truth. She's not going to have any dim suspicion of the truth. By God! I'd kill anybody, even you, who told her. She's not to know. She must never know." In his sudden fit of passion he sprang to his feet and towered over me with clenched fists,—the sputtering flames casting a weird Brocken shadow on wall and ceiling of the fog-darkened room—I shrank into my chair, for he seemed not a man but one of the primal forces of nature. He shouted in the same deep, shaken voice.

"Adrian is dead. The child is dead. But the book lives. You understand." His great fist touched my face. "The book lives. You have seen it."

"Very well," said I, "I've seen it."

"You swear you've seen it?"

"Yes," said I, in some bewilderment.

He turned away, passed his hand over his forehead and through his hair, and walked for a little about the room.

"I'm sorry, Hilary, old chap, to have lost control of myself. It's a matter of life and death. I'm all right now. But you understand clearly what I mean?"

"Certainly. I'm to swear that I saw the manuscript. I'm to lend myself to a pious fraud. That's all right for the present. But it can't last forever."

Jaffery thrust both hands in his pockets and bent and fixed the steel of his eyes on me. I should not like to be Jaffery's enemy.

"It can. And it's going to. I'll see to that."

"What do you mean?" I asked. "There's no book. We can't conjure something out of nothing."

"There is a book, damn you," he roared fiercely, "and you've seen it, and I've got it. And I'm responsible for it. And what the hell does it matter to you what becomes of it?"

"Very well," said I. "If you insist, I can wash my hands of the whole matter. I saw a completed manuscript. You are my co-executor and trustee. You took it away. That's all I know. Will that do for you?"

"Yes. And I'll give you a receipt. Whatever happens, you're not responsible. I can burn the damned thing if I like. Do anything I choose. But you've seen the outside of it."

He went to the writing table by the gloomy window and scribbled a memorandum and duplicate, which we both signed. Each pocketed a copy. Then he turned on me.

"I needn't mention that you're not going to give a hint to a human soul of what you have seen this day?"

I faced him and looked into his eyes. "What do you take me for? But you're forgetting. . . . There is one human soul who must know."

He was silent for a minute or two. Then, with his great-hearted smile:

"You and Barbara are one," said he.

Presently, after a little desultory talk, he took a folded paper from his pocket and shook it out before me. I recognized the top sheet of the blotting-pad on which Adrian had written thrice: "God: A Novel: By Adrian Boldero."

"We had better burn this," said he; and he threw it into the fire.

CHAPTER XII

The slow weeks passed. Fog gave way to long rain and rain to a touch of frost and timid spring sunshine; and it was only then that Doria emerged from the Valley of the Shadow. The first time they allowed me to visit her, I stood for a fraction of a second, almost in search of a human occupant of the room. Lying in the bed she looked such a pitiful scrap, all hair and eyes. She smiled and held droopingly out to me the most fragile thing in hands I have ever seen.

"I'm going to live, after all, they tell me."

"Of course you are," I answered cheerily. "It's the season for things to find they're going to live. The crocuses and aconite have already made the discovery."

She sighed. "The garden at Northlands will soon be beautiful. I love it in the spring. The dancing daffodils—"

"We'll have you down to dance with them," said I.

"It's strange that I want to live," she remarked after a pause. "At first I longed to die—that was why my recovery was so slow. But now—odd, isn't it?"

"Life means infinitely more than one's own sorrow, no matter how great it is," I replied gently.

"Yes," she assented. "I can live now for Adrian's memory."

I suppose most women in Doria's position would have said much the same. In ordinary circumstances one approves the pious aspiration. If it gives them temporary comfort, why, in Heaven's name, shouldn't they have it? But in Doria's case, its utterance gave me a kind of stab in the heart. By way of reply I patted her poor little wrist sympathetically.

"When will the book be out?" she asked.

"I'm afraid I don't quite know," said I.

"I suppose they're busy printing it."

"Jaffery's in charge," I replied, according to instructions.

"He must get it out at once. The early spring's the best time. It won't do to wait too long. Will you tell him?"

"I will," said I.

I don't think I have ever loathed a thing so wholly as that confounded ghost of a book. Naturally it was the dominant thought in the poor child's mind. She had already worried Barbara about it. It formed the subject of nearly her first question to me. I foresaw trouble. I could not plead bland ignorance forever; though for the present I did not know the nature of Jaffery's scheme. Anyhow I redeemed my promise and gave him Doria's message. He received it with a grumpy nod and said nothing. He had become somewhat grumpy of late, even when I did not broach the disastrous topic, and made excuses for not coming down to Northlands.

I attributed the unusual moroseness to London in vile weather. At the best of times Jaffery grew impatient of the narrow conditions of town; yet there he was week after week, staying in a poky set of furnished chambers in Victoria Street, and doing nothing in particular, as far as I could make out, save riding on the tops of motor-omnibuses without an overcoat.

After his silent acknowledgment of the message, he stuffed his pipe thoughtfully—we were in the smoking-room of a club (not the Athenæum) to which we both belonged—and then he roared out:

"Do you think she could bear the sight of me?"

"What do you mean?" I asked.

"Well"—he grinned a little—"I'm not exactly a kind of sick-room flower."

"I think you ought to see her—you're as much trustee and executor as I am. You might also save Barbara and myself from nerve-racking questions."

"All right, I'll go," he said.

The interview was only fairly successful. He told her that the book would be published as soon as possible.

"When will that be?" she asked.

Jaffery seemed to be as vague as myself.

"Is it in the printer's hands?"

"Not yet."

"Why?"

He explained that Adrian had practically finished the novel; but here and there it needed the little trimming and tacking together, which Adrian would have done had he lived to revise the manuscript. He himself was engaged on this necessary though purely mechanical task of revision.

"I quite agree," said Doria to this, "that Adrian's work could not be given out in an imperfect state. But there can't be very much to do, so why are you taking all this time over it?"

"I'm afraid I've been rather busy," said he.

Which tactless, though I admit unavoidable, reply did not greatly please Doria. When she saw Barbara, to whom she related this conversation, she complained of Jaffery's unfeeling conduct. He had no right to hang up Adrian's great novel on account of his own wretched business. Letting the latter slide would have been a tribute to his dead friend. Barbara did her best to soothe her; but we agreed that Jaffery had made a bad start.

A short while afterwards I was in the club again and there I came across Arbuthnot, the manager of Jaffery's newspaper, whom I had known for some years—originally I think through Jaffery. I accepted the offer of a seat at his luncheon table, and, as men will, we began to discuss our common friend.

"I wonder what has come over him lately," said he after a while.

"Have you noticed any difference?" I was startled.

"Yes. Can't make him out."

"Poor Adrian Boldero's death was a great shock."

"Quite so," Arbuthnot assented. "But Jaff Chayne, when he gets a shock, is the sort of fellow that goes into the middle of a wilderness and roars. Yet here he is in London and won't be persuaded to leave it."

"What do you mean?" I asked.

"We wanted to send him out to Persia, and he refused to go. We had to send young Brodie instead, who won't do the work half as well."

"All this is news to me," said I.

"And it was a first-class business with armed escorts, caravans, wild tribes—a matter of great danger and subtle politics—railways, finance—the whole hang of the international situation and internal conditions—a big scoop—everything that usually is butter and honey to Jaff Chayne—an ideal job for him in every way. But no. He was fed up with scalliwagging all over the place. He wanted a season in town!"

At the idea of Jaffery yearning to play the Society butterfly I could not help laughing. Jaffery lounging down Bond Street in immaculate vesture! Jaffery sipping tea at afternoon At Homes! Jaffery dancing till three o'clock in the morning! It was all very comic, and Arbuthnot seeing the matter in that aspect laughed too. But, on the other hand, it was all very incomprehensible. To Jaffery a job was a sacred affair, the meaning of his existence. He was a Mercury who took himself seriously. The more remote and rough and uncomfortable and dangerous his mission, the more he liked it. He had never spared himself. He had been a model special correspondent ever ready at a moment's notice to set off to the ends of the earth. And now, all of a sudden, behold him declining a task after his own heart, and, as I gathered from Arbuthnot, of the greatest political significance, and thereby endangering his peculiar and honourable position on the paper.

"If it had been any other man alive who had turned us down like that," said Arbuthnot, "we would have chucked him altogether. In fact we didn't tell him that we wouldn't."

It was very mysterious; all the more so because Jaffery had never been a man of mystery, like Adrian. I went away wondering. If it had occurred to me at the time that I was destined to play Boswell to Jaffery's Johnson, perhaps I might have gone straight to him and demanded a solution of my difficulties. As it was, in my unawakened condition, I did nothing of the kind. I spent an hour or two looking up something in the British Museum, stopped at the bootmaker's to give an order concerning Susan's riding-boots (*vide* diary) and drove home to dinner, to a comfortable chat with Barbara, during which I gave her an account of the day's doings, and eventually to the peaceful slumber of the contented and inoffensive man.

A fortnight or so passed before I saw Jaffery again. Happening to be in Westminster in the forenoon—I had come up to town on business—I mounted to his cheerless eyrie in Victoria Street, and rang the bell. A dingy servitor in a dress suit, on transient duty, admitted me, and I found Jaffery collarless and minus jacket and waistcoat, smoking a pipe in front of the fire. It wasn't even a good coal fire. Some austere former tenant had installed an electric radiator in the once comfort-giving grate. But Jaffery did not seem to mind. The remains of breakfast were on the table which the dingy servitor began to clear. Jaffery rose from the depths of his easy chair like an agile mammoth.

"Hullo, hullo, hullo!"

His usual greeting. We shook hands and commended the weather. When the alien attendant had departed, he began to curse London. It was a hole for sick dogs, not for sound men. He loathed its abominable suffocation.

"Then why the deuce do you stay in it?"

He shrugged his shoulders. "I can't do anything else."

This gave me an opening to satisfy my curiosity.

"I understood you could have gone to Persia."

He frowned and tugged his red beard. "How did you know that?"

"Arbuthnot—" I began.

"Arbuthnot?" he boomed angrily. "What the blazes does he mean by telling you about my affairs? I'll punch his damned head!"

"Don't," said I. "Your hands are so big and he's so small. You might hurt him."

"I'd like to hurt him. Why can't he keep his infernal tongue quiet?"

He proceeded to wither up the soul of Arbuthnot with awful anathema. Then in his infantile way he shouted: "I didn't want any of you to know anything about it."

"Why?" I asked.

"Because I didn't."

"But I suppose you wanted to go to Persia?"

He paused in his lumbering walk about the little room and collecting a litter of books and papers and a hat or two and a legging from a sofa, pitched it into a corner.

"Here. Sit down."

I had been warming my back at the fire hitherto and surveying the half-formal, half-unkempt sitting-room. It was by no means the comfortable home from Harrod's Stores that Barbara had prescribed; and he had not attempted to furnish it in slap-up style with the heads of game and skins and modern weapons which lay in the London Repository. It was the impersonal abode of the male bird of passage.

"Sit down," said he, "and have a drink."

I declined, alleging the fact that a philosophically minded country gentleman of domestic habits does not require alcohol at half past eleven in the morning, except under the stress of peculiar circumstances.

"I'm going to have one anyway!"

He disappeared and presently reëntered with a battered two-handled silver quart pot bearing defaced arms and inscription, a rowing trophy of Cambridge days, which he always carried about with him on no matter what lightly equipped expedition—it is always a matter of regret to me that Jaffery, as I have mentioned before, missed his seat in the Cambridge boat; but when one despoils a Proctor of his square cap and it is found the central feature of one's rooms beneath a glass shade such as used to protect wax flowers from the dust, what can one expect from the priggish judgment of university authority?—he reëntered, with this vessel full of beer. He nodded, drank a huge draught and wiped his moustache with his hand.

"Better have some. I've got a cask in the bedroom."

"Good God!" said I, aghast. "What else do you keep there? A side of bacon and a Limburger cheese and Bombay duck?"

Now just imagine a civilised gentleman keeping a cask of beer in his bedroom.

Jaffery laughed and took another swig and called me a long, lean, puny-gutted insect; which was not polite, but I was glad to hear the deep "Ho! ho! ho!" that followed his vituperation.

"All the same," said I, reclining on the cleared sofa and lighting a cigarette, "I should like to know why you missed one of the chances of your life in not going out to Persia."

He stood, for a moment or two, scrabbling in whisker and beard; and, turning over in his mind, I suppose, that Barbara was my wife, and Susan my child, and I myself an inconsiderable human not evilly disposed towards him, he apparently decided not to annihilate me.

"It was hell, Hilary, old chap, to chuck the Persian proposition," said he, his hands in his trouser pockets, looking out of the window at the infinitely reaching landscape of the chimney pots of south London, their grey smoke making London's unique pearly haze below the crisp blue of the March sky. "Just hell!" he muttered in his bass whisper, and craning round my neck I could, with the tail of my eye, catch his gaze, which was very wistful and seemed directed not at the opalescent mystery of the London air, but at the clear vividness of the Persian desert. Away and away, beyond the shimmering sand, gleamed the frosted town with white walls, white domes, white minarets against the horizon band of topaz and amethystine vapours. And in his nostrils was the immemorable smell of the East, and in his ears the startling jingle of the harness and the pad of the camels, and the guttural cries of the drivers, and in his heart the certainty of plucking out the secret from the soul of this strange land. . . .

At last he swung round and throwing himself into the armchair enquired politely after the health of Barbara and Susan. As far as the Persian journey was concerned the palaver was ended. He did not intend to give me his reasons for staying in England and I could not demand them more insistently. At any rate I had discovered the cause of his grumpiness. What creature of Jaffery's temperament could be contented with a soft bed in the centre of civilisation, when he had the chance of sleeping in verminous caravanserais with a saddle for pillow? In spite of his amazing predilections, Jaffery was very human. He would make a great sacrifice without hesitation; but the consequences of the sacrifice would cause him to go about like a bear with a sore head.

And the cause of the sacrifice? Obviously Doria. Once having been admitted to her bedside, he went there every day. Flowers and fruit he had sent from the very beginning in absurd profusion; a grape for Doria failed in adequacy unless it was the size of a pumpkin. Now he brought the offerings personally in embarrassing bulk. One offering was a gramophone which nearly drove her mad. Even in its present stage of development it offends the sensitive ear; but in its early days it was an instrument of torturing cacophony. And Jaffery, thinking the brazen strains music of the spheres, would turn on the hideous engine, when he came to see her, and would grin and roar and expect her to shew evidence of ravished senses. She did her best, poor child, out of politeness and recognition of his desire to alleviate her lot; but I don't think the gramophone conveyed to her heart the poor dear fellow's unspoken message. But gently criticising the banality of the tunes the thing played and sending him forth in quest of records of recondite and "unrecorded" music, she succeeded in mitigating the terror. To the present moment, however, I don't think Jaffery has realised that she had a higher æsthetic equipment than the hypnotised fox-terrier in the advertisement. . . . Jaffery also bought her puzzles and funny penny pavement toys and gallons of eau-de-cologne (which came in useful), and expensive scent (which she abominated), and stacks of new novels, and a fearsome machine of wood and brass and universal joints, by means of which an invalid could read and breakfast and write and shave all at the same time. The only thing he did not give her—the thing she craved more than all—was a fresh-bound copy of Adrian's book.

Obviously, as I have remarked, it was Doria that kept him out of Persia. But I could not help thinking that this same Persian journey might have afforded a solution of the whole difficulty. Despatched suddenly to that vaguely known country, he could have taken the mythical manuscript to revise on the journey: the convoy could have been attacked by a horde of Kurds or such-like desperadoes, all could have been slain save a fortunate handful, and the manuscript could have been looted as an important political document and carried off into Eternity. Doria would have hated Jaffery forever after; but his chivalrous aim would have been accomplished. Adrian's honour would have been safe. But this simple way out never occurred to him. Apparently he thought it wiser to sacrifice his career and remain in London so as to buoy Doria up with false hope, all the time praying God to burn down St. Quentin's Mansions (where he lived) and Adrian's portmanteau of rubbish and himself all together.

Suddenly, as soon as Doria could be moved, Mr. Jornicroft stepped in and carried her to the south of France. Barbara and Jaffery and myself saw her off by the afternoon train at Charing Cross. She was to rest in Paris for the night and the next day, and proceed the following night to Nice. She looked the frailest thing under the sun. Her face was startling ivory beneath her widow's headgear. She had scarcely strength to lift her head. Mr. Jornicroft had made luxurious arrangements for her comfort—an ambulance carriage from St. John's Wood, a special invalid compartment in the train; but at the station, as at Doria's wedding, Jaffery took command. It was his great arms that lifted her feather-weight with extraordinary sureness and gentleness from the carriage, carried her across the platform and deposited her tenderly on her couch in the compartment. Touched by his solicitude she thanked him with much graciousness. He bent over her—we were standing at the door and could not choose but hear:

"Don't you remember what I said the first day I met you?"

"Yes."

"It stands, my dear; and more than that." He paused for a second and took her thin hand. "And don't you worry about that book. You get well and strong."

He kissed her hand and spoiled the gallantry by squeezing her shoulder—half her little body it seemed to be—and emerging from the compartment joined us on the platform. He put a great finger on the arm of the rubicund, thickset, black-moustached Jornicroft.

"I think I'll come with you as far as Paris," said he. "I'll get into a smoker somewhere or the other."

"But, my dear sir"—exclaimed Mr. Jornicroft in some amazement—"it's awfully kind, but why should you?"

"Mrs. Boldero has got to be carried. I didn't realise it. She can't put her feet to the ground. Some one has got to lift her at every stage of the journey. And I'm not going to let any damned clumsy fellow handle her. I'll see her into the Nice train to-morrow night—perhaps I'll go on to Nice with you and fix her up in the hotel. As a matter of fact, I will. I shan't worry you. You won't see me, except at the right time. Don't be afraid."

Mr. Jornicroft, most methodical of Britons, gasped. So, I must confess, did Barbara and I. When Jaffery met us at the station he had no more intention of escorting Doria to Nice than we had ourselves.

"I can't permit it—it's too kind—there's no necessity—we'll get on all right!" spluttered Mr. Jornicroft.

"You won't. She has got to be carried. You're not going to take any risks."

"But, my dear fellow—it's absurd—you haven't any luggage."

"Luggage?" He looked at Mr. Jornicroft as if he had suggested the impossibility of going abroad without a motor veil or the Encyclopædia Britannica. "What the blazes has luggage got to do with it?" His roar could be heard above the din of the hurrying station. "I don't want *luggage*." The humour of the proposition appealed to him so mightily that he went off into one of his reverberating explosions of mirth.

"Ho! ho! ho!" Then recovering—"Don't you worry about that."

"But have you enough on you—it's an expensive journey—of course I should be most happy—"

Jaffery stepped back and scanned the length of the platform and beckoned to an official, who came hurrying towards him. It was the station master.

"Have you ever seen me before, Mr. Winter?"

The official laughed. "Pretty often, Mr. Chayne."

"Do you think I could get from here to Nice without buying a ticket now?"

"Why, of course, our agent at Boulogne will arrange it if I send him a wire."

"Right," said Jaffery. "Please do so, Mr. Winter. I'm crossing now and going to Nice by the Côte d'Azur Express to-morrow night. And see after a seat for me, will you?"

"I'll reserve a compartment if possible, Mr. Chayne."

The station master raised his hat and departed. Jaffery, his hands stuffed deep in his pockets, beamed upon us like a mountainous child. We were all impressed by his lordly command of the railway systems of Europe. It was a question of credit, of course, but neither Mr. Jornicroft, solid man that he was, nor myself could have undertaken that journey with a few loose shillings in his possession. For the first time since Adrian's death I saw Jaffery really enjoying himself.

And that is how Jaffery without money or luggage or even an overcoat travelled from London to Nice, for no other purpose than to save Doria's sacred little body from being profaned by the touch of ruder hands.

Having carried her at every stage beginning with the transfer from train to steamer at Folkestone and ending with a triumphant march up the stairs to the third floor of the Cimiez hotel, he took the first train back straight through to London.

He returned the same old grinning giant, without a shadow of grumpiness on his jolly face.

CHAPTER XIII

About this time a bolt came from the blue or a bomb fell at our feet—the metaphor doesn't matter so long as it conveys a sense of an unlooked-for phenomenon. True, in relation to cosmic forces, it was but a trumpery bolt or a squib-like bomb; but it startled us all the same. The admirable Mrs. Considine got married. A retired warrior, a recent widower, but a celibate of twenty years standing owing to the fact that his late wife and himself had occupied separate continents (*on avait fait continent à part,* as the French might say) during that period, a Major-General fresh from India, an old flame and constant correspondent, had suddenly swooped down upon the boarding-house in Queen's Gate and, in swashbuckling fashion, had abducted the admirable and unresisting lady. It was a matter of special license, and off went the tardily happy pair to Margate, before we had finished rubbing our eyes.

It was grossly selfish on the part of Mrs. Considine, said Barbara. She thought her—no; perhaps she didn't think her—God alone knows the convolutions of feminine mental processes—but she proclaimed her anyhow—an unscrupulous woman.

"There's Liosha," she said, "left alone in that boarding-house."

"My dear," said I, "Mrs. Jupp—I admit it's deplorable taste to change a name of such gentility as Considine for that of Jupp, but it isn't unscrupulous—Mrs. Jupp did not happen to be charged with a mission from on High to dry nurse Liosha for the rest of her life."

"That's where you're wrong," Barbara retorted. "She was. She was the one person in the world who could look after Liosha. See what she's done for her. It was her duty to stick to Liosha. As for those two old faggots marrying, they ought to be ashamed of themselves."

Whether they were ashamed of themselves or not didn't matter. Liosha remained alone in the boarding-house. Not all Barbara's indignation could turn Mrs. Jupp into the admirable Mrs. Considine and bring her back to Queen's Gate. What was to be done? We consulted Jaffery, who as Liosha's trustee ought to have consulted us. Jaffery pulled a long face and smiled ruefully. For the first time he realised—in spite of tragic happenings—the comedy aspect of his position as the legal guardian of two young, well-to-do and attractive widows. He was the last man in the world to whom one would have expected such a fate to befall. He too swore lustily at the defaulting duenna.

"I thought it was all fixed up nicely forever," he growled.

"Everything is transitory in this life, my dear fellow," said I. "Everything except a trusteeship. That goes on forever."

"That's the devil of it," he growled.

"You must get used to it," said I. "You'll have lots more to look after before you've done with this existence!"

His look hardened and seemed to say: "If you go and die and saddle me with Barbara, I'll punch your head."

He turned his back on me and, jerking a thumb, addressed Barbara.

"Why do you take him out without a muzzle? Now you've got sense. What shall I do?"

Then Liosha superb and smiling sailed into the room.

I ought to have mentioned that Barbara had convened this meeting at the boarding-house. The room into which Liosha sailed was the elegant *"bonbonnière"* of a chamber known as the "boudoir." There was a great deal of ribbon and frill and photograph frame and artful feminine touch about it, which Liosha and, doubtless, many other inmates thought mightily refined.

Liosha kissed Barbara and shook hands with Jaffery and me, bade us be seated and put us at our ease with a social grace which could not have been excelled by the admirable Mrs. Considine (now Jupp) herself. That maligned lady had performed her duties during the past two years with characteristic ability. Parenthetically I may remark that Liosha's table-manners and formal demeanour were now irreproachable. Mrs. Considine had also taken up the Western education of the child of twelve at the point at which it had been arrested, and had brought Liosha's information as to history, geography, politics and the world in general to the standard of that of the average schoolgirl of fifteen. Again, she had developed in our fair barbarian a natural taste in dress, curbing, on her emergence from mourning, a fierce desire for apparel in primary colours, and leading her onwards to an appreciation of suaver harmonies. Again she had run her tactful hand over Liosha's stockyard vocabulary, erasing words and expressions that might offend Queen's Gate and substituting others that might charm; and she had done it with a touch of humour not lost on Liosha, who had retained the sense of values in which no child born and bred in Chicago can be deficient.

"I suppose you're all fussed to death about this marriage," she said pleasantly. "Well, I couldn't help it."

"Of course not, dear," said Barbara.

"You might have given us a hint as to what was going on," said Jaffery.

"What good could you have done? In Albania if the General had interfered with your plans, you might have shot him from behind a stone and everyone except Mrs. Considine would have been happy; but I've been taught you don't do things like that in South Kensington."

"Whoever wanted to shoot the chap?"

"I, for one," said Barbara. "What are we to do now?"

"Find another dragon," said Jaffery.

"But supposing I don't want another dragon?"

"That doesn't matter in the least. You've got to have one."

"Say, Jaff Chayne," cried Liosha, "do you think I can't look after myself by this time? What do you take me for?"

I interposed. "Rather a lonely young woman, that's all. Jaffery, in his tactless way, by using the absurd term 'dragon,' has missed the point altogether. You want a companion, if only to go about with, say to restaurants and theatres."

"I guess I can get heaps of those," said Liosha, a smile in her eyes. "Don't you worry!"

"All the more reason for a dragon."

"If you mean somebody who's going to sit on my back every time I talk to a man, I decidedly object. Mrs. Considine was different and you're not going to find another like her in a hurry. Besides—I had sense enough to see that she was going to teach me things. But I don't want to be taught any more. I've learned enough."

"But it's just a woman companion that we want to give you, dear," said Barbara. "Her mere presence about you is a protection against—well, any pretty young woman living alone is liable to chance impertinence and annoyance."

Liosha's dark eyes flashed. "I'd like to see any man try to annoy me. He wouldn't try twice. You ask Mrs. Jardine"—Mrs. Jardine was the keeper of the boarding-house—"she'll tell you a thing or two about my being able to keep men from annoying me."

Barbara did, afterwards, ask Mrs. Jardine, and obtained a few sidelights on Liosha's defensive methods. What they lacked in subtlety they made up in physical effectiveness. There were not many spruce young gentlemen who, after a week's residence in that establishment, did not adopt a peculiarly deferential attitude towards Liosha.

"Still," said Jaffery, "I think you ought to have somebody, you know."

"If you're so keen on a dragon," replied Liosha defiantly, "why not take on the job yourself?"

"I? Good Lord! Ho! ho! ho!"

Jaffery rose to his feet and roared with laughter. It was a fine joke.

"There's a lot in Liosha's suggestion," said Barbara, with an air of seriousness.

"You don't expect me to come and live here?" he cried, waving a hand to the frills and ribbons.

"It wouldn't be a bad idea," said I. "You would get all the advantages and refining influences of a first-class English home."

He pivoted round. "Oh, you be—"

"Hush," said Barbara. "Either you ought to stay here and look after Liosha more than you do—"

He protested. Wasn't he always looking after her? Didn't he write? Didn't he drop in now and then to see how she was getting on?

"Have you ever taken the poor child out to dinner?" Barbara asked sternly.

He stood before her in the confusion of a schoolboy detected in a lapse from grace, stammering explanations. Then Liosha rose, and I noticed just the faintest little twitching of her lip.

"I don't want Jaff Chayne to be made to take me out to dinner against his will."

"But—God bless my soul! I should love to take you out. I never thought of it because I never take anybody out. I'm a barbarian, my dear girl, just like yourself. If you wanted to be taken out, why on earth didn't you say so?"

Liosha regarded him steadily. "I would rather cut my tongue out."

Jaffery returned her gaze for a few seconds, then turned away puzzled. There seemed to be an unnecessary vehemence in Liosha's tone. He turned again and approached her with a smiling face.

"I only meant that I didn't know you cared for that sort of thing, Liosha. You must forgive me. Come and dine with me at the Carlton this evening and do a theatre afterwards."

"No, I wont!" cried Liosha. "You insult me."

Her cheeks paled and she shook in sudden wrath. She looked magnificent. Jaffery frowned.

"I think I'll have to be a bit of a dragon after all."

I recalled a scene of nearly two years before when he had frowned and spoken thus roughly and she had invited him to chastise her with a cleek. She did not repeat the invitation, but a sob rose in her throat and she marched to the door, and at the door, turned splendidly, quivering.

"I'm not going to have you or any one else for a dragon. And"—alas for the superficiality of Mrs. Considine's training—"I'm going to do as I damn well like."

Her voice broke on the last word, as she dashed from the room. I exchanged a glance with Barbara, who followed her. Barbara could convey a complicated set of instructions by her glance. Jaffery pulled out pouch and pipe and shook his head.

"Woman is a remarkable phenomenon," said he.

"A more remarkable phenomenon still," said I, "is the dunderheaded male."

"I did nothing to cause these heroics."

"You asked her to ask you to ask her out to dinner."

"I didn't," he protested.

I proved to him by all the rules of feminine logic that he had done so. Holding the match over the bowl of his pipe, he puffed savagely.

"I wish I were a cannibal in Central Africa, where women are in proper subjection. There's no worry about 'em there."

"Isn't there?" said I. "You just ask the next cannibal you meet. He is confronted with the Great Conundrum, even as we are."

"He can solve it by clubbing his wife on the head."

"Quite so," said I. "But do you think the poor fellow does it for pleasure? No. It worries him dreadfully to have to do it."

"That's specious rot, and platitudinous rubbish such as any soft idiot who's been glued all his life to an armchair can reel off by the mile. I know better. A couple of years ago Liosha would have eaten out of my hand, to say nothing of dining with me at the Canton. It's all this infernal civilisation. It has spoiled her."

"You began this argument," said I, "with the proposition that woman was a remarkable phenomenon—a generalisation which includes woman in fig-leaves and woman in diamonds."

"Oh, dry up," said Jaffery, "and tell me what I ought to do. I didn't want to hurt the girl's feelings. Why should I? In fact I'm rather fond of her. She appeals to me as something big and primitive. Long ago, if it hadn't been that poor old Prescott—you know what I mean—I gave up thinking of her in that way at once—and now I just want to be friends—we have been friends. She's a jolly good sort, and, if I had thought of it, I would have taken her about a bit. . . . But what I can't stand is these modern neurotics—"

"You called them heroics—"

"All the same thing. It's purely artificial. It's cultivated by every modern woman. Instead of thinking in a straight line they're taught it's correct to think in a corkscrew. You never know where to have 'em."

"That's their artfulness," said I. "Who can blame them?"

Meanwhile Liosha, pursued by Barbara, had rushed to her bedroom, where she burst into a passion of tears. Jaff Chayne, she wailed, had always treated her like dirt. It was true that her father had stuck pigs in the stockyards; but he was of an old Albanian family, quite as good a family as Jaff Chayne's. It had numbered princes and great chieftains, the majority of whom had been most gloriously slain in warfare. She would like to know which of Jaff Chayne's ancestors had died out of their feather beds.

"His grandfather," said Barbara, "was killed in the Indian Mutiny, and his father in the Zulu War."

Liosha didn't care. That only proved an equality. Jaff Chayne had no right to treat her like dirt. He had no right to put a female policeman over her. She was a free woman—she wouldn't go out to dinner with Jaff Chayne for a thousand pounds. Oh, she hated him; at which renewed declaration she burst into fresh weeping and wished she were dead. As a guardian of young and beautiful widows Jaffery did not seem to be a success.

Barbara, in her wise way, said very little, and searched the paraphernalia on the dressing table for eau-de-cologne and such other lotions as would remove the stain of tears. Holding these in front of Liosha, like a stern nurse administering medicine, she waited till the fit had subsided. Then she spoke.

"You ought to be ashamed of yourself, Liosha, going on like a silly schoolgirl instead of a grown-up woman of the world. I wonder you didn't announce your intention of assassinating Jaffery."

"I've a good mind to," replied Liosha, nursing her grievance.

"Well, why don't you do it?" Barbara whipped up a murderous-looking knife that lay on a little table—it was the same weapon that she had lent the Swiss waiter. "Here's a dagger." She threw it on the girl's lap. "I'll ring the bell and send a message for Mr. Chayne to come up. As soon as he enters you can stick it into him. Then you can stick it into me. Then if you like you can go downstairs and stick it into Hilary. And having destroyed everybody who cares for you and is good to you, you'll feel a silly ass—such a silly ass that you'll forget to stick it into yourself."

Liosha threw the knife into a corner. On its way it snicked a neat little chip out of a chair-back.

"What do you want me to do?"

"Clean your face," said Barbara, and presented the materials.

Sitting on the bed and regarding herself in a hand-mirror Liosha obeyed meekly. Barbara brought the powder puff.

"Now your nose. There!" For the first time Barbara smiled. "Now you look better. Oh, my dear girl!" she cried, seating herself beside Liosha and putting an arm round her waist. "That's not the way to deal with men. You must learn. They're only overgrown babies. Listen."

And she poured into unsophisticated but sympathetic ears all the duplicity, all the treachery, all the insidious cunning and all the serpent-like wisdom of her unscrupulous sex. What she said neither I nor any of the sons of men are ever likely to know! but so proud of belonging to that nefarious sisterhood, so overweening in her sex-conceit did she render Liosha, that when they entered the little private sitting-room next door whither, according to the instructions conveyed by Barbara's parting glance downstairs, I had dragged a softly swearing Jaffery, she marched up to him and said serenely:

"If you really do want me to dine with you, I'll come with pleasure. But the next time you ask me, please do it in a decent way."

I saw mischief lurking in my wife's eye and shook my head at her rebukingly. But Jaffery stared at Liosha and gasped. It was all very well for Doria and Barbara to be ever putting him in the wrong: they were daughters of a subtle civilisation; but here was Liosha, who had once asked him to beat her, doing the same—woman was a more curious phenomenon than ever.

"I'm sorry if my manners are not as they should be," said he with a touch of irony. "I'll try to mend 'em. Anyhow, it's awfully good of you to come."

She smiled and bowed; not the deep bow of Albania, but the delicate little inclination of South Kensington. The quarrel was healed, the incident closed. He arranged to call for her in a taxi at a quarter to seven. Barbara looked at the clock and said that we must be going. We rose to take our leave. Maliciously I said:

"But we've settled nothing about a remplaçante for Mrs. Considine."

"I guess we've settled everything," Liosha replied sweetly. "No one can replace Mrs. Considine."

I quite enjoyed our little silent walk downstairs. Evidently Jaffery's theory of primitive woman had been knocked endways; and, to judge by the faint knitting of her brow, Barbara was uneasily conscious of a mission unfulfilled. Liosha had gained her independence.

Our friends carried out the evening's programme. Liosha behaved with extreme propriety, modelling her outward demeanour upon that of Mrs. Considine, and her attitude towards Jaffery on a literal interpretation of Barbara's reprehensible precepts. She was so dignified that Jaffery, lest he should offend, was afraid to open his mouth except for the purpose of shovelling in food, which he did, in astounding quantity. From what both of us gathered afterwards—and gleefully we compared notes—they were vastly polite to each other. He might have been entertaining the decorous wife of a Dutch Colonial Governor from whom he desired facilities of travel. The simple Eve travestied in guile took him in completely. Aware that it was her duty to treat him like an overgrown baby and mould him to her fancy and twist him round her finger and lead him whithersoever she willed, making him feel all the time that he was pointing out the road, she did not know how to begin. She sat tongue-tied, racking her brains to loss of appetite; which was a pity, for the maître d'hôtel, given a free hand by her barbarously ignorant host, had composed a royal menu. As dinner proceeded she grew shyer than a chit of sixteen. Over the quails a great silence reigned. Hers she could not touch, but she watched him fork, as it seemed to her, one after the other, whole, down his throat: and she adored him for it. It was her ideal of manly gusto. She nearly wept into her *Fraises Diane*—vast craggy strawberries (in March) rising from a drift of snow impregnated by all the distillations of all the flowers of all the summers of all the hills—because she would have given her soul to sit beside him on the table with the bowl on her lap and feed him with a tablespoon and, for her share of it, lick the spoon after his every mouthful. But it had been drummed into her that she was a woman of the world, the fashionable and all but incomprehensible world, the English world. She looked around and saw a hundred of her sex practising the well-bred deportment that Mrs. Considine had preached. She reflected that to all of those women gently nurtured in this queer English civilisation, equally remote from Armour's stockyards and from her Albanian fastness, the wisdom that Barbara had imparted to her a few hours before was but their A.B.C. of life in their dealings with their male companions. She also reflected—and for the reflection not Mrs. Considine or Barbara, only her woman's heart was responsible—that to the man whom she yearned to feed with great tablespoonfuls of delight, she counted no more than a pig or a cow—her instinctive similes, you must remember, were pastoral—or that peculiar damfool of a sister of his, Euphemia.

When I think of these two children of nature, sitting opposite to one another in the fashionable restaurant trying to behave like super-civilised dolls, I cannot help smiling. They were both so thoroughly in earnest; and they bored themselves and each other so dreadfully. Conversation patched sporadically great expanses of silence and then they talked of the things that did not interest them in the least. Of course they smiled at each other, the smirk being essential to the polite atmosphere; and of course Jaffery played host in the orthodox manner, and Liosha acknowledged attentions with a courtesy equally orthodox. But how much happier they both would have been on a bleak mountain-side eating stew out of a pot! Even champagne and old brandy failed to exercise mellowing influences. The twain were petrified in their own awful correctitude. Perhaps if they had proceeded to a musical comedy or a farce or a variety entertainment where Jaffery could have expanded his lungs in laughter, their evening as a whole might have been less dismal. But a misapprehension as to the nature of the play had caused Jaffery to book seats for a gloomy drama with an ironical title, which stupefied them with depression.

When they waited for the front door of the house in Queen's Gate to open to their ring, Liosha in her best manner thanked him for a most enjoyable evening.

"Most enjoyable indeed," said Jaffery. "We must have another, if you will do me the honour. What do you say to this day week?"

"I shall be delighted," said Liosha.

So that day week they repeated this extraordinary performance, and the week after that, and so on until it became a grim and terrifying fixture. And while Jaffery, in a fog of theory as to the Eternal Feminine, was trying to do his duty, Liosha struggled hard to smother her own tumultuous feelings and to carry out Barbara's prescription for the treatment of overgrown babies; but the deuce of it was that though in her eyes Jaffery was pleasantly overgrown, she could not for the life of her regard him as a baby. So it came to pass that an unnatural pair continued to meet and mystify and misunderstand each other to the great content of the high gods and of one unimportant human philosopher who looked on.

"I told you all this artificiality was spoiling her," Jaffery growled, one day. "She's as prim as an old maid. I can't get anything out of her."

"That's a pity," said I.

"It is." He reflected for a moment. "And the more so because she looks so stunning in her evening gowns. She wipes the floor with all the other women."

I smiled. You can get a lot of quiet amusement out of your friends if you know how to set to work.

CHAPTER XIV

It was a gorgeous April day—one of those days when young Spring in madcap masquerade flaunts it in the borrowed mantle of summer. She could assume the deep blue of the sky and the gold of the sunshine, but through all the travesty peeped her laughing youth, the little tender leaves on the trees, the first shy bloom of the lilac, the swelling of the hawthorn buds, the pathetic immature barrenness of the walnuts.

And even the leafless walnuts were full of alien life, for in their hollow boles chippering starlings made furtive nests, and in their topmost forks jackdaws worked with clamorous zeal. A pale butterfly here and there accomplished its early day, and queen wasps awakened from their winter slumber in cosy crevices, the tiniest winter-palaces in the world, sped like golden arrow tips to and from the homes they had to build alone for the swarms that were to come. The flower beds shone gay with tulips and hyacinths; in the long grass beyond the lawn and under the trees danced a thousand daffodils; and by their side warmly wrapped up in furs lay Doria on a long cane chair.

She could not literally dance with the daffodils as I had prophesied, for her full strength had not yet returned, but there she was among them, and she smiled at them sympathetically as though they were dancing in her honour. She was, however, restored to health; the great circles beneath her eyes had disappeared and a tinge of colour shewed beneath her ivory cheek. Beside her, in the first sunbonnet of the year, sat Susan, a prim monkey of nine. . . . Lord! It scarcely seemed two years since Jaffery came from Albania and tossed the seven year old up in his arms and was struck all of a heap by Doria at their first meeting. So thought I, looking from my study-table at the pretty picture some thirty yards, away. And once again—pleasant self repetition of history—Jaffery was expected. Doria, fresh from Nice, had spent a night at her father's house and had come down to us the evening before to complete her convalescence. She had wanted to go straight to the flat in St. John's Wood and begin her life anew with Adrian's beloved ghost, and she had issued orders to servants to have everything in readiness for her arrival, but Barbara had intervened and so had Mr. Jornicroft, a man of limited sympathies and brutal common sense. All of us, including Jaffery, who seemed to regard advice to Doria as a presumption only equalled by that of a pilgrim on his road to Mecca giving hints to Allah as to the way to run the universe, had urged her to give up the abode of tragic memories and find a haven of quietude elsewhere. But she had indignantly refused. The home of her wondrous married life was the home of her widowhood. If she gave it up, how could she live in peace with the consciousness ever in her brain that the Holy of Holies in which Adrian had worked and died was being profaned by vulgar tread? Our suggestions were callous, monstrous, everything that could arise from earth-bound non-percipience of sacred things. We could only prevail upon her to postpone her return to the flat until such time as she was physically strong enough to grapple with changed conditions.

The pink sunbonnet was very near the dark head; both were bending over a book on Doria's knee—*Les Malheurs de Sophie*, which Susan, proud of her French scholarship, had proposed to read to Doria, who having just returned from France was supposed to be the latest authority on the language. I noticed that the severity of this intellectual communion was mitigated by Susan's favourite black kitten, who, sitting on its little haunches, seemed to be turning over pages rather rapidly. Then all of a sudden, from nowhere in particular, there stepped into the landscape (framed, you must remember, by the jambs of my door) a huge and familiar figure, carrying a great suit-case. He put this on the ground, rushed up to Doria, shook her by both hands, swung Susan in the air and kissed her, and was still laughing and making the welkin ring—that is to say, making a thundering noise—when I, having sped across the lawn, joined the group.

"Hello!" said I, "how did you get here?"

"Walked from the station," said Jaffery. "Came down by an earlier train. No good staying in town on such a morning. Besides—" He glanced at Doria in significant aposiopesis.

"And you lugged that infernal thing a mile and a half?" I asked, pointing to the suit-case, which must have weighed half a ton. "Why didn't you leave it to be called for?"

"This? This little *sachet*?" He lifted it up by one finger and grinned.

Susan regarded the feat, awe-stricken. "Oh, Uncle Jaff, you are strong!"

Doria smiled at him admiringly and declared she couldn't lift the thing an inch from the ground with both her hands.

"Do you know," she laughed, "when he used to carry me about, I felt as if I had been picked up by an iron crane."

Jaffery beamed with delight. He was just a little vain of his physical strength. A colleague of his once told me that he had seen Jaffery in a nasty row in Caracas during a revolution, bend from his saddle and wrench up two murderous villains by the armpits, one in each hand, and dash their heads together over his horse's neck. But that is the sort of story that Jaffery himself never told.

Barbara, who, flitting about the house on domestic duty, had caught sight of him through a window, came out to greet him.

"Isn't it glorious to have her back?" he cried, waving his great hand towards Doria. "And looking so bonny. Nothing like the South. The sunshine gets into your blood. By Jove! what a difference, eh? Remember when we started for Nice?"

He stood, legs apart and hands on hips, looking down on her with as much pride as if he had wrought the miracle himself.

"Get some more chairs, dear," said Barbara.

By good fortune seeing one of the gardeners in the near distance, I hailed him and shouted the necessary orders. That is the one disadvantage of summer: during the whole of that otherwise happy season, Barbara expects me to be something between a scene-shifter and a Furniture Removing Van.

The chairs were fetched from a far-off summer house and we settled down. Jaffery lit his pipe, smiled at Doria, and met a very wistful look. He held her eyes for a space, and laid his great hand very gently on hers.

"I know what you're thinking of," he said, with an arresting tenderness in his deep voice. "You won't have to wait much longer."

"Is it at the printer's?"

"It's printed."

Barbara and I gave each a little start—we looked at Jaffery, who was taking no notice of us, and then questioningly at each other. What on earth did the man mean?

"From to-morrow onwards, till publication, the press will be flooded with paragraphs about Adrian Boldero's new book. I fixed it up with Wittekind, as a sort of welcome home to you."

"That was very kind, Jaffery," said Doria; "but was it necessary? I mean, couldn't Wittekind have done it before?"

"It was necessary in a way," said Jaffery. "We wanted you to pass the proofs."

Doria smiled proudly. "Pass Adrian's proofs? I? I wouldn't presume to do such a thing."

"Well, here they are, anyway," said Jaffery.

And to the bewilderment of Barbara and myself, he snapped open the hasps of his suit-case and drew out a great thick clump of galley-proofs fastened by a clip at the left hand top corner, which he deposited on Doria's lap. She closed her eyes and her eyelids fluttered as she fingered the precious thing. For a moment we thought she was going to faint. There was breathless silence. Even Susan, who had been left out in the cold, let the black kitten leap from her knee, and aware that something out of the ordinary was happening, fixed her wondering eyes on Doria. Her mother and I wondered even more than Susan, for we had more reason. Of what manuscript, in heaven's name, were these the printed proofs? Was it possible that I had been mistaken and that Jaffery, in the assiduity of love, had made coherence out of Adrian's farrago of despair?

Jaffery touched Doria's hand with his finger tips. She opened her eyes and smiled wanly, and looked at the front slip of the long proofs. At once she sat bolt upright.

"'*The Greater Glory.*' But that wasn't Adrian's title. His title was '*God.*' Who has dared to change it?"

He drew out a great thick clump of galley-proofs.

Her eyes flashed; her little body quivered. She flamed an incarnate indignation. For some reason or other she turned accusingly on me.

"I knew nothing of the change," said I, "but I'm very glad to hear of it now."

Many times before had I been forced to disclaim knowledge of what Jaffery had been doing with the book.

"Wittekind wouldn't have the old title," cried Jaffery eagerly. "The public are very narrow minded, and he felt that in certain quarters it might be misunderstood."

"Wittekind told dear Adrian that he thought it a perfect title."

"Our dear Adrian," said I, pacifically, "was a man of enormous will-power and perhaps Wittekind hadn't the strength to stand up against him."

"Of course he hadn't," exclaimed Doria. "Of course he hadn't when Adrian was alive: now Adrian's dead, he thinks he is going to do just as he chooses. He isn't! Not while I live, he isn't!"

Jaffery looked at me from beneath bent brows and his eyes were turned to cold blue steel.

"Hilary!" said he, "will you kindly tell Doria what we found on Adrian's blotting pad—the last words he ever wrote?"

What he desired me to say was obvious.

"Written three or four times," said I, "we found the words: 'The Greater Glory: A Novel by Adrian Boldero.'"

"What has become of the blotting pad?"

"The sheet seemed to be of no value, so we destroyed it with a lot of other unimportant papers."

"And I came across further evidence," said Jaffery, "of his intention to rename the novel."

Doria's anger died away. She looked past us into the void. "I should like to have had Adrian's last words," she whispered. Then bringing herself back to earth, she begged Jaffery's pardon very touchingly. Adrian's implied intention was a command. She too approved the change. "But I'm so jealous," she said, with a catch in her voice, "of my dear husband's work. You must forgive me. I'm sure you've done everything that was right and good, Jaffery." She held out the great bundle and smiled. "I pass the proofs."

Jaffery took the bundle and laid it again on her lap. "It's awfully good of you to say that. I appreciate it tremendously. But you can keep this set. I've got another, with the corrections in duplicate."

She looked at the proofs wistfully, turned over the long strips in a timid, reverent way, and abruptly handed them back.

"I can't read it. I daren't read it. If Adrian had lived I shouldn't have seen it before it was published. He would have given me the finally bound book—an advance copy. These things—you know—it's the same to me as if he were living."

The tears started. She rose; and we all did the same.

"I must go indoors for a little. No, no, Barbara dear. I'd rather be alone." She put her arm round my small daughter. "Perhaps Susan will see I don't break my neck across the lawn."

Her voice ended in a queer little sob, and holding on to Susan, who was mighty proud of being selected as an escort, walked slowly towards the house. Susan afterwards reported that, dismissed at the bedroom door, she had lingered for a moment outside and had heard Auntie Doria crying like anything.

Barbara, who had said absolutely nothing since the miraculous draught of proofs, advanced, a female David, up to Goliath Jaffery.

"Look here, my friend, I'm not accustomed to sit still like a graven image and be mystified in my own house. Will you have the goodness to explain?"

Jaffery looked down on her, his head on one side.

"Explain what?"

"That!"

She pointed to the proofs of which I had possessed myself and was eagerly scanning. Unblenching he met her gaze.

"That is the posthumous novel of Adrian Boldero, which I, as his literary executor, have revised for the press. Hilary saw the rough manuscript, but he had no time to read it."

They looked at one another for quite a long time.

"Is that all you're going to tell me?"

"That's all."

"And all you're going to tell Hilary?"

"Telling Hilary is the same as telling you."

"Naturally."

"And telling you is the same as telling Hilary."

"By no manner of means," said Barbara tartly. She took him by the sleeve. "Come and explain."

"I've explained already," said Jaffery.

Barbara eyed him like a syren of the cornfields. "I'm going to dress a crab for lunch. A very big crab."

Jaffery's face was transfigured into a vast, hairy smile. Barbara could dress crab like no one else in the world. She herself disliked the taste of crab. I, a carefully trained gastronomist, adored it, but a Puckish digestion forbade my consuming one single shred of the ambrosial preparation. Doria would pass it by through sheer unhappiness. And it was not fit food for Susan's tender years. Old Jaff knew this. One gigantic crab-shell filled with Barbara's juicy witchery and flanked by cool pink, meaty claws would be there for his own individual delectation. Several times before had he taken the dish, with a "One man, one crab. Ho! ho! ho!" and had left nothing but clean shells.

"I'm going to dress this crab," said Barbara, "for the sake of the servants. But if you find I've put poison in it, don't blame me."

She left us, her little head indignantly in the air. Jaffery laughed, sank into a chair and tugged at his pipe.

"I wish Doria could be persuaded to read the thing," said he.

"Why?" I asked looking up from the proofs.

"It's not quite up to the standard of 'The Diamond Gate.'"

"I shouldn't suppose it was," said I drily.

"Wittekind's delighted anyhow. It's a different *genre*; but he says that's all the better."

Susan emerged from my study door on to the terrace.

"My good fellow," said I, "yonder is the daughter of the house, evidently at a loose end. Go and entertain her. I'm going to read this wonderful novel and don't want to be disturbed till lunch."

The good-humoured giant lumbered away, and Susan finding herself in undisputed possession took him off to remote recesses of the kitchen garden, far from casual intruders. Meanwhile I went on reading, very much puzzled. Naturally the style was not that of "The Diamond Gate," which was the style of Tom Castleton and not of Adrian Boldero. But was what I read the style of Adrian Boldero? This vivid, virile opening? This scene of the two derelicts who hated one another, fortuitously meeting on the old tramp steamer? This cunning, evocation of smells, jute, bilge water, the warm oils of the engine room? This expert knowledge so carelessly displayed of the various parts of a ship? How had Adrian, man of luxury, who had never been on a tramp steamer in his life, gained the knowledge? The people too were lustily drawn. They had a flavour of the sea and the breeziness of wide spaces; a deep-lunged folk. So that I should not be interrupted I wandered off to a secluded nook of the garden down the drive away from the house and gave myself up to the story. From the first it went with a rare swing, incident following incident, every trait of character presented objectively in fine scorn of analysis. There were little pen pictures of grim scenes faultless in their definition and restraint. There was a girl in it, a wild, clean-limbed, woodland thing who especially moved my admiration. The more I read the more fascinated did I become, and the more did I doubt whether a single line in it had been written by Adrian Boldero.

After a long spell, I took out my watch. It was twenty past one. We lunched at half-past. I rose, went towards the house and came upon Jaffery and Susan. The latter I despatched peremptorily to her ablutions. Alone with Jaffery, I challenged him.

"You hulking baby," said I, "what's the good of pretending with me? Why didn't you tell me at once that you had written it yourself?"

He looked at me anxiously. "What makes you think so?"

"The simple intelligence possessed by the average adult. First," I continued, as he made no reply but stood staring at me in ingenuous discomfort, "you couldn't have got this out of poor Adrian's mush; secondly, Adrian hadn't the experience of life to have written it; thirdly, I have read many brilliant descriptive articles in *The Daily Gazette* and have little difficulty in recognising the hand of Jaffery Chayne."

"Good Lord!" said he. "It isn't as obvious as all that?"

I laughed. "Then you did write it?"

"Of course," he growled. "But I didn't want you to know. I tried to get as near Tom Castleton as I could. Look here"—he gripped my shoulder—"if it's such a transparent fraud, what the blazes is going to happen?"

To some extent I reassured him. I was in a peculiar position, having peculiar knowledge. Save Barbara, no other soul in the world had the faintest suspicion of Adrian's tragedy. The forthcoming book would be received without shadow of question as the work of the author of "*The Diamond Gate.*" The difference of style and treatment would be attributed to the marvellous versatility of the dead genius. . . . Jaffery's brow began to clear.

"What do you think of it—as far as you've gone?"

My enthusiastic answer expressed the sincerity of my appreciation. He positively blushed and looked at me rather guiltily, like a schoolboy detected in the act of helping an old woman across the road.

"It's awful cheek," said he, "but I was up against it. The only alternative was to say the damn thing had been lost or burnt and take the consequences. Somehow I thought of this. I had written about half of it all in bits and pieces about three or four years ago and put it aside. It wasn't my job. Then I pulled it out one day and read it and it seemed rather good, so, having the story in my head, I set to work."

"And that's why you didn't go to Persia?"

"How the devil could I go to Persia? I couldn't write a novel on the back of a beastly camel!"

He walked a few steps in silence. Then he said with a rumble of a laugh.

"I had an awful fright about that time. I suddenly dried up; couldn't get along. I must have spent a week, night after night, staring at a blank sheet of paper. I thought I had bitten off more than I could chew and was going the way of Adrian. By George, it taught me something of the Hades the poor fellow must have passed through. I've been in pretty tight corners in my day and I know what it is to have the cold fear creeping down my spine; but that week gave me the fright of my life."

"I wish you had told me," said I, "I might have helped. Why didn't you?"

"I didn't like to. You see, if this idea hadn't come off, I should have looked such a stupendous ass."

"That's a reason," I admitted.

"And I didn't tell you at first because you would have thought I was going off my chump. I don't look the sort of chap that could write a novel, do I? You would have said I was attempting the impossible, like Adrian. You and Barbara would have been scared to death and you would have put me off."

Franklin came from the house. Luncheon was on the table. We hurried to the dining-room. Jaffery sat down before a gigantic crab.

"Is it all right?" he asked.

"Doria has interceded for you," said Barbara. "You owe her your life."

Doria smiled. "It's the least I could do for you."

Jaffery grinned by way of delicate rejoinder and immersed himself in crab. From its depths, as it seemed, he said:

"Hilary has read half the book."

"What do you think of it?" Barbara asked.

I repeated my dithyrambic eulogy. Doria's eyes shone.

"I do wish you could see your way to read it," said Jaffery.

"I would give my heart to," said Doria. "But I've told you why I can't."

"Circumstances alter cases," said I, platitudinously. "In happier circumstances you would have been presented with the novelist's fine, finished product. As it happens, Jaffery has had to fill up little gaps, make bridges here and there. I'm sure if you had been well enough," I added, with a touch of malice, for I had not quite forgiven his leaving me in the dark, "Jaffery would have consulted you on many points."

I was very anxious to see what impression the book would make upon her. Although I had reassured Jaffery, I could, scarcely conceive the possibility of the book being taken as the work of Adrian.

"Of course I would," said Jaffery eagerly. "But that's just it. You weren't equal to the worry. Now you're all right and I agree with Hilary. You ought to read it. You see, some of the bridges are so jolly clumsy."

Doria turned to my wife. "Do you think I would be justified?"

"Decidedly," said Barbara. "You ought to read it at once."

So it came to pass that, after lunch, Doria came into my study and demanded the set of proofs. She took them up to her bedroom, where she remained all the afternoon. I was greatly relieved. It was right that she should know what was going to be published under Adrian's name.

In Jaffery's presence, I disclosed to Barbara the identity of the author. He said to her much the same as he had said to me before lunch, with, perhaps, a little more shamefacedness. Were it not for reiteration upon reiteration of the same things in talk, life would be a stark silence broken only by staccato announcement of facts. At last Barbara's eyes grew uncomfortably moist.

Impulsively she flew to Jaffery and put her arms round his vast shoulders—he was sitting, otherwise she could not have done it—and hugged him.

"You're a blessed, blessed dear," she said; and ashamed of this exhibition of sentiment she bolted from the room.

Jaffery, looking very shy and uncomfortable, suggested a game of billiards.

To Barbara and myself awaiting our guests in the drawing-room before dinner, the first to come was Doria, whom we hadn't seen since lunch; an arresting figure in her low evening dress; you can imagine a Tanagra figure in black and white ivory. Her face, however, was a passion of excitement.

"It's wonderful," she cried. "More than wonderful. Even I didn't know till to-day what a great genius Adrian was. All these things he describes—he never saw them. He imagined, created. Oh, my God! If only he had lived to finish it." She put her two hands before her eyes and dashed them swiftly away—"Jaffery has done his best, poor fellow. But oh! the bridges he speaks of—they're so crude, so crude! I can see every one. The murder—you remember?"

It occurred in the first part of the novel. I had read it. Three or four splashes of blood on the page instead of ink and the thing was done. Admirable. The instinctive high light of the artist.

"I thought it one of the best things in the book," said I.

"Oh!" she waved a gesture of disgust. "How can you say so? It's horrible. It isn't Adrian. I can see the point where he left it to the imagination. Jaffery, with no imagination, has come in and spoiled it. And then the scene on the Barbary Coast of San Francisco, where Fenton finds Ellina Ray, the broken-down star of London musical comedy. Adrian never wrote it. It's the sort of claptrap he hated. He has often told me so. Jaffery thought it was necessary to explain Ellina in the next chapter, and so in his dull way, he stuck it in."

That scene also had I read. It was a little flaming cameo of a low dive on the Barbary Coast, and a presentation of the thing seen, somewhat journalistic, I admit—but such as very few journalists could give.

"That's pure Adrian," said I brazenly.

"It isn't. There are disgusting little details that only a man that had been there could have mentioned. Oh! do you suppose I don't know the difference between Adrian's work and that of a penny-a-liner like Jaffery?"

The door opened and Jaffery appeared. Doria went up to him and took him by the lapels of his dress coat.

"I've read it. It's a work of genius. But, oh! Jaffery, I do want it to be without a flaw. Don't hate me, dear—I know you've done all that mortal man could do for Adrian and for me. But it isn't your fault if you're not a professional novelist or an imaginative writer. And you, yourself, said the bridges were clumsy. Couldn't you—oh!—I loathe hurting you, dear Jaffery—but it's all the world, all eternity to me—couldn't you get one of Adrian's colleagues—one of the famous people"—she rattled off a few names—"to look through the proofs and revise them—just in honour of Adrian's memory? Couldn't you, dear Jaffery?" She tugged convulsively at the poor old giant's coat. "You're one of the best and noblest men who ever lived or I couldn't say this to you. But you understand, don't you?"

Jaffery's ruddy face turned as white as chalk. She might have slapped it physically and it would have worn the same dazed, paralysed lack of expression.

"My life," said he, in a queer toned voice, that wasn't Jaffery's at all, "my life is only an expression of your wishes. I'll do as you say."

"It's for Adrian's sake, dear Jaffery," said Doria.

Jaffery passed his great glazed hand over his stricken face, from the roots of his hair to the point of his beard, and seemed to wipe therefrom all traces of day-infesting cares, revealing the sunny Reubens-like features that we all loved.

"But apart from my amateur joining of the flats, you think the book's worthy of Adrian?"

"Oh, I do," she cried passionately. "I do. It's a work of genius. It's Adrian in all his maturity, in all his greatness!"

The door opened.

"Dinner is served, madam," said Franklin.

CHAPTER XV

When, by way of comforting Jaffery, I criticised Doria's outburst, he fell upon me as though about to devour me alive. After what he had done for her, said I, given up one of the great chances of his career, carried her bodily from London to Nice, and made her a present of a brilliant novel so as to save Adrian's memory from shame, she ought to go on her knees and pray God to shower blessings on his head. As it was, she deserved whipping.

Jaffery called me, among other things, an amazing ass—he has an Eastern habit of, facile vituperation—and roared about the drawing-room. The ladies, be it understood, had retired.

"You don't seem to grip the elements of the situation. You haven't the intelligence of a rabbit. How in Hades could she know I've written the rotten book? She thinks it's Adrian's. And she thinks I've spoiled it. She's perfectly justified. For the little footling services I rendered her on the journey, she's idiotically grateful—out of all proportion. As for Persia, she knows nothing about it—"

"She ought to," said I.

"If you tell her, I'll break your neck," roared Jaffery.

"All right," said I, desiring to remain whole. "So long as you're satisfied, it doesn't much matter to me."

It didn't. After all, one has one's own life to live, and however understanding of one's friends and sympathetically inclined towards them one may be, one cannot follow them emotionally through all their bleak despairs and furious passions. A man doing so would be dead in a week.

"It doesn't seem to strike you," he went on, "that the poor girl's mental and moral balance depends on the successful carrying out of this ghastly farce."

"I do, my dear chap."

"You don't. I wrote the thing as best I could—a labour of love. But it's nothing like Tom Castleton's work—which she thinks is Adrian's. To keep up the deception I had to crab it and say that the faults were mine. Naturally she believes me."

"All right," said I, again. "And when the book is published and Adrian's memory flattered and Doria is assured of her mental and moral balance—what then?"

"I hope she'll be happy," he answered. "Why the blazes do you suppose I've worried if it wasn't to give her happiness?"

I could not press my point. I could not commit the gross indelicacy of saying: "My poor friend, where do you come in?" or words to that effect. Nor could I possibly lay down the proposition that a living second husband—stretching the imagination to the hypothesis of her taking one—is but an indifferent hero to the widow who spends her life in burning incense before the shrine of the demigod husband who is dead. We can't say these things to our friends. We expect them to have common sense as we have ourselves. But we don't, and—for the curious reason, based on the intense individualism of sexual attraction, that no man can appreciate, save intellectually, another man's desire for a particular woman—we can't realize the poor, fool hunger of his heart. The man who pours into our ears a torrential tale of passion moves us not to sympathy, but rather to psychological speculation, if we are kindly disposed, or to murderous inclinations if we are not. On the other hand, he who is silent moves us not at all. In any and every case, however, we entirely fail to comprehend why, if Neæra is obdurate, our swain does not go afield and find, as assuredly he can, some complaisant Amaryllis.

I confess, honestly, that during this conversation I felt somewhat impatient with my dear, infatuated friend. There he was, casting the largesse of his soul at the feet of a blind woman, a woman blinded by the bedazzlement of a false fire, whose flare it was his religion to intensify. There he was doing this, and he did not see the imbecility of it! In after time we can correlate incidents and circumstances, viewing them in a perspective more or less correct. We see that we might have said and done a hundred helpful things. Well, we know that we did not, and there's an end on't. I felt, as I say, impatient with Jaffery, although—or was it because?—I recognised the bald fact that he was in love with Doria to the maximum degree of besottedness.

You see, when you say to a man: "Why do you let the woman kick you?" and he replies, with a glare of indignation: "She has deigned to touch my unworthy carcass with her sacred boot!" what in the world are you to do, save resume the interrupted enjoyment of your cigar? This I did. I also found amusement in comparing his meek wooing, like that of an early Italian amorist, with his rumbustious theories as to marriage by capture and other primitive methods of bringing woman to heel.

Doria, seeing him unresentful of kicking, continued to kick (when Barbara wasn't looking—for Barbara had read her a lecture on the polite treatment of trustees and executors) and made him more her slave than ever. He fetched and carried. He read poetry. He was Custodian of the Sacred Rubbers, when the grass was damp. He shielded her from over-rough incursions on the part of Susan. He chanted the responses in her Litany of Saint Adrian. He sacrificed his golf so that he could sit near her and hold figurative wool for her to unwind. It was very pretty to watch them. The contrast between them made its unceasing appeal. Besides, Doria did not kick all the time; there were long spells during which, touched by the giant's devotion, she repaid it in tokens of tender regard. At such times she was as fascinating an elf as one could wish to meet on a spring morning. He could bring, like no one else, the smile into her dark, mournful eyes. There is no doubt that, in her way and as far as her Adrian-bound emotional temperament permitted, she felt grateful to Jaffery. She also felt safe in his company. He was like a great St. Bernard dog, she declared to Barbara.

These idyllic relations continued unruffled for some days, until a letter arrived from the eminent novelist to whom, with Doria's approval, Jaffery had sent the proofs.

"A marvellous story," was the great man's verdict; "singularly different from 'The Diamond Gate,' only resembling it in its largeness of conception and the perfection of its kind. The alteration of a single word would spoil it. If an alien hand is there, it is imperceptible."

At this splendid tribute Jaffery beamed with happiness. He tossed the letter to Barbara across the breakfast table.

"No alien hand perceptible. Ho! ho! ho! But it's stunning, isn't it? I do believe the old fraud of a book is going to win through. This ought to satisfy Doria, don't you think so?"

"It ought to," said Barbara. "I'll send it up to her room."

But Doria with Adrian's impeccability on the brain—and how could a work of Adrian's be impeccable when an alien hand, however imperceptible, had touched it?—was not satisfied. Towards noon, when she came downstairs, she met Jaffery on the terrace, with a familiar little knitting of the brow before which his welcoming smile faded.

"It's all right up to a point," she said, handing him back the letter. "Nobody with the rudiments of a brain could fail to recognise the merits of Adrian's work. But no novelist is possessed of the critical faculty."

"Then why," asked Jaffery, after the way of men, "did you ask me to send him the novel?"

"I took it for granted he had common sense," replied Doria, after the way of women.

"And he hasn't any?"

"Read the thing again."

Jaffery scanned the page mechanically and looked up: "Well, what's to be done now?"

"I should like to compare the proofs with Adrian's original manuscript. Where is it?"

Here was the question we had all dreaded. Jaffery lied convincingly.

"It went to the printers, my dear, and of course they've destroyed it."

"I thought everything was typed nowadays."

"Typing takes time," replied Jaffery serenely. "And I'm not an advocate of feather-beds and rose-water baths for printers. As I wanted to rush the book out as quickly as possible, I didn't see why I should pamper them with type. Have you the original manuscript of 'The Diamond Gate'?"

"No," said Doria.

"Well—don't you see?" said Jaffery, with a smile.

For the first time I praised Old Man Jornicroft. He had brought up his daughter far from the madding mechanics of the literary life. To my great relief, Doria swallowed the incredible story.

"It was careless of you not to have given special instructions for the manuscript to be saved, I must say. But if it's gone, it's gone. I'm not unreasonable."

"I think you are," said Barbara, who had been arranging flowers in the drawing-room, and had emerged onto the terrace. "You made Jaffery submit his careful editing to an expert, and you're honourably bound to accept the expert's verdict."

"I do accept it," she retorted with a toss of her head and a flash of her eyes. "Have I ever said I didn't? But I'm at liberty to keep to my own opinion."

Jaffery scratched his whiskers and beard and screwed up his face as he did in moments of perplexity.

"What exactly do you want changed?" he asked.

"Just those few coarse touches you admit are yours."

"Adrian wanted to get an atmosphere of rye-whisky and bad tobacco—not tea and strawberries." The eminent novelist's encomium had aroused the artist's pride in his first-born. An altered word would spoil the book. "My dear girl," said he, stretching out his great hand, from beneath which she wriggled an impatient shoulder, "my dear Doria," said he, very gently, "the possessor of the Order of Merit is both a critic and a man of common sense. Anyway, he knows more about novels than either of us do. If it weren't for him I would give you the proofs to blue pencil as much as you liked. But I'm sure you would make a thundering mess of it."

Doria made a little gesture—a bit of a shrug—a bit of a resigned flicker of her hands.

"Of course, do as you please, dear Jaffery. I'm quite alone, a woman with nobody to turn to"—she smiled with her lips, but there was no coordination of her eyes—"as I said before, I pass the proofs."

She went quickly through the drawing-room door into the house, leaving Jaffery still scratching a red whisker.

"Oh, Lord!" said he, ruefully, "I've gone and done it now!"

He turned to follow her, but Barbara interposed her small body on the threshold.

"Don't be a silly fool, Jaff. You've pandered quite enough to her morbid vanity. It's your book, isn't it? You have given it birth. You know better than anybody what is vital to it. Just you send those proofs straight back to the publisher. If you let her persuade you to change one word, as true as I'm standing here, I'll tell her the whole thing, and damn the consequences!"

My exquisite Barbara's rare "damns" were oaths in the strictest sense. They connoted the most irrefragable of obligations. She would no more think of breaking a "damn" than her marriage vows or a baby's neck.

"Of course, I'm not going to let her touch the thing," said Jaffery. "But I don't want her to look on me as a bullying brute."

"It would be better, both for you and her, if she did," snapped Barbara. "The ordinary woman's like the dog and the walnut tree. It's only the exceptional woman that can take command."

I, who had been sitting calm, on the low parapet beneath the tenderly sprouting wistaria arbour, broke my philosophic silence.

"Observe the exceptional woman," said I.

For a day or so Doria stood upon her dignity, treating Jaffery with cold politeness. In the mornings she allowed him to wrap her up in her garden chair and attend to her comforts, and then, settled down, she would open a volume of Tolstoi and courteously signify his dismissal. Jaffery with a hang-dog expression went with me to the golf-course, where he drove with prodigious muscular skill, and putted execrably. Had it not been a question of good taste, to say nothing of human sentiment, I would have reminded him that the thing he was hitting so violently was only a little white ball and not poor Adrian's skull. If ever a man was loyal to a dead friend Jaffery Chayne was loyal to Adrian Boldero. But poor old Jaffery was being checked in every vital avenue, not by the memory of the man whom he had known and loved, but by his cynical and masquerading ghost. It is not given to me, thank God! to know from direct speech what Jaffery thought of Adrian—for Jaffery is too splendid a fellow to have ever said a word in depreciation of his once living friend and afterward dead rival; but both I, who do not aspire to these Quixotic heights and only, with masculine power of generalisation, deduce results from a quiet eye's harvest of mundane phenomena, and Barbara, whose rapier intuition penetrates the core of spiritual things, could, with little difficulty, divine the passionate struggle between love and hatred, between loyalty and tenderness, between desire and duty that took place in the soul of this chivalrous yet primitive and vastly appetited gentleman.

You may think I am trying to present Jaffery as a hero of romance. I am not. I am merely trying to put before you, in my imperfect way, a barbarian at war with civilised instincts; a lusty son of Pantagruel forced into the incongruous rôle of Sir Galahad. . . . During the term of his punishment he behaved in a bearish and most unheroic manner. At last, however, Doria forgave him, and, smiling on him once more, permitted him to read Tolstoi aloud to her. Whereupon he mended his manners.

The day following this reconciliation was a Sunday. We had invited Liosha (as we constantly did) to lunch and dine. She usually arrived by an early train in the forenoon and returned by the late train at night. But on Saturday evening, she asked Barbara, over the telephone, for permission to bring a friend, a gentleman staying in the boarding house, the happy possessor of a car, who would motor her down. His name was Fendihook. Barbara replied that she would be delighted to see Liosha's friend, and of course came back to us and speculated as to who and what this Mr. Fendihook might be.

"Why didn't you ask her?" said I.

"It would scarcely have been polite."

We consulted Jaffery. "Never heard of him," he growled. "And I don't like to hear of him now. That young woman's running loose a vast deal too much."

"What an old dog in the manger you are!" cried Barbara; and thus started an old argument.

On Sunday morning we saw Mr. Fendihook for ourselves. I met the car, a two-seater, which he drove himself, at the front door, and perceived between a motoring cap worn peak behind and a tightly buttoned Burberry coat a pink, fleshy, clean shaven face, from the middle of which projected an enormous cigar. I helped Liosha out.

"This is Mr. Fendihook."

"Commonly called Ras Fendihook, at your service," said he.

I smiled and shook hands and gave the car into the charge of my chauffeur, who appeared from the stable-yard. In the hall, aided by Franklin, Mr. Ras Fendihook divested himself of his outer wrappings and revealed a thickset man of medium height, rather flashily attired. I know it is narrow-minded, but I have a prejudice against a black and white check suit, and a red necktie threaded through a gold ring.

"Against the rules?" he asked, holding up his cigar, a very good one, on which he had retained the band.

"By no means," said I, "we smoke all over the house."

"Tiptop!" He looked around the hall. "You seem to have a bit of all right here."

"I told you you would like it. Everybody does," said Liosha. "Ah, Barbara, dear!" She ran up the stairs to meet her. We followed. Mr. Fendihook was presented. I noticed, with a little shock, that he had kept on his gloves.

"Very kind of you to let me come down, madam. I thought a bit of a blow would do our fair friend good."

Barbara took off Liosha, looking very handsome and fresh beneath the motor-veil, to her room, leaving me with Mr. Fendihook. As he preceded me into the drawing-room I saw a bald patch like a tonsure in the middle of a crop of coarse brown hair. Again he looked round appreciatively and again he said "Tiptop!" He advanced to the open French window.

"Garden's all right. Must take a lot of doing. Who are our friends? The long and the short of it, aren't they?"

He alluded to Jaffery and Doria, who were strolling on the lawn. I told him their names.

"Jaffery Chayne. Why, that's the chap Mrs. Prescott's always talking about, her guardian or something."

"Her trustee," said I, "and an intimate friend of her late husband."

"Ah!" said he, with a twinkle in his eyes which, I will swear, signified "Then there was a Prescott after all!" He waved his cigar. "Introduce me." And as I accompanied him across the lawn—"There's nothing like knowing everybody—getting it over at once. Then one feels at home."

"I hope you felt at home as soon as you entered the house," said I.

"Of course I did, old pal," he replied heartily. "Of course I did." And the amazing creature patted me on the back.

I performed the introductions. Mr. Fendihook declared himself delighted to make the acquaintance of my friends. Then as conversation did not start spontaneously, he once more looked around, nodded at the landscape approvingly, and once more said "Tiptop!"

"That's what I want to have," he continued, "when I can afford to retire and settle down. None of your gimcrack modern villas in a desirable residential neighbourhood, but an English gentleman's country house."

"It's your ambition to be an English gentleman, Mr. Fendihook?" queried Doria.

He laughed good-humouredly. "Now you're pulling my leg."

I saw that he was not lacking in shrewdness.

Susan, never far from Jaffery during her off-time, came running up.

"Hallo, is that your young 'un?" Mr. Fendihook asked. "Come and say how d'ye do, Gwendoline."

Susan advanced shyly. He shook hands with her, chucked her under the chin and paid her the ill compliment of saying that she was the image of her father. Jaffery stood with folded arms holding the bowl of his pipe in one hand and looked down on Mr. Fendihook as on some puzzling insect.

"Do you mind if I take off my gloves?" our strange visitor asked.

"Pray do," said I. The sight of the fellow wandering about a garden bareheaded and gloved in yellow chamois leather had begun to affect my nerves. He peeled them off.

"Look here, Gwendoline Arabella, my dear," he cried. "Catch!"

He made a feint of throwing them.

"Haven't you caught 'em?"

"No."

She stared at the man open-mouthed, for behold, his hands were empty.

"Tut, tut!" said he. "Perhaps you can catch a handkerchief." He flicked a red silk handkerchief from his pocket, crumpled it into a ball and threw; but like the gloves it vanished. "Now where has it gone to?"

Susan, who had shrunk beneath Jaffery's protecting shadow, crept forward fascinated. Mr. Fendihook took a sudden step or two towards a flower bed.

"Why, there it is!"

He stretched out a hand and there before our eyes the handkerchief hung limp over the pruned top of a standard rose.

"Jolly good!" exclaimed Jaffery.

"I hope you don't mind. I like amusing kiddies. Have you ever talked to angels, Araminta? No? Well, I have. Look."

He threw half-crowns up into the air until they disappeared into the central blue, and then held a ventriloquial conversation, not in the best of taste, with the celestial spirits, who having caught the coins announced their intention of sticking to them. But threats of reporting to headquarters prevailed, and one by one the coins dropped and jingled in his hand. We applauded. Susan regarded him as she would a god.

"Can you do it again?" she asked breathlessly.

"Lord bless you, Eustacia, I can keep on doing it all day long."

He balanced his cigar on the tip of his nose and with a snap caught it in his mouth. He turned to me with a grin, which showed white strong teeth. "More than you could do, old pal!"

"You must have practised that a great deal," said Doria.

"Two hours a day solid year in and year out—not that trick alone, of course. Here!" he burst into a laugh. "I'm blowed if you know who I am—I'm the One and Only Ras Fendihook—Illusionist, Ventriloquist, and General Variety Artist. Haven't you ever seen my turn?"

We confessed, with regret, that we had missed the privilege.

"Well, well, it's a queer world," he said philosophically. "You've never heard of me—and perhaps you two gentlemen are big bugs in your own line—and I've never heard of you. But anyhow, I never asked you, Mr. Chayne, to catch my gloves."

"I haven't your gloves," said Jaffery, with his eye on Susan.

"You have. You've got 'em in your pocket."

And diving into Jaffery's jacket pocket, he produced the wash-leather gloves.

"There, Petronella," said he, "that's the end of the matinée performance."

Susan looked at him wide-eyed. "I'm not at all tired."

"Aren't you? Then don't let that big black dog there chase the little one."

He pointed with his finger and from behind the old yew arbour came the shrill clamour of a little dog in agony. It brought Barbara flying out of the house. Liosha followed leisurely. The yelping ceased. Mr. Ras Fendihook went to meet his hostess. Doria, Jaffery and I looked at one another in mutual and dismayed comprehension.

"Old pal," quoted Doria.

I glanced apprehensively across the strip of lawn. "I hope, for his sake, he's not calling Barbara 'old girl.'"

"He calls everybody funny names," Susan chimed in. "See what a lot he called me."

"Does your Royal Fairy Highness approve of him?" asked Jaffery.

"I should think so, Uncle Jaff," she replied fervently. "He's—he's *marvelious!*"

"He is," said Jaffery, "and even that jewel of language doesn't express him."

"My dear," said I, "you stick close to him all day, as long as mummy will let you."

I have never got the credit I deserved for the serene wisdom of that suggestion. All through lunch, all through the long afternoon until it was Susan's bedtime, her obedience to my command saved over and over again a tense situation. To the guest in her house Barbara was the perfection of courtesy. But beneath the mask of convention raged fury with Liosha. A woman can seldom take a queer social animal for what he is and suck the honey from his flowers of unconventionality. She had never heard a man say "Right oh!" to a butler when offered a second helping of pudding. She had never dreamed of the possibility of a strange table-neighbour laying his hand on hers and requesting her to "take it from me, my dear." It sent awful shivers down her spine to hear my august self alluded to as her "old man." She looked down her nose when, to the apoplectic joy of Susan (supposed to be on her primmest behaviour at meals), he, with a significant wink, threw a new potato into the air, caught it on his fork and conveyed it to his mouth. Her smile was that of the polite hostess and not of the enthusiastic listener when he told her of triumphs in Manchester and Cincinnati. To her confusion, he presupposed her intimate acquaintance with the personalities of the World of Variety.

"That's where I came across little Evie Bostock," he said confidentially. "A clipper, wasn't she? Just before she ran off with that contortionist—you know who I mean—handsome chap—what's his name?—oh, of course you know him."

My poor Barbara! Daughter of a distinguished Civil servant, a K.C.B., assumed to be on friendly terms with a Boneless Wonder!

"But indeed I don't, Mr. Fendihook," she replied pathetically.

"Yes, yes, you must." He snapped his fingers. "Got it. Romeo! You must have heard of Romeo."

I sniggered—I couldn't help it—at Barbara's face. He went on with his reminiscences. Barbara nearly wept, whilst I, though displeased with Liosha for introducing such an incongruous element into my family circle, took the rational course of deriving from the fellow considerable entertainment. Jaffery would have done the same as myself, had not his responsibility as Liosha's guardian weighed heavily upon him. He frowned, and ate in silence, vastly. Doria, like my wife, I could see was shocked. The only two who, beside myself, enjoyed our guest were Susan and Liosha. Well, Susan was nine years old and a meal at which a guest broke her whole decalogue of table manners at once—to say nothing of the performance of such miracles as squeezing an orange into nothingness, without the juice running out, and subsequently extracting it from the neck of an agonised mother—was a feast of memorable gaudiness. Susan could be excused. But Liosha? Liosha, pupil of the admirable Mrs. Considine? Liosha, descendant of proud Albanian chieftains who had lain in gory beds for centuries? How could she admire this peculiarly vulgar, although, in his own line, peculiarly accomplished person? Yet her admiration was obvious. She sat by my side, grand and radiant, proud of the wondrous gift she had bestowed on us. She acclaimed his tricks, she laughed at his anecdotes, she urged him on to further exhibition of prowess, and in a magnificent way appeared unconscious of the presence at the table of her trustee and would-be dragon, Jaffery Chayne.

After lunch Susan obeyed my instructions and stuck very close to Mr. Fendihook. Doria retired for her afternoon rest. Jaffery, having invited Liosha to go for a long walk with him and she having declined, with a polite smile, on the ground that her best Sunday-go-to-meeting long gown was not suitable for country roads, went off by himself in dudgeon. Barbara took Liosha aside and cross-examined her on the subject of Mr. Fendihook and as far as hospitality allowed signified her non-appreciation of the guest. After a time I took him into the billiard room, Susan following. As he was a brilliant player, giving me one hundred and fifty in two hundred and running out easily before I had made thirty, he found less excitement in the game than in narrating his exploits and performing tricks for the child. He did astonishing things with the billiard balls, making them run all over his body like mice and balancing them on cues and juggling with them five at a time. I think that day he must have gone through his whole répertoire.

The party assembled for tea in the drawing-room. Fendihook's first words to Liosha were:

"Hallo, my Balkan Queen, how have you been getting on?"

"Very well, thank you," smiled Liosha.

He turned to Jaffery. "She's not up to her usual form to-day. But sometimes she's a fair treat! I give you my word."

He laughed loudly and winked. Jaffery, whose agility in repartee was rather physical than mental, glowered at him, rumbled something unintelligible beneath his breath, and took tea out to Doria, who was established on the terrace.

"Seems to have got the pip," Mr. Fendihook remarked cheerfully.

Barbara, with icy politeness, offered him tea. He refused, explaining that unless he sat down to a square meal, which, in view of the excellence of his lunch, he was unable to do, he never drank tea in the afternoon.

"Could I have a whisky and soda, old pal?"

The drink was brought. He pledged Barbara—"And may I drink to the success of that promising little affair"—he jerked a backward thumb—"between our pippy friend and the charming widow?"

Barbara had passed the gasping stage.

"Mr. Chayne," she said in the metallic voice that, before now, had made strong men grow pale, "Mr. Chayne stands in the same relation of trustee to Mrs. Boldero as he does to Mrs. Prescott."

But Fendihook was undismayed. "Some fellows have all the luck! Here's to him, and here's to you, Sheba's Queen."

He nodded to Liosha and pulled at his drink. But Liosha did not respond. A hard look appeared in her eyes and the knuckles of her hand showed white. Presently she rose and went onto the terrace, where she found Jaffery fixing a rebellious rug round Doria's feet. And this is what happened.

"Jaff Chayne," she said, "I want to have a word with you. You'll excuse me, Doria, but Jaff Chayne's as much my trustee as he is yours. I have business to talk."

Doria eyed her coldly. "Talk as much business as you like, my dear girl. I'm not preventing you." Jaffery strode off with Liosha. As soon as they were out of earshot, she said:

"Are you going to marry her?"

"Who?"

"Doria."

Jaffery bent his brows on her. He was not in his most angelic mood.

"What the blazes has that got to do with you? Just you mind your own business."

"All right," she retorted, "I will."

"Glad to hear it," said he. "And now I want a word with you. What do you mean by bringing that howling cad down here?"

"It's you who howl, not he. He's a very kind gentleman and very clever and he makes me laugh. He's not like you."

"He's a performing gorilla," cried Jaffery.

They were both exceedingly angry, and having walked very fast, they found themselves in front of the gate of the walled garden. Instinctively they entered and had the place to themselves.

"And a confounded bounder of a gorilla at that!" Jaffery continued.

"How dare you speak so of my friend?"

"You ought to be ashamed of yourself for having such a friend. And you're just going to drop him. Do you understand?"

"Shan't!" said Liosha.

"You shall. You're not going to be seen outside the house with him."

There was battle clamorous and a trifle undignified. They said the same things over and over again. Both had worked themselves into a fury.

"I forbid you to have anything to do with the fellow."

"You, Jaff Chayne, told me to mind my own business. Just you mind yours."

"It is my business," he shouted, "to see that you don't disgrace yourself with a beast of a fellow like that."

"What did you say? Disgrace myself?" She drew herself up magnificently. "Do you think I would disgrace myself with any man living? You insult me."

"Rot!" cried Jaffery. "Every woman's liable to make a blessed fool of herself—and you more than most."

"I know one that's not going to make a fool of herself," she taunted, and flung an arm in the direction of the house.

Jaffery blazed. "You leave me alone."

"And you leave me alone."

They glared inimically into each other's eyes. Liosha turned, marched superbly away, opened the garden door and, passing through, slammed it in his face. It had been a very pretty, primitive quarrel, free from all subtlety. Elemental instinct flamed in Jaffery's veins. If he could have given her a good sound thrashing he would have been a happy man. This accursed civilisation paralysed him. He stood for a few moments tearing at whiskers and beard. Then he started in pursuit, and overtook her in the middle of the lawn.

"Anyhow, you'll take the infernal fellow away now and never bring him here again."

"It's Hilary's house, not yours," she remarked, looking straight before her.

"Well, ask him."

"I will. Hilary!"

At her hail and beckon I left the terrace where Mr. Fendihook had been discoursing irrepressibly on the Bohemian advantages of widowhood to a quivering Doria, and advanced to meet her, a flushed and bright-eyed Juno.

"Would you like me to bring Ras Fendihook here again?"

"Tell her straight," said Jaffery.

Even Susan, looking from one to the other, would have been conscious of storms. I took her hand.

"My dear Liosha," said I, "our social system is so complicated that it is no wonder you don't appreciate the more delicate ramifications—"

"Oh! Talk sense to her," growled Jaffery.

"Mr. Fendihook is not quite"—I hesitated—"not quite the kind of person, my dear, that we're accustomed to meet."

"I know," said Liosha, "you want them all stamped out in a pattern, like little tin soldiers."

"I see the point of your criticism, and it's true, as far as it goes."

"Oh, go on—" Jaffery interrupted.

"But—" I continued.

"You'd rather not see him again?"

"No," roared Jaffery.

"I'm talking to Hilary, not you," said Liosha. She turned to me. "You and Barbara would like me to take him away right now?"

I still held her hand, which was growing moist—and I suppose mine was too—and I didn't like to drop it, for fear of hurting her feelings. I gave it a great squeeze. It was very difficult for me. Personally, I enjoyed the frank, untrammelled and prodigiously accomplished scion of a vulgar race. As a mere bachelor, isolated human, meeting him, I should have taken him joyously, if not to my heart, at any rate to my microscope and studied him and savoured him and got out of him all that there was of grotesqueness. But to every one of my household, save Susan who did not count, he was—I admit, deservedly—an object of loathing. So I squeezed Liosha's hand.

"The beginning and end of the matter, my dear," said I, "is that he's not quite a gentleman."

"All right," said Liosha, liberating herself. "Now I know."

She left me and sailed to the terrace. I use the metaphor advisedly. She had a way of walking like a full-rigged ship before a breeze.

"Ras Fendihook, it's time we were going."

Mr. Fendihook looked at his watch and jumped up.

"We must hook it!"

Barbara asked conventionally: "Won't you stay to supper?"

"Great Scott, no!" he exclaimed. "No offence meant. You're very kind. But it's Ladies' Night at the Rabbits and I'm Buck Rabbit for the evening and the Queen of Sheba's coming as my guest."

"Who are the Rabbits?" asked Doria.

Even I had heard of this Bohemian confraternity; and I explained with a learned inaccuracy that evoked a semi-circular grin on the pink, fleshy face of Mr. Ras Fendihook.

"Ouf! Thank goodness!" said Barbara as the two-seater scuttered away down the drive.

"Yes, indeed," said Doria.

Jaffery shook his fist at the disappearing car.

"One of these days, I'll break his infernal neck!"

"Why?" asked Doria, on a sharp note of enquiry.

"I don't like him," said Jaffery. "And he's taking her out to dine among all that circus crowd. It's damnable!"

"For the lady whose father stuck pigs in Chicago," said Doria. "I should think it was rather a rise in the social scale."

And she went indoors with her nose in the air. To every one save the puzzled Jaffery it was obvious that she disapproved of his interest in Liosha.

CHAPTER XVI

"The Greater Glory" came out in due season, puzzled the reviewers and made a sensation; a greater sensation even than a legitimate successor to "The Diamond Gate" dictated by the spirit of Tom Castleton. The contrast was so extraordinary, so inexplicable. It was generally concluded that no writer but Adrian Boldero, in the world's history, had ever revealed two such distinct literary personalities as those that informed the two novels. The protean nature of his genius aroused universal wonder. His death was deplored as the greatest loss sustained by English letters since Keats. The press could do nothing but hail the new book as a masterpiece. Barbara and myself, who, alone of mortals, knew the strange history of the two books, did not agree with the press. In sober truth "The Greater Glory" was not a work of genius; for, after all, the only hallmark of a work of genius that you can put your finger on is its haunting quality. That quality Tom Castleton's work possessed; Jaffery Chayne's did not. "The Greater Glory" vibrated with life, it was wide and generous, it was a capital story; but, unlike "The Diamond Gate," it could not rank with "The Vicar of Wakefield" and "David Copperfield." I say this in no way to disparage my dear old friend, but merely to present his work in true proportion. Published under his own name it would doubtless have received recognition; probably it would have made money; but it could not have met with the enthusiastic reception it enjoyed when published under the tragic and romantic name of Adrian Boldero.

Of course Jaffery beamed with delight. His forlorn hope had succeeded beyond his dreams. He had fulfilled the immediate needs of the woman he loved. He had also astonished himself enormously.

"It's darned good to let you and Barbara know," said he, "that I'm not a mere six foot of beef and thirst, but that I'm a chap with brains, and" — he turned over a bundle of press-cuttings—"and 'poetic fancy' and 'master of the human heart' and 'penetrating insight into the soul of things' and 'uncanny knowledge of the complexities of woman's nature.' Ho! ho! ho! That's me, Jaff Chayne, whom you've disregarded all these years. Look at it in black and white: 'uncanny knowledge of the complexities of a woman's nature'! Ho! ho! ho! And it's selling like blazes."

It did not enter his honest head to envy the dead man his fresh ill-gotten fame. He accepted the success in the large simplicity of spirit that had enabled him to conceive and write the book. His poorer human thoughts and emotions centred in the hope that now Adrian's restless ghost would be laid forever and that for Doria there would open a new life in which, with the past behind her, she could find a glory in the sun and an influence in the stars, and a spark in her own bosom responsive to his devotion. For the tumultuous moment, however, when Adrian's name was on all men's tongues, and before all men's eyes, the ghost walked in triumphant verisimilitude of life. At all the meetings of Jaffery and Doria, he was there smiling beneath his laurels, whenever he was evoked; and he was evoked continuously. Either by law of irony or perhaps for intrinsic merit, the bridges to whose clumsy construction Jaffery, like an idiot, had confessed, had been picked out by many reviewers as typical instances of Adrian Boldero's new style. Such blunders were flies in Doria's healing ointment. She alluded to the reviewers in disdainful terms. How dared editors employ men to write on Adrian's work who were unable to distinguish between it and that of Jaffery Chayne?

One day, when she talked like this, Barbara lost her temper.

"I think you're an ungrateful little wretch. Here has Jaffery sacrificed his work for three months and devoted himself to pulling together Adrian's unfinished manuscript and making a great success of it, and you treat him as if he were a dog."

Doria protested. "I don't. I *am* grateful. I don't know what I should do without Jaffery. But all my gratitude and fondness for Jaffery can't alter the fact that he has spoiled Adrian's work; and when I hear those very faults in the book praised, I am fit to be tied."

"Well, go crazy and bite the furniture when you're all by yourself," said Barbara; "but when you're with Jaffery try to be sane and civil."

"I think you're horrid!" Doria exclaimed, "and if you weren't the wife of Adrian's trusted friend, I would never speak to you again."

"Rubbish!" said Barbara. "I'm talking to you for your good, and you know it."

Meanwhile Jaffery lingered on in London, in the cheerless little eyrie in Victoria Street, with no apparent intention of ever leaving it. Arbuthnot of *The Daily Gazette* satirically enquiring whether he wanted a job or still yearned for a season in Mayfair he consigned, in his grinning way, to perdition. Change was the essence of holiday-making, and this was his holiday. It was many years since he had one. When he wanted a job he would go round to the office.

"All right," said Arbuthnot, "and, in the meantime, if you want to keep your hand in by doing a fire or a fashionable wedding, ring us up."

Whereat Jaffery roared, this being the sort of joke he liked.

The need of a holiday amid the bricks and mortar of Victoria Street may have impressed Arbuthnot, but it did not impress me. I dismissed the excuse as fantastic. I tackled him one day, at lunch, at the club, assuming my most sceptical manner.

"Well," said he, "there's Doria. Somebody must look after her."

"Doria," said I, "is a young woman, now that she is in sound health, perfectly capable of looking after herself. And if she does want a man's advice, she can always turn to me."

"And there's Liosha."

"Liosha," I remarked judiciously, "is also a young woman capable of looking after herself. If she isn't, she has given you very definitely to understand that she's going to try. Have you had any more interesting evenings out lately?"

"No," he growled. "She's offended with me because I warned her off that low-down bounder."

"I think you did your best," said I, "to make her take up with him."

He protested. We argued the point, and I think I got the best of the argument.

"Well, anyhow," he said with an air of infantile satisfaction, "she can't marry him."

"Who's going to prevent her, if she wants to?"

"The law of England." He laughed, mightily pleased. "The beggar is married already. I've found that out. He's got three or four wives in fact— oh, a dreadful hound—but only one real one with a wedding ring, and she lives up in the north with a pack of children."

"All the more dangerous for Liosha to associate with such a villain."

He waved the suggestion aside. No fear of that, said he. It was not Liosha's game. Hers was an Amazonian kind of chastity. Here I agreed with him.

"All the less reason," said I, "for you to stay in London, so as to look after her."

"But I don't like her to be seen about in the fellow's company. She'll get a bad name."

"Look here," said I, "the idea of a vast, hairy chap like you devoting his life to keeping a couple of young widows out of mischief is too preposterous. Try me with something else."

Then, being in good humour, he told me the real reason. He was writing another book.

He was writing another novel and he did not want any one to know. He was getting along famously. He had had the story in his head for a long time. Glad to talk about it; sketched the outline very picturesquely. Perhaps I was more vitally interested in the development of the man Jaffery than in the story. A queer thing had happened. The born novelist had just discovered himself and clamoured for artistic self-expression. He was writing this book just because he could not help it, finding gladness in the mere work, delighting in the mechanics of the thing, and letting himself go in the joy of the narrative. What was going to become of it when written, I did not enquire. It was rather too delicate a matter. Jaffery Chayne could be nothing else than Jaffery Chayne. A new novel published by him would resemble "The Greater Glory" as closely as "Pendennis" resembles "Philip." And then there would be the deuce to pay. If he published it under his own name, he would render himself liable to the charge of having stolen a novel from the dead author of "The Greater Glory," and so complicate this already complicated web of literary theft; and if he threw sufficient dust into the eyes of Doria to enable him to publish under Adrian's name, he would be performing the task of the altruistic bees immortalised by Virgil.

Anyhow, there he was, perfectly happy, pegging away at his novel, looking after Doria, pretending to look after Liosha, and enjoying the society of the few cronies, chiefly adventurous birds of passage like himself, who happened to be passing through London. Being a man of modest needs, save need of mere bulk of simple food, he found his small patrimony and the savings from his professional earnings quite adequate for amenable existence. When he wanted healthy, fresh air he came down to us to see Susan; when he wanted anything else he went to see Doria, which was almost daily.

Doria was living now in the flat surrounded by the Lares and Penates consecrated by Adrian. Now and then for purposes of airing and dusting, she entered the awful room—neither servants nor friends were allowed to cross the threshold; but otherwise it was always locked and the key lay in her jewel case. Adrian was the focus of her being. She put heavy tasks on Jaffery. There was to be a fitting monument on Adrian's grave, over which she kept him busy. In her blind perversity she counted on his coöperation. It was he who carried through negotiations with an eminent sculptor for a bust of Adrian, which in her will, made about that time, she bequeathed to the nation. She ordered him to see to the inclusion of Adrian in the supplement to the Dictionary of National Biography. . . . And all the time Jaffery obeyed her sovereign behests without a murmur and without a hint that he desired reward for his servitude. But, to those gifted with normal vision, signs were not wanting that he chafed, to put it mildly, under this forced worship of Adrian; and to those who knew Jaffery it was obvious that his one-sided arrangement could not last forever. Doria remained blind, taking it for granted that every one should kiss the feet of her idol and in that act of adoration find august recompense. That the man loved her she was fully aware; she was not devoid of elementary sense; but she accepted it, as she accepted everything else, as her due, and perhaps rather despised Jaffery for his meekness. Why, again, she disregarded what her instinct must have revealed to her of the primitive passions lurking beneath the exterior of her kind and tender ogre, I cannot understand. For one thing, she considered herself his intellectual superior; vanity perhaps blinded her judgment. At all events she did not realise that a change was bound to come in their relations. It came, inevitably.

One day in June they sat together on the balcony of the St. John's Wood flat, in the soft afternoon shadow, both conscious of queer isolation from the world below, and from the strange world masked behind the vast superficies of brick against which they were perched. Jaffery said something about a nest midway on a cliff side overlooking the sea. He also, in bass incoherence, formulated the opinion that in such a nest might he found true happiness. The pretty languor of early summer laughed in the air. Their situation, 'twixt earth and heaven, had a little sensuous charm. Doria replied sentimentally:

"Yes, a little house, covered with clematis, on a ledge of cliff, with the sea-gulls wheeling about it—bringing messages from the sunset lands across the blue, blue sea—" Poor dear! She forgot that sea lit by a westering sun is of no colour at all and that the blue water lies to the east; but no matter; Jaffery, drinking in her words, forgot it likewise. "Away from everything," she continued, "and two people who loved—with a great, great love—"

Her eyes were fixed on the motor omnibuses passing up and down Maida Vale at the end of her road. Her lips were parted—the ripeness of youth and health rendered her adorable. A flush stained her ivory cheek— you will find the exact simile in Virgil. She was too desirable for Jaffery's self-control. He bent forward in his chair—they were sitting face to face, so that he had his back to the motor omnibuses—and put his great hand on her knee.

"Why not we two?"

It was silly, sentimental, schoolboyish—what you please; but every man's first declaration of love is bathos—the zenith of his passion connoting perhaps the nadir of his intelligence. Anyhow the declaration was made, without shadow of mistake.

Doria switched her knee away sharply, as her vision of sunset and gulls and blue sea and a clematis-covered house vanished from before her eyes, and she found herself on her balcony with Jaff Chayne.

"What do you mean?" she asked.

"You know very well what I mean."

He rose like a leviathan and made a step towards her. The three-foot balustrade of the balcony seemed to come to his ankles. She put out a hand.

"Oh, don't do that, Jaff. You might fall over. It makes me so nervous."

He checked himself and stood up quite straight. Again he felt as if she had dealt him a slap in the face.

"You know very well what I mean," he repeated. "I love you and I want you and I'll never be happy till I get you."

She looked away from him and lifted her slender shoulders.

"Why spoil things by talking of the impossible?"

"The word has no meaning. Doesn't exist," said Jaffery.

"It exists very much indeed," she returned, with a quick upward glance.

"Not with an obstinate devil like me."

He leaned against the low balustrade. She rose.

"You'll drive me into hysterics," she cried and fled to the drawing-room.

He followed, impatiently. "I'm not such an ass as to fall off a footling balcony. What do you take me for?"

"I take you for Adrian's friend," she said, very erect, brave elf facing horrible ogre—and, either by chance or design, her hand touched and held the tip of a great silver-framed photograph of her late husband.

"I think I've proved it," said Jaffery.

"Are you proving it now? What value can you attach to Adrian's memory when you say such things to me?"

"I'm saying to you what every honest man has the right to say to the free woman he loves."

"But I'm not a free woman. I'm bound to Adrian."

"You can't be bound to him forever and ever."

"I am. That's why it's shameful and dishonourable of you,"—his blue eyes flashed dangerously and he clenched his hands, but heedless she went on—"yes, mean and base and despicable of you to wish to betray him. Adrian—"

"Oh, don't talk drivel. It makes me sick. Leave Adrian alone and listen to a living man," he shouted, all the pent-up intellectual disgusts and sex-jealousies bursting out in a mad gush. "A real live man who would walk through Hell for you!" He caught her frail body in his great grasp, and she vibrated like a bit of wire caught up by a dynamo. "My love for you has nothing whatever to do with Adrian. I've been as loyal to him as one man can be to another, living and dead. By God, I have! Ask Hilary and Barbara. But I want you. I've wanted you since the first moment I set eyes on you. You've got into my blood. You're going to love me. You're going to marry me, Adrian or no Adrian."

He bent over her and she met the passion in his eyes bravely. She did not lack courage. And her eyes were hard and her lips were white and her face was pinched into a marble statuette of hate. And unconscious that his grip was giving her physical pain he continued:

"I've waited for you. I've waited for you from the moment I heard you were engaged to the other man. And I'll go on waiting. But, by God!"—and, not knowing what he did, he shook her backwards and forwards—"I'll not go on waiting for ever. You—you little bit of mystery—you little bit of eternity—you—you—ah!"

With a great gesture he released her. But the poor ogre had not counted on his strength. His unwitting violence sent her spinning, and she fell, knocking her head against a sofa. He uttered a gasp of horror and in an instant lifted her and laid her on the sofa, and on his knees beside her, with remorse oversurging his passion, behaved like a penitent fool, accusing himself of all the unforgivable savageries ever practised by barbaric male. Doria, who was not hurt in the least, sat up and pointed to the door.

"Go!" she said. "Go. You're nothing but a brute."

Jaffery rose from his knees and regarded her in the hebetude of reaction.

"I suppose I am, Doria, but it's my way of loving you."

She still pointed. "Go," she said tonelessly. "I can't turn you out, but if Adrian was alive—Ha! ha! ha!—" she laughed with a touch of hysteria. "How do you dare, you barren rascal—how do you dare to think you can take the place of a man like Adrian?"

"Go! You are nothing but a brute."

The whip of her tongue lashed him to sudden fury. He picked her up bodily and held her in spite of struggles, just as you or I would hold a cat or a rabbit.

"You little fool," said he, "don't you know the difference between a man and a—"

Realisation of the tragedy struck him as a spent bullet might have struck him on the side of the head. He turned white.

"All right," said he in a changed voice. "Easy on. I'm not going to hurt you."

He deposited her gently on the sofa and strode out of the room.

CHAPTER XVII

If the old song be true which says that it is not so much the lover who woos as the lover's way of wooing, Jaffery seemed to have thrown away his chances by adopting a very unfortunate way indeed. Doria proved to Barbara, urgently summoned to a bed of prostration and nervous collapse, that she would never set eyes again upon the unqualifiable savage by whom her holiest sentiments had been outraged and her person disgracefully mishandled. She poured out a blood-curdling story into semi-sympathetic ears. Barbara made short work of her contention that Jaffery ought to have respected her as he would have respected the wife of a living friend, characterising it as morbid and indecent nonsense; and with regard to the physical violence she declared that it would have served her right had he smacked her.

"If you want to be faithful to the memory of your first husband, be faithful," she said. "No one can prevent you. And if a good man comes along with an honourable proposal of marriage, tell him in an honourable way why you can't marry him. But don't accept for months all a man has to give, and then, when he tells you what you've known perfectly well all along, treat him as if he were making shameful proposals to you—especially a man like Jaffery; I have no patience with you."

Doria wept. No one understood her. No one understood Adrian. No one understood the bond there was between them. Of that she was aware. But when it came to being brutally assaulted by Jaffery Chayne, she really thought Barbara would sympathise. Wherefore Barbara, rather angry at being brought up to London on a needless errand, involving loss of dinner and upset of household arrangements, administered a sleeping-draught and bade her wake in the morning in a less idiotic frame of mind.

"Perhaps I behaved like a cat," Barbara said to me later—to "behave like a cat" is her way of signifying a display of the vilest phases of feminine nature—"but I couldn't help it. She didn't talk a great deal of sense. It isn't as if I had never warned her about the way she has been treating Jaffery. I have, heaps of times. And as for Adrian—I'm sick of his name—and if I am, what must poor old Jaff be?"

This she said during a private discussion that night on the whole situation. I say the whole situation, because, when she returned to Northlands, she found there a haggard ogre who for the first time in his life had eaten a canary's share of an excellent dinner, imploring me to tell him whether he should enlist for a soldier, or commit suicide, or lie prone on Doria's doormat until it should please her to come out and trample on him. He seemed rather surprised—indeed a trifle hurt—that neither of us called him a Satyr. How could we take his part and not Doria's—especially now that Barbara had come from the bedside of the scandalously entreated lady? He boomed and bellowed about the drawing-room, recapitulating the whole story.

"But, my good friend," I remonstrated, "by the showing of both of you, she taunted you and insulted you all ends up. You—'a barren rascal'—you? Good God!"

He flung out a deprecatory hand. What did it matter? We must take this from her point of view. He oughtn't to have laid hands on her. He oughtn't to have spoken to her at all. She was right. He was a savage unfit for the society of any woman outside a wigwam.

"Oh, you make me tired," cried Barbara, at last. "I'm going to bed. Hilary, give him a strait-waistcoat. He's a lunatic."

The household resources not including a strait-waistcoat, I could not exactly obey her, but as he had come down luggageless, and with a large disregard of the hours of homeward trains, I lent him a suit of my meagre pyjamas, which must have served the same purpose.

He left the next morning. Heedless of advice he called on Doria and was denied admittance. He wrote. His letter was returned unopened. He passed a miserable week, unable to work, at a loose end in London-during the height of the season. In despair he went to *The Daily Gazette* office and proclaimed himself ready for a job. But for the moment the earth was fairly calm and the management could find no field for Jaffery's special activities. Arbuthnot again offered him reports of fires and fashionable weddings, but this time Jaffery did not enjoy the fine humour of the proposal. He blistered Arbuthnot with abuse, swung from the newspaper office, and barged mightily down Fleet Street, a disturber of traffic. Then he came down to Northlands for a while, where, for want of something to do, he hired himself out to my gardener and dug up most of the kitchen garden. His usual occupation of romping with Susan was gone, for she lay abed with some childish ailment which Barbara feared might turn into German measles. So when he was not perspiring over a spade or eating or sleeping he wandered about the place in his most restless mood. At nights he ransacked my library for gazetteers and atlases wherein he searched for abominable places likely to afford the explorer the most horrible life and the bleakest possible death. He was toying with the idea of making a jaunt on his own account to Thibet, when a merciful Providence gave him something definite to think about.

It was Saturday morning. I was shaving peacefully in my dressing-room when Jaffery, after thunderously demanding admittance, rushed in, clad in bath gown and slippers, flourishing a letter.

"Read that."

I recognised Liosha's handwriting. I read:

"Dear Jaff Chayne,

"As you are my Trustee, I guess I ought to tell you what I'm going to do. I'm going to marry Ras Fendihook—"

I looked up. "But you told me the man was married already."

"He is. Read on."

"We are going to be married at once. We are going to be married at Havre in France. Ras says that because I am a widow and an Albanian it would be an awful trouble for me to get married in England, and I would have to give up half my money to Government. But in France, owing to different laws, I can get married without any fuss at all. I don't understand it, but Ras has consulted a lawyer, so it's all right. I suppose when I am married you won't be my trustee any more. So, dear Jaff Chayne, I must say good-bye and thank you for all your great kindness to me. I am sorry you and Barbara and Hilary don't like Ras, which his real name really is Erasmus, but you will when you know him better.

"Yours affectionately,

"LIOSHA PRESCOTT."

The amazing epistle took my breath away.

"Of all the infernal scoundrels!" I cried.

"There's going to be trouble," said Jaffery, and his look signified that it was he who intended to cause it.

"But why Havre of all places in the world?" said I.

"I suppose it's the only one he knows," replied Jaffery. "He must have once gone to Paris by that route. It's the cheapest."

I glanced through the letter again, and I felt a warm gush of pity for our poor deluded Liosha.

"We must get her out of this."

"Going to," said Jaffery. "Let us have in Barbara at once."

I opened the communicating door and threw the letter into the room where she was dressing. After a moment or two she appeared in cap and peignoir, and the three of us in dressing-gowns, I with lather crinkling over one-half of my face, held first an indignation meeting, and then a council of war.

"I never dreamed the brute would do this," said Jaffery. "He couldn't offer her marriage in the ordinary way without committing bigamy, and I know she wouldn't consent to any other arrangement; so he has invented this poisonous plot to get her out of England."

"And probably go through some fool form of ceremony," said Barbara.

"But how can she be such a thundering idiot as to swallow it?" asked Jaffery.

I was going to remark that women would believe anything, but Barbara's eye was upon me. Yet Liosha's unfamiliarity with the laws and formalities of English marriage was natural, considering the fact that, not so very long before, she was placidly prepared to be sold to a young Albanian cutthroat who met his death through coming to haggle over her price. I myself had found unworthy amusement in telling her wild fables of English life. Her ignorance in many ways was abysmal. Once having seen a photograph in the papers of the King in a bowler-hat she expressed her disappointment that he wore no insignia of royalty; and when I consoled her by saying that, by Act of Parliament, the King was obliged to wear his crown so many hours a day and therefore wore it always at breakfast, lunch and dinner in Buckingham Palace, she accepted my assurance with the credulity of a child of four. And when Barbara rebuked me for taking advantage of her innocence, she was very angry indeed. How was she to know when and where not to believe me?

"She is fresh and ingenuous enough," said I, "to swallow any kind of plausible story. And her ingenuousness in writing you a full account of it is a proof."

"She has given the whole show away," said Jaffery. He smiled. "If Fendihook knew, he would be as sick as a dog."

"And the poor dear is so honest and truthful," said Barbara. "She thought she was doing the honourable thing in letting you know."

"No doubt modelling herself on Mrs. Jupp, late Considine," said I.

"Who let us know at the last minute," said Barbara with a quick knitting of the brow.

"Precisely," said I.

"Good Lord!" cried Jaffery. "Do you think she's gone off with the fellow already?"

"You had better ring up Queen's Gate and find out."

He rushed from the room. I hastily finished shaving, while Barbara discoursed to me on the neglect of our duties with regard to Liosha.

Presently Jaffery burst in like a rhinoceros.

"She's gone! She went on Thursday. And this is Saturday. Fendihook left last Sunday. Evidently she has joined him."

We regarded each other in dismay.

"They're in Havre by now," said Barbara.

"I'm not so sure," said Jaffery, sweeping his beard from moustache downward. This I knew to be a sign of satisfaction. When he was puzzled he scrabbled at the whisker. "I'm not so sure. Why should he leave the boarding-house on Sunday? I'll tell you. Because his London engagement was over and he had to put in a week's engagement at some provincial music-hall. Theatrical folks always travel on Sunday. If he was still working in London and wanted to shift his lodgings he wouldn't have chosen Sunday. We can easily see by the advertisements in the morning paper. His London engagement was at the Atrium."

"I've got the *Daily Telegraph* here," said Barbara.

She fetched it from her room, in the earthquake-stricken condition to which she, as usual, had reduced it, and after earnest search among the ruins disinterred the theatrical advertisement page. The attractions at the Atrium were set out fully; but the name of Ras Fendihook did not appear.

"I'm right," said Jaffery. "The brute's not in town. Now where did she write from?" He fished the envelope from his bath-gown pocket. "Postmark, 'London, S.W., 5.45 p.m.' Posted yesterday afternoon. So she's in London." He glanced at the letter, which was written on her own note-paper headed with the Queen's Gate address, and then held it up before us. "See anything queer about this?"

We looked and saw that it was dated "Thursday."

"There's something fishy," said he. "Can I have the car?"

"Of course."

"I'm going to run 'em both to earth. I want Barbara to come along. I can tackle men right enough, but when it comes to women, I seem to be a bit of an ass. Besides—you'll come, won't you?"

"With pleasure, if I can get back early this afternoon."

"Early this afternoon? Why, my dear child, I want you to be prepared to come to Havre—all over France, if necessary."

"You've got rather a nerve," said I, taken aback by the vast coolness of the proposal.

"I have," said he curtly. "I make my living by it."

"I'd come like a shot," said Barbara, "but I can't leave Susan."

"Oh, blazes!" said Jaffery. "I forgot about that. Of course you can't." He turned to me. "Then Hilary'll come."

"Where?" I asked, stupidly.

"Wherever I take you."

"But, my dear fellow—" I remonstrated.

He cut me short. "Send him to his bath, Barbara dear, and pack his bag, and see that he's ready to start at ten sharp."

He strode out of the door. I caught him up in the corridor.

"Why the deuce," I cried, "can't you do your manhunting by yourself?"

"There are two of 'em and you may come in useful." He faced me and I met the cold steel in his eyes. "If you would rather not help me to save a woman we're both fond of from destruction, I can find somebody else."

"Of course I'll come," said I.

"Good," said he. "Ask Barbara to order a devil of a breakfast."

He marched away, looking in his bath-gown like twenty Roman heroes rolled into one, quite a different Jaffery from the noisy, bellowing fellow to whom I had been accustomed. He spoke in the normal tones of the ordinary human, very coldly and incisively.

I rejoined Barbara. "My dear," said I, "what have we done that we should be dragged into all these acute discomforts of other people's lives?"

She put her hand on my shoulder. "Perhaps, my dear boy, it's just because we've done nothing—nothing otherwise to justify our existence. We're too selfishly, sluggishly happy, you and I and Susan. If we didn't take a share of other people's troubles we should die of congestion of the soul."

I kissed her to show that I understood my rare Barbara of the steady vision. But all the same I fretted at having to start off at a moment's notice for anywhere—perhaps Havre, perhaps Marseilles, perhaps Singapore with its horrible damp climate, which wouldn't suit me—anywhere that tough and discomfort-loving Jaffery might choose to ordain. And I was getting on so nicely with my translation of Firdusi. . . .

"Don't forget," said I, departing bathwards, "to tell Franklin to put in an Arctic sleeping-bag and a solar topee."

We drove first to the house in Queen's Gate and interviewed Mrs. Jardine, a pretentious woman with gold earrings and elaborately done black hair, who seemed to resent our examination as though we were calling in question the moral character of her establishment. She did not know where Mr. Fendihook and Mrs. Prescott had gone. She was not in the habit of putting such enquiries to her guests.

"But one or other may have mentioned it casually," said I.

"Mr. Fendihook went away on Sunday and Mrs. Prescott on Thursday. It was not my business to associate the two departures in any way."

By pressing the various points we learned that Fendihook was an old client of the house. During Mrs. Considine's residence he had been touring in America. It had been his habit to go and come without much ceremonial. As for Liosha, she had given up her rooms, paid her bill and departed with her trunks.

"When did she give notice to leave you?"

"I knew nothing of her intentions till Thursday morning. Then she came with her hat on and asked for her bill and said her things were packed and ready to be brought downstairs."

"What address did she give to the cabman?"

Mrs. Jardine did not know. She rang for the luggage porter. Jaffery repeated his question.

"Westminster Abbey, sir," answered the man.

I laughed. It seemed rather comic. But every one else regarded it as the most natural thing in the world. Jaffery frowned on me.

"I see nothing to laugh at. She was obeying instructions—covering up her tracks. When she got to Westminster she told the driver to cross the bridge—and what railway station is the other end of the bridge?"

"Waterloo," said I.

"And from Waterloo the train goes to Southampton, and from Southampton the boat leaves for Havre. There's nothing funny, believe me."

I said no more.

The porter was dismissed. Jaffery drew the letter from his pocket.

"On the other hand she was in London yesterday afternoon in this district, for here is the 5:45 postmark."

"Oh, I posted that letter," said Mrs. Jardine.

"You?" cried Jaffery. He slapped his thigh. "I said there was something fishy about it."

"There was nothing fishy, as you call it, at all, Mr. Chayne, and I'm surprised at your casting such an aspersion on my character. I had a short letter from Mrs. Prescott yesterday enclosing four other letters which she asked me to stamp and post, as I owed her fourpence change on her bill."

"Where did she write from?" Jaffery asked eagerly.

"Nowhere in particular," said the provoking lady.

"But the postmark on the envelope."

She had not looked at the postmark and the envelope had been destroyed.

"Then where is she?" I asked.

"At Southampton, you idiot," said Jaffery. "Let us get there at once."

So after a visit to my bankers—for I am not the kind of person to set out for Santa Fé de Bogotà with twopence halfpenny in my pocket—and after a hasty lunch at a restaurant, much to Jaffery's impatient disgust—"Why the dickens," cried he, "did I order a big breakfast if we're to fool about wasting time over lunch?"—but as I explained, if I don't have regular meals, I get a headache—and after having made other sane preparations for a journey, including the purchase of a toothbrush, an indispensable toilet adjunct, which Franklin, admirable fellow that he is, invariably forgets to put into my case, we started for Southampton. And along the jolly Portsmouth Road we went, through Guildford, along the Hog's Back, over the Surrey Downs rolling warm in the sunshine, through Farnham, through grey, dreamy Winchester, past St. Cross, with its old-world almshouse, through

Otterbourne and up the hill and down to Southampton, seventy-eight miles, in two hours and a quarter. Jaffery drove.

We began our search. First we examined the playbills at the various places of entertainment. Ras Fendihook was not playing in Southampton. We went round the hotels, the South-Western, the Royal, the Star, the Dolphin, the Polygon—and found no trace of the runaways. Jaffery interviewed officials at the stations and docks, dapper gentlemen with the air of diplomatists, tremendous fellows in uniform, policemen, porters, with all of whom he seemed to be on terms of familiar acquaintance; but none of them could trace or remember such a couple having crossed by the midnight boats of Thursday or Friday. Nor were their names down on the list of those who had secured berths in advance for this Saturday night.

"You're rather at fault," said I, rather maliciously, not displeased at my masterful friend's failure.

"Not a bit," said he. "Fendihook's leaving on Sunday certainly means that he was starting to fulfill a provincial engagement on Monday. If it was a week's engagement, he crosses to-night. We've only to wait and catch them. If it was a three nights' engagement, which is possible, he and Liosha crossed on Thursday night. In that case we'll cross ourselves and track them down."

"Even if we have to go over the Andes and far away," I murmured.

"Even so," said he. "Now listen. If he's had a week's engagement he must be finishing to-night. In order to catch the boat he must be working in the neighbourhood. Savvy? The only possible place besides this is Portsmouth. We'll run over to Portsmouth, only seventeen miles."

"All right," said I, with a wistful look back at my peaceful, comfortable home, "let us go to Portsmouth. I'll resign myself to dine at Portsmouth. But supposing he isn't there?" I asked, as the car drove off.

"Then he went to Havre on Thursday."

"But suppose he's at Birmingham. He would then take to-morrow night's boat."

"There isn't one on Sundays."

"Then Monday night's boat."

"Well, if he does, won't we be there on Tuesday morning to meet him on the quay? Lord!" he laughed, and brought his huge grip down on my leg above the knee, thereby causing me physical agony, "I should like to take you on an expedition. It would do you a thundering lot of good."

We arrived at Portsmouth, where we conducted the same kind of enquiries as at Southampton. Neither there nor at adjoining Southsea could we find a sign of the Variety Star, Ras Fendihook, and still less of the obscure Liosha. We dined at a Southsea hotel. We dined very well. On that I insisted—without much expenditure of nervous force. Jaffery rails at me for a Sybarite and what not, but I have never seen him refuse viands on account of succulency or wine on account of flavour. We had a quart of excellent champagne, a pint of decent port and a good cigar, and we felt that the gods were good. That is how I like to feel. I felt it so gratefully that when Jaffery suggested it was time to start back to Southampton in order to waylay the London train at the docks, on the off-chance of our fugitives having come down by it, and to catch the Havre boat ourselves, I had not a weary word to say. I cheerfully contemplated the prospect of a night's voyage to Havre. And as Jaffery (also humanised by good cheer) had been entertaining me with juicy stories of China and other mythical lands, I felt equal to any daredevil adventure.

We went back to Southampton and collected our luggage at the South-Western Hotel—the hotel porter in charge thereof. Our uncertainty as to whether we would cross or not horribly disturbed his dull brain. Ten shillings and Jaffery's peremptory order to stick to his side and obey him slavishly took the place of intellectual workings. It was nearly midnight. We walked through the docks, a background of darkness, a foreground of confusing lights amid which shone vivid illuminated placards before the brightly lit steamers—"St. Malo"—"Cherbourg"—"Jersey"—"Havre." At the quiet gangway of the Havre boat we waited. The porter deposited our bags on the quay and stood patiently expectant like a dog who lays a stick at its master's feet.

One London train came in. The carriage doors opened and a myriad ants swarmed to the various boats. At the Havre boat I took the fore, he the aft gangway. Thousands passed over, men and women, vague human forms encumbered with queer projecting excrescences of impedimenta. They all seemed alike—just a herd of Britons, impelled by irrational instinct, like the fate-driven lemmings of Norway, to cross the sea. And all around, weird in the conflicting lights, hurried gnome-like figures mountainously laden, and in the confusion of sounds could be heard the slither and thud of trunks being conveyed to the hold. At last the tail of the packed wedge disappeared on board and the gangway was clear. I went to the aft gangway to Jaffery and the porter. Neither of us had seen Fendihook or Liosha.

A second train produced results equally barren.

There was nothing to do but carry out the prearranged plan. We went aboard followed by the porter with the luggage.

My method of travel has always been to arrange everything beforehand with meticulous foresight. In the most crowded trains and boats I have thus secured luxurious accommodation. To hear therefore that there were no berths free and that we should have to pass the night either on the windy deck or in the red-plush discomfort of the open saloon caused me not unreasonable dismay. I had to choose and I chose the saloon. Jaffery, of course, chose the raw winds of heaven. All night I did not get a wink of sleep. There was a gross fellow in the next section of red-plush whose snoring drowned the throb of the engines. Stewards long after they had cleared away the remains of supper from the long central table chinked money at the desk and discussed the racing stables of the world with a loudly dressed, red-faced man who, judging from the popping of corks, absorbed whiskies and sodas at the rate of three a minute. I understood then how thoughts of murder arose in the human brain. I devised exquisite means of removing him from a nauseated world. Then there was a lamp which swung backwards and forwards and searched my eyeballs relentlessly, no matter how I covered them.

What was I doing in this awful galley? Why had I left my wife and child and tranquil home? The wind freshened as soon as we got out to sea. There were horrible noises and rattling of tins and swift scurrying of stewards. The ship rolled, which I particularly hate a ship to do. And I was fully dressed and it seemed as if all the tender parts of my body were tied up with twine. What was I doing in this galley?

When I awoke it was broad daylight, and Jaffery was grinning over me and all was deathly still.

"Good God!" I cried, sitting up. "Why has the ship stopped? Is there a fog?"   ¬

"Fog?" he boomed. "What are you talking of? We're alongside of Havre."

"What time is it?" I asked.

"Half-past six."

"A Christian gentleman's hour of rising is nine o'clock," said I, lying down again.

He shook me rudely. "Get up," said he.

The sleepless, unshaven, unkempt, twine-bound, self-hating wreck of Hilary Freeth rose to his feet with a groan.

"What a ghastly night!"

"Splendid," said Jaffery, ruddy and fresh. "I must have tramped over twenty miles."

There was an onrush of blue-bloused porters, with metal plate numbers on their arms. One took our baggage. We followed him up the companion onto the deck, and joined the crowd that awaited the releasing gangway. I stood resentful in the sardine pack of humans. The sky was overcast. It was very cold. The universe had an uncared-for, unswept appearance, like a house surprised at dawn, before the housemaids are up. The forced appearance of a well-to-do philosopher at such an hour was nothing less than an outrage. I glared at the immature day. The day glared at me, and turned down its temperature about twenty degrees. From fool thoughtlessness I had not put on my overcoat, which was now far away in charge of the blue-bloused porter. I shivered. Jaffery was behind me. I glanced over my shoulder.

"This is our so-called civilisation," I said bitterly.

At the sound of my voice a tall woman in the rank five feet deep from us turned instinctively round, and Liosha and I looked into each other's eyes.

CHAPTER XVIII

Jaffery caught sight of her at the same time and gripped my arm. Her eyes travelling from mine to his flashed indignant anger. Then she turned haughtily. We tried to edge nearer her, but she was just beyond the convergence of two side currents which pushed us even further away. The gangway was fixed and the movement of the conglomerate mass began. Presently Jaffery again seized my arm.

"There's the brute waiting for her."

And there on the quay, with a flower in his buttonhole and a smile on his fat face, stood Mr. Ras Fendihook. He met her at the foot of the gangway, and obviously told at once of our presence, sought us anxiously with his gaze; then with an air of bravado waved his hat—a hard white felt—and cried out: "Cheer O!" We did not respond. He grinned at us and linking his arm through Liosha's joined the stream of passengers hurrying across the stones to the custom-sheds.

"Stop," Jaffery roared.

They turned, as indeed did everybody within earshot. Fendihook would have gone on, but Liosha very proudly drew him out of the stream into a clear space and, prepared for battle, awaited us. When we had struggled our slow way down and reached the quay she advanced a few steps looking very terrible in her wrath.

"How dare you follow me?"

"Come further away from the crowd," said Jaffery, and with an imperious gesture he swept the three of us along the quay to the stern of the boat, where only a few idle sailor men were lounging, and a sergeant de ville was pacing on his leisurely beat.

"I said you would make a fool of yourself one of these days if I didn't play dragon," he said, at a sudden halt. "I've come to play dragon with a vengeance." He marched on Fendihook. "Now you."

"How d'ye do, old cock? Didn't expect you here," he said jauntily.

"Don't be insolent," replied Jaffery in a remarkably quiet tone. "You know very well why I'm here."

"Jaff Chayne—" Liosha began.

He waved her off. "Take her away, Hilary."

"Come," said I. "I'll tell you all about it."

"He has got to tell me, not you."

"I certainly don't know why the devil you're here," said Fendihook, with sudden nastiness.

"I've come to save this lady from a dirty blackguard."

"How are you going to do it?"

Jaffery addressed Liosha. "You said in your letter—"

"You wrote to him, you crazy fool, after all my instructions?" snarled Fendihook.

"You said in your letter you were going to marry this man."

"Sure," said Liosha.

"And are you going to marry this lady?"

"Certainly."

"Why didn't you marry her in England?"

"I told you in my letter," said Liosha. "See here—we don't want any of your interference." And she planted herself by the side of her abductor, glaring defiance at Jaffery.

Jaffery smiled. "You told her that because she was a widow and an Albanian she would find considerable obstacles in her way and would forfeit half her money to the Government. You lying little skunk!"

The vibration in Jaffery's voice arrested Liosha. She looked swiftly at Fendihook.

"Wasn't it true what you told me?"

"Of course not," I interposed. "You were as free to marry in England as Mrs. Considine."

She paid no attention to me.

"Wasn't it true?" she repeated.

Fendihook laughed in vulgar bluster. "You didn't take all that rot seriously, you silly cuckoo?"

Liosha drew a step away from him and regarded him wonderingly. For the first time doubt as to his straight-dealing rose in her candid mind.

"She did," said Jaffery. "She also took seriously your promise to marry her in France."

"Well, ain't I going to marry her?"

"No," said Jaffery. "You can't."

"Who says I can't?"

"I do. You've got a wife already and three children."

"I've divorced her."

"You haven't. You've deserted her, which isn't the same thing. I've found out all about you. You shouldn't be such a famous character."

Liosha stood speechless, for a moment, quivering all over, her eyes burning.

"He's married already—" she gasped.

"Certainly. He decoyed you here just to seduce you."

Liosha made a sudden spring, like a tigress, and had it not been for Jaffery's intervening boom of an arm, her hands would have been round Fendihook's throat.

"Steady on," growled Jaffery, controlling her with his iron strength. Fendihook, who had started back with an oath, grew as white as a sheet. I tapped him on the arm.

"You had better hook it," said I. "And keep out of her way if you don't want a knife stuck into you. Yes," I added, meeting a scared look, "you've been playing with the wrong kind of woman. You had better stick to the sort you're accustomed to."

"Thank you for those kind words," said he. "I will."

"It would be wise also to keep out of the way of Jaffery Chayne. With my own eyes I've seen him pick up a man he didn't like and"—I made an expressive gesture—"throw him clean away."

"Right O!" said he.

He nodded, winked impudently and walked away. A thought struck me. I overtook him.

"Where are you staying in Havre?"

He looked at me suspiciously. "What do you want to know for?"

"To save you from being murdered, as you would most certainly be if we chanced upon the same hotel."

"I'm staying at the Phares—the swagger one on the beach near the Casino."

"Excellent," said I. "Go on swaggering. Good-bye."

"Good-bye, old pal," said he.

He tilted his white hat to a rakish angle and marched away.

I rejoined Jaffery and Liosha. He still held her wrists; but she stood unresisting, tense and rigid, with averted head, looking sidewise down. Her lip quivered, her bosom heaved. Jaffery had mastered her fury, but now we had to deal with her shame and humiliation.

"Let her go!" I whispered.

Jaffery freed her. She rubbed her wrists mechanically, without moving her head. I wished Barbara had been there; she would have known exactly what to do. As it was, we stood by her, somewhat helplessly.

"*Monsieur,*" said a voice close by, and we saw our little blue-bloused porter. He explained that he had been seeking us everywhere. If we did not make haste we would lose the Paris train.

I replied that as we were not going to Paris, we were not pressed for time; but this little outside happening broke the situation.

"Better give this fellow your luggage ticket, Liosha," said Jaffery.

She looked about her bewildered and then I noticed on the ground a leather satchel which she had been carrying. I picked it up. She extracted the ticket and we all went to the custom-house.

"What's the programme now?" I asked Jaffery.

"Hotel," said he. "This poor girl will want a rest. Besides, we'll have to stay the night."

"Our friend is staying at the Hotel des Phares."

"Then we'll go to Tortoni's."

An ordinary woman would have drawn down the motor veil which she wore cockled-up on her travelling hat; but Liosha, grandly unconcerned with such vanities, showed her young shame-stricken face to all the world. I felt intensely sorry for her. She realised now from what a blatant scoundrel she had been saved; but she still bitterly resented our intervention. "I felt as if I was stripped naked walking between them"—that was her primitive account later of her state of mind.

"Barbara," said I, "sent you her very dear love."

She nodded, without looking at me.

"Barbara would have come too, if Susan had not been ill."

She gave a little start. I thought she was about to speak; but she remained silent. We entered the customs-shed, when she attended mechanically to her declarations.

On emerging free into the open air again, we found that the cheery sun had pierced the morning clouds and gave promise of a glorious day. The luggage was piled on the hotel omnibus. We took an open cab and rattled through the narrow flag-paved streets of the harbour quarter of the town. As we emerged into a more spacious thoroughfare, suddenly from a gaudy column at the corner flared the name of Ras Fendihook. I caught the heading of the *affiche*: "Music-Hall-Eldorado." Part of the mystery was solved. Jaffery had been right in his deduction that he had left London on a professional engagement; but we had not thought of an engagement out of England. I had a correct answer now to my question: "Why Havre of all places?" Jaffery sitting with Liosha on the back seat of the victoria saw it too and we exchanged glances. But Liosha had eyes for nothing save her hands tightly clasped in her lap. We passed another column before we entered the Place Gambetta, where already at that early hour, above its wide terrace, the striped awning of Tortoni's was flung. We alighted at the hotel and ordered our three rooms; coffee and roll to be taken up to madame; we men would eat our petit déjeuner downstairs. Liosha left us without saying a word.

Bathed, shaved, changed, refreshed by the good *café au lait*, gladdened by the sunshine and smugly satisfied with our morning's work, quite a different Hilary Freeth sat with Jaffery on the terrace from the sleepless wreck he had awakened two hours before. My urbane dismissal of Ras Fendihook lingered suave in my memory. The glow of conscious heroism warmed me, even like last night's dinner, to sympathy with my kind. After despatching, by the chasseur, a long telegram to Barbara, and sending up to Liosha's room a bunch of red roses we bought at a florist's hard by, I surrendered myself idly to the contemplation of the matutinal Sunday life of provincial France, while Jaffery smoked his pipe and uttered staccato maledictions on Mr. Ras Fendihook.

I love provincial France. It is narrow, it is bourgeois, it is regarding of its *sous*, it is what you will. But it lives a spacious, out-of-door, corporate life. On Sundays, it does not bury itself, like provincial England, in a cellular house. It walks abroad. It indulges in its modest pleasures. It is serious, it is intensely conscious of family, but it can take deep breaths of freedom. It is not Sundayfied into our vacuous boredom. It clings to the picturesque, in which it finds its dignified delight. The little soldier clad in blue tunic and red trousers struts along with his *fiancée* or *maîtresse* on his arm; the cuirassier swaggers by in brass helmet and horsehair plume; the cavalry officer, dapper in light blue, with his pretty wife, drinks syrup at a neighbouring table in your café. The work-girls, even on Sunday, go about bareheaded, as though they were at home in the friendly street. The curé in shovel hat and cassock; the workmen for whom Sunday happens not to be the *jour de repos hebdomadaire* ordained by law, in their blue *sarreau*; the peasants from outlying villages—the men in queer shell-jackets with a complication of buttons, the women in dazzling white caps astonishingly gauffered; the lawyer in decent black, with his white cambric tie; the fat and greasy citizen with fat and greasy wife and prim, pig-tailed little daughter clad in an exiguous cotton frock of loud and unauthentic tartan, and showing a quarter of an inch of sock above high yellow boots; the superb pair of gendarmes with their cocked hats, wooden epaulettes and swords; the white-aproned waiters standing by café tables—all these types are distinct, picked out pleasurably by the eye; they give a cheery sense of variety; the stage is dressed.

So when Jaffery asked me what in the world we were going to do all day, I replied:

"Sit here."

"Don't you want to see the place?"

"The place," said I, "is parading before us."

"We might hire a car and run over to Etretat."

"There's Liosha," I objected. "We can't leave her alone and she's not in a mood for jaunts."

"She won't leave her room to-day, poor girl. It must be awful for her. Oh, that swine of a blighter!"

His wrath exploded again over the iniquitous Fendihook. For the dozenth time we went over the story.

"What on earth are we going to do with her?" he asked. "She can't go back to the boarding-house."

"For the time being, at any rate, I'll take her down to Barbara."

"Barbara's a wonder," said he fervently. "And do you know, Hilary, there's the makings of a devilish fine woman in Liosha, if one only knew the right way to take her."

The right way, I think, was known to me, but I did not reveal it. I assented to Jaffery's proposition.

"She has a vile temper and the mind and facile passions of a Spanish gipsy, but she has stunning qualities. She's the soul of truth and honour and as straight as a die. And brave. This has been a nasty knock for her; but I don't mind betting you that as soon as she has pulled herself together she'll treat the thing quite in a big way."

And as if to prove his assertion, who should come sailing towards us past the long line of empty tables but Liosha herself. Another woman would have lain weeping on her bed and one of us would have had to soothe her and sympathise with her, and coax her to eat and cajole her into revisiting the light of day. Not so Liosha. She arrayed herself in fresh, fawn-coloured coat and skirt, fitting close to her splendid figure, which she held erect, a smart hat with a feather, and new white gloves, and came to us the incarnation of summer, clear-eyed as the morning, our roses pinned in her corsage. Of course she was pale and her lips were not quite under control, but she made a valiant show.

We arose as she approached, but she motioned us back to our chairs.

"Don't get up. I guess I'll join you."

We drew up a chair and she seated herself between us. Then she looked steadily and unsmilingly from one to the other.

"I want to thank you two. I've been a damn fool."

"Well, old girl," said Jaffery kindly, "I must own you've been rather indiscreet."

"I've been a damn fool," she repeated.

"Anyhow it's over now. Thank goodness," said I. "Did you eat your breakfast?"

She made a little wry face. No, she could not touch it. What would she have now? I sent a waiter for café-au-lait and a brioche and lectured her on the folly of going without proper sustenance. The ghost of a smile crept into her eyes, in recognition, I suppose, of the hedonism with which I am wrongly credited by my friends. Then she thanked us for the roses. They were big, like her, she said. The waiter set out the little tray and the *verseur* poured out the coffee and milk. We watched her eat and drink. Having finished she said she felt better.

"You've got some sense, Hilary," she admitted.

"Tell me," said Jaffery. "How did we come to miss you on the boat? We watched the London trains carefully."

"I came from Southsea about an hour before the boat started and went to bed at once."

"Southsea? Why, we were there all the evening," said I. "What were you doing at Southsea?"

"Staying with Emma—Mrs. Jupp. The General lives there. I couldn't stick that boarding-house by myself any longer so I wrote to Emma to ask her to put me up."

"So that's why you went on Thursday?"

"That's why."

"Pardon me if I'm inquisitive," said I, "but did you take Mrs. Considine—I mean Mrs. Jupp—into your confidence?"

"Lord no! She's not my dragon any longer. She knew I was going to Havre—to meet friends. Of course I had to tell her that. But Jaff Chayne was the only person that had to know the truth."

We questioned her as delicately as we could and gradually the intrigue that had puzzled us became clear. Ras Fendihook left London on Sunday for a fortnight's engagement at the Eldorado of Havre. As there was no Sunday night boat for Southampton he had to travel to Havre via Paris. Being a crafty villain, he would not run away with Liosha straight from London. She was to join him a week later, after he had had time to spy out the land and make his nefarious schemes for a mock marriage. His fortnight up, he was sailing away again to America. Liosha was to accompany him. In all probability, for I delight in thinking the worst of Mr. Ras Fendihook, he would have found occasion, towards the end of his tour, of sending her on a fool's errand, say, to Texas, while he worked his way to New York, where he would have an unembarrassed voyage back to England, leaving Liosha floundering helplessly in the railway network of the United States. I have made it my business to enquire into the ways of this entertaining but unholy villain. This is what I am sure he would have done. One girl some half dozen years before he had left penniless in San Francisco and the door over which burns the Red Lamp swallowed her up forever.

For the present, however, Liosha was to join him in Havre. Not a soul must know. He gave sordid instructions as to secrecy. As Jaffery had guessed, he had instigated the comic destination of Westminster Abbey. Although her open nature abhorred the deception, she obeyed his instructions in minor details and thought she was acting in the spirit of the intrigue when she enclosed the letters to Mrs. Jardine to be posted in London. By risking discovery of her secret during her visit to the admirable lady at Southsea and by ingenuously disclosing the plot to Jaffery she showed herself to be a very sorry conspirator.

She spoke so quietly and bravely that we had not the heart to touch upon the sentimental side of her adventure. As we could not stay in Havre all day at the risk of meeting Mr. Ras Fendihook, who might swagger into the town from his swagger hotel on the *plage*, we carried out Jaffery's proposal, hired an automobile and drove to Etretat. We came straight from inland into the tiny place, so coquettish in its mingling of fisher-folk and fashion, so cut off from the coast world by the jagged needle gates jutting out on each side of the small bay and by the sudden grass-grown bluff rising above them, so cleanly sparkling in the sunshine, and for the first time Liosha's face brightened. She drew a deep breath.

"Oh, let us all come and live here."

We laughed and wandered among the tarred, up-turned boats wherein the fishermen store their tackle and along the pebbly beach where a few belated bathers bobbed about in the water and up the curious steps to the terrace and listened to the last number of the orchestra. Then lunch at the clean, old-fashioned Hotel Blanquet among the fishing boats; and afterwards coffee and liqueurs in the little shady courtyard. Jaffery was very gentle with Liosha, treating her tenderly like a bruised thing, and talked of his adventures and cracked little jokes and attended solicitously to her wants. Several times I saw her raise her eyes in shy gratitude, and now and then she laughed. Her healthy youth also enabled her to make an excellent meal, and after it she smoked cigarettes and sipped *crème de menthe* with frank gusto. To me she appeared like a naughty child who instead of meeting with expected punishment finds itself coddled in affectionate arms. All resentment had died away. Unreservedly she had laid herself as a "damn fool" at our feet—or rather at Jaffery's feet, for I did not count for much. Instead of blundering over her and tugging her up and otherwise exacerbating her wounds, he lifted her with tactful kindness to her self-respect. For the first time, save when Susan was the connecting-link, he entered into a spiritual relation with Liosha. She fulfilled his prophecy— she was dealing with a soul-shrivelling situation in a big way. He admired her immensely, as his great robust nature admired immense things. At the same time he realised all in her that was sore and grievously throbbing and needed the delicate touch. I shall never forget those few hours.

To dream away a summer's afternoon had no place, however, in Jaffery's category of delights. He must be up and doing. I have threatened on many restless occasions to rig up at Northlands a gigantic wheel for his benefit similar to that in which Susan's white mice take futile exercise. If there was such a wheel he must, I am sure, get in and whirl it round; just as if there is a boat he must row it, or tree to be felled he must fell it, or a hill to be climbed he must climb it. At Etretat, as it happens, there are two hills. He stretched forth his hand to one, of course the highest, crowned by the fishermen's chapel and ordained an ascent. Liosha was in the chastened mood in which she would have dived with him to the depths of the English Channel. I, with grudging meekness and a prayer for another five minutes devoted to the deglutition of another liqueur brandy, acquiesced.

It was not such an arduous climb after all. A light breeze tempered the fury of the July sun. The grass was crisp and agreeable to the feet. The smell of wild thyme mingling with the salt of the low-tide seaweed conveyed stimulating fragrance. When we reached the top and Jaffery suggested that we should lie down, I protested. Why not walk along the edge of the inspiring cliffs?

"It's all very well for you, who've slept like a log all night," said he throwing his huge bulk on the ground, "but Liosha and I need rest."

Liosha stood glowing on the hilltop and panting a little after the quick ascent. A little curly strand on her forehead played charmingly in the wind which blew her skirts close around her in fine modelling. I thought of the Winged Victory.

"I'm not a bit tired," she said.

But seeing Jaffery definitely prone with his bearded chin on his fists, she glanced at me as though she should say: "Who are we to go contrary to his desires?" and settled down beside him.

So I stretched myself, too, on the grass and we watched the dancing sea and the flashing sails of fishing boats and the long plume from a steamer in the offing and the little town beneath us and the tiny golfers on the cliff on the other side of the bay, and were in fact giving ourselves up to an idyllic afternoon, when suddenly Liosha broke the spell.

"If I had got hold of that man this morning I think I would have killed him."

Since leaving Havre we had not referred to unhappy things.

"It would have served him right," said Jaffery.

"I did strike him once."

"Oh?" said I.

"Yes." She looked out to sea. There was a pause. I longed to hear the details of the scene, which could not have lacked humorous elements. But she left them to my imagination. "After that," she continued, "he saw I was an honest woman and talked about marriage."

Jaffery's fingers fiddled with bits of grass. "What licks me, my dear," said he, "is how you came to take up with the fellow."

She shrugged her shoulders—it was the full shrug of the un-English child of nature. "I don't know," she said, with her gaze still far away. "He was so funny."

"But he was such a bounder, old lady," said Jaffery, in gentle remonstrance.

"You all said so. But I thought you didn't like him because he was different and could make me laugh. I guess I hated you all very much. You seemed to want me to behave like Euphemia, and I couldn't behave like Euphemia. I tried very hard when you used to take me out to dinner."

Jaffery looked at her comically. But all he said was: "Go on."

"What can I say?"—she shrugged her shoulders again. "With him I hadn't to be on my best behaviour. I could say anything I liked. You all think it dreadful because I know, like everybody else, how children come into the world, and can make jokes about things like that. Emma used to say it was not ladylike—but he—he did not say so. He laughed. His friends used to laugh. With him and his friends, I could, so to speak, take off my stays"—she threw out her hands largely—"ouf!"

"I see," said Jaffery, frowning at his blades of grass.

"But between liking, figuratively, to take off your corsets in a crowd of Bohemians and wanting to marry the worst of them lies a big difference. You must have got fond of the fellow," he added, in a low voice.

I said nothing. It was their affair. I was responsible to Barbara for her safe deliverance and here she was delivered. My attitude, as you can understand, was solely one of kindly curiosity. Liosha, for some moments, also said nothing. Rather feverishly she pulled off her new white gloves and cast them away; and I noticed an all but imperceptible something—something, for want of a better word, like a ripple—sweep through her, faintly shaking her bosom, infinitesimally ruffling her neck and dying away in a flush on her cheek.

"You loved the fellow," said Jaffery, still picking at the grass-blades.

She bent forward, as she sat; hovered over him for a second or two and clutched his shoulder.

"I didn't," she cried. "I didn't." She almost screamed. "I thought you understood. I would have married anybody who would have taken me out of prison. He was going to take me out of prison to places where I could breathe." She fell back onto her heels and beat her breast with both hands. "I was dying for want of air. I was suffocating."

Her intensity caught him. He lumbered to his feet.

"What are you talking about?"

She rose, too, almost with a synchronous movement. An interested spectator, I continued sitting, my hands clasped round my knees.

"The little prison you put me into. I felt this in my throat"—and forgetful of the admirable Mrs. Considine's discipline she mimed her words startlingly—"I was sick—sick—sick to death. You forget, Jaff Chayne, the mountains of Albania."

"Perhaps I did," said he, with his steady eyes fixed on her. "But I remember 'em now. Would you like to go back?"

She put her hands for a few seconds before her face, as though to hide swift visions of slaughtered enemies, then dashed them away. "No. Not now. Not after—No. But mountains, freedom—anything unlike prison. Oh, I've gone mad sometimes. I've wanted to take up a fender and smash things."

"I've felt like that myself," said Jaffery.

"And what have you done?"

"I've broken out of prison and run away."

"That's what I did," said Liosha.

Then Jaffery burst into his great laugh and held her hands and looked at her with kindly, sympathetic mirth in his eyes. And Liosha laughed, too.

"We're both of us savages under our skins, old lady. That's what it comes to."

No more was said of Ras Fendihook. The man's broad, flashy good-humour had caught her fancy; his vagabond life stimulated her imagination of wider horizons; he promised her release from the conventions and restrictions of her artificial existence; she was ready to embark with him, as his wife, into the Unknown; but it was evident that she had not given him the tiniest little scrap of her heart.

"Why didn't you tell me all this long ago?" asked Jaffery.

"I tried to be good to please you—you and Barbara and Hilary, who've been so kind to me."

"It's all this infernal civilisation," he declared. "My dear girl, I'm as much fed up with it as you are; I want to go somewhere and wear beads."

"So do I," said Liosha.

I thought of Barbara's lecture on the whole duty of woman and I chuckled. The attitude in which I was, my hands clasped round my knees, consorted with sardonic merriment. I was checked, however, a moment afterwards, by the sight of my barbarians in the perfect agreement of babyhood calmly walking away from me along the cliff road. I jumped to my feet and pursued them.

"At any rate while you're with me," I panted, "you'll observe the decencies of civilised life."

CHAPTER XIX

"*Arrêtez! 'Arrêtez!*" roared Jaffery all of a sudden.

We had just passed the Havre Casino on our way back from Etretat. The chauffeur pulled up. Jaffery flung open the door, leaped out and disappeared. In a few seconds we heard his voice reverberating from side to side of the Boulevard Maritime.

"Hullo! hullo! hullo!"

I raised myself and, looking over the back of the car, saw Jaffery in characteristic attitude, shaking a strange man by the shoulders and laughing in delighted welcome. He was a squat, broad, powerful-looking fellow, with a heavy black beard trimmed to a point, and wearing a curiously ill-fitting suit of tweeds and a bowler-hat. I noticed that he carried neither stick nor gloves. The ecstasies of encounter having subsided, Jaffery dragged him to the car.

"This is my good old friend, Captain Maturin," he shouted, opening the door. "Mrs. Prescott. Mr. Freeth. Get in. We'll have a drink at Tortoni's."

Captain Maturin, unconfused by Jaffery's unceremonious whirling, took off his hat very politely and entered the car in a grave, self-possessed manner. He had clear, unblinking, grey-green eyes, the colour of a stormy sea before the dawn. I was for surrendering him my seat next Liosha, but with a courteous "Pray don't," he quickly established himself on the small seat facing us, hitherto occupied by Jaffery. Jaffery jumped up in front next the chauffeur and leaned over the partition. The car started.

"Captain and I are old shipmates." All Havre must have heard him. "From Christiania to Odessa, with all the Baltic and Mediterranean ports thrown in. In the depth of winter. Remember?"

"It was five years ago," said Captain Maturin, twisting his head round. "We sailed from the port of Leith on the 27th of December."

"And by gosh! Didn't it blow? Gales the whole time, there and back."

"It was as dirty a voyage as ever I made," said Captain Maturin.

"A ripping time, anyhow," said Jaffery.

"Weren't you very seasick?" I asked.

"Ho! ho! ho!" Jaffery roared derisively.

"Mr. Chayne's pretty tough, sir," said the Captain with a grave smile. "He has missed his vocation. He's a good sailor lost."

"Remember that night off Vigo?"

"I don't ever want to see such another, Mr. Chayne. It was touch and go." Captain Maturin's smile faded. No commander likes to think of the time when a freakish Providence and not his helpless self was responsible for the saving of his ship.

"He was on the bridge sixty hours at a stretch," said Jaffery.

"Sixty hours?" I exclaimed.

"Thousands have done it before and thousands have done it since, myself included. On this occasion Mr. Chayne saw it through with me."

Two days and nights and a day without sleep; standing on a few planks, holding on to a rail, while you are tossed up and down and from side to side and drenched with dashing tons of ice-cold water and fronting a hurricane that blows ice-tipped arrows, and all the time not knowing from one minute to the next whether you are going to Kingdom come—No. It is my idea of duty, but not my idea of fun. And even as duty—I thanked merciful Heaven that never since the age of nine, when I was violently sick crossing to the Isle of Wight, have I had the remotest desire to be a mariner, either professional or amateur. I looked at the two adventurers wonderingly; and so did Liosha.

"I love the sea," she said. "Don't you?"

"I can't say I do, ma'am. I've got a wife and child at Pinner, and I grow sweet peas for exhibition. All of which I can't attend to on board ship."

He said it very seriously. He was not the man to talk flippantly for the entertainment of a pretty woman.

"But if he's a month ashore, he fumes to get back," boomed Jaffery.

"It's the work I was bred to," replied the Captain soberly. "If a man doesn't love his work, he's not worth his salt. But that's not saying that I love the sea."

With such discourse did we beguile the short journey to the Hotel, Restaurant and Café Tortoni in the Place Gambetta. The terrace was thronged with the good Havre folks, husbands and wives and families enjoying the Sunday afternoon *apéritif*.

"Now let us have a drink," cried Jaffery, huge pioneer through the crowd. Liosha would have left us three men to our masculine devices. But Jaffery swept her along. Why shouldn't we have a pretty woman at our table as well as other people? She flushed at the compliment, the first, I think, he had ever paid her. A waiter conjured a vacant table and chairs from nowhere, in the midst of the sedentary throng. For Liosha was brought grenadine syrup and soda, for me absinthe, at which Captain Maturin, with the steady English sailor's suspicion of any other drink than Scotch whisky, glanced disapprovingly. Jaffery, to give himself an appetite for dinner, ordered half a litre of Munich beer.

"And now, Captain," said he genially, "what have you been doing with yourself? Still on the Baltic-Mediterranean?"

"No, Mr. Chayne. I left that some time ago. I'm on the Blue Cross Line—Ellershaw & Co.—trading between Havre and Mozambique."

"Where's Mozambique?" Liosha asked me.

I looked wise, but Captain Maturin supplied the information. "Portuguese East Africa, ma'am. We also run every other trip to Madagascar."

"That's a place I've never been to," said Jaffery.

"Interesting," said the Captain. He poured the little bottle of soda into his whisky, held up his glass, bowed to the lady, and to me, exchanged a solemnly confidential wink with Jaffery, and sipped his drink. Under Jaffery's questioning he informed us—for he was not a spontaneously communicative man—that he now had a very good command: steamship *Vesta*, one thousand five hundred tons, somewhat old, but sea-worthy, warranted to take more cargo than any vessel of her size he had ever set eyes on.

"And when do you sail?" asked Jaffery.

"To-morrow at daybreak. They're finishing loading her up now."

Jaffery drained his tall glass mug of beer and ordered another.

"Are you going to Madagascar this trip?"

"Yes, worse luck."

"Why worse luck?" I asked.

"It cuts short my time at Pinner," replied Captain Maturin.

Here was a man, I reflected, with the mystery and romance of Madagascar before him, who sighed for his little suburban villa and plot of garden at Pinner. Some people are never satisfied.

"I've not been to Madagascar," said Jaffery again.

Captain Maturin smiled gravely. "Why not come along with me. Mr. Chayne?"

Jaffery's eyes danced and his smile broadened so that his white teeth showed beneath his moustache. "Why not?" he cried. And bringing down his hand with a clamp on Liosha's shoulder—"Why not? You and I. Out of this rotten civilisation?"

Liosha drew a deep breath and looked at him in awed amazement. So did I. I thought he was going mad.

"Would you like it?" he asked.

"Like it!" She had no words to express the glory that sprang into her face.

Captain Maturin leaned forward.

"I'm sorry, Mr. Chayne, we've no license for passengers, and certainly there's no accommodation for ladies."

Jaffery threw up a hand. "But she's not a lady—in your silly old sailor sense of the term. She's a hefty savage like me. When you had me aboard, did you think of having accommodation for a gentleman? Ho! ho! ho! At any rate," said he, at the end of the peal, "you've a sort of spare cabin? There's always one."

"A kind of dog-hole—for you, Mr. Chayne."

Jaffery's keen eye caught the Captain's and read things. He jumped to his feet, upsetting his chair and causing disaster at two adjoining and crowded tables, for which, dismayed and bareheaded—Jaffery could be a very courtly gentleman when he chose—he apologized in fluent French, and, turning, caught Captain Maturin beneath the arm.

"Let us have a private palaver about this."

They threaded their way through the tables to the spaciousness of the Place Gambetta. Liosha followed them with her glance till they disappeared; then she looked at me and asked breathlessly:

"Hilary! Do you think he means it?"

"He's demented enough to mean anything," said I.

"But, seriously." She caught my wrist, and only then did I notice that her hands were bare, her gloves reposing where she had cast them on the hillside at Etretat. "Did he mean it? I'd give my immortal soul to go."

I looked into her eyes, and if I did not see stick, stark, staring craziness in them I don't know what stick, stark, staring craziness is.

"Do you know what you're letting yourself in for?" said I, pretending to believe in her sanity. "Here's a rotten old tub of a tramp—without another woman on board, with all the inherited smells of all the animals in Noah's Ark, including the descendants of all the cockroaches that Noah forgot to land, with a crew of Dagoes and Dutchmen, with awful food, without a bath, with a beast of an unventilated rabbit-hutch to sleep in—a wallowing, rolling, tossing, pitching, antiquated parody of a steamer, a little trumpery cockleshell always wet, always shipping seas, always slithery, never a dry place to sit down upon, with people always standing, sixty hours at a time, without sleep, on the bridge to see that she doesn't burst asunder and go down—a floating—when she does float—a floating inferno of misery— here it is—I can tell you all about it—any child in a board school could tell you—an inferno of misery in which you would be always hungry, always sleepless, always suffering from indigestion, always wet through, always violently ill and always dirty, with your hair in ropes and your face bloused by the wind—to say nothing of icebergs and fogs and the cargo of cotton goods catching fire, and the wheezing mediæval boilers bursting and sending you all to glory—"

I paused for lack of breath. Liosha, who, elbows on table and chin on hands, had listened to me, first with amusement, then with absorbed interest, and lastly with glowing rapture, cried in a shaky voice:

"I should love it! I should love it!"

"But it's lunatic," said I.

"So much the better."

"But the proprieties."

She shifted her position, threw herself back in her chair, and flung out her hands towards me.

"You ought to be keeping Mrs. Jardine's boarding-house. What have Jaff Chayne and I to do with proprieties? Didn't he and I travel from Scutari to London?"

"Yes," said I. "But aren't things just a little bit different now?"

It was a searching question. Her swift change of expression from glow to defensive sombreness admitted its significance.

"Nothing is different," she said curtly. "Things are exactly the same." She bent forward and looked at me straight from beneath lowering brows. "If you think just because he and I are good friends now there's any difference, you're making a great mistake. And just you tell Barbara that."

"I will do so—" said I.

"And you can also tell her," she continued, "that Liosha Prescott is not going to let herself be made a fool of by a man who's crazy mad over another woman. No, sirree! Not this child. Not me. And as for the proprieties"—she snapped her fingers—"they be—they be anything'd!"

To this frank exposition of her feelings I could say nothing. I drank the remainder of my absinthe and lit a cigarette. I fell back on the manifest lunacy of the Madagascar voyage. I urged, somewhat anti-climatically after my impassioned harangue, its discomfort.

"You'll be the fifth wheel to a coach. Your petticoats, my dear, will always be in the way."

"I needn't wear petticoats," said Liosha.

We argued until a red, grinning Jaffery, beaming like the fiery sun now about to set, appeared winding his way through the tables, followed by the black-bearded, grey-eyed sea captain.

"It's all fixed up," said he, taking his seat. "The Cap'en understands the whole position. If you want to come to 'Jerusalem and Madagascar and North and South Amerikee,' come."

"But this is midsummer madness," said I.

"Suppose it is, what matter?" He waved a great hand and fortuitously caught a waiter by the arm. "*Même chose pour tout le monde.*" He flicked him away. "Now, this is business. Will you come and rough it? The *Vesta* isn't a Cunard Liner. Not even a passenger boat. No luxuries. I hope you understand."

"Hilary has been telling me just what I'm to expect," said Liosha.

"We'll do our best for you, ma'am," said Captain Maturin; "but you mustn't expect too much. I suppose you know you'll have to sign on as one of the crew?"

"And if you disobey orders," said I, "the Captain can tie you up to the binnacle, and give you forty lashes and put you in irons."

"I guess I'll be obedient, Captain," said Liosha, proud of her incredulity.

"I don't allow my ship's company to bring many trunks and portmanteaux aboard," smiled Captain Maturin.

"I'll see to the dunnage," said Jaffery.

"The *what?*" I asked.

"It's only passengers that have luggage. Sailor folk like Liosha and me have dunnage."

"I see," said I. "And you bring it on board in a bundle together with a parrot in a cage."

Earnest persuasion being of no avail, I must have recourse to light mockery. But it met with little response. "And what," I asked, "is to become of the forty-odd *colis* that we passed through the customs this morning?"

"You can take 'em home with you," said Jaffery. He grinned over his third foaming beaker of dark beer. "Isn't it a blessing I brought him along? I told him he'd come in useful."

"But, good Lord!" I protested, aghast, "what excuse can I, a lone man, give to the Southampton customs for the possession of all this baggage? They'll think I've murdered my wife on the voyage and I shall be arrested. No. There is the parcel post. There are agencies of expedition. We can forward the luggage by *grande vitesse* or *petite vitesse*—how long are you likely to be away on this Theophile Gautier voyage—'*Cueillir la fleur de neige. Ou la fleur d'Angsoka*'?"

"Four months," said Captain Maturin.

"Then if I send them by the Great Swiftness, they'll arrive just in time."

I love my friends and perform altruistic feats of astonishing difficulty; but I draw the line at being personally involved in a nightmare of curved-top trunks and green canvas hat-containing crates belonging to a woman who is not my wife.

There followed a conversation on what seemed to me fantastic, but to the others practical details, in which I had no share. A suit of oilskins and sea-boots for Liosha formed the subject of much complicated argument, at the end of which Captain Maturin undertook to procure them from marine stores this peaceful Sunday night. Liosha, aglow with excitement and looking exceedingly beautiful, also mentioned her need of thick jersey and woollen cap and stout boots not quite so tempest-defying as the others; and these, too, the foolish and apparently infatuated mariner promised to provide. We drifted mechanically, still talking, into the interior of the Café-Restaurant, where we sat down to a dinner which I ordered to please myself, for not one of the others took the slightest interest in it. Jaffery, like a schoolboy son of Gargamelle, shovelled food into his mouth—it might have been tripe, or bullock's heart or chitterlings for all he knew or cared. His jolly laugh served as a bass for the more treble buzz and clatter of the pleasant place. I have never seen a man exude such plentiful happiness. Liosha ate unthinkingly, her elbows on the table, after the manner of Albania, her hat not straight—I whispered the information as (through force of training) I should have whispered it to Barbara, with no other result than an impatient push which rendered it more piquantly crooked than ever. Captain Maturin went through the performance with the grave face of another classical devotee to duty; but his heart—poor fellow!—was not in his food. It was partly in Pinner, partly in his antediluvian tramp, and partly in the prospect of having as cook's mate during his voyage the superbly vital young woman of the stone-age, now accidentally tricked out in twentieth century finery, who was sitting next to him.

Captain Maturin took an early leave. He had various things to do before turning in—including, I suppose, the purchase of his cook's mate's outfit—and he was to sail at five-thirty in the morning. If his new deck-hand and cook's mate would come alongside at five or thereabouts, he would see to their adequate reception.

"You wouldn't like to ship along with me, too, Mr. Freeth?" said he, with a grip like—like any horrible thing that is hard and iron and clamping in a steamer's machinery—and athwart his green-grey eyes filled with wind and sea passed a gleam of humour—"There's still time."

"I would come with pleasure," said I, "were it not for the fact that all my spare moments are devoted to the translation of a Persian poet."

If I am not urbane, I am nothing.

He went. Liosha bade me good-bye. She must retire early. The rearrangement of her luggage—"dunnage," I corrected—would be a lengthy process. She thanked me, in her best Considine manner, for all the trouble I had taken on her account, sent her love to Barbara and to Susan, whose sickness, she trusted, would be transitory, expressed the hope that the care of her belongings would not be too great a strain upon my household—and then, like a flash of lightning, in the very middle of the humming restaurant filled with all the notabilities and respectabilities of Havre, she flung her generous arms around my neck in a great hug, and kissed me, and said: "Dear old Hilary, I do love you!" and marched away magnificently through the staring tables to the inner recesses of the hotel.

Puzzledom reigned in Havre that night. English people are credited in France with any form of eccentricity, so long as it conforms with traditions of *le flègme britannique*; but there was not much *flègme* about Liosha's embrace, and so the good Havrais were mystified.

There was no following Liosha. She had made her exit. To have run after her were an artistic crime; and in real life we are more instinctively artistic and dramatic than the unthinking might suppose. Besides, there was the bill to pay. We sat down again.

"That little chap never seems to have any luck," said Jaffery. "He's one of the finest seamen afloat, with a nerve of steel and a damnable way of getting himself obeyed. He ought to be in command of a great liner instead of a rotten old tramp of fifteen hundred tons."

I beamed. "I'm glad you call it a rotten old tramp. I described it in those terms to Liosha."

"Oh!" said Jaffery. "Precious lot you know about it." He yawned cavernously. "I'll be turning in soon, myself."

It was not yet ten o'clock. "And what shall I do?" I asked.

"Better turn in, too, if you want to see us off."

"My dear Jaff," said I, "you have always bewildered me, and when I contemplate this new caprice I am beyond the phenomenon of bewilderment. But in one respect my mind retains its serene equipoise. Nothing short of an Act of God shall drag me from my bed at half-past four in the morning."

"I wanted to give you a few last instructions."

"Give them to me now," said I.

He handed me the key of his chambers. "If you wouldn't mind tidying up, some day—I left my papers in a deuce of a mess."

"All right," said I.

"And I had better give you a power of attorney, in case anything should crop up."

He called for writing materials, and scribbled and signed the document, which I put into my letter case.

"And what about letters?"

"Don't want any. Unless"—said he, after a little pause, frowning in the plenitude of his content—"if you and Barbara can make things right again with Doria—then one of you might drop me a line. I'll send you a schedule of dates."

"Still harping on my daughter?" said I.

"You may think it devilish funny," he replied; "but for me there's only one woman in the world."

"Let us have a final drink," said I.

We drank, chatted a while, and went to bed.

When I awoke the next morning the *Vesta* was already four hours on her way to Madagascar.

CHAPTER XX

I have one failing. Even I, Hilary Freeth, of Northlands in the County of Berkshire, Esquire, Gent, have one failing, and I freely confess it. I cannot keep a key. Were I as other men are—which, thank Heaven, I am not—I might wear a pound or so of hideous ironmongery chained to my person. This I decline to do, with the result that, as I say, I cannot keep a key. Of all the household stowaway places under my control (and Barbara limits their number) only one is locked; and that drawer containing I know not what treasures or rubbish is likely to continue so forever and ever—for the key is lost. Such important documents as I desire to place in security I send to bankers or solicitors, who are trained from childhood in the expert use of safes and strong-boxes. My other papers the world can read if it choose to waste its time; at any rate, I am not going to lock them up and have the worry of a key preying on my mind. I should only lose it as I lost the other one. Now, by a freak of fortune, the key of Jaffery's flat remained in the suit-case wherein I had flung it at Havre, until it was fished out by Franklin on my arrival at Northlands.

"For goodness' sake, my dear," said I to Barbara, "take charge of this thing."

But she refused. She had too many already to look after. I must accept the responsibility as a moral discipline. So I tied a luggage label to the elusive object, inscribed thereon the legend, "Key of Jaffery's flat," and hung it on a nail which I drove into the wall of my library.

"Besides," said Barbara, satirically watching the operation, "I am not going to have anything to do with this crack-brained adventure."

"To hear you speak," said I, for she had already spoken at considerable length on the subject, "one would think that I could have prevented it. If Jaffery chooses to go Baresark and Liosha to throw her cap over the topmasts, why in the world shouldn't they?"

"I suppose I'm conventional," said Barbara. "And from the description you have given me of the boat, I'm sure the poor child will be utterly miserable, and she'll ruin her hands and her figure and her skin."

I wished I had drawn a little less lurid picture of the steamship *Vesta*.

As soon as business or idleness took me to town, I visited St. Quentin's Mansions, and after consultation with the porter, who, knowing me to be a friend of Mr. Chayne's, assured me that I need not have burdened myself with the horrible key, I entered Jaffery's chambers. I found the small sitting-room in very much the same state of litter as when Jaffery left it. He enjoyed litter and hated the devastating tidiness of housemaids. Give a young horse with a long, swishy tail a quarter of an hour's run in an ordinary bachelor's rooms, and you will have the normal appearance of Jaffery's home. As I knew he did not want me to dust his books and pictures (such as they were) or to make order out of a chaos, of old newspapers, or to put his pipes in the rack or to remove spurs and physical culture apparatus from the sofa, or to bestow tender care upon a cannon ball, an antiquated eighteen or twenty-pounder, which reposed—most useful piece of furniture—in the middle of the hearth-rug, or to see to the comfortless electric radiator that took the place of a grate, I let these things be, and concentrated my attention on his papers which lay loose on desk and table. This was obviously the tidying up to which he had referred. I swept his correspondence into one drawer. I gathered together the manuscript of his new novel and swept it into another. On the top of a pedestal bookcase I discovered the original manuscript of "The Greater Glory," neatly bound in brown paper and threaded through with red tape. This I dropped into the third drawer of the desk, which already contained a mass of papers. I went into his bedroom, where I found more letters lying about. I collected them and looked around. There seemed to be little left for me to do. I noticed two photographs on his dressing-table—one of his mother, whom I remembered, and, one of Doria—these I laid face downwards so that the light should not fade them. I noticed also a battered portmanteau from beneath the lid of which protruded three or four corners of scribbling paper, and lastly my eyes fell upon the offending beer-barrel in a dark alcove. The basin set below the tap, in order to catch the drip, was nearly full. In four months' time the room would be flooded with sour and horrible beer. Full of the thought, I deposited the letters in the drawer with the rest of the correspondence, and, leaving the flat, summoned the lift, and in Jaffery's name presented a delighted porter with the contents of a nine-gallon cask. I went away in the rich glow that mantles from man's heart to check when he knows that he has made a friend for life. It was only afterwards, when I got home, and hung the labelled key on my library wall, that I realised that old Jaffery and myself had, at least, one thing in common—videlicet, the keyless habit. I had often suspected that deep in our souls lurked some hidden *trait-d'union*. Now I had found it.

And looking back on that wreck of a room, I reflected how congenial Jaffery must have found his surroundings on board the *Vesta*. The weather had changed from summer calm to storm. The gentleman from the meteorological office who writes for the newspapers talked about cyclonic disturbances, and reported gales in the channel and on the west coasts of France. The same was likely to continue. The wind blew hard enough in Berkshire, what must it have done in the Bay of Biscay? As a matter of fact, as we learned from a picture postcard from Jaffery and a short letter from Liosha posted at Bordeaux, and from their lips considerably later—for impossible as it may seem, they did not go to the bottom or die of scurvy or the cannibal's pole-axe—they had made their way from Havre in an ever-increasing tempest, during which they apparently had not slept or put on a dry rag. Heavy seas washed the deck, and kept out the galley fires, so that warm food had not been procurable. It seemed that every horror I had prophesied had come to pass. I should have pitied them, but for the blatant joyousness of their communications. "I was not seasick a minute, and I have never been so happy in my life," wrote Liosha. "Hilary should have been with us," wrote Jaffery. "It would have made a man of him. Liosha in splendid fettle. She goes about in men's clothes and oilskins and can turn her hand to anything when she isn't lashed to a stanchion." You can just imagine them having cast off all semblance of Christians and wallowing in wet and dirt. . . .

About this time, according to the sequence of events recorded in my all too scraggy diary, Doria came to us for a week-end, her first visit since Jaffery's outrageous conduct. She was glad to make friends with us once more, and to prove it showed the pleasanter side of her character. She professed not to have forgiven Jaffery; but she referred to the terrible episode in less vehement terms. It was obvious to us both that she missed him more than she would confess, even to herself. In her reconstituted existence he had stood for an essential element. Unconsciously she had counted on his devotion, his companionship, his constant service, his bulky protection from the winds of heaven. Now that she had driven him away, she found a girder wanting in her life's neat structure, which accordingly had begun to wobble uncomfortably. After all, she had provoked the man (this with some reluctance she admitted to Barbara), and he had only picked her up and shaken her. He had had no intention of dashing out her brains or even of giving her a beating. In her heart she repented. Otherwise why should she take so ill Jaffery's flight with Liosha, which she characterised as abominable, and Liosha's flight with Jaffery, which she characterised as monstrous?

"I can't talk to Barbara about it," she said to me on the Sunday morning, perching herself on the corner of my library table, a disrespectful trick which she had caught from my wife, while I sat back in my writing-chair. "Barbara seems to be bemused about the woman. One would think she was a kind of saint, incapable of stain."

"In one specific way," I replied, "I think she is."

"Oh, rubbish, Hilary!" she smiled, and swung her little foot. "You, a man of the world, how can you talk so? First she runs off with that dreadful fellow and a few hours afterwards runs off with Jaffery. What respectable woman—well, what honest woman, according to the term of the lower classes—would run away with two men within twenty-five hours?"

"She went off with Fendihook, honourably, thinking he was going to marry her. She has joined Jaffery honourably, too, because there's no question of marriage or anything else between them."

"*Sancta simplicitas!*" She shook her head from side to side and looked at me pityingly. "I'll allow Jaffery is just a fool. But she isn't. The best one can say for her is that she has no moral sense. I know the type."

"Where have you studied it, my dear?" I asked.

She coloured, taken aback, but after half a second she replied with her ready sureness:

"In my father's drawing-room among city people and in my own among literary people."

"H'm!" said I. "Lioshas don't grow on every occasional chair."

"You're as bemused as Barbara."

"I haven't studied what you call the type," I replied. "But I've studied an individual, which you haven't."

She swung off the table. "Oh, well, have it your own way—Paul and Virginia, if you like. What does it matter to me?"

"Yes, my dear," said I. "That's just it—what the dickens does it matter to you?"

"Nothing at all." She snapped a dainty finger and thumb.

"You've turned Jaffery out of your house," I continued, with malicious intent. "You've sworn never to set eyes on him again. You've banished him beyond your horizon. His doings now can be no concern of yours. If he chose to elope with the fat woman in a freak museum, why shouldn't he? What would it have to do with you?"

"Only this," said Doria, coming back to the table corner but not sitting on it. "It would make Jaffery's declaration to me all the more insulting."

"'Having known me to decline'?" I quoted.

"Precisely."

She tossed her head, in her wounded pride. But unknowingly she had swallowed my bait. I had hooked my little fish. I smiled to myself. She was eaten up with jealousy.

"Well," said I, "you remember the French proverb about the absent being always in the wrong. Let us wait until they come back and hear what they've got to say for themselves."

She put her hands behind her back. As she stood, her little black and ivory head was not much above the level of mine. "What they may say is a matter of perfect indifference to me."

I bent forward. "I think I ought to tell you what Jaffery's—practically—last words to me were: 'There's only one woman in the world for me.' Meaning you." She broke away with a laugh. "And to prove it, he elopes with the fat woman! Oh, Hilary"—with the tips of her fingers she brushed my hair—"you really are a simple old dear!"

"All the same—" I began.

"All the same," she interrupted, "this is a very untidy conversation. I didn't come in here to talk, but to borrow a copy of Baudelaire, if you have one."

She turned to scan my shelves. I joined her and took down *Les Fleurs du Mal*. She thanked me, tucked the book under her arm, and went out.

Rather uncharitably I rejoiced in her soreness. It was good discipline. It would give her a sense of values. Should she ever get Jaffery back again, with no Liosha hanging round his neck, I was certain that not only would she forgive past mishandling, but for the sake of keeping him would put up with a little more. Whether she would marry him was another story. I had every reason to believe that she would not. Adrian reigned her bosom's lord. In her worshipping fidelity she never wavered. She regarded a second marriage with horror. That was comprehensible enough, with her husband but seven months dead. No, should she ever get Jaffery back, I didn't think she would marry him; but beyond doubt she would treat him with more consideration and respect. These, of course, were my conjectures and deductions (confirmed by Barbara) from the patent fact that she found herself lost without Jaffery and that she was furiously jealous of Liosha.

It was several weeks before we saw her again. August arrived. Barbara and I played the ever-fresh summer comedy. I swore by all my gods I would not leave Northlands. I went on vowing until I arrived with a mountain of luggage, a wife and a child and a maid at a great hotel on the Lido. Our days were unimportant. We bathed in the Adriatic. We revisited familiar churches and picture galleries in Venice. We mingled with a cosmopolitan crowd and developed the complexions (not only in our faces) of an Othello family. Doria, too, made holiday abroad. Every August, Mr. Jornicroft repaired the ravages of eleven months' civic and other feasting at Marienbad, and Doria, as she had done before her marriage, accompanied him. She and Barbara exchanged letters about nothing in particular. The time passed smoothly.

Once or twice we had word from our runagates. The fury of the sea having subsided after they had left Bordeaux, they had settled down to the normal life of shipboard, and Jaffery took his turn with the hands, coiled ropes, sweated over cargo, and kept his watch. Liosha, we were given to understand, besides helping in the galley and the cabin and swabbing decks, found much delight in painting the ship's boats with paint which Jaffery had bought for the purpose at Bordeaux. She had struck up a friendship with the first mate, who, possessing a camera, had taken their photographs. They sent us one of the two standing side by side, and a more villainous-looking yet widely smiling pair you could not wish to see. Both wore sailors' caps and jerseys and sea-boots, and Barbara's keen eye detected the fact that Liosha, for freedom's sake, had cut a foot or so off the bottom of her skirt without taking the trouble to hem up the edge, which, now frayed, hung about her calves in disgraceful fringes.

"I think you were wrong, my dear," said I. "The poor thing looks anything but utterly miserable."

"I'm sure I was right about her hands and skin," she maintained.

"Well, it's her own skin."

"More's the pity," Barbara retorted.

What on earth she meant, I do not know; but, as usual, she had the last word.

The middle of September found us back in England, and shortly afterwards Doria returned also, and resumed her lonely life in the Adrian-haunted flat. But by and by she grew restless, complaining that no one but her father, of whose society she had wearied, was in town, and went off on a series of country-house visits. The flat, I suspected, for all its sacred memories, was dull without Jaffery. She still maintained her unrelenting attitude, and spoke scornfully of him; but once or twice she asked when this mad voyage would be over, thereby betraying curiosity rather than indifference.

Meanwhile the autumn publishing season was in full swing. Wittekind's list of new novels in its deep black framing border stared at you from the advertisement pages of every periodical you picked up, and so did the list of every other publisher. Day after day Doria's eyes fell on this announcement of Wittekind, and day after day her indignation swelled at the continued omission of "The Greater Glory." All these nobodies, these ephemeral scribblers, were being thrust flamboyantly on public notice and her Adrian, the great Sun of the firm, was allowed to remain in eclipse. For what purpose had he lived and died if his memory was treated with this dark ingratitude? I strove to reason with her. Adrian's book had been prodigally advertised in the spring. It had sold enormously. It was still selling. There was no need to advertise it any longer. Besides, advertisement cost money, and poor Wittekind had to do his duty by his other authors. He had to push his new wares. "Tradesman!" cried Doria. If he wasn't, I remonstrated, if he wasn't a tradesman in a certain sense, an expert in the art of selling books, how could Adrian's novels have attained their wide circulation? It was to his interest to increase that circulation as much as possible. Why not let him run his very successful business his own way? Doria loftily assured me that she had no interest in his business, in the mere vulgar number of copies sold. Adrian's glory was above such sordid things. Of far higher importance was it that his name should be kept, like a beacon, before the public. Not to do so was callous ingratitude and tradesman's niggardliness on the part of Wittekind. Something ought to be done. I confessed my inability to do anything.

"I know you have nothing to do with the literary side of the executorship. Jaffery undertook it. And now, instead of looking after his duties, he has gone on this impossible voyage."

Here was another grievance against the unfortunate Jaffery. I might have asked her who drove him to Madagascar, for had she been kind, he would have made short work of Liosha, after having rescued her from Fendihook, and would have returned meekly to Doria's feet. But what would have been the use? I was tired of these windy arguments with Doria, and worn out with the awful irony of upholding our poor Adrian's genius.

"I'm sorry he's not here," said I, somewhat tartly, "because he might have prevailed upon you to listen to common sense."

A little while after this, another firm of publishers announced an *édition de luxe* of the works of a brilliant novelist cut off like Adrian in the flower of his age. It was printed on special paper and illustrated by a famous artist, and limited to a certain number of copies. This set Doria aflare. From Scotland, where she was paying one of her restless visits, she sent me the newspaper cutting. If the commercial organism, she said, that passed with

Wittekind for a soul would not permit him to advertise Adrian's spring book in his autumn list, why couldn't he do like Mackenzie & Co., and advertise an *édition de luxe* of Adrian's two novels? And if Mackenzie & Co. thought it worth while to bring out such an edition of an entirely second-rate author, surely it would be to Wittekind's advantage to treat Adrian equally sumptuously. I advised her to write to Wittekind. She did. Accompanied by a fury of ink, she sent me his most courteous and sensible answer. Both books were doing splendidly. There was every prospect of a golden aftermath of cheap editions. The time was not ripe for an *édition de luxe*. It would come, a pleasurable thing to look forward to, when other sales showed signs of exhaustion.

"He talks about exhaustion," she wrote. "I suppose he means when he sends the volumes to be pulped, 'remainder or waste'—there's a foolish woman here who evidently has written a foolish book, and has shown me her silly contract with a publisher. 'Remainder or waste.' That's what he's thinking of. It's intolerable. I've no one, dear Hilary, to turn to but you. Do advise me."

I sent her a telegram. For one thing, it saved the trouble of concocting a letter, and, for another, it was more likely to impress the recipient. It ran:

"I advise you strongly to go to Wittekind yourself and bite him."

I was rather pleased at the humour—may I venture to qualify it as mordant?—of the suggestion. Even Barbara smiled. Of course, I was right. Let her fight it out herself with Wittekind.

But I have regretted that telegram ever since.

CHAPTER XXI

Luckily, I have kept most of Jaffery's letters written to me from all quarters of the globe. Excepting those concerned with the voyage of the *S.S. Vesta*, they were rare phenomena. Ordinarily, if I heard from him thrice a year I had to consider that he was indulging in an orgy of correspondence. But what with Doria and Adrian and Liosha, and what with Barbara and myself being so intimately mixed up in the matters which preoccupied his mind, the voyage of the *Vesta* covered a period of abnormal epistolary activity. Instead of a wife, our amateur sailor found a post office at every port. He wrote reams. He had the journalist's trick of instantaneous composition. Like the Ouidaesque hero, who could ride a Derby Winner with one hand, and stroke a University Crew to victory with the other, Jaffery could with one hand hang on to a rope over a yawning abyss, while with the other he could scribble a graphic account of the situation on a knee-supported writing-pad. In ordinary circumstances—that is to say in what, to Jaffery, were ordinary circumstances—he performed these literary gymnastics for the sake of his newspaper; but the voyage of the *Vesta* was an exceptional affair. Save incidentally—for he did send descriptive articles to *The Daily Gazette*—he was not out on professional business. The gymnastics were performed for my benefit—yet with an ulterior motive. He had sailed away, not on a job, but to satisfy a certain nostalgia, to escape from civilisation, to escape from Doria, to escape from desire and from heartache . . . and the deeper he plunged into the fatness of primitive life, the closer did the poor ogre come to heartache and to desire. He wrote spaciously, in the foolish hope that I would reply narrowly, following a Doria scent laid down with the naïveté of childhood. I received constant telegrams informing me of dates and addresses—I who, Jaffery out of England, never knew for certain whether he was doing the giant's stride around the North Pole or horizontal bar exercise on the Equator. It was rather pathetic, for I could give him but little comfort.

Besides the letters, he (and Liosha) deluged us with photographs taken chiefly by the absurd second mate, from which it was possible to reconstruct the *S.S. Vesta* in all her dismalness. You have seen scores of her rusty, grimy congeners in any port in the world. You have only to picture an old, two-masted, well-decked tramp with smokestack and foul clutter of bridge-house amidships, and fore and aft a miserable bit of a deck broken by hatches and capstans and donkey-engines and stanchions and chains and other unholy stumbling blocks and offences to the casual promenader. From the photographs and letters I learned that the dog-hole, intended by the Captain for Jaffery, but given over to Liosha, was away aft, beneath a kind of poop and immediately above the scrunch of the propeller; and that Jaffery, with singular lack of privacy, bunked in the stuffy, low cabin where the officers took their meals and relaxations. The more vividly did they present the details of their life, the more heartfelt were my thanksgivings to a merciful Providence for having been spared so dreadful an experience.

Our two friends, however, found indiscriminate joy in everything; I have their letters to prove it. And Jaffery especially found perpetual enjoyment in the vagaries of Liosha. For instance, here is an extract from one of his letters:

"It's a grand life, my boy! You're up against realities all the time. Not a sham within the horizon. You eat till you burst, work till you sleep, and sleep till you're kicked awake. You should just see Liosha. Maturin says he has only met one other woman sailor like her, and that was the daughter of a trader sailing among the Islands, who had lived all her life since birth on his ship and had scarcely slept ashore. She's as much born to it as any shell-back on board. She has the amazing gift of looking part of the tub, like the stokers and the man at the wheel. Unlike another woman, she's never in the way, and the more work you can give her to do, the happier she is. She's in magnificent health and as strong as a horse. At first the hands didn't know what to make of her; now she's friends with the whole bunch. The difficulty is to keep her from overfamiliar intercourse with them, for though she signed on as cook's mate, she eats in the cabin with the officers, and between the cabin and the fo'c'sle lies a great gulf. They come and tell her about their wives and their girls and what rotten food they've got—'Everybody has got rotten food on board ship, you silly ass!' quoth Liosha. 'What do you expect—sweetbreads and ices?'—and what soul-shattering blighters they've shipped with, and what deeds of heroism (mostly imaginary) they have performed in pursuit of their perilous calling. They're all children, you know, when you come to the bottom of them, these hell-tearing fellows—children afflicted with a perpetual thirst and a craving to punch heads—and Liosha's a child, too; so there's a kind of freemasonry between them.

"There was the devil's own row in the fo'c'sle the other evening. The first mate went to look into it and found Liosha standing enraptured at the hatch looking down upon a free fight. There were knives about. The mate, being a blasphemous and pugilistic dog, soon restored order. Then he came up to Liosha—you and Barbara should have seen her—it was sultry, not a breath of air—and she just had on a thin bodice open at her throat and the sleeves rolled up and a short ragged skirt and was bareheaded.

"'Why the Hades didn't you stop 'em, missus?'

"For some reason or the other, the whole ship's company, except the skipper and myself, call her 'missus.' She gazed on him like an ox-eyed Juno; you know her way.

"'Why should I interfere with their enjoyment?'

"'Enjoyment—!' he gasped. 'Oh, my Gawd!' He flung out his arms and came over to me. I was smoking against the taffrail. 'There they was trying to cut one another's throats, and she calls it enjoyment.'

"He went off spluttering. I watched Liosha. A Dutchman—what you would call a Swede—a hulking beggar, came up from the fo'c'sle very much the worse for wear. Liosha says:

"'Mr. Andrews was very angry, Petersen.'

"He grinned. 'He was, missus.'

"'What was it all about?'

"He explained in his sea-English, which is not the English of that mildewed Boarding House in South Kensington. Bill Figgins had called him a — —, he had retaliated, and the others had taken a hand, too."

It is I who suppress the actual words reported by Jaffery. But, believe me, they were enough to annoy anybody.

"She shouted down the stairway. 'Here you, Bill Figgins, come on deck for a minute.'

"A lean, wiry, black-looking man-spawn of the Pool of London, emerged.

"'what's the matter?'

"'Why did you call Petersen a — —?' she asked pleasantly and word-perfect.

"''Cos he is one.'

"'He isn't,' said Liosha. 'He's a very nice man. And so are you. And you both fought fine; I was looking on, and I was mad not to see the end of it. But Mr. Andrews doesn't like fighting. So see here, if you two don't shake hands, right now, and make friends and promise not to fight again, I'll not speak a word to either of you for the rest of the voyage.'

"If I had tackled them like this, hefty chap that I am, they would have consigned me to a shambles of perdition. And if any other woman had attempted it, even our valiant Barbara, they would have told her in perhaps polite, but anyhow forcible, terms to mind her own business. In either case they would have resented to the depths of their simple souls the alien interference. But with Liosha it was different. Of course sex told. Naturally. But she was a child like themselves. She had looked on, placidly, and had caught the flash of knives without turning a hair. They felt that if she were drawn into a mêlée she would use a knife with the best of them. I'm panning out about this, because it seems so deuced interesting and I should like to know what you and Barbara think. Do you remember Gulliver? For all the world it was like Glumdalclitch making the peace between two little nine-year-old Brobdingnagians. The two men looked at each other sheepishly. Half a dozen grinning heads appeared at the fo'c'sle hatch. You never saw anything so funny in your life. At last the lean Bill Figgins stuck out his hand sideways to the Dutchman, without looking at him.

"'All right, mate.'

"And the Swede shook it heartily, and the grimy hands cried 'Bravo, missus!' and Liosha, turning and catching sight of me just a bit abaft the funnel beneath the bridge, for the first time, swung up the deck towards me, as pleased as Punch.'"

Here is another extract. . . . Well, wait for a minute.

Jaffery's letters are an embarrassment of riches. If I printed them in full they would form a picturesque handbook to the coast of the African continent from Casablanca in Morocco, all the way round by the Cape of Good Hope to Port Said. But Jaffery, in his lavish way, duplicated these travel-pictures in articles to *The Daily Gazette*, which, supplemented by memory, he has already published in book form for all the world to read. Therefore, if I recorded his impressions of Grand Bassam, Cape Lopez, Boma, Matadi, Delagoa Bay, Montirana, Mombasa and other apocalyptic places, I should be merely plagiarising or infringing copyright, or what-not; and in any case I should be introducing matter entirely irrelevant to this chronicle. You must just imagine the rusty *Vesta* wallowing along, about nine knots an hour, around Africa, disgorging cotton goods and cheap jewelry at each God-forsaken port, and making up cargo with whatever raw material could find a European market. If I had gone this voyage, I would tell you all about it; but you see, I remained in England. And if I subjected Jaffery's correspondence to microscopic examination, and read up blue books on the exports and imports of all the places on the South African coast line, and told you exactly what was taken out of the *S.S. Vesta* and what was put into her, I cannot conceive your being in the slightest degree interested. To do so, would bore me to death. To me, cargo is just cargo. The transference of it from ship to shore and from shore to ship is a matter of awful noise and perspiring confusion. I have travelled, in so-called comfort, as a first-class passenger to Africa. I know all about it. Generally, the ship cannot get within quarter of a mile of the shore. On one side of it lies a fleet of flat-bottomed lighters manned by glistening and excited negroes. On board is a donkey-engine working a derrick with a Tophetical clatter. Vast bales and packing cases are lifted from the holds. A dingily white-suited officer stands by with greasy invoice sheets, while another at the yawning abyss whence the cargo emerges makes the tropical day hideous with horrible imprecations. And the merchandise swings over the side and is received in the lighter, by black uplifted arms, in the midst of a blood-curdling babel of unmeaning ferocity. That is all that unloading cargo means to me; and I cannot imagine that it means any more to any of the sons or daughters of men who are not intimately concerned in a particular trade. . . . You must imagine, I say, the *S.S. Vesta* repeating this monotonous performance; Jaffery and Liosha and the little, black-bearded skipper, all clad in decent raiment, going ashore, and being entertained scraggily or copiously by German, French, Portuguese, English, fever-eyed commissioners, who took them on the *tour du propriétaire*, among the white wooden government buildings, the palm-covered huts of the natives, and shewed them the Mission Chapels and the new Custom Houses and the pigeon-like fowls and the little dirty naked nigger children, and the exiguity of their stock of glass and china, and the yearning of their souls for the fleshpots of the respective Egypts to which they belonged. You must imagine this. If anything relevant to the story of Jaffery, which, as you will remember, is all that I have to relate, happened at any of these ports, I should tell you. I should have chapter and verse for it in Jaffery's letters. But as far as I can make out, the moment they put foot on shore, they behaved like the best-conducted globe-trotters who dwell habitually in a semi-detached residence in Peckham Rye. I know Jaffery will be furious when he reads this. But great is the Truth, and it shall prevail. It was on the sea, away from ports and mission stations and exiles hungering for the last word of civilisation, and shore-going clothes, that life as depicted by Jaffery swelled with juiciness; and to my taste, the juiciest parts of his letters are those humoristically concerned with the doings of Liosha.

As to his hopeless passion for Doria, he says very little. When Jaffery put pen to paper he was objective, loving to describe what he saw and letting what he felt go hang. In consequence the shy references to Doria were all the more poignant by reason of their rarity. But Liosha was the central figure in many a picture.

Here, I say, is another extract:

> "Liosha continues to thrive exceedingly. But there's one thing that worries me about her. What the blazes are we going to do with her after this voyage? No doubt she would like to

keep on going round and round Africa for the rest of her life. But I can't go with her. I must get back and begin to earn my living. And I don't see her settling down to afternoon tea and respectability again. I think I'll have to set her up as a gipsy with a caravan and a snarling tyke for company. How a creature with her physical energy has managed to lie listless for all these months I can't imagine. It shews strength of character anyway. But I don't see her putting in another long stretch. . . .

"She has taken her position as cook's mate seriously, and shares the galley with the cook, a sorrow-stricken little Portugee whose wife ran away with another man during the last trip. He pours out his woes to her while she wipes away the tears from the lobscouse. I don't know how she stands it, for even I, who've got a pretty strong stomach, draw the line at the galley. But she loves it. Now and again, when it's my watch—I'm on the starboard watch, you know—I see her turn out in the morning at two bells. She stands for a few moments right aft of her cabin-door, and fills her lungs. And the wind tugs at her hair beneath her cap, and at her skirts, and the spindrift from the pale grey sea of dawn stings at her face; and then she lurches like a sailor down the wet, slanting deck—and I can tell you, she looks a devilish fine figure of a woman. And soon afterwards there comes from the galley the smell of bacon and eggs—my son, if you don't know the conglomerate smell of fried bacon and eggs, bilge water, and the salt of the pure early morning ocean, your ideas of perfume are rudimentary. She and the Portugee between them, he contributing the science and she the good-will, give us excellent grub; of course you would turn your nose up at it—but you've never been hungry in your life! and there hasn't been a grumble in the cabin. Maturin has offered her the permanent job. Certainly she looks after us and attends to our comforts in a way sailor men on tramps aren't accustomed to. She's a great pal of the second mate's and at night they play spoiled-five at a corner of the table, with the greasiest pack of cards you ever saw, and she's perfectly happy.

"Now and again we discuss the future, without arriving at any result. A day or two ago I chaffed her about marriage. She considered the matter gravely.

"'I guess I'll have to. I'm twenty-four. But I haven't had much luck so far, have I?'

"I replied: 'You won't always strike wrong 'uns.'

"'I don't know what kind of a man I'm going to strike,' she said. 'Not any of those little billy-goats in dinner jackets I used to meet at Mrs. Jardine's. No, sirree. And no more Ras Fendihooks!'

"She rose—we had been sitting on the cabin sky-light—and leaned over the taffrail and looked wistfully out to sea. I joined her. She was silent for a bit. Then she said:

"'I guess I'm not going to marry at all; for I'm not going to marry a man I don't love, and I couldn't love a man who couldn't beat me—and there ain't many. That's the kind of fool way I'm built.'

"She turned and left me. I suppose she meant it. Liosha doesn't talk through her hat. But if she ever does fall in love with a man who can beat her, there'll be the devil to pay. Liosha in love would be a tornado of a spectacle. But I shouldn't like it. Honest—I shouldn't like it. I've got so used to this clean great Amazon of a Liosha, that I should loathe the fellow were he as decent a sort as you please."

It is curious to observe how, as the voyage proceeded, Jaffery's horizon gradually narrowed to the small shipboard circle, just as an invalid's interests become circumscribed by the walls of his sick-room. He tells us of childish things, a catch of fish, a quarrel between the first and second mate over Liosha, second having accused first of a disrespectful attitude towards the lady, the sail-cloth screen rigged up aft behind which Liosha had her morning tub of sea-water, the stubbing of Liosha's toe and her temporary lameness, the illness of the Portugee cook and Liosha's supremacy in the galley. And he wrote it all with the air of the impresario vaunting the qualities of his prima donna, nay more—with a fatuous air of proprietorship, as though he himself had created Liosha.

Here is the beginning of another letter, addressed to us both:

"A thousand thanks, dearest people, for what you tell me of Doria. If she just misses me a little bit, all may be well. I've bought some jolly gold barbaric ornaments that she may accept when I reach home; and do try to persuade her that the poor old bear is rough only on the outside.

"Things going on just as usual. Liosha has got a monkey given her by the donkey-man. . . .

There follows a description of the monkey and its antics, and a long account of a chase all over the ship, in which all the ship's company including the captain took part, to the subversion of discipline and navigation. But you see—he switches off at once to Liosha and the trivial records of the humdrum day.

At last he had something less trivial to write about. They were in the Mozambique Channel, making for Madagascar:

"Now that this darned cabin table is comparatively straight, I can scribble a few lines to you. We've had a beast of a time. The dirtiest weather ever since we left Beira and the cranky old tub rolling and pitching and standing on her head as I've never known ship do before. Consequence was the cargo got shifted and there was a list to port, so that every time she ducked that side, she shipped half the channel. Skies black as thunder and the sea the colour of inky water. We had the devil's own job getting the cargo straight. Just imagine a black rolling dungeon full of great packing cases weighing about half a ton each all gone murderous mad. Just imagine getting down among them, as practically all hands had to do, save the engine-room, and sweating and fighting and straining and lashing for hour after hour. And half the time the port side of the lame old duck under water. How she didn't turn turtle is known only to Allah and Maturin; and One is great and the other's a damned fine sailor. Of course, I had to go down into the inferno of the hold like the others. Part of the day's work; but I didn't like it; no one liked it.

"When the order was given all hands tumbled up to the hatchway and began swarming down the iron ladder. It was a swaying, staggering crowd. When you stand on a wet deck at an angle of forty-five degrees one way and thirty degrees another and constantly shifting both angles, with nothing but a rope lashed athwart the ship to catch hold of, your mind is pretty well concentrated on yourself. I know mine was. I slipped and wallowed on my belly hanging on to the rope like grim death till my turn came for the ladder. I got my feet on the rungs. I was all right, when looking up into the livid daylight whom do you think I saw calmly preparing to follow me? Liosha. I hadn't noticed her. She had sea-boots and a jersey and looked just like a man. I roared:

"'Clear out. This is no place for you.'

"'I'm coming. Go along down.'

"She put her foot on the rung just below my face. I gripped as much of her ankle as the stiff leather allowed.

"'Clear out. Don't be a fool.'

"Andrews, the first mate, poured out a flood of blasphemy. What the this, that and the other were we waiting for?

"'Mr. Andrews,' I shouted, 'send this woman to her cabin.'

"'Oh, go to hell! Tumble down every one of you, or I'll damn soon make you,' cried Andrews.

"He was in a vile temper, being responsible for the snugness of the cargo, and the cargo lay about as snug as a dormitory of devils. He was sorry afterwards, poor chap, for his lack of courtesy, but at the moment he didn't care who went down into the hold, or who was killed, so long as this infernal cargo was righted and the crazy old tub didn't go down.

"So I descended. It was ordained. Liosha followed. And once down we were carried away out of ourselves by a nightmare of toil and peril. Andrews and second were there yelling orders. We obeyed in some subconscious way. How we heard I don't know. For peace and quiet give me a battlefield. Twenty men in semi-darkness, scarce able to stand, fighting blind, mad forces of half a ton each. The huge crates of deal seemed so innocent and harmless on the quay-side, but charging about that swaying, rocking lower deck, they looked malignant, like grimy blocks of Hell's anger. I don't know what I did. All I can say is that I never before felt my muscles about to snap—queer feeling that—and I think I'm about as tough as they make 'em.

"Liosha worked as well as any man in the bunch. I only caught sight of her now and then . . . you see what we had to do, don't you? . . . We had to secure all these infernal things that were running amuck and ease up the rest of the cargo that had got jammed on the port side. There were accidents. Three or four were knocked out. Petersen, the Swede, had his leg crushed. I don't know what was wrong at the time. He was working next me, and a roll of the ship brought an ugly crate over him. He couldn't get up. He looked ghastly. So I took him on my back and clawed my way up the iron ladder and reached the deck somehow, and staggered along, barging into everything—it was blowing half a gale—and once I fell and he screamed like a pig, poor devil. But I picked him up and got him into the fo'c'sle and stuck him in a bunk. The Portugee cook, sick of fever—I think he's a blighted malingerer—was the only creature there. I routed him out, in the dim mephitic place reeking of sour bedding, and put Petersen in his charge. Then I went back through the drenching seas to the hatch. There was just enough room for a man's body to squeeze through down the ladder. I went down into the same hell-broth of sweat and confusion. The ground you stood upon might have been the back of a super-Titanic butterfly. Stability was a nonexistent term. It was a helpless scuttering surge of men and vast wooden cubes. Most of the men had torn off their upper garments and fought half naked, the sweat glistening on their skins in the feeble light. Soon the heat became unbearable and I too tore off jersey and shirt. Liosha joined me and we worked together without speaking. Her long thick hair had come down and she had hastily tied it in a knot, just as you might tie a knot in a towel, and she had thrown off things like everybody else and only a flimsy cotton, sleeveless bodice, or whatever it's called, drenched through and sticking to her, made a pretence of covering her from her waist.

"You had to get like flies round these infernal things and wait your time—if you could—for the roll, and push and then scramble with ropes and make fast; awl at the same time dance out of the way of the slithering hulks that bore down on you with fantastic murderousness. And through it all thundered the roaring of the storm, the grind of the engines, the shattering of the propeller lifted above the waves, and the shrieks and creakings of every plank and plate of this steam-driven old Noah's Ark.

"We had just, with exhausted muscles, made a whole stack fast, and were standing by, panting, haggard eyed, the sweat running down anyhow, twenty of us, Dagoes, Dutchmen, Englishmen, in the dim twilight—just a shaft of pale illumination coming slick down the ladder where the hatch was open,—hanging on to edges and corners of cargo, when suddenly the ship, caught on top of a wave, vibrated in a sickening shudder, plunged, and then with an impetus of cataclysm wallowed to starboard. Andrews shrieked, 'Stand clear!' Most of the men leaped and flung themselves away. But I stumbled and fell. Before I realized the danger of a vast sliding crate, two strong arms were curled round my waist and I was flung aside, to slither and roll down the swaying deck until I was stopped by the bulkhead. When I picked myself up, I saw half the men securing the crate and the other half grovelling around something on the deck. It was Liosha. She lay white and senseless with blood streaming from her head.

Before I realized the danger . . . I was flung aside.

"In a mortal funk I took her up the ladder with the help of another fellow, and carried her to her cabin. I never before realised the appalling length of this vessel. We got her into her bunk aft; I sent the other chap for brandy and first-aid appliances from the ship's stores, and did what I could to discover how far she was injured. . . .

"Thank God, nothing worse had happened than a nasty scalp wound. But her escape had been miraculous. She had saved my life; for as I lay on the deck, the crate charging direct would have squashed my skull into jelly, and crushed my body against the side of the hold. A fraction of a second later and it would have been her skull and her body instead of mine; but she just managed to roll practically clear until she got caught by the swerving side of the crate. I hope you'll understand what a heroic thing she did. She faced what seemed to be certain death for me; and it is thanks to Liosha that I'm able to tell you that I'm alive. And she, God bless her, walks about with her head bandaged, among an adoring ship's company, and refuses to admit having done anything wonderful."

And, indeed, to confirm Jaffery's last statement, here is a bit of a scrawl from Liosha—her complete account of the incident:

"We've just had the most awful storm I ever did see. The cargo go loose in the hold and we had to fix it up. I got a cut on the head and had to stay in bed till the storm finished. I must say it gave me an awful headache, but there I guess I'm better now."

Well, that seems to be the most exciting thing that happened to them. Afterwards, in the mind of each, it loomed as the great event in the amazing voyage. A man does not forget having his life saved by a woman at the risk of her own; and a woman, no matter how heroic in action and how magnanimous in after modesty, does not forget it either. Although he had been credited (to his ingenuous delight) by reviewers of "The Greater Glory" with uncanny knowledge of the complexities of a woman's nature, I have never met a more dunder-headed blunderer in his dealings with women. He perceived the symptoms of this unforgetfulness on Liosha's part, but seems to have been absolutely fogged in diagnosis.

"Liosha flourishes," he writes in one of his last *Vesta* letters, "like a virgin forest of green bay trees. Gosh! She's splendid. I take back and swallow every presumptuous word I've said about her. And, I suppose, owing to our knockabout sort of intimacy, she has adopted a protective, motherly attitude towards me. In her great, spacious, kind way, she gives you the impression that she owns Jaffery Chayne, and knows exactly what is for his good. Women's ways are wonderful but weird."

He must have thought himself vastly clever with his alliterative epigram. But he hadn't the faintest idea of the fount of Liosha's motherliness.

"Owing to our knockabout sort of intimacy"! Oh, the silly ass!

CHAPTER XXII

It was not until the end of October that Doria completed her round of country-house visits and returned to the flat in St. John's Wood. The morning after her arrival in town she took my satirical counsel and called at Wittekind's office, and, I am afraid, tried to bite that very pleasant, well-intentioned gentleman. She went out to do battle, arraying herself in subtle panoply of war. This I gather from Barbara's account of the matter. She informs me that when a woman goes to see her solicitor, her banker, her husband's uncle, a woman she hates, or a man who really understands her, she wears in each case an entirely different kind of hat. Judging from a warehouse of tissue-paper-covered millinery at the top of my residence, which I once accidentally discovered when tracking down a smell of fire, I know that this must be true. Costumes also, Barbara implies, must correspond emotionally with the hats. I recognised this, too, as philosophic truth; for it explained many puzzling and apparently unnecessary transformations in my wee wife's personal appearance. And yet, the other morning when I was going up to town to see after some investments, and I asked her which was the more psychological tie, a green or a violet, in which to visit my stockbroker, she lost as much of her temper as she allows herself to lose and bade me not he silly. . . . But this has nothing to do with Doria.

Doria, I say, with beaver cocked and plumes ruffled, intent on striking terror into the heart of Wittekind, presented herself in the outer office and sent in her card. At the name of Mrs. Adrian Boldero, doors flew open, and Doria marched straight away into Wittekind's comfortably furnished private room. Wittekind himself, tall, loose-limbed, courteous, the least tradesman-like person you can imagine, rose to receive her. For some reason or the other, or more likely against reason, she had pictured a rather soapy, smug little man hiding crafty eyes behind spectacles; but here he was, obviously a man of good breeding, who smiled at her most charmingly and gave her to understand that she was the one person in the world whom he had been longing to meet. And the office was not a sort of human *charcuterie* hung round with brains of authors for sale, but a quiet, restful place to which valuable prints on the walls and a few bits of real Chippendale gave an air of distinction. Doria admits to being disconcerted. She had come to bite and she remained to smile. He seated her in a nice old armchair with a beautiful back—she was sensitive to such things—and spoke of Adrian as of his own blood brother. She had not anticipated such warmth of genuine feeling, or so fine an appreciation of her Adrian's work.

"Believe me, my dear Mrs. Boldero," said he, "I am second only to you in my admiration and grief, and there's nothing I wouldn't do to keep your husband's memory green. But it is green, thank goodness. How do I know? By two signs. One that people wherever the English language is spoken are eagerly reading his books—I say reading, because you deprecate the purely commercial side of things; but you must forgive me if I say that the only proof of all their reading is the record of all their buying. And when people buy and read an author to this prodigious extent, they also discuss him. Adrian Boldero's name is a household word. You want advertisement and an *édition de luxe*. But it is only the little man that needs the big drum."

"But still, Mr. Wittekind," Doria urged, "an *édition de luxe* would be such a beautiful monument to him. I don't care a bit about the money," she went on with a splendid disregard of her rights that would have sent a shiver down the incorporated back of the Incorporated Society of Authors, "I'm only too willing to contribute towards the expense. Please understand me. It's a tribute and a monument."

"You only put up monuments to those who are dead," said Wittekind.

"But my husband—"

"—isn't dead," said he.

"Oh!" said Doria. "Then—"

"The time for your *édition de luxe* is not yet."

"Yet? But—you don't think Adrian's work is going to die?"

She looked at him tragically. He reassured her.

"Certainly not. Our future sumptuous edition will be a sign that he is among the immortals. But an *édition de luxe* now would be a wanton *Hic jacet*."

All of this may have been a bit sophistical, but it was sound business from the publisher's point of view, and conveyed through the medium of Wittekind's unaffected urbanity it convinced Doria. I listened to her account of it with a new moon of a smile across my soul—or across whatever part of oneself one smiles with when one's face is constrained to immobility.

"I'm so glad I plucked up courage to come and see you, Mr. Wittekind," she said. "I feel much happier. I'm quite content to leave Adrian's reputation in your hands. I wish, indeed, I had come to see you before." "I wish you had," said he.

"Mr. Chayne has been most kind; but—"

"Jaffery Chayne isn't you," he laughed. "But all the same, he's a splendid fellow and an admirable man of business."

"In what way?" she asked, rather coldly.

"Well—so prompt."

"That's the very last word I should apply to him. He took an unconscionable time," said Doria.

"He had a very difficult and delicate work of revision to do. Your husband's work was a first draft. The novel had to be pulled together. He did it admirably. That sort of thing takes time, although it was a labour of love."

"It merely meant writing in bits of scenes. Oh, Mr. Wittekind," she cried, reverting to an old grievance, "I do wish I could see exactly what he wrote and what Adrian wrote. I've been so worried! Why do your printers destroy authors' manuscripts?"

"They don't," said Wittekind. "They don't get them nowadays. They print from a typed copy."

"'The Greater Glory' was printed from my husband's original manuscript."

Wittekind smiled and shook his head. "No, my dear Mrs. Boldero. From two typed copies—one in England and one in America."

"Mr. Chayne told me that in order to save time he sent you Adrian's original manuscript with his revisions."

"I'm sure you must have misunderstood him," said Wittekind. "I read the typescript myself. I've never seen a line of your husband's manuscript."

"But 'The Diamond Gate' was printed from Adrian's manuscript."

"No, no, no. That, too, I read in type."

Doria rose and the colour fled from her cheeks and her great dark eyes grew bigger, and she brought down her little gloved hand on the writing desk by which the publisher, cross-kneed, was sitting. He rose, too.

"Mr. Chayne has definitely told me that both Adrian's original manuscripts went to the printers and were destroyed by the printers."

"It's impossible," said Wittekind, in much perplexity. "You're making some extraordinary mistake."

"I'm not. Mr. Chayne would not tell me a lie."

Wittekind drew himself up. "Neither would I, Mrs. Boldero. Allow me."

He took up his "house" telephone. "Ask Mr. Forest to come to me at once." He turned to Doria. "Let us get to the bottom of this. Mr. Forest is my literary adviser—everything goes through his hands."

They waited in silence until Mr. Forest appeared. "You remember the Boldero manuscripts?"

"Of course."

"What were they, manuscript or typescript?"

"Typescript."

"Have you even seen any of Mr. Boldero's original manuscript?"

"No."

"Do you think any of it has ever come into the office?"

"I'm sure it hasn't."

"Thank you, Mr. Forest."

The reader retired.

"You see," said Wittekind.

"Then where are the original manuscripts of 'The Diamond Gate' and 'The Greater Glory'?"

"I'm very sorry, dear Mrs. Boldero, but I have no means of knowing."

"Mr. Chayne said they were sent here, and used by the printers and destroyed by the printers."

"I'm sure," said Wittekind, "there's some muddling misunderstanding. Jaffery Chayne, in his own line, is a distinguished man—and a man of unblemished honour. A word or two will clear up everything."

"He's in Madagascar."

"Then wait till he comes back."

Doria insisted—and who in the world can blame her for insisting?

"You may think me a silly woman, Mr. Wittekind; but I'm not—not to the extent of an hysterical invention. Mr. Chayne has told me definitely that those two manuscripts came to your office, that the books were printed from them and that they were destroyed by the printers."

"And I," said Wittekind, "give you my word of honour—and I have also given you independent testimony—that no manuscript of your husband's has ever entered this office."

"Suppose they had come in his handwriting, would they have been destroyed?"

"Certainly not. Every sheet would have been returned with the proofs. Typed copy may or may not be returned."

"But autograph copy is valuable?"

"Naturally."

"The manuscripts of Adrian's novels might be worth a lot of money?"

"Quite a lot of money."

"So you don't think Mr. Chayne destroyed them?"

"It's an act of folly of which a literary man like Mr. Chayne would be incapable."

"And you've never seen any of it?"

"I've given you my word of honour."

"Then it's very extraordinary," said Doria.

"It is," said Wittekind, stiffly.

She thrust out her hand and flashed a generous glance.

"Forgive me for being bewildered. But it's so upsetting. You have nothing whatever to do with it. It's all Jaffery Chayne." She looked up at the loosely built, kindly man. "It's for him to give explanations. In the meanwhile, I leave my dear, dear husband's memory in your hands—to keep green, as you say" —tears came into her eyes—"and you will, won't you?"

The pathos of her attitude dissolved all resentment. He bent over her, still holding her hand.

"You may be quite sure of that," said he. "Even we publishers have our ideals—and our purest is to distribute through the world the works of a man of genius."

So Doria having telephoned for permission to come and see us on urgent business, arrived at Northlands late in the afternoon, full of the virtues of Wittekind and the vices of Jaffery. She gave us a full account of her interview and appealed to me for explanations of Jaffery's extraordinary conduct. I upbraided myself bitterly for having counselled her to bite Wittekind. I ought, instead, to have thrown every possible obstacle in the way of her meeting him. I ought to have foreseen this question of the manuscripts, the one weak spot in our web of deception. Now I may be a liar when driven by necessity from the paths of truth, but I am not an accomplished liar. It is not my fault. Mere providence has guided my life through such gentle pastures that I have had no practice worth speaking of. Barbara, too, is an amateur in mendacity. Both of us were sorely put to it under Doria's indignant and suspicious cross-examination.

"You saw the original manuscript of 'The Greater Glory'?"

"Yes," I lied.

"Did you see the original manuscript of 'The Diamond Gate'?"

"No," I lied again.

"Was it among Adrian's papers?"

"Not to my knowledge. Probably if Adrian didn't send it to the printers, he destroyed it."

"I don't believe he destroyed it. Jaffery has got it, and he has also got the manuscript of 'The Greater Glory.' What does he want them for?"

"That's a leading question, my dear, which I can't answer, because I don't know whether he has them or not. In fact, I know nothing whatever about them."

"It sounds horrid and ungracious, Hilary, after all you've done for me," said Doria, "but I really think you ought to know something."

From her point of view, and from any outside person's point of view, she was perfectly right. My bland ignorance was disgraceful. If she had brought an action against us for recovery of these wretched manuscripts and we managed to keep the essential secret, both counsel and judge would have flayed me alive. . . . Put yourself in her place for a minute—God knows I tried to do so hard enough—and you will see the logic of her position, all through. She was not a woman of broad human sympathies and generous outlook; she was intense and narrow. Her whole being had been concentrated on Adrian during their brief married life; it was concentrated now on his memory. To her, as to all the world, he flamed a dazzling meteor. Her faults, which were many and hard to bear with, all sprang from the bigotry of love. Nothing had happened to cloud her faith. She had come up against many incomprehensible things: the delay in publication of Adrian's book; the change of title; the burning of Adrian's last written words on the blotting pad; the vivid pictures that were obviously not Adrian's; the consignment to a printer's Limbo of the original manuscripts; my own placid disassociation from the literary side of the executorship. She had accepted them—not without protest; but she had in fact accepted them. Now she struck a reef of things more incomprehensible still. Jaffery had lied to her outrageously. I, for one, hold her justified in her indignation.

But what on earth could I do? What on earth could my poor Barbara do? We sat, both of us, racking our brains for some fantastic invention, while Doria, like a diminutive tragedy queen, walked about my library, inveighing against Jaffery and crying for her manuscripts. And I dared not know anything at all about them. She had every reason to reproach me.

Barbara, feeling very uncomfortable, said: "You mustn't blame Hilary. When Adrian died each of the executors took charge of a special department. Jaffery Chayne did not interfere with Hilary's management of financial affairs, and Hilary left Jaffery free with the literary side of things. It has worked very well. This silly muddle about the manuscripts doesn't matter a little bit."

"But it does matter," cried Doria.

And it did. Now that she knew that those sacred manuscripts written by the dear, dead hand had not been destroyed by printers, every fibre of her passionate self craved their possession. We argued futilely, as people must, who haven't the ghost of a case.

"But why has Jaffery lied?"

"The manuscript of 'The Diamond Gate,'" I declared, again perjuring myself, "has nothing whatever to do with Jaffery and me. As I've told you it was not among Adrian's papers which we went through together. We're narrowed down to 'The Greater Glory.' Possibly," said I, with a despairing flash, "Jaffery had to pull it about so much and deface it with his own great scrawl, that he thought it might pain you to see it, and so he told you that it had disappeared at the printer's. Now that I remember, he did say something of the kind."

"Yes, he did," said Barbara.

Doria brushed away the hypothesis. "You poor things! You're merely saying that to shield him. A blind imbecile could see through you"—I have already apologised to you for our being the unconvincing liars that we were—"you know nothing more about it than I do. You ought to, as I've already said. But you don't. In fact, you know considerably less. Shall I tell you where the manuscripts are at the present moment?"

"No, my dear," said Barbara, in the plaintive voice of one who has come to the end of a profitless talk; for you cannot imagine how utterly wearied we were with the whole of the miserable business. "Let us wait till Jaffery comes home. It won't be so very long."

"Yes, Doria," said I, soothingly. "Barbara's right. You can't condemn a man without a hearing?"

Doria laughed scornfully. "Can't I? I'm a woman, my dear friend. And when a woman condemns a man unheard she's much more merciful than when she condemns him after listening to his pleadings. Then she gets really angry, and perhaps does the man injustice."

I gasped at the monstrous proposition; but Barbara did not seem to detect anything particularly wrong about it.

"At any rate," said I, "whether you condemn him or not, we can't do anything until he comes home. So we had better leave it at that."

"Very well," said Doria. "Let us leave it for the present. I don't want to be more of a worry to you dear people than I can help. But that's where Adrian's manuscripts are, both of them"—and she pointed to the key of Jaffery's flat hanging with its staring label against my library wall.

Of course it was rather mean to throw the entire onus on to Jaffery. But again, what could we do? Doria put her pistol at our heads and demanded Adrian's original manuscripts. She had every reason to believe in their existence. Wittekind had never seen them. Vandal and Goth and every kind of Barbarian that she considered Jaffery to be, it was inconceivable that he had deliberately destroyed them. It was equally inconceivable that he had sold the precious things for vulgar money. They remained therefore in his possession. Why did he lie? We could supply no satisfactory answer; and the more solutions we offered the more did we confirm in her mind the suspicion of dark and nefarious dealings. If it were only to gain time in order to think and consult, we had to refer her to the absent Jaffery.

"My dear," said I to Barbara, when we were alone, "we're in a deuce of a mess."

"I'm afraid we are."

"Henceforward," said I, "we're going to live like selfish pigs, with no thought about anybody but ourselves and our own little pig and about anything outside our nice comfortable sty."

"We'll do nothing of the kind," said Barbara.

"You'll see," said I. "I'm a lion of egotism when I'm roused."

We dined and had a pleasant evening. Doria did not raise the disastrous topic, but talked of Marienbad and her visits, and discussed the modern tendencies of the drama. She prided herself on being in the forefront of progress, and found no dramatic salvation outside the most advanced productions of the Incorporated Stage Society. I pleaded for beauty, which she called wedding-cake. She pleaded for courage and truth in the presentation of actual life, which I called dull and stupid photography which any dismal fool could do. We had quite an exciting and entirely profitless argument.

"I'm not going to listen any longer," she cried at last, "to your silly old early Victorian platitudes!"

"And I," I retorted, "am not going to be browbeaten in my own home by one-foot-nothing of crankiness and chiffon."

So, laughingly, we parted for the night, the best of friends. If only, I thought, she could sweep her head clear of Adrian, what a fascinating little person she might be. And I understood how it had come to pass that our hulking old ogre had fallen in love with her so desperately.

The next morning I was in the garden, superintending the planting of some roses in a new, bed, when Doria, in hat and furs, came through my library window, and sang out a good-bye. I hurried to her.

"Surely not going already? I thought you were at least staying to lunch."

No; she had to get back to town. The car, ordered by Barbara, was waiting to take her to the station.

"I'll see you into the train," said I.

"Oh, please don't trouble."

"I will trouble," I laughed, and I accompanied her down the slope to the front door where stood Barbara by the car and Franklin with the luggage. Doria and I drove to the station. For the few minutes before the train came in we walked up and down the platform. She was in high spirits, full of jest and laughter. An unwonted flush in her cheeks and a brightness in her deep eyes rendered her perfectly captivating.

"I haven't seen you looking so well and so pretty for ever such a long time," I said.

The flush deepened. "You and Barbara have done me all the good in the world. You always do. Northlands is a sort of Fontaine de Jouvence for weary people."

That was as graceful as could be. And when she shook hands with me a short while afterwards through the carriage window, she thanked me for our long-sufferance with more spontaneous cordiality than she had ever before exhibited. I returned to my roses, feeling that, after all, we had done something to help the poor little lady on her way. If I had been a cat, I should have purred. After an hour or so, Barbara summoned me from my contemplative occupation.

"Yes, dear?" said I, at the library window.

"Have you written to Rogers?"

Rogers was a plumber.

"He's a degraded wretch," said I, "and unworthy of receiving a letter from a clean-minded man."

"Meanwhile," said Barbara, "the servants' bathroom continues to be unusable."

"Good God!" said I, "does Rogers hold the cleanliness of this household in his awful hands?"

"He does."

"Then I will sink my pride and write to him."

"Write now," said Barbara, leading me to my chair. "You ought to have done it three days ago."

So with three days' bathlessness of my domestic staff upon my conscience, and with Barbara at my elbow, I wrote my summons. I turned in my chair, holding it up in my hand.

"Is this sufficiently dignified and imperious?"

I began to declaim it. "Sir, it has been brought to my notice that the pipes—". I broke off short. "Hullo!" said I, my eyes on the wall, "what has become of the key of Jaffery's flat?"

There was the brass-headed nail on which I had hung it, impertinently and nakedly bright. The labelled key had vanished.

"You've got it in your pocket, as usual," said Barbara.

I may say that I have a habit of losing things and setting the household from the butler to the lower myrmidons of the kitchen in frantic search, and calling in gardeners and chauffeurs and nurses and wives and children to help, only to discover that I have had the wretched object in my pocket all the time. So accustomed is Barbara to this wolf-cry that if I came up to her without my head and informed her that I had lost it, she would be profoundly sceptical.

But this time I was blameless. "I haven't touched it," I declared, "and I saw it this morning."

"I don't know about this morning," said Barbara. "But I grant you it was there yesterday evening, because Doria drew our attention to it."

"Doria!" I cried, and I rose, with mouth agape, and our eyes met in a sudden stare.

"Good Heavens! do you think she has taken it?"

"Who else?" said I. "She came out from here to say good-bye to me in the garden. She had the opportunity. She was preternaturally animated and demonstrative at the station—your sex's little guileful way ever since the world began. She had the stolen key about her. She's going straight to Jaffery's flat to hunt for those manuscripts."

"Well, let her," said Barbara. "We know she can't find them, because they don't exist."

"But, my darling Barbara," I cried, "everything else does. And everything else is there. And there's not a blessed thing locked up in the place!"

"Do you mean—?" she cried aghast.

"Yes, I do. I must get up to town at once and stop her."

"I'll come with you," said Barbara.

So once more, on altruistic errand, I motored post-haste to London. We alighted at St. Quentin's Mansions. My friend the porter came out to receive us.

"Has a lady been here with a key of Mr. Chayne's flat?"

"No, sir, not to my knowledge."

We drew breaths of relief. Our journey had been something of a strain.

"Thank goodness!" said Barbara.

"Should a lady come, don't allow her to enter the flat," said I.

And there, in a wilderness of ransacked drawers and strewn papers, . . . lay a tiny, black, moaning heap of a woman.

"I shouldn't give a strange lady entrance in any case," said the porter.

"Good!" said I, and I was about to go. But Barbara, with her ready common-sense, took me aside and whispered:

"Why not take all these compromising manuscripts home with us?"

In my letter case I had the half-forgotten power of attorney that Jaffery had given me at Havre. I shewed it to the porter.

"I want to get some things out of Mr. Chayne's flat."

"Certainly, sir," said the porter. "I'll take you up."

We ascended in the lift. The porter opened Jaffery's door. We entered the sitting-room. And there, in a wilderness of ransacked drawers and strewn papers, with her head against the cannon-ball on the hearthrug, lay a tiny, black, moaning heap of a woman.

CHAPTER XXIII

If a ministering angel walks abroad through this world of many sorrows, it is my wife Barbara. To her and to her alone did the soul-stricken little creature owe her life and her reason. For a fortnight she scarcely left Doria's room, sleeping for odd hours anywhere, and snatching meals with the casual swiftness of a swallow. For a whole fortnight she wrestled with the powers of darkness, which like Apollyon straddled quite over all the breadth of the way, and by sheer valiancy and beauty of heart, she made them spread forth their dragon's wings and speed them away so that Doria for a season saw them no more. How she fought and with what weapons, who am I to tell you? These things are written down; but in a Book which no human eye can see.

We carried her moaning and distraught from that room of awful revelation, put her into the car, and brought her back to Northlands. It was the only thing to be done. Barbara's instinct foresaw madness if we took her to the flat in St. John's Wood. Her father's house, her natural refuge, was equally impossible. For what explanation could we have given to the worthy but uncomprehending man? He would have called in doctors to minister to a mind afflicted with a disease beyond their power of diagnosis. Unless, of course, we made public the facts of the tragedy; which was unthinkable. Barbara's instinct pierced surely through the gloom. The first coherent words that Doria said were:

"Let me stay with you for a little. I've nowhere in the world to go. I can't ask father—and I can't go back home. It would drive me mad."

Of course it would have driven her mad to return to the haunted flat— haunted now by no gracious ghost, but by an Unutterable Presence, the thought of which, even in her quiet, lavender-scented country bedroom, made her scream of nights. For she knew all. To save her reason, Barbara, with her wonderful tenderness, had bridged over the chasms between her stark peaks of discovery. She knew all that we knew. Further attempts at deception would have been vain cruelty. Barbara could palliate the offence; she could show how irresistible had been the temptation; she could prove how our love for Adrian had been unshaken by disastrous knowledge and urge that Doria's love should be unshaken likewise; she could apply all the healing remedies of which she only has the secret—but she could not leave the poor soul to stumble blindly in uncertainty.

Doria could never enter her dishallowed paradise again. Even I, when I went through the place in order to make arrangements for closing it altogether, felt a teeth-chattering shiver in the condemned cell where Adrian had worked out his doom. It had been sacrosanct; not a thing had been disturbed; there was the iron safe empty, but yet a grim receptacle of abominable secrets; the quill pen, its point stained with idle ink, lay on the office writing-table. And the blotting-pad was still there under a clump of dusty, unused scribbling-paper. On a little stool in the corner stood the half-emptied decanter of brandy and a glass and a syphon of soda-water. . . . Goodness knows, I'm not a superstitious or even an imaginative man; I had been in that room before and had hated it, on account of its poignant associations; nothing transcendental had affected me; but now I shuddered, physically shuddered, as though the cubic space were informed with a spirit in the torture of an everlasting despair. Doria not knowing, he could have borne his punishment. But now Doria knew. He had lost her love, the rock on which he had built his hope of salvation. He was damned to eternity. It is the supreme and unspeakable horror of eternal life that you cannot dash your head against a wall and plunge into nothingness. Yet he tried. The awful Presence of Adrian was dashing his head against those bare and ghastly walls. . . .

I never was so glad to breathe God's honest November fog again. Of course my affright was a silly matter of nerves. But I would not have slept in that flat for anything in the world.

I had to make, of course, another expedition to Jaffery's chambers, in order to restore to order the chaos that Doria had made. She had ransacked every drawer in the place and strewn the contents of the old portmanteau, Adrian's mass of incoherent manuscript, about the floor. I did what I ought to have done on my first visit; I brought the tragic lumber to Northlands, and having made a bonfire in a corner of the kitchen garden, burned the whole lot. Why Jaffery had not got rid of the evidence of Adrian's guilt, I could not at the time imagine. It was only later that I heard the trivial and mechanical reason. He could not burn the papers in his flat, because he had no fire—only the electric radiator. You try, in these circumstances, to destroy five or six thousand sheets of thick paper, and see how you get on. Jaffery had his idea, when he transferred the manuscript from Adrian's study; on his next voyage he would take the portmanteau with him, weight it with the cannon-ball, which he used after his bath for physical exercise, and throw it overboard. By singular ill-luck, he had started on his two voyages that year—if a channel crossing can be termed a voyage—at a moment's notice. In each case he had not had occasion to call at his chambers, and the destroying journey had yet to be made. As for discovery of the secrets lying in unlocked receptacles, who was there to discover them? Such friends as he had would never pry into his private concerns; and as for housemaids and waiters and porters, the whole matter to them was unintelligible. While he was living in St. Quentin's Mansions, he considered himself secure. When he realised, at Havre, that he would be absent for some months, he put things into my charge. That I bitterly regretted not having put tinder lock and key or taken steps to destroy papers and manuscripts, I need not say. For a long time I felt the guiltiest wretch outside prison in the three kingdoms. If I had been a wild man of the jungle like Jaffery, it would not have mattered; but I have always prided myself on being—not the last word, for that would not be consonant with my natural modesty—but, say, the penultimate word of our modern civilisation; and the memory of having acted like an ingenuous child of nature still burns whenever it floats across my brain. Metaphorically, Jaffery and I sobbed with remorse on each other's bosoms, and called ourselves all the picturesque synonyms for careless fools we could think of; but that, naturally, did not a bit of good to anybody.

The fact was accomplished. Our dear Humpty-Dumpty had had his great fall, and not all the king's horses and all the king's men could ever set Humpty-Dumpty up again.

Greek tragedies are all very well in their way. They are vastly interesting in the inevitableness of their prearranged doom. *Moi qui vous parle*, I have read all of them; and I like them. I have even seen some of them acted. I have seen, for instance, the Agamemnon given by the boys of Bradfield College, in their model open-air Greek theatre, built out of a chalk-pit, and I have sat gripped from beginning to end by the tremendous drama. I am not talking foolishly. I know as much as the ordinary man need know about Greek tragedy. But in spite of Aristotle (who ought to have been strangled at birth, like all other bland doctrinaires—and of all the doctrinaires on art, there has none been so blandly egregious since the early morning long ago when the pre-historic artist who drew an elk on the omoplate of a bison was clubbed by the superior person of his day who could not draw for nuts)—in spite of Aristotle and the rest of the theorists, I assert that, as far as my experience goes, in the ordinary wary modern life to which we are accustomed, doom and inevitableness do not matter a hang. If we have any common-sense we can dodge them. Most of us do. Of course, if a woman marries a congenital idiot there are bound to be ructions—here we are entering the domain of pathology, which is as doomful as you please; but in our ordinary modern life ninety per cent. of the tragedies are determined by sheer million to one fortuities. The history of our great criminal trials, for instance, is a romance of coincidence. It is your melodramatist and not your Aristotelian purist that knows what he's talking about when he writes a play. He only has to look about him and draw what happens in real life. That there may be an Eternal Puckish Malice arranging and deranging human destinies is another question. I am neither a theologian nor a metaphysician, and I do not desire to discuss the subject. I only maintain that, had it not been for sheer chance, Adrian's secret would never have been discovered a second time. I cannot see any doom about it. A series of sheer, silly accidents on the part of Jaffery and myself had brought Doria face to face with these incriminating papers. As for her having gained access to the flat without the porter's knowledge, that had been calculation on her part. She had watched at the street entrance until he had taken some one up in the lift, and then she had mounted the interminable stairs.

I could have caught Jaffery by letter at Genoa or Marseilles; but in view of his imminent return, I did not write to him. What useful purpose would have been served? He would have left the steamship *Vesta* and travelled post-haste overland, dragging with him a resentful Liosha, and rushed like a mad bull into an upheaval in which he could have no place. We had arranged by correspondence that, after he had parted from the good Captain Maturin at Havre, he would come straight to us, in order to leave Liosha temporarily in our care. For what else could be done with her? Let him bring her, then, according to programme. It would be far better, we agreed, Barbara and I, to let them fulfil their lunatic adventure undisturbed, and on Jaffery's arrival at Northlands to break the disastrous tidings. It would give us time to watch Doria and see what direction the resultant of the forces now tearing her soul would take.

"Let Jaffery stay away as long as possible," said Barbara. "I can't be bothered with him. I wish his old voyage could be extended for a year."

The first time I met Doria, when she crawled out of her room, a great pity smote my heart. The ivory of her face had turned to wax, and she had dwindled into a fragile reed, and in her eyes quivered the apprehension of an ill-treated dog. I put my arm round her and hugged her reassuringly, not knowing what else to do, and mumbled a few silly words. Then I settled her down before the drawing-room fire, and rushed out into the garden and cut the last poor lingering autumn roses, and, returning, cast them into her lap. And we talked hard about the roses; and I told her which were Madame Abel Chatenay, which Marquise de Salisbury, and which Frau Karl Druska, which Lady Ursula and which Lady Hillingdon. We did not refer at all to unhappy things.

It was only some days afterwards that she ventured to raise the veil of her awful desolation. But she had no need to tell me. Any fool could have divined it. Together with far less shattering of idols has many a woman's reason been brought down. And in our poor Doria's case it was not only the shattering of idols.

"Hilary, dear," she said, with a mournful attempt at a smile. "I can't go on living here for ever."

"Why not?" I asked. "This is a vast barrack of a place, and you're only just a bit of a wee white mouse. And we love our pets. Why do you want to go?"

We were walking up and down the drive. It was a warm, damp morning and the trees shaken by the mild southwester shed their leaves around us in a golden shower; and the leaves that had fallen lay sodden on the grass borders. Here and there a surviving blossom of antirrhinum swaggered among its withered brethren as if to maintain the illusion of summer. A partridge or two whirred across the path from copse to meadow. The gentle sadness of the autumn day had moved her to discourse on the mutability of mundane things. Hence, by chain of association, I suppose, her sudden remark.

"I don't want to go," she replied. "I should like to stay in the dreamy peace of Northlands for ever. But I have been a pet for such a long time—for years, and I've shown myself to be such a bad pet—biting the hand that fed me."

I bade her not talk foolishly. She moved her small shoulder.

"It's true. While the three of you—you and Barbara and Jaffery—were doing for me what has never been done for another human being, I was all the time snarling and snapping. I can't make out how you can bear the sight of me." She clenched her hands and straightened her arms down tense. "The thought of it scorches me," she cried suddenly.

"Whatever you did, dear," said I, "was so natural; and we understood it all. How could we blame you?"

We had, in fact, blamed her on many occasions, not being as gods to whom human hearts are open books; but this was not the occasion on which to tell her so. I don't like the devil being called the father of lies. I am convinced that the discoverer of mendacity was a warm-hearted philanthropist, who has never received due credit, and that the devil having seized hold of his discovery perverted it to his own diabolical uses. It is the sort of plagiaristic thing that devils, whether they promote ancient Gehennas or modern companies, have been doing since the world began.

"That doesn't make it any the easier to me," said Doria. "The horrible things I said and did—the ghastliness of it—"

"My dear girl," I interrupted, as kindly as I could. "Don't let this mere fringe of tragedy worry you."

She laughed shrilly, with a set, white face; which is the most unmirthful kind of laugh you can imagine.

"Don't you know that it's the fringe that is the maddening irritation? The big central thing numbs and stupefies, when it doesn't kill. And for some reason"—she threw out her little gloved hands—"the big thing hasn't killed me—it has paralysed me. The springs of feeling"—she clutched her bosom—"are dried up. My heart is withered and dead. I can't explain. For all the dead things I'm not responsible. I've gone through Hell the last two or three weeks and they've been burned up altogether. But what hasn't been burned up is the fringe, as you call it. That's only red-hot. It scorches me, and I can't sleep for the torture of it. . . ." She stopped, and fronting me laid an appealing touch on my arm. "Oh, Hilary, forgive me. I didn't mean to go on in this wild way. I thought I had a better hold on myself."

"I don't see," said I, "why you shouldn't unburden your heart to one who has proved himself to be a friend not only of yours, but of Adrian."

She released me, and with a wide gesture, swayed across the gravel path. I stepped to her side and mechanically we walked on, a few paces, before either of us spoke.

"I have told you," she said at last. "I have no heart to unburden. There never was an Adrian."

"There was indeed," said I, warmly.

"Yours. Not mine."

"Have you no forgiveness for him, then?" I asked earnestly.

She halted again and looked at me and at the back of her great eyes gleamed black ice.

"No," she said.

I went straight to bed-rock.

"He was the father of your dead child," said I.

Her small frame heaved and she looked away from me down the drive. "I can only thank God that the child didn't live."

Barbara had told me something of the fear in which she seemed to hold Adrian's memory. But I had not in the least realised it till now when I heard the profession from her own lips. In fact, I know that she had never yet spoken to Barbara with such passionate directness.

"You oughtn't to say such a thing, Doria," I said sternly.

"I am as God made me."

"Adrian loved you. He sinned for your sake—in order to get you."

She dismissed the argument with a gesture.

"You must have pity on him," I insisted, "for the unspeakable torment of those months of barrenness, of abortive attempts at creation."

She was silent for a moment. Having reached the front gates we turned and began to walk up the drive. Then she said:

"Yes, I do pity him. It's enough to tear one's brain out,—his when he was alive—and mine now. The thought of it will freeze my soul for all eternity. I can't tell you what I feel." She cast out her hands imploringly to the autumn fields. "I pity him as I would pity some one remote from me—a criminal whom I might have seen done to death by awful tortures. It's a matter of the brain, not of the heart. No. I have all the understanding. But I can't find the pardon."

"That will come," said I.

"In the next world, perhaps, not in this."

Her tone of finality forbade argument. Besides what was there to argue about? She had said: "There never was an Adrian." From her point of view, she was mercilessly right.

"It's horrible to think," she went on after a pause, "that all this time I've been living, first on stolen property and now on charity—Jaffery's charity— and he hasn't even had a word of thanks. Quite the contrary." Again she laughed the shrill, dead laugh. "You see, I must go home—to my father's— I'm strong enough now—and start my life, such as it is, all over again. I can't touch another penny of the Wittekind money. Castleton's people and Jaffery must be paid."

"Tom Castleton," I said, "was alone in the world, and Jaffery's not the man to take back a free gift beautifully given. If you don't like to keep the money—I appreciate your feelings—you can devote it to philanthropic purposes."

"Yes, I might do that," she agreed. "But is this fraud—this false reputation—to go on forever?"

"I'm afraid it must," said I. "Nobody would be benefited by throwing such a bombshell of scandal into society. If anybody living were suffering from wrong it might be different. But there's no reason to blacken unnecessarily the name you bear."

"Then you really think I should be justified in keeping the secret?" she asked anxiously.

"I think it would be outrageous of you to do anything else," said I.

"That eases my mind. If it were essential for me to make things public, I would do it. I'm not a coward. But I should die of the disgrace."

"To poor Adrian," said I.

She flashed a quick, defiant glance.

"To me."

"To Adrian," I insisted, smitten with a queer inspiration. "He sinned—the unpardonable sin, if you like. But he expiated it. He's expiating it now. And you love him. And it's for his sake, not yours, that you shrink from public disgrace. You were so irrevocably wrapped up in him"—I pursued my advantage—"that you feel yourself a partner in his guilt. Which means that you love him still."

She raised a stark, terror-stricken face. I touched her shoulder. Then, all of a sudden, she collapsed, and broke into an agony of sobs and tears. I drew her to a desolate rustic bench and put my arm round her and let her sob herself out.

After that we did not speak of Adrian.

CHAPTER XXIV

At last news came from Havre of the end of the preposterous voyage.

"Crossing to-night. Coming straight to you. Send car to meet us Reading. Local trains beastly. Both fit as elephants. Love to all.

"JAFFERY."

Such was the telegram. I wired to Southampton acquiescence in his proposal. It was far more sensible to come direct to Reading than to make a détour through London. Rooms were got ready. In the one destined for Liosha, we had already stowed the cargo of trunks which the Great Swiftness had delivered in the nick of time. The next day I took the car to Reading and waited for the train.

From the far end of it I saw two familiar figures descend, and a moment afterwards the station resounded with a familiar roar.

"Hullo! hullo! hullo!"

Jaffery, red-bearded, grinning, perhaps a bit mightier, hairier, redder than ever, his great hands uplifted, rushed at me and shook me in his lunatic way, so that train, passengers, porters and Liosha all rocked and reeled before my eyes. He let me go, and, before I could recover, Liosha threw her arms round my neck and kissed me. A porter who picked up my hat restored me to mental equipoise. Then I looked at them, and anything more splendid in humanity than that simple, happy pair of gigantic children I have never seen in my life. I, too, felt the laughter of happiness swell in my heart, for their gladness at the sight of me was so true, so unaffected, and I wrung their hands and laughed aloud foolishly. It is good to be loved, especially when you've done nothing particular to deserve it. And in their primitive way these two loved me.

"Isn't she fit?" roared Jaffery.

"Magnificent," said I.

She was. The thick tan of exposure to wind and sun gave her a gipsy swarthiness beneath which glowed the rich colour of health. When I had parted from her at Havre there had been just a thread of soft increase in her generous figure; but now all superfluous flesh had hardened down into muscle, and the superb lines proclaimed her splendour. And there seemed to be more authority in her radiant face and a new masterfulness and a quicker intelligence in her brown eyes. I noticed that it was she who first broke away from the clamour of greeting and gave directions as to the transport of their "dunnage." Jaffery followed her with the tail of his eye; then turned to me with a bass chuckle.

"We're a sort of Jaff Chayne and Co., according to her, and she thinks she's managing director. Ho! ho! ho!" He put his arm round my shoulder and suddenly grew serious. "How's everybody?"

"Flourishing," said I.

"And Doria?"

"At Northlands."

"She knows I'm coming?"

"Yes," said I.

Liosha joined us, accompanied by a porter, carrying their exiguous baggage. We walked to the exit, without saying much, and settled ourselves in the limousine, my guests in the back seat, I on one of the little chairs facing them. We started.

"My dear old chap," said I, leaning forward. "I've got something to tell you. I didn't like to write about it. But it has got to be told, and I may as well get it over now."

It was a subdued and half-scared Jaffery who greeted Barbara and Susan at our front door. The jollity had gone out of him. He was nothing but a vast hulk filled with self-reproach. It was his fault, his very grievous and careless fault for having postponed the destruction of the papers, and for having left them loose and unsecured in his rooms. He all but beat his breast. If Doria had died of the shock his would be the blame. He saluted Barbara with the air of one entering a house of mourning.

"You mustn't look so woe-begone," she said. "Something like this was bound to happen. I have dreaded it all along—and now it has happened and the earth hasn't come to an end."

We stood in the hall, while Franklin divested the visitors of their outer wraps and trappings.

"And, Liosha," Barbara continued, throwing her arms round as much of Liosha as they could grasp—she had already kissed her a warm welcome—

"it's a shame, dear, to depress you the moment you come into the place. You'll wish you were at sea again."

"I guess not," said Liosha. "I know now I'm among folks who love me. Isn't that true, Susan?"

"Daddy loves you and mummy loves you and I adore you," cried Susan.

Whereupon there was much hugging of a spoiled monkey.

We went upstairs. At the drawing-room door Barbara gave me one of her queer glances, which meant, on interpretation, that I should leave her alone with Jaffery for a few minutes so that she could pour the balm of sense over his remorseful soul, and that in the meantime it would be advisable for me to explain the situation to Liosha. Aloud, she said, before disappearing:

"Your old room, Liosha, dear—you'll find everything ready."

In order to carry out my wife's orders, I had to disentangle Susan from Liosha's embrace and pack her off rueful to the nursery. But the promise to seat her at lunch between the two seafarers brought a measure of consolation.

"Come into the library, Liosha," said I, throwing the door open. I followed her and settled her in an armchair before a big fire; and then stood on the hearthrug, looking at her and feeling rather a fool. I offered her refreshment. She declined. I commented again on her fine physical appearance and asked her how she was. I drew her attention to some beautiful narcissi and hyacinths that had come from the greenhouse. The more I talked and the longer she regarded me in her grave, direct fashion, the less I knew how to tell her, or how much to tell her, of Doria's story. The drive had been a short one, giving time only for a narration of the facts of the discovery. Liosha, although accepting my apology, had sat mystified; also profoundly disturbed by Jaffery's unconcealed agitation. Her life with him during the past four months had drawn her into the meshes of the little drama. For her own sake, for everybody's sake, we could not allow her to remain in complete ignorance. . . . I gave her a cigarette and took one myself. After the first puff, she smiled.

"You want to tell me something."

"I do. Something that is known only to four people in the world—and they're in this house."

"If you tell me, I guess it'll be known only to five," said Liosha.

To have questioned the loyalty of her eyes would have been to insult truth itself.

"All right," said I. "You'll be the fifth and last." And then, as simply as I could, I told her all there was to know. She grasped the literary details more quickly than I had anticipated. I found afterwards that the long months of the voyage had not been entirely taken up with the cooking of bacon and the swabbing of decks; there had been long stretches of tedium beguiled by talk on most things under heaven, and aided by her swift and jealous intelligence her mental horizon had broadened prodigiously through constant association with a cultivated man. . . . When I reached the point in my story where Jaffery gave up the Persian expedition, she gripped the arms of her chair, and her lips worked in their familiar quiver.

"He must have loved her to do that," she said in a low voice.

I went on, and the more involved I became in the disastrous affair, the more was I convinced that it would be better for her to understand clearly the imbroglio of Jaffery and Doria. You see, I knew all along, as all along I hope I have given you to understand—ever since the day when she asked him to beat her with a golf-stick—that the poor girl loved Jaffery, heart and soul. I knew also that she made for herself no illusions as to Jaffery's devotion to Doria. On that point her words to me at Havre had left me in no doubt whatever. But since Havre all sorts of extraordinary things had happened. There had been their intimate comradeship in the savagery (from my point of view) of the last few months. There was now Doria's awful change of soul-attitude towards Adrian. It was right that Liosha should be made aware of the emotional subtleties that underlay the bare facts. It seemed cruel to tell her of the last scene, so pathetic, so tragic, so grotesque, between the man she loved and the other woman. But her unflinching bravery and her great heart demanded it. And as I told her, walking nervously about the room, she followed me with her steadfast eyes.

"So that's why Jaff Chayne came abroad with me."

"I suppose so," said I.

"If I had been a man I should have strangled her, or flung her out of the window."

"I dare say. But you wouldn't have been Jaff Chayne."

"That's true," she assented. "No man like him ever walked the earth. And how a woman could be so puppy-blind as not to see it, I can't imagine."

"Her head was full of another man, you see."

"Oh yes, I see," she said with a touch of contempt. "And such a man! You were fond of him I know. But he was a sham. He used to look on me, I remember, as an amusing sort of animal out of the Zoological Gardens. It never occurred to him that I had sense. He was a fool."

Intimately as we had known Liosha, this was the first time she had ever expressed an opinion regarding Adrian. We had assumed that, having touched her life so lightly, he had been but a shadowy figure in her mind, and that, save in so far as his death concerned us, she had viewed him with entire indifference. But her keen feminine brain had picked out the fatal flaw in poor Adrian's character, the shallow glitter that made us laugh and the want of vision from which he died.

"Go on," said Liosha.

I continued. In justice to Doria, I elaborated her reasons for setting Adrian on his towering pinnacle. Liosha nodded. She understood. False gods, whatever degree of godhead they usurped, had for a time the mystifying power of concealing their falsehood. And during that time they were gods, real live dwellers on Olympus, flaming Joves to poor mortal Semeles. Liosha quite understood.

I ended, more or less, a recapitulation of what she had heard, uncomprehending, in the car.

"And that's how it stands," said I.

I was rather shaken, I must confess, by my narrative, and I turned aside and lit another cigarette. Liosha remained silent for a while, resting her cheek on her hand. At last she said in her deep tones:

"Poor little devil! Good God! Poor little devil!"

Tears flooded her eyes.

"By heavens," I cried, "you're a good creature."

"I'm nothing of the sort," said Liosha. She rose. "I guess I must have a clean up before lunch," and she made for the door.

I looked at my watch. "You just have time," said I.

I opened the door for her to pass out, and fell a-musing in front of the fire. Here was a new Liosha, as far apart from the serene young barbarian who had come to us two and a half years before blandly characterising Euphemia as a damn fool because she would not let her buy a stocked chicken incubator and take it to the Savoy Hotel, as a prairie wolf from the noble Great Dane. Her nature had undergone remarkable developments. As Jaffery had prophesied at Havre, she treated things in a big way, and she had learned restraint, not the restraint of convention, for not a convention would have stopped her from doing what she chose, but the restraint of self-discipline. And she had learned pity. A year ago she would not have wept over Doria, whom she had every woman's reason for hating. A new, generous tenderness had blossomed in her heart. If all the cutthroats of

Albania who had murdered her family had been brought bound and set on their knees with bared necks before her and she had been presented with a sharp sword, I doubt whether she would have cut off one single head.

A tap at the window aroused me. It was Jaffery in the rain, which had just begun to fail, seeking admittance. I let him in.

"This is an awful business, old man," he said gloomily.

From which I gather that for once Barbara's soothing had been of little avail.

"Have you seen Doria yet?" I asked.

He shook his head. "Barbara is with her. She's coming in to lunch."

At the anti-climax, I smiled. "That shews she's not quite dead yet."

But to Jaffery it was no smiling matter. "Look here, Hilary," he said hoarsely, "don't you think it would be better for me to cut the whole thing and go away right now?"

"Go away—?" I stared at him. "What for?"

"Why should I force myself on that poor, tortured child? Think of her feelings towards me. She must loathe the sound of my name."

"Jaff Chayne," said I, "I believe you're afraid of mice."

He frowned. "What the blazes do you mean?"

"You're in a blue funk at the idea of meeting Doria."

"Rot," said Jaffery.

But he was.

Franklin summoned us to luncheon. We went into the drawing-room where the rest of our little party were assembled, Susan and her governess, Liosha, Barbara and Doria. Doria stepped forward valiantly with outstretched hand, looking him squarely in the face.

"Welcome back, Jaffery. It's good to see you again."

Jaffery grew very red and bending over her hand muttered something into his beard.

"You'll have to tell me about your wonderful voyage."

"There was nothing so wonderful about it," said Jaffery.

That was all for the moment, for Barbara hustled us into the dining-room. But the terrible meeting that both had dreaded was over. Nobody had fainted or shed tears; it was over in a perfectly well-bred way. At lunch Susan, between Liosha and Jaffery, became the centre of attention and saved conversation from constraint.

To Doria, who had lingered at Northlands, in order to lose no time in setting herself right with Jaffery,—her own phrase—the ordinary table small-talk would have been an ordeal. As it was, she sat on my left, opposite Liosha, lending a polite ear to the answers to Susan's eager questions. The child had not received such universal invitation to chatter at mealtime since she had learned to speak. But, in spite of her inspiring assistance, a depressing sense of destinies in the balance pervaded the room, and we were all glad when the meal came to an end. Susan, refusing to be parted from her beloved Liosha, carried her off to the nursery to hear more fairy-tales of the steamship *Vesta*. Barbara and Doria went into the drawing-room, where Jaffery and I, after a perfunctory liqueur brandy, soon joined them. We talked for a while on different things, the child's robustious health, the garden, the weather, our summer holiday, much in the same dismal fashion as assembled mourners talk before the coffin is brought downstairs. At last Barbara said:

"I must go and write some letters."

And I said: "I'm going to have my afternoon nap."

Both the others cried out with simultaneous anxiety and scarlet faces:

"Oh, don't go, Barbara, dear."

"Can't you cut the sleep out for once?"

"I must!" said Barbara.

"No," said I.

And we left our nervous ogre and our poor little elf to fight out between themselves whatever battle they had to fight. Perhaps it was cold-blooded cruelty on our part. But these two had to come to mutual understanding sooner or later. Why not at once? They had the afternoon before them. It was pouring with rain. They had nothing else to do. In order that they should be undisturbed, Barbara had given orders that we were not at home to visitors. Besides, we were actuated by motives not entirely altruistic. If I seem to have posed before you as a noble-minded philanthropist, I have been guilty of careless misrepresentation. At the best I am but a not unkindly, easy-going man who loathes being worried. And I (and Barbara even more than myself) had been greatly worried over our friends' affairs for a considerable period. We therefore thought that the sooner we were freed from these worries the better for us both. Deliberately we hardened our hearts against their joint appeal and left them together in the drawing-room.

"Whew!" said I, as we walked along the corridor. "What's going to happen?"

"She'll marry him, of course."

"She won't," said I.

"She will. My dear Hilary, they always do."

"If I have any knowledge of feminine character," said I, "that young woman harbours in her soul a bitter resentment against Jaffery."

"If," she said. "But you haven't."

"All right," said I.

"All right," said Barbara.

We paused at the library door. "What," I asked, "is going to become of Liosha?"

Barbara sighed. "We're not out of this wood yet."

"And with Liosha on our hands, I don't think we ever shall be."

"I should like to shake Jaffery," said Barbara.

"And I should like," said I, "to kick him."

CHAPTER XXV

So, as I have said, we left those two face to face in the big drawing-room. The man in an agony of self-reproach, helpless pity and realised failure; the woman—as it seemed to me, smoking reflectively in my library armchair, for sleep was impossible—the woman in the calm of desperation. The man who had performed a thousand chivalrous acts to shield her from harm, who lavished on her all the devotion and tenderness of his simple heart; the woman who owed him her life, and, but for fool accident and her own lack of faith in him, would still be owing him the twilight happiness of her Fool's Paradise. They had not met, or exchanged written words, since the early summer day at the St. John's Wood flat, when he had told her that he loved her, and by the sheer mischance of his hulking strength had thrown her to the ground; since that day when she had spat out at him her hatred and contempt, when she had called him "a barren rascal," and had lashed him into fury; when, white with realisation that the secret was about to escape from his lips, he had laid her on the sofa and had gone blindly into the street. Now facing each other for the first time after many months, they remembered all too poignantly that parting. The barren rascal who stood before her was the man who had written every word of Adrian's triumphant second novel, and had given it to her out of the largesse of his love. And he had borne with patience all her imperious strictures and had obeyed all her crazy and jealous whims. He had fooled her—quixotically fooled her, it is true—but fooled her as never woman had been fooled in the world before. And knowing Adrian to be the barren rascal, all the time, never had he wavered in his loyalty, never had he uttered one disparaging word. And he had secured the insertion of a life of Adrian in the next supplement to the Dictionary of National Biography; and he had helped her to set up that staring white marble monument in Highgate Cemetery, with its lying inscription. Never had human soul been invested in such a Nessus shirt of irony. No wonder she had passed through Hell-fire. No wonder her soul had been scorched and shrivelled up. No wonder the licking fires of unutterable shame kept her awake of nights. And if she writhed in the flaming humiliation of it all when she was alone, what was that woman's anguish of abasement when she stood face to face, and compelled to speech, with the man whose loving hand had unwittingly kindled that burning torment?

The poor human love for Adrian was not dead. That secret I had plucked out of her heart a few weeks ago in the garden. How did she regard the man who must have held Adrian in the worst of contempt, the contempt of pity? She hated him. I was sure she hated him. I could not take my mind off those two closeted together. What was happening? Again and again I went over the whole disastrous story. What would be the end? I wearied myself for a long, long time with futile speculation.

My library door opened, and Liosha, bright-eyed, with quivering lip and tragic face, burst in, and seeing me, flung herself down by my side and buried her head on the arm of the chair and began to cry wretchedly.

"My dear, my dear," said I, bewildered by this tornado of misery. "My dear," said I, putting an arm round her shoulders, "what is the matter?"

"I'm a fool," she wailed. "I know I'm a fool, but I can't help it. I went in there just now. I didn't know they were there. Susan's music mistress came and I had to go out of the nursery—and I went into the drawing-room. Oh, it's hard, Hilary, dear—it's damned hard."

"My poor Liosha," said I.

"There doesn't seem to be a place in the world for me."

"There's lots of places in our hearts," I said as soothingly as I could. But the assurance gave her little comfort. Her body shook.

"I wish the cargo had killed me," she said.

I waited for a little, then rose and made her sit in my chair. I drew another near her.

"Now," said I. "Tell me all about it."

And she told me in her broken way.

She walked into the drawing-room thinking to find Barbara. Instead, she sailed into a surging sea of passion. Doria crouched on a sofa hiding her face—the flame, poor little elf in the Nessus shirt, had been lapping her round, and with both hands outstretched she motioned away Jaffery who stood over her.

"Don't touch me, don't touch me! I couldn't bear it!" she cried; and then, aware of Liosha's sudden presence, she started to her feet. Liosha did not move. The two women glared at each other.

"What do you mean by coming in here?" cried Doria.

"You had better leave us, Liosha," said Jaffery sombrely.

But Liosha stood firm. The spurning of Jaffery by Doria struck a chord of the heroic that ran through her strange, wild nature. If this man she loved was not for her, at least no other woman should scorn him. She drew herself up in her full-bosomed magnificence.

"Instead of telling him not to touch you, you little fool, you ought to fall at his feet. For what he has done for you, you ought to steal the wide world and give it to him. And you refuse your footling little insignificant self. If you had a thousand selves, they wouldn't be enough for him."

"Stop!" shouted Jaffery.

She wheeled round on him. "Hold your tongue, Jaff Chayne. I guess I've the right, if anybody has, to fix up your concerns."

"What right?" Doria demanded.

"Never mind." She took a step forward. "Oh, no; not that right! Don't you dare to think it. Jaff Chayne doesn't care a tinker's curse for me that way. But I have a right to speak, Jaff Chayne. Haven't I?"

Jaffery's mind went back to the Bedlam of the slithering cargo. He turned to Doria.

"Let her say what she wants."

"I want nothing!" cried Liosha. "Nothing for myself. Not a thing! But I want Jaff Chayne to be happy. You think you know all he has done for you, but you don't. You don't know a bit. They offered him thousands of pounds to go to Persia, and he would have come back a great man, and he didn't go because of you."

"Persia? I never heard of that," said Doria.

"The job didn't suit me," Jaffery growled.

"And you told her all about it?"

"No, he didn't," said Liosha. "Hilary told me to-day."

"I take your word for it," said Doria coldly. "It only shows that I'm under one more obligation than I thought to Mr. Chayne."

From what I could gather, the word "obligation" infuriated Liosha. She uttered an avalanche of foolish things. And Jaffery (for what is man in a woman's battle but an impotent spectator?) looked in silence from one to the other; from the little ivory, black and white Tanagra figure to the great full creature whom he had seen, but a few days ago, with the salt spray in her hair and the wind in her vestments. And at last she said:

"If I were a woman like you and wouldn't marry a man who loved me like Jaff Chayne, and who had done for me all that Jaff Chayne had done for you, I'd pray to God to blast me and fill my body with worms."

And then she burst out of the room, and, like a child seeking protection, came and threw herself down by my side.

What happened when she left them I know, because Jaffery kept me up till three o'clock in the morning narrating it to me, while he poured into his Gargantuan self hogsheads of whisky and soda.

When Liosha had gone, they eyed one another for a while in embarrassing silence, until Doria spoke:

"She misunderstood—when she came in. Quite natural. It was your touch of pity that I couldn't bear. I wasn't repelling you, as she seemed to think."

"It cut me to the heart to see you in such grief," said Jaffery. "I only thought of comforting you."

"I know." She sat on a chair by the window and looked out at the pouring rain.

"Tell me," she said, without turning round, "what did she mean by saying she had the right to interfere in your affairs?"

"She saved my life at the risk of her own," replied Jaffery.

"I see. And you saved my life once; so perhaps you have rights over me."

"That would be damnable!" he cried. "Such a thought has never entered my head."

"It is firmly fixed in mine," said Doria.

She sat for a while, with knitted brows deep in thought. Jaffery stood dejectedly by the fire, his hands in his pockets. Presently she rose.

"Besides saving my life and doing for me the things I know, there must be many things you've done for me that I never heard of—like this sacrifice of the Persian expedition. Liosha was right. I ought to go on my knees to you. But I can't very well do that, can I?"

"No," replied Jaffery, scrabbling at whiskers and beard. "That would be stupid. You mustn't worry about me at all. Whatever I did for you, my dear, I'd do a thousand times over again!"

"You must have your reward, such as it is. God knows you have earned it."

"Don't talk about rights or rewards," said he. "As I've said repeatedly this afternoon, I've forfeited even your thanks."

"And I've said I forgive you—if there's anything to forgive," she smiled, just a little wearily. "So that is wiped out. All the rest remains. Let us bury all past unhappiness between us two."

"I wish we could. But how?"

"There is a way."

"What is that?"

"You make things somewhat hard for me. You might guess. But I'll tell you. Liosha again was right. . . . If you want me still, I will marry you. Not quite yet; but, say, in six months' time. You are a great-hearted, loyal man"—she continued bravely, faltering under his gaze—"and I will learn to love you and will devote my life to making you happy."

She glanced downwards with averted head, awaiting some outcry of gladness, surrendering herself to the quick clasp of strong arms. But no outcry came, and no arms clasped. She glanced up, and met a stricken look in the man's eyes.

For Jaffery could not find a word to utter. A chill crept about his heart and his blood became as water. He could not move; a nightmare horror of dismay held him in its grip. The inconceivable had happened. He no longer desired her. The woman who had haunted his thoughts for over two years, for whom he had made quixotic sacrifices, for whom he had made a mat of his great body so that she should tread stony paths without hurt to her delicate feet, was his now for the taking—nobly self-offered—and with all the world as an apanage he could not have taken her. The phenomenon of sex he could not explain. Once he had desired her passionately. The ivory-white of her daintiness had fired his blood. He had fought with beasts. He had wrestled with his soul in the night watches. He had loved her purely and sweetly, too. But now, as she stood before him, recoiling a little from his fixed stare of pain, though she had suffered but little loss in beauty and in that of her which was desirable, he realised, in a kind of paralysis, that he desired her no more, that he loved her no more with the idealised love he had given to the elfin princess of his dreams. Not that he would not still do her infinite service. The pathos of her broken life moved him to an anguish of pity. For her soothing he would give all that life held for him, save one thing—which was no longer his to give. Another man glib of tongue and crafty of brain might have lied his way out of an abominable situation. But

Jaffery's craft was of the simplest. He could not trick the dead love into smiling semblance of life. His nature was too primitive. He could only stare in spellbound affright at the icy barrier that separated him from Doria.

"I see," she said tonelessly, moving slowly away from him. "Your feelings have changed. I am sorry."

Then he found power of motion and speech. He threw out his arms. "My God, dear, forgive me he groaned, and sat down and clutched his head in his hands. She returned to the window and looked out at the rain. And there she fought with her woman's indignant humiliation. And there was a long, dead silence, broken only by the faintly heard notes of Susan's piano in the nursery and the splash of water on the terrace.

Presently all that was good in Doria conquered. She crossed the room and laid a light hand on Jaffery's head. It was the finest moment in her life.

"One can't help these things. I know it too well. And no hearts are broken. So it's all for the best."

He groaned again. "I didn't know. I'd like to shoot myself."

She smiled, conscious of feminine superiority. "If you did, I should die, too. I tell you, it's all for the best. I love you as I never loved you before. I usen't to love you a little bit. But I should have had to learn to love you as a wife—and it might have been difficult."

A moment afterwards she appeared in the library, serenely matter-of-fact. Liosha started round in her chair and looked defiantly at her rival.

"Would both of you mind coming into the drawing-room for a minute?"

We followed her. She held the door, which I was about to shut, and left it open. Before Jaffery had time to rise at our entrance, I caught sight of him sitting as she had left him, great clumps of his red hair sticking through his fingers. His face was a picture of woe. I can imagine nothing more like it than that of a conscience smitten lion. Doria ran her arm through mine and kept me near the doorway.

"I've asked Jaffery to marry me," she said, in a steady voice, "and he doesn't want to. It's because he loves a much better woman and wants to marry her."

Then while Jaffery and Liosha gasped in blank astonishment, she swung me abruptly out of the room and slammed the door behind her.

"There," she said, and flung up her little bead, "what do you think of that?"